THE LOW ROAD

THE DI ALEC MCKAY SERIES
BOOK 7

ALEX WALTERS

BLOODHOUND
— BOOKS —

First published in 2025 by Bloodhound Books.

www.bloodhoundbooks.com

Print ISBN: 978-1-917449-6-32

This one has to be dedicated to the memory of Andy Victor.
Thanks for more than 50 years of extraordinary friendship, Andy.

CHAPTER ONE

A t least at this time of the year Sheila didn't have to drive the last stretch in the dark.

She hated the journey in winter. Often it would be raining, a threat of sleet or snow on the higher stretches, her eyes fixed on the blurred rear lights of the vehicles in front. She could cope with that. She was a nervous but cautious driver, staying well below the speed limits, keeping a safe distance from the car in front, alert for any incident.

That wasn't the real problem.

The real problem was the stream of idiot drivers who saw any concession to the weather as a sign of weakness. The ones who bombed up to the rear of her car, tailgating intimidatingly inches behind her until they exhausted their limited patience, overtaking on the next blind bend. Or the ones performing similar manoeuvres in the opposite direction, heading towards her, headlights on full beam, sliding back into their own lane only because other drivers slowed enough to allow it.

She couldn't understand why people drove like that. She'd been involved in one fatal collision, years ago. She hadn't been driving and now she'd almost blanked out the incident. But it

1

had been a long time before she'd wanted to drive herself, and she was constantly aware of the risks.

She much preferred travelling during the spring and summer months. It was well past midsummer now, but still light until late. The weather was always mixed in Scotland, but this year they'd been lucky. The downside was the tourist season. The Scottish schools weren't back for another week or two, and the English ones were well into their summer holidays. On top of that, there were the foreign visitors. Germans, Dutch and Americans in their hire cars and camper vans, trying to remember which side to drive on. The road was much busier than in winter, and the idiots never went away.

She'd been later than usual leaving this afternoon. Her mother's condition was deteriorating by the week, though she refused to acknowledge it. Every time Sheila visited there was a new problem, another area she needed support with. It wouldn't be long until Sheila would have to decide whether her mother was still fit to look after herself at home. There was nothing wrong with her brain, fortunately, no sign of the dementia that dogged so many people of her age. But physically she was growing weaker, and she was struggling with the demands of living alone.

Sheila had considered moving back down there. But her work was in Inverness. She couldn't carry out much of it remotely, and she couldn't face doing this trip as a daily commute. The other option was to bring her mother to Inverness. But she'd have a battle prising her out of the bungalow. It was something that, at least for the moment, she was trying not to think about.

Perhaps because it was later than usual, the road seemed unusually quiet tonight. There were a few lorries, the odd camper van, a scattering of cars, but long stretches where she'd seen no other vehicles.

She relaxed a little as she drew nearer to Inverness, knowing that home was in sight. She wasn't sure how she'd kept this up, week after week, in the months since her father had died. It had become a habit, something she got on with because she had no choice. But more than once over the weeks she'd worried she might risk nodding off at the wheel.

She was sure she'd been paying full attention today, but she didn't know where the car had come from. When she'd last looked in the rear-view mirror, there'd been nothing in sight. Now, as she glanced across, she was startled to see a large SUV close to her bumper, filling the whole of the rear windscreen. Another numpty.

She couldn't understand why the car wasn't overtaking. The road was straight with decent visibility, nothing coming towards them. She lifted her foot from the accelerator, slowing to encourage the driver to pull past. But the car showed no sign of moving out. Instead, it came even closer. She felt it bump gently into the rear of her car.

Sheila's hands tightened on the wheel. What the hell was the driver doing? This wasn't your run-of-the-mill idiot. This was someone genuinely trying to intimidate her.

She pressed her foot on the accelerator, hoping to gain herself some space and time, though there was no way she could outpace a vehicle like that. The SUV dropped back, and Sheila wondered briefly whether the collision had been accidental. Maybe someone who really had nodded off at the wheel.

That thought didn't last more than a second or two. Almost immediately, the SUV drew closer again. This time Sheila felt an even stronger bump against the rear of her car. Again, it dropped back slightly. Before she could decide how to react, the SUV pulled out as if to overtake her.

'Just go,' Sheila muttered. 'Just bugger off and leave me alone.'

The car was level with her. She resisted the temptation to glance over at the driver, forcing herself to concentrate on the road. 'Just go,' she said again.

The SUV swung to the left, catching her wing. Her little hatchback was no match for a bloody great truck like that. She hit the brakes, trying to drop back, but the SUV remained level. It swung again, forcing her off the main carriageway. Involuntarily she pulled to the left. She realised too late that the land beyond the narrow hard shoulder fell away. The drop wasn't steep but the ground was uneven. As the car slid from the road, she felt it tipping. Out of her control, the car's momentum rolled it over, dropping onto a steeper stretch of ground, gathering speed as it bounced down the hillside towards a thicket of trees. She closed her eyes, unable to do anything but pray, feeling the sickening pull of her stomach as the car fell further and faster. Then there was a crash of impact, and she knew nothing more.

CHAPTER TWO

'Ach, just ignore them. They've been churning out that bollocks for years.'

DCI Helena Grant watched Alec McKay prowl restlessly around her office like an animal in search of sustenance. She'd once have found it irritating, but now she was accustomed to it. The time to worry was when Alec chose to sit calmly in front of her. 'It's easy for you to say,' she said. 'It's not personal for you.'

'It has been, though,' McKay pointed out. 'More than once. Never seems to occur to those buggers that they're writing about actual human beings.'

'At least they don't name any names,' Grant said. 'Not yet, anyway.'

'They never will. Too much risk of defamation.'

'There's no risk of defamation with Rory.'

McKay stopped pacing, seemingly chastened by what she'd said. 'Aye, you've a point there. I wasn't thinking.'

She smiled to show no offence had been taken. 'You're probably right, though. So far it's nothing but vague assertions and innuendo. But they've launched a reader campaign to get the case reopened.'

'Of course they have.' McKay had finally sat down opposite her and was riffling aimlessly through the paperwork on her desk. 'It's what they do to sell papers now they've given up on proper news. Nothing's going to happen unless they can magic up some new evidence.'

'They're hinting they do have something.'

'If they have, they've an obligation to share it with us,' McKay said. 'I'll believe it when I see it. Even if they have stumbled across something new, that doesn't necessarily reflect badly on the original inquiry.'

'Except it'll give them another opportunity to take a pop at the police. They can never resist that.'

'That goes with the territory. No bugger loves the polis. We're either fascists, racists or too lazy to get off our arses. Take your pick.'

'I can always depend on you for a balanced view, Alec.'

'It's why you value my company.'

'That'll be it.' She picked up the newspaper they'd been discussing. One of the national tabloids, its Scottish edition had spent the previous few days highlighting the supposed shortcomings of a twenty-year-old murder investigation. The initial trigger for the story had been a true crime podcast which had insinuated – on the basis of no substantive evidence, as far as Grant could see – that the wrong man might have been convicted. The story, such as it was, had been picked up and amplified by the newspaper with a more sensationalist spin. They'd kept it running with increasingly hysterical headlines, culminating in the launch of a campaign for the investigation to be reopened.

Neither the podcast nor the newspaper had so far produced any new information or evidence. There had undoubtedly been gaps and inconsistencies in the prosecution case but the evidence had been sufficiently compelling that the jury had rapidly returned a unanimous guilty verdict. In the absence of new information, the conviction seemed as safe as it could be.

Even so, the case had personal resonance for Helena Grant. The senior investigating officer had been her late husband, Rory Grant, at the time a Detective Superintendent in the Major Investigations Team. Although there'd been no mention of Rory or any other individual officers in the newspaper account, Grant was finding it difficult not to view the coverage as an implied attack on Rory's integrity or competence.

McKay gestured towards the front page. 'I mean, look at the state of that. There's barely a proper news story in the whole rag. It's all soap stars or numpties who've been on some reality show. They'll get bored in a few days and move on to some shite about the royal family.'

'I hope you're right.'

'You should know by now, Hel. I'm always right.'

'In your own head.'

McKay was back on his feet again. He walked over to the window, staring at the Inverness cityscape. McKay was always like this when things were quiet, a creature deprived of his natural habitat. Not that he'd be short of work to be getting on with, but it would be the kind of administration he preferred to ignore.

She was probably obsessing with the newspaper story for similar reasons. There were times in this job when they barely had a moment to think, when they were working every available hour. But there were occasional times when the pace slackened. It was what made the job possible, but she worked inefficiently at times like this, too easily distracted by nonsense like this news story.

McKay turned back from the window and sat back down. He tapped the front of the newspaper. 'If they wanted to campaign about something, they'd be better off focusing on the state of the A9.'

'I never had you down as a campaigner for road improvements.'

'Oh, Christ, I'm not. Though don't get me started on the bloody potholes. But something like that RTC over the weekend, it makes you realise how fragile life is.'

'Are you discovering a new philosophical streak, Alec? Is this some sort of midlife crisis?'

'I'm well past all that. But I was reading the details. That poor wee woman.'

'I haven't looked at it,' Grant said. 'What's the story?'

'Car went off the road a little way before the Slochd summit. No obvious reason for it. Straight stretch, decent visibility. The driver might have been speeding, but there's no evidence of that from the previous average speed cameras she'd passed.'

'Who was she?'

'Woman called Sheila McGivern. Late thirties. Unmarried. They've tracked down her next of kin, her mother, who lives in Kingussie. She was coming back from there. She drove down from Inverness to visit her mother every weekend.'

'Maybe just tired then.'

'Quite possible. If you nodded off on that road you'd know about it.'

'Any suspicious circumstances?'

'Hard to say yet. McGivern didn't have any significant medical conditions. It's possible there might be something she hadn't told her mother about. Obviously, they're getting the car checked out, and the collision analysts are looking at the forensics. Initial view is that there could have been another vehicle involved.'

'So we might be talking dangerous or reckless driving. Failure to stop.'

'Or worse.'

Grant laughed. 'So that's why you're so interested. You'd love that, wouldn't you? You're getting excited already at the prospect.'

'A man can dream.'

'A man can find ways of avoiding the form-filling he ought to be getting on with.'

'Aye, well, that too. But you can tell how desperate I am that I'm even following up an RTC.'

'They're not exactly uncommon on the A9. The speed cameras have made a difference, but there are still too many idiots on the road.'

McKay tapped the newspaper again. 'That's my point. If they want a bloody campaign, maybe focus on something half-useful rather than this crap.'

She smiled indulgently. 'I never thought I'd see the day. Alec McKay, road safety warrior. If you're not careful, I'll have you transferred to traffic.'

CHAPTER THREE

S he was into her rhythm now. Ginny sometimes thought it wouldn't happen, but it always did. The moment when everything came together, and the running felt effortless and energising, rather than something she was forcing herself to do.

Not that she had to make much of an effort during the summer months. It was harder in winter, when the days shrank almost to nothing and she ran in darkness, using a head torch and taking only the most familiar routes. Now, even this early in the morning, she was sprinting in full daylight, the sun low in the south-eastern sky, long shadows stretching over the firth as she pounded the shore. It was the season she enjoyed most. July drifting seamlessly into August; the barley fading from green to yellow as the harvest drew closer; a faint breeze from the sea.

Normally she'd have slipped into the familiar state of mind brought on by the exercise. It went with that sense of perfect rhythm. The moment when her mind emptied of its extraneous thoughts and concerns. It wasn't that she stopped thinking. Often, this was the time when, unprompted, her brain generated its best and most creative ideas. She recalled moments when she'd experienced an insight that had helped progress an investigation or resolve an issue that had been plaguing her for weeks. In this mindset, her head could explore channels of its own, like a wave finding its own unique way up the beach.

Today that was eluding her. Physically, she had found that ideal rhythm. Mentally, her mind remained stubbornly snagged on more immediate concerns.

That wasn't surprising. Normally she was beset by nothing more than the usual work and domestic concerns. A challenging investigation. Alec McKay being a pain in the backside. Some work that needed doing on the house. Stuff that was frustrating or irritating, but nothing genuinely worrying. Issues she could easily offload as she slipped into the rhythm.

This was different. This was something that might change everything. Something she didn't know how to face.

Ginny had decided to shorten her usual run today. She wanted to be back in time to prepare a decent breakfast, make sure they had time to get organised, and get their brains in the right place for the day to come. They had to be at the hospital by 9am. Then there'd no doubt be endless waiting around until they carried out the biopsy. Ginny wouldn't be able to wait with Isla, so she'd find somewhere to get a coffee until Isla called to say it was done. It would be a day of boredom and mild anxiety rather than anything worse. But it was a day Ginny was dreading.

It had started with almost nothing. A small painless swelling on Isla's neck. She'd ignored it at first. It was only when she'd mentioned it in passing to Ginny that she'd been persuaded to get it checked out. There'd been the usual difficulties getting a GP appointment. Ginny could only pray that the resulting delays would not have any serious implications.

The GP had clearly been worried, even though she'd made the usual reassuring noises. What had been more concerning to

ALEX WALTERS

Ginny was how quickly they'd been booked in for the hospital appointment. The GP had been characteristically vague about the possible implications of the swelling, but had eventually told Isla her major concern was that it might be indicative of Hodgkin lymphoma, a cancer of the lymphatic system.

If that turned out to be the case, the bad news was that it was a relatively aggressive form of cancer. The good news was that it was very treatable, typically through some combination of chemotherapy and radiotherapy. If it did turn out to be lymphoma, the major question, as far as Ginny could judge, was whether they'd caught it in time.

But that was getting ahead of herself. Today's appointment was simply to carry out a biopsy. Only after that would Isla receive a diagnosis. Today might be the end of her worries, or the start of a much more protracted battle.

As she approached the grey stone edifice of Fort George, the army garrison that dominated this side of the Moray Firth, Ginny turned back towards home. Another twenty minutes saw her turning into the gate of the cottage she shared with Isla. As she stopped to find her keys, she glanced at her watch. Still not 7am. Ginny had always been an early riser, and was generally in the office not much after 7.30am. It was normally the time of day when she felt most alive and awake, even if it generally led Alec McKay to admonish her for being 'so fucking cheerful'.

Today, she had no concerns about being in the office. She showered and took her time preparing two bowls of home-made muesli, adding fresh raspberries and yoghurt. She put on a pot of coffee and made her way upstairs to wake Isla.

She'd expected Isla still to be sleeping, but she was already sitting up. Ginny placed Isla's mug of coffee on the bedside table and sat down on the edge of the bed. 'How are you doing?'

'Physically, fine. Emotionally – not so much. I didn't sleep brilliantly, as you probably noticed.'

Ginny took Isla's hand. 'It's almost certainly nothing. But if it isn't we can face it together.'

'I know. And I'm more than grateful that you're here. Although that means I'm imposing my worries on you.'

'That's the point of it, though, isn't it? The point of being together.'

'I know. And it does make it easier.'

'We need to deal with it as it comes. You get a shower. Breakfast's ready. Let's focus on the practicalities.'

'Fair enough, Mrs Sensible.' Isla smiled. 'And thanks. This isn't fun, but it'd be a million times worse if I was on my own.'

CHAPTER FOUR

'I'm saying it makes me feel uncomfortable, that's all.'

'I hope you're not looking for more money, Craig. If that's what this is about, it's a non-starter. We're paying you more than the going rate as it is.'

That was bollocks and they both knew it, but it was the game you had to play in this business. If Craig Fairlie pressed harder, he could probably squeeze a few more quid out of the newspaper. On the other hand, he was in this for the longer term. He wanted to build a decent relationship so they'd trust him with stories from his patch. That was partly why he was concerned about the way they were using this one. He'd expected they'd run his feature as a one-off. Hugh Preston had been more than happy with that. It had given his podcast some national publicity, a sheen of borrowed credibility, and he'd gained a stack more listeners. The newspaper had filled a couple of pages with a story likely to appeal to their usually ignored Highland readership. Win–win.

He hadn't expected the newspaper to keep running with the story, never mind turn it into a bloody campaign. Preston had been furious. It was one thing for the paper to use his material with acknowledgement, but the follow-up pieces had downplayed the origins of the story while drifting further into the realm of speculation. His fury, understandably enough, had been directed at Fairlie, the local journalist commissioned to write the follow-up articles, rather than towards Colin Wishaw, the features editor who'd decided to extract the maximum from the story.

Fairlie was sitting in what generally constituted his office: a corner in a bar in an Inverness backstreet. The place was quiet in the daytime even at the height of summer. It wasn't a place to attract the tourists, other than the occasional American looking for 'local colour'. In this place, the colour in question was mainly a nicotine-stained beige, even though no one had smoked in there for years. Ally, the landlord, wasn't one for change. The usual crowd filled the place in the evening, and a handful of regulars, of which Fairlie was one, kept the place ticking over during the day. No one was likely to come close enough to listen to Fairlie's telephone conversation. 'It's not that, Colin. You know that.'

'I mean, if you're not happy to continue, we can always stop. Pity, though, because I reckon we can keep this one running for a while. Reader feedback's been very positive. Or we could find someone else to cover it.'

There it was. The usual casual threat. Don't try to be too clever, sonny. People like you are two a penny. If you don't want to write it, someone else will. Even if that someone was some hack from Glasgow who knew bugger all about life up here. 'I just want to make sure we're doing it properly. That we're not stretching the material beyond what it's worth.'

They both knew this was exactly what they were doing. The original podcast had raised some questions about the police investigation into the notorious O'Donnell case, twenty years before. The case had been controversial at the time, and there'd been criticism of the initial lack of progress made by the police. Hugh Preston's contention was that, in the face of growing media and political pressure, the police had used every means possible, legitimate or otherwise, to secure a conviction.

In truth, Fairlie had been largely unimpressed by the case that Preston had presented. The supposed new evidence came from a single source, whose identity Preston refused to divulge, quite possibly, Fairlie thought, because he didn't know it himself. The suggestion was that, in the face of inconsistencies and gaps in the available witness statements, forensic and other evidence had been fabricated or misused to ensure the prosecution case was as watertight as possible. This was little more than an assertion, although the source had provided examples of the supposed actions that had been taken. Fairlie hadn't found any of this particularly compelling. The account was intriguing, but there was nothing so far to justify a reopening of the investigation.

Preston claimed his source had promised more substantive material which would be explored in a follow-up edition of the podcast. Preston was keen to build interest, and initially he'd been quite happy to use the newspaper to help him achieve that. But as the story had increasingly been taken out of his hands, Preston had grown suspicious of Fairlie's motives and become less co-operative.

The result was that Fairlie's subsequent stories had been of even less substance than the original feature. Fairlie was a decent writer and he'd done his best to conceal how little material they actually had, but he was incapable of spinning any gold without at least a few scraps of straw to work with.

Wishaw gave an exasperated sigh on the other end of the line. 'You're an old hand. You know how this works. We've had more reader feedback on this story than almost anything we've done in the last couple of years. People were fascinated by the original inquiry, and this has rekindled that interest. It doesn't matter if there's nothing much in it. If it goes nowhere, we can just imply that, as ever, the police are looking after their own. If somehow we do manage to get a result from this, we're the good guys doing our bit to uphold justice.'

'You're a cynical bastard, Colin.'

'How long have you been in this business? Don't pretend I'm telling you anything you don't already know.'

'I just want to make sure we keep Hugh Preston onside. If there is a real story here, he's the one who's got it. He's already feeling frozen out.'

'Do you really think he's got something?'

'I honestly don't know. He's got a source, or he claims he has. But I've no idea whether there's anything there.'

'We're giving the guy free publicity for his bloody podcast. What more does he want?'

'He doesn't trust us. He thinks we'll run off with the story, and his stuff will end up looking second hand.' And in fairness, Fairlie thought, he's probably not wrong. Wishaw would shaft anyone for a decent story.

'So do your best to keep him on board. But maybe get some insurance.'

'Insurance?'

'You're a fucking reporter, Craig. If there really is a story out there, you should be digging for it yourself, not relying on some two-bit podcaster.'

'I have been. Or at least I've been trying. But you know what it's like. The police close ranks on stuff like this.'

In reality, Fairlie's digging had been half-hearted so far. He'd focused most of his energy on squeezing as much as he could out of Preston's initial work. He'd made a few calls to contacts in the force, and received a fairly frosty response. But Wishaw had a point. If they wanted to keep this story running, they couldn't depend on Preston to come up with the goods.

'That's why we use a local guy like you. You've got the inside track. More than any of our stringers down here.'

Another implied threat, Fairlie thought. If you can't give us some added value, we might as well use one of our local tame freelancers. 'It's early days. There are plenty of people I can talk to. If there's anything there, one of them should be able to tell me.'

'Good to hear. We can make a lot of capital out of this if we play it right. You'll be able to bask in the shared glory.'

Too right, Fairlie thought, given that I'll be the one doing most of the work. He exchanged a few more semi-barbed pleasantries with Wishaw before ending the call. His pint sat almost untouched on the table beside him. Fairlie wasn't really one for drinking, especially in the daytime, but he felt obliged to sip his way through a beer or two to keep Ally happy. He took a large mouthful and flicked through the contact list on his phone. Time to call in some favours.

CHAPTER FIVE

'Some people have called you a populist and an opportunist. How would you respond to that?'

Iain Pennycook gave a broad smile. 'I've been living with those accusations for my whole political career. It reassures me I'm on the right track. It means I'm addressing issues that matter to ordinary people. The issues too often ignored in Westminster and, I'm sorry to say, in Holyrood.'

Charlotte Kent nodded encouragingly. 'You think this is one of those issues?'

'There's no doubt about it. You ask anyone who lives in this part of the Highlands. We're dependent on that road, and people are becoming scared to use it.'

'So what's the solution?'

Pennycook knew he had to frame his response carefully. Kent was young but she was one of the better media interviewers in these parts, probably destined for a glittering career down south in due course. He'd seen her tie some politicians up in knots. It was clear she disliked him both personally and politically, though she'd tried hard to maintain a facade of neutrality. She'd have no hesitation in tripping him up given half a chance. 'I'm not going to offer pat solutions to the problem. There's no single answer. But the first priority should be to finish duelling the whole road. And in my view that means not just the stretch from Perth to Inverness, but further north too.'

'All of which requires substantial investment at a time when public borrowing is at a record high.'

'That's the stock response, but there's always money to be found when it suits those in power. The people of the Highlands are never treated as a priority. We're taken for granted.' Pennycook leaned forward, adopting the more serious demeanour he knew always played well with his target audience. 'Look, Charlotte, I'm not doing this because I want to be popular. There are plenty of people – the metropolitan elite, if you like – who dislike me. I speak the truth. I tell it like it is. I do it because I genuinely care about the people I represent. The so-called ordinary people who keep this country going.'

'Some would say that you don't represent anyone,' Kent said. 'You hold no elected position, and you've been singularly unsuccessful so far in acquiring one.'

'The system is stacked against those of us who aren't part of the establishment. But I've had more impact over the last decade than most mainstream politicians you can name. I focus on the issues that matter.'

''What do you expect your campaign to achieve?'

'To save lives. I know this is going to be a long haul. We're already experiencing the dirty tricks, the smear tactics, the usual attacks I face whenever I raise my head above the parapet.'

Kent looked at him sceptically. 'Why would anyone want to smear you over an issue like this? Surely everyone would agree with your objectives, even if they might differ on how achievable they are.'

'You'd have to ask them that. Just as you'd have to ask them why so much of the work on the A9 has been late and over budget. We'll keep on fighting and campaigning until something's done. Last year was one of the highest on record for deaths on that road. Whenever there's another serious collision, people are terrified that the victim could be a relative or friend. No one should have to live with that fear. Something must be done.'

'And you seriously think you're the man to do it?'

For once, her tone slightly betrayed her bias, Pennycook thought. She'd sounded more patronising than she'd intended, and that never went down well with his supporters. 'I *seriously* do, Charlotte.' He gave the second word a slightly ironic emphasis. 'Someone will have to take this on, and I'm the only one in the frame. I owe it to the people up here to do everything in my power to prevent more unnecessary deaths.'

'Are you intending to stand for Holyrood in the next elections?'

She'd clearly intended to surprise him with the sudden switch of topic, but it was a question he'd expected and prepared for. 'I've been mulling that over, and I haven't yet reached a decision. On the one hand, it would provide me with a platform to communicate my views to the widest possible audience. On the other – and this is something I'm very conscious of – I do think parliament is little more than a talking shop.'

'Perhaps you could be the one to change that?' Kent gave him a mischievous smile.

She was taking the piss now, Pennycook thought. 'I think some things are beyond even my capabilities. I'm better devoting my energies to causes like the one we've been discussing today. But I am weighing up the options. When I do make a decision, you'll be one of the first to know.'

'We all look forward to hearing your decision. And I'm sure

everyone wishes you well with this campaign. I don't think even those who disagree with your politics would deny it's a worthy cause.'

'I appreciate your open-mindedness, Charlotte.'

'We aim to give everyone a fair hearing, Mr Pennycook.' He could almost hear the unspoken *even you.* 'Thank you for taking the time to talk to us today.' She cut to a pre-recorded promotional trail. 'Thanks, Iain. Good stuff. I see there's been another one.'

'Another one?'

'Fatal accident on the A9. Early this morning.'

Pennycook raised an eyebrow. 'Must have hit the news after I left the house. Proves my point, though. That's two this week. It can't go on. Where was this one?'

'Same area as the one at the weekend, I understand. Just a mile or two up the road.'

'One of the single-carriageway sections, I assume.'

'I imagine so. Anyway, good luck with your campaign. Come back and update us when you can.'

Pennycook could see Kent was preparing to go back on air, so he waved an airy farewell and exited the studio. He'd have to find out more about this latest collision. Every death was a personal tragedy, of course. That went without saying. But every death on that road would boost their cause, enable them to put more pressure on the authorities. Charlotte Kent would no doubt think that attitude cynical. As far as Pennycook was concerned, it was just realistic. It was how you got things done.

CHAPTER SIX

'Still not given up then?' McKay said.

Jock Henderson looked at the cigarette he was holding between nicotine-stained fingers. 'Only a matter of time till they're banned entirely. I'm making the most of them while I can.'

'If the lung disease doesn't get you first. Are you allowed to smoke here?'

'Why do you think I'm standing so far away?'

'I thought it was because you're a good delegator. Get the juniors to do the heavy lifting.'

'We're not all lazy buggers. I've been doing my fair share over there.'

They were standing on the roadside. Ahead of them, several hundred yards further down the road, was the site of that morning's serious collision. McKay could see the remains of a crushed red saloon car and, towering above it, the front of a seemingly barely dented HGV. 'What's the story?'

Henderson finished his cigarette and dropped the butt onto the tarmac, squashing it with his shoe. 'Surprised this one's brought you out, Alec.'

McKay looked around, taking in the clear blue sky, the dense surroundings of pine and firs, the hills and moorland beyond. 'Lovely day. I fancied a trip out.'

'Aye, and I've just been awarded a knighthood for services to optimism and good humour. Don't give me that bollocks.'

'It's an unexplained death, isn't it? Nothing much else going on back at the ranch so I thought I'd take a look.'

'If I'd known things were that quiet, I'd have had you seconded to my lot.' Henderson was a senior examiner, responsible for crime scene investigation. He and McKay went back longer than either of them wanted to admit, and they'd maintained the same barbed double act for years.

'If I'd known you were that desperate for talent, I'd have volunteered. So what is the story?' McKay gestured towards the two vehicles.

'What do you think? Another bloody head-on. Car driver and passenger probably killed instantly. Truck driver's not in a good way either. He was unconscious when the first responders arrived. Shipped up to Raigmore as soon as the ambulance got here.'

'Another vehicle involved?'

'Too early to be sure. Collision happened at around 5am. So it would have been fully light. Good weather conditions. Dry road. Fairly straight stretch of road with decent visibility. Not easy to see what would have caused the driver to be on the wrong side of the road.'

'Age of the driver?'

'Need to get that checked out. State they were in it was difficult to tell. But not elderly, if that's what you're getting at.'

'Just thinking of heart attacks, strokes, maybe just poor eyesight.'

'That sort of thing's possible at any age. One for the pathologist. The other option's some sort of vehicle failure, but again we can get that checked out. But more likely, given the history of this road, just another bloody stupid bit of overtaking.'

'Although, as you say, good visibility. Why would you overtake in the face of a bloody great lorry?'

'Maybe because some people are – and I'm using the technical term here, you understand – fucking numpties.'

'That's definitely a consideration. Still doesn't smell right to me, though.'

'I know what you mean. This kind of collision, there's usually another vehicle involved. Someone tries to overtake, misjudges it, next thing they know they're flies on a windscreen. But in those situations, unless the overtaken vehicle somehow gets caught up in the crash, they're usually the ones who stop and call it in. They're not to blame and they've nothing to hide. In this case, if there was a third vehicle, the driver's just buggered off.'

McKay was staring past the two vehicles as if the answer to the mystery might lie in that direction. 'Might have been traumatised by the experience. Not thinking straight. Maybe we'll hear from them later.'

Henderson had lit another cigarette. 'You still haven't told me why you're here.'

'Just intrigued, Jock. We've had four fatals in the last couple of weeks. Even by the standards of this bloody road, that's unusual. Especially in the middle of summer and a stretch of half-decent weather.'

'Tourist bampots?' Henderson suggested. 'People not used to driving on the proper side of the road? It's very much that time of year.'

'That was my first thought. But all the drivers involved were locals. Don't know about this one?'

'We've checked on the registered keeper of the car. One Gavin McCann. Address in Tain. We haven't confirmed he was actually driving, but it seems most likely. So, yes, probably a local. That's all we know about him so far, and we don't know who the passenger was. The truck driver was from near Stirling, and there's no reason to think he was at fault. It was the car on the wrong side of the road. But so what? It just means we're going through a worse than usual patch. Maybe it'll finally persuade the powers-that-be to do something about it.' Henderson paused. 'You've obviously been spending time on this. Things really that quiet for you?'

'Everyone needs a hobby,' McKay said. 'Anything to get away from the bureaucracy. You know me, Jock.'

'Aye, all too well. Never happy unless you've got something to get your teeth into. I think you're barking up the wrong tree here, though. We're most likely dealing with whatever's the collective noun for fuckwits.'

'A man's got to dream. It's what keeps me going in this job. Assume we'll know more if the truck driver pulls through.'

'Imagine so. We've got the collision analysts working on the scene, and the car'll be shipped off to the vehicle examiners in due course. There should be a fair bit to work with.' He stubbed out his cigarette. 'Best be getting back. Buggers will think I'm not pulling my weight.'

'Heaven forbid.' McKay watched as Henderson made his ungainly way back to the scene of the collision. He was always fascinated by the way Henderson moved. It was as if the man had never quite grown accustomed to his own limbs. But Henderson was almost certainly right. There was nothing here beyond a series of personal tragedies.

Except somehow McKay didn't quite feel that. He'd been looking back at the previous recent RTCs on this road. In all cases, the investigations were still ongoing and so far inconclusive. Today's was the only one involving a head-on collision. In the previous instances, no other vehicles had been present at the scene, although in a couple of cases the collision analysts had identified evidence that indicated the possible involvement of another vehicle. The collisions had all happened on stretches of the road with no police cameras, and, despite public appeals, no witnesses had come forward. Today's crash didn't exactly fit the same pattern, but there were unexplained aspects here too.

McKay had long ago learned to trust his copper's gut, recognising that it was nothing more or less than the product of his years of experience. His subconscious brain was capable of spotting links and patterns long before his conscious mind had even begun to engage.

Even so, this time he hesitated. If there really was a pattern here, he wasn't sure how it would make any sense. He was also conscious of his own desire to conjure some sort of major crime out of the currently rather empty fresh air. As he'd told Jock Henderson, a man's got to dream.

But he also has to take care that the dream is something more than wishful thinking.

CHAPTER SEVEN

'I mean, it's possible. Anything's *possible*. But I can't say I've ever heard of anything like that. Have you?'

McKay was silent, reflecting on the oddities he had witnessed in the course of his career. 'No,' he finally admitted. 'Not really.'

Adam Sutherland was a short, heavily built man, sitting behind his desk with the air of a benevolent monarch surveying his territory. He led the team of collision investigators employed by the force. He was widely respected for his technical expertise and experience, but McKay had never found him an easy man to like. A wee bit too chippy, always seeing a slight where none was intended. But maybe it just took one to know one.

'Don't get me wrong. We've more than enough eejits out there. But mostly it's because they're drunk or high or think they're Lewis bloody Hamilton. Not to mention the ones who think they're indestructible because they've reached nineteen years old without killing themselves. But I've never come across anything like you're suggesting.'

McKay was sitting opposite him, trying his hardest not to roam around the room the way he did in Helena Grant's office.

Sutherland wasn't the type who'd respond positively to someone peering at his shelves and papers. 'But you do think there's something odd about this latest batch of RTCs? That's what you said on the phone.'

'I never like jumping to conclusions. We're still working on these investigations.'

'But?'

'There are often aspects of collisions that can't be fully explained. Usually it comes down to a moment's carelessness or inattention, or some factor we can't trace after the fact. An animal running into the road, something like that. It's odd to find a succession of crashes that aren't straightforwardly explicable. But odd things happen.'

'Not as odd as someone engineering them deliberately?'

'I can't see it. It would be hellishly difficult to engineer something like that. You'd need extraordinary driving skills, not to mention nerves of steel.'

'Or to not care whether you lived or died.'

'You'd still need to be a bloody good driver. And you couldn't expect to get away with it for long. Even if you managed not to kill yourself, eventually there'd be a witness. In this latest one, if the lorry driver pulls through, he'll be able to give us a good idea of what happened. Assuming he remembers.'

McKay nodded. 'What do the headshrinkers call it? Dissociative amnesia?'

'Something like that. People often block out memories of traumatic moments. Of course, it can sometimes be convenient for the buggers not to remember.'

'There's no suggestion the truck driver did anything wrong, though?'

'Not so far. On the right side of the road. Tachograph indicates he wasn't speeding. He hadn't been on the road long so unlikely to be tired. It was the car on the wrong side of the road. Unless the medics find he was over the limit or something, the truck driver doesn't look to have been at fault. But the poor bastard will still feel some responsibility. I don't have any sympathy for the idiot overtakers or the speed merchants or the drunks who kill themselves. But they can leave behind a hell of a lot of collateral damage. Not just other deaths and casualties, but the emotional scars.'

'Very lyrical, Adam.'

'You see too much of it in this seat. But the short answer is that you're barking up the wrong tree. I can't envisage any link between these cases.' He hesitated, as if unsure how to phrase his next question. 'From everything I've heard about you, you don't seem the fanciful type. Why are you interested in this?'

'Just a gut thing, really. I went up to look at the aftermath of this morning's incident and it seemed odd. I couldn't work out how the collision could have taken place. I had a quick skim of the files on the other recent cases, and none of them seemed to have an obvious cause. But I'm not the expert here. I just thought it was worth chatting them over with you.'

'Aye, I'm the expert. The work's still ongoing. We haven't finished all the vehicle examinations. We haven't had all the post-mortem reports. We may be able to get more GPS data on the vehicles' movements. We might have more witnesses come forward.'

'Your gut's more experienced in this area than mine is.'

'Not to mention bigger.' Sutherland laughed. 'No, Alec. I know it would make a good headline. Killer on the road and all that. But, trust me, it's bollocks. It couldn't happen. Not in a million years.'

CHAPTER EIGHT

'You psychic or something, Alec?'
'If I am, it's never brought me any luck on the lottery.
Why'd you ask?' McKay was at his desk, working his way less
than half-heartedly through a series of online forms. He'd forced
himself to come in early, leaving Chrissie sleeping contentedly,
to get on with this. He was now on his fourth coffee and sixth
biscuit, but still only on his second form. At this rate, he'd be
finished some time shortly before the next millennium.

Helena Grant stood in the doorway of the open-plan office,
brandishing a newspaper. 'Thought you might be amused to see
this.'

'That rag's always good for a laugh. What is it? More on the
bloody O'Donnell case?'

'That was the other rag.'

'They're all interchangeable. Same old shite, however you
slice it.'

'This one's set up its own campaign.'

'Don't they bother with news any more? No, stupid
question. What's this one about?'

She dropped the paper on McKay's desk. 'They've

obviously been listening to Alec McKay, road safety warrior. Campaign to improve safety standards on the A9.'

'Not something anyone would readily disagree with, at least not in principle. Maybe different if you're having to stump up the money, but that's why I'm not a politician.'

'Speaking of which, do you want to know who's heading up the campaign?'

'I'm guessing you're going to tell me.'

'Only Iain Pennycook.'

'You're joking? The unflushable one? He's back again?'

'I don't think he ever really went away.'

'Just lurking somewhere planning his next grift. I don't know why anyone takes him seriously.'

'He knows how to play the populist card, doesn't he? Don't think it pays to underestimate him.'

'He's not stupid. He's just shameless.' McKay's first dealings with Pennycook went back a couple of decades. In those days, McKay had still been in uniform and Pennycook had been not much more than a grifter and scam artist in Inverness. He'd already had a record for minor offences – teenage shoplifting and opportunistic theft – and was eventually sent down for a series of major credit card frauds. McKay had had several contacts with him, and quickly categorised Pennycook as a loud-mouthed smart-arse about half as clever as he thought he was. Nothing he'd seen in the intervening years had caused him to change that opinion.

In fairness to Pennycook – not a phrase McKay had ever been heard to use – the man had served his time and presumably learned his lesson. It wasn't exactly that he'd gone straight. It was more that he now directed his questionable talents towards less directly criminal objectives. He'd first come to public attention as a noisy campaigner against Scottish independence. McKay hadn't had much of an opinion on that one way or the other, or if he did he preferred to keep it to himself. Pennycook had quickly become something of a media figure, partly because of his relative youth – he was still only in his early thirties at the time – and partly because of his undoubted eloquence. He could pontificate persuasively on almost any political topic, generally unhindered by any great knowledge or understanding of the matter in question.

Pennycook's support for the Union was only one aspect of his espoused politics, which embraced a range of broadly conservative causes. He'd avoided the minefields of party politics, and claimed he was simply speaking for the downtrodden everyman in the face of the overbearing elite. The latter group encompassed elected politicians, the media, the legal profession, the teaching profession, most global businesses, and anyone else it suited Pennycook to criticise.

McKay had never paid much attention to politics, and most of this had washed over him. But it became impossible to ignore Pennycook. He was constantly on television and radio, banging on about his hobby horse of the moment, and his beaming smile frequently shone out from the front pages of the Scottish press. On a couple of occasions he'd made a big play of considering entering the Scottish Parliament as an independent 'just to give the place a shake-up'. But the idea had been quietly dropped, possibly because the polls had indicated that Pennycook stood little chance of being elected.

As far as McKay could judge, the only cause Iain Pennycook was really interested in was the promoting and publicising of Iain Pennycook. His high-profile campaigns raised substantial funding from the public, and McKay suspected a large proportion of that went into Pennycook's own pockets. There was no suggestion anything he did was fraudulent or illegal, but McKay had little doubt the man was fleecing his followers.

Over the years, Pennycook had jumped from cause to cause, aiming to be in the centre of the spotlight wherever it might move. He'd loudly supported the No campaign in the 2014 independence vote, and equally loudly supported Brexit in the subsequent EU referendum. In more recent years, he'd jumped on the 'culture wars' bandwagon, pontificating about wokeness and cancellation.

On the face of it, the A9 campaign seemed oddly parochial for Pennycook. He'd preferred to focus on issues that could attract support from the whole of Scotland, particularly in the densely-populated Central Belt. The quality of the A9 and other major roads in the region was important to those living in the Highlands, but would have less resonance elsewhere.

But perhaps that was the point. Pennycook had recently made a lot of noise about moving back to Inverness, arguing that the Highlands and Islands were ignored and short-changed not only by Westminster but also by Holyrood. It was possible that, in the face of diminishing returns further south, Pennycook was seeking to build a new power-base up here.

'He was my first collar, you know?' McKay mused now. 'Arrested him for using a stolen credit card.'

'Was that the conviction that got him sent down?' Grant asked. 'Does that mean you're single-handedly responsible for the Iain Pennycook phenomenon.'

'Not guilty. He got a suspended sentence for that one. It was the next conviction that did for him, if I remember correctly.'

'I suppose this is a decent enough cause even if he's mainly using it to line his own pockets. I won't be sorry if it deflects interest from the O'Donnell campaign.'

'It'll do that all right. I've no time for the man but Pennycook's an effective rabble-rouser. If he wants attention – and that's usually all he wants – he'll get it.'

'I hope so. The last thing I want is Rory's name being dragged through the mud after all these years.'

'It won't come to that,' McKay said. 'Rory was a good cop. As professional as anyone I've met in the force. He wouldn't have had anything to hide.'

'Do you think I don't know that? But if someone in the team was playing games, he wouldn't necessarily have been aware. He was the SIO so he'd have carried the can regardless. That's how it works. You know that.'

'One reason I've never sought promotion. That and the fact that no bugger in their right mind would ever risk giving it to me. Speaking of promotions, I believe we're finally due to get a new Area Commander in the next few weeks?'

'So I've heard. We need a safe pair of hands after everything that happened.'

The previous Area Commander, Mike Everly, had been killed in the line of duty in what McKay knew to have been questionable circumstances. As far as McKay was aware, there'd never been any inquiry into those circumstances. Certainly nobody had bothered to seek McKay's opinion on the matter, though that wasn't so surprising. All he knew was that it would be a scandal that Everly's transgressions were ignored if the reputation of a thoroughly decent cop like Rory Grant was tarnished.

'Someone who wants a quiet life,' McKay agreed. 'That's usually why they come up here.'

'I just want someone who lets us get on with our work.'

McKay looked at the complicated online form on the screen in front of him and sighed. 'Aye. There's a danger we might have to do exactly that.'

CHAPTER NINE

G ordon Rennie was standing awkwardly in the doorway, looking as if he'd never been in a bar before. He'd been a cop for thirty plus years before his retirement so that seemed unlikely, Craig Fairlie thought. Maybe he was out of practice.

Fairlie rose from his seat in the corner and waved Rennie over. 'Good to see you, Gordon. What can I get you?'

Rennie was still looking round at the dark interior of the pub, his expression suggesting he'd no idea why he was in here. 'I'm driving. Better stick to something soft. Fizzy water, maybe.'

'Fizzy water it is. Don't worry, I'm not expecting us to eat here. Ally doesn't stretch to much more than crisps. Even then he sees anything beyond salt and vinegar as pretentiously cosmopolitan. But I thought we might chat in here first. It's quiet and no one's likely to be listening.'

This was true enough. At 11.30am they were the only people in the place apart from Ally polishing glasses behind the bar. A few of the regulars would drift in as the day went on, but they mostly made a point of ignoring one another, sitting in distant corners of the room to minimise the risk of anyone interacting with them. It was that kind of place.

Rennie sat himself at the table, while Fairlie fetched the water. When he returned a few moments later, Rennie was leafing aimlessly through the newspaper Fairlie had left on the table. 'Page 4,' he said. 'The headline's "How much did the police really know about Simon O'Donnell's killer?"' Fairlie raised his hands. 'Not one of mine, I'm relieved to say. It's almost content free.' He'd left the paper on the table deliberately, knowing that – if he hadn't seen it already – Rennie wouldn't be able to resist looking for today's coverage of the O'Donnell story. He wanted to make a point. If Rennie didn't co-operate with Fairlie, the story would continue to run anyway but Rennie wouldn't have any opportunity to influence the content.

'The whole thing's scandalous,' Rennie said. 'There's nothing in it at all. Bloody rag.' He looked up at Fairlie, as if remembering who he was talking to. 'No offence.'

'None taken.' Fairlie took a tiny sip of his previously untouched pint. 'You're right. But I'd rather work with them than against them. That's why I wanted to talk to you.'

'It doesn't matter what I say to you. They'll still print the same salacious nonsense anyway.'

'That's not true, Gordon. No newspaper wants to print anything that's factually untrue.' This was rubbish, as Fairlie well knew. These kinds of papers would publish anything they thought they could get away with. 'If we can give them the real story, they'll go with it.'

'Even if the real story isn't likely to sell papers? Police did a decent job in difficult circumstances and put a dangerous killer behind bars. Not exactly sexy, is it?'

'Depends how we sell it. There was huge interest in the case at the time. The details of the investigation were fascinating. Even a straight retelling of the story would bring in readers.

And if this podcaster does have genuine evidence of police wrongdoing—'

'There was no police wrongdoing.'

Fairlie held up his hand. 'I said *if*. You can't know every detail of the case. Isn't it possible that one of your colleagues cut corners somewhere?'

Rennie hesitated. 'Anything's possible, obviously. But I saw no evidence of anything of that kind.'

'That's my point. I'm sure you and the vast majority of your colleagues on the case were completely straight. But if someone in that team did something dodgy and our podcaster friend has evidence of that, then it's better we present that evidence in context.'

'How do you mean?'

'As you say, the real story is that the police conducted a successful investigation in challenging circumstances. If there also happened to be some questionable behaviour, the public isn't going to care too much.'

Rennie looked unconvinced. 'Depends how you tell the story, doesn't it?'

'That's my point. Look, Gordon, if you work with me we can help control the narrative. You know me. You've worked with me over the years. I've always played straight with you, haven't I?'

'Aye, I suppose,' Rennie conceded grudgingly.

'There you are then. I'm not going to shaft you over this one. You're better off trusting me than some half-arsed podcaster who's never been closer to a police investigation than watching *Shetland* on TV. All I want is the story from the police perspective. I won't name you, and the whole thing can be off the record.'

'Maybe. As long as I can trust you not to bring my name into it.'

'All off the record unless you expressly agree otherwise.'

'I want the story told properly. And fairly.'

'I'm a reporter. Not a sensationalist. Not someone who churns out regurgitated press releases. But someone who's prepared to carry out serious journalism where it matters.' This was mostly bollocks – Fairlie had churned out plenty of regurgitated press releases in his time – but it seemed to be impressing Rennie.

'Okay,' Rennie said finally. 'So what is it you want to know?'

'Talk me through the O'Donnell case from your perspective. I've carried out plenty of research on it since I became involved in all this, but I've only got access to what's in the public domain. I want to know the real story. Tell me it as if I'm hearing it for the first time.'

Rennie was silent for a moment, clearly thinking back to events that had happened more than two decades before. 'Everyone who was around then knows the basics. It shook the whole area. O'Donnell was what you might describe as a respectable nobody. I mean, he'd done well enough for himself. Decently paid job. Working for the police, ironically enough, which is one of the reasons why the case became so notorious. He was part of the police family, even in a civilian role. He had a nice house up near Beauly. Still fairly young and unmarried. But he wasn't particularly wealthy. There was no reason why he should have been targeted.'

'There were various theories at the time,' Fairlie said.

'Numerous theories. And they've carried on proliferating ever since. But none of them had any substance as far as we could tell. Just the usual conspiracist nonsense that always comes out of the woodwork with a case like that. Exacerbated by the fact that he worked for the police. As far as we could ascertain O'Donnell was just what he appeared to be. A middle ranking finance manager with what was then the Northern

Constabulary. A man with no significant profile except in a limited professional sphere.'

Rennie took a sip of his water before continuing. 'O'Donnell was alone in the house at the time of the break-in. The pathologist couldn't pin down the precise time of death, but it happened some time in the small hours of the Sunday morning. O'Donnell's place was a new-build bungalow. Nice place with a decent garden. I suppose I could see why a housebreaker might think it was worth trying, though as it turned out there wasn't much worth stealing.'

'A lot of housebreakers are just trying to steal enough to fund their next hit,' Fairlie pointed out.

'Not sure this one even yielded that much. The break-in took place at the rear of the house. The security wasn't great. The intruder forced open a window and gained entry through that.'

So far Rennie hadn't mentioned the name of the man who'd ultimately been convicted of O'Donnell's murder. Fairlie assumed that wasn't accidental.

'The break in wasn't exactly subtle, and would have made some noise. But O'Donnell was asleep at the other end of the house. He probably didn't hear anything until the intruder entered his bedroom. That's where the sequence of events becomes murky. When O'Donnell's body was discovered, the house had been ransacked. Drawers pulled on to the floor, cupboards emptied, everything you could imagine. We think that must have happened after O'Donnell's death. Our assumption was that the intruder made an initial circuit of the house and disturbed O'Donnell in the bedroom. Then they continued the burglary after O'Donnell was dead.'

'That would take a pretty cool head.'

'Or the opposite. It might have indicated a panicked reaction. Wanting to get something out of the whole mess. Or it might have suggested someone who wasn't too fazed by what they'd just done.' He stopped again to take a mouthful of water, leaving the last sentence hanging in the air.

'The body wasn't discovered until the Monday evening after O'Donnell failed to turn into work. One of his colleagues had tried to contact him and been concerned by the lack of response. He wasn't the type to be absent without good reason, so she called round to check he was okay. She found the front door standing open. I can't imagine what it must have been like for her. To be faced with – that.'

'The descriptions were pretty graphic,' Fairlie said.

'I don't think they really conveyed a sense of what it was like. It was unbelievable. Just utterly savage.'

'And O'Donnell was still in bed?'

'On the bed, anyway. There was no evidence he'd offered any resistance or been involved in a struggle. The killer had simply attacked him. Stabbing him multiple times before finally attempting to cut his throat.'

It was perhaps time to engineer a break, Fairlie thought. He looked at his watch. 'How about we get some food before places get too busy? What sort of thing do you fancy?'

Rennie's expression suggested he was struggling to understand the question. 'Anything,' he said finally. 'Whatever you prefer. Anything's fine.'

CHAPTER TEN

McKay sighed. 'You're telling me he didn't make it?'

DC Josh Carlisle still looked like a fresh-faced youth, though he must be well into his thirties by now. He had the air of a man who'd one day develop a set of jowls and move effortlessly from unfeasible youth to late middle age with no intervening period of aging. He'd worked with McKay for a few years and grown accustomed to the older man's ways, but he still looked nervous in McKay's presence. In fairness, McKay thought, most people did. 'I think I might be saying something more than that.'

McKay gestured for him to sit down. Carlisle looked as if he'd inadvertently walked into a trap. He glanced nervously across the open-plan office to where Ginny Horton was typing at her computer, perhaps hoping she might come to his assistance.

'So what are you saying?'

'That there might be suspicious circumstances.'

'Suspicious circumstances?'

'The consultant wasn't happy to sign off the death certificate. The patient had been responding well to treatment and had recovered consciousness. They'd taken him off the ICU and moved him into a private room because they knew we'd want to interview him.'

'What were the consultant's concerns?'

'Initially just that the death was unexpected. His first worry was that they'd missed some internal injury. He can't be sure of that till they've carried out the post-mortem, but he thinks it's unlikely.'

'So how does he think the patient died?' McKay paused. 'And – no disrespect, Josh – how come you're the person telling me all this?'

Carlisle looked even less comfortable than when he'd first approached McKay. 'A mate of mine was part of the initial response team. He thought we'd want to be forewarned, given it could be heading in our direction...'

'It may be doing that quite literally, son,' McKay murmured. 'Don't say a word till we've heard what Helena has to say.' He rose as Helena Grant made her way across the office towards them. 'Morning, Helena.'

'Does the standing up indicate an unexpected outbreak of male gallantry, Alec? Or are you trying to make an escape?'

'I was going to find you a seat, given that Josh here seems to be occupying the only one available and you look like a woman bearing important news.'

She glanced suspiciously from McKay to Carlisle, who'd jumped awkwardly to his feet at McKay's words. 'Sit down, Josh. Alec's winding you up. I'm perfectly capable of getting my own seat.' She grabbed one from an unoccupied desk and called over to Horton. 'You might want to listen to this, Ginny, if you're not in the middle of something.'

'Nothing that can't wait.' Horton dragged her own seat over to McKay's desk.

'Remind me to book a meeting room next time,' McKay said.

'You like the attention, Alec,' Grant said. 'Especially as I come bearing news that will be music to your ears.'

'You finally managed to swing me early retirement?'

'Be careful what you wish for. No, we have a suspicious death.'

'The truck driver from the A9 collision?'

Grant's eyes flicked from McKay to Carlisle and back again. McKay maintained his innocent smile. 'Grapevine working overtime, I see,' she said.

'Aye. But I don't know any detail so your time here isn't wasted.'

'That's very reassuring. I'd hate to be superfluous. But you're right as always. It's the lorry driver. Chap called Brian Renton. Died in Raigmore this afternoon. Consultant refused to sign the death certificate without a post-mortem. He felt he couldn't assign a straightforward cause of death.'

'Maybe they missed something,' Horton suggested.

'Consultant acknowledges that. They were still conducting tests, so it's possible there was some internal injury they hadn't identified.'

'But?' McKay prompted.

'There are signs the death might have been due to external factors. In a word, asphyxiation.'

'Asphyxiation?'

'Most probably suffocation.'

'Most probably?'

'Don't ask me for details,' Grant said. 'Something to do with blood vessels and bruising. Apparently the symptoms in question aren't specific to asphyxiation so he's not prepared to commit himself beyond that. But he thinks it's a possibility we should consider, pending the pathologist's findings.'

'You don't think he's just trying to cover up for his own negligence?'

'If he'd wanted a quiet life, he could just have signed the certificate.'

'Fair point.' McKay said. 'But what's he suggesting? That someone entered the patient's room and stuck a pillow across his face?'

'Would it even be possible?' Horton said. 'They must have decent security in a place like that, surely?'

'Pretty decent,' Grant agreed. 'But it's difficult when you've got the public coming and going all the time.'

'Hell of a risk, though,' McKay said.

'I suppose you'd have to pick your moment. But yes. Would need some nerve.'

Some thought had been stirring in the back of McKay's mind as Grant had been speaking, though he hadn't pinned it down. 'Where do things stand? In terms of an investigation, I mean.'

'We're treating the room as a crime scene for the moment. Examiner's going over it. Don't know what they'll find but any forensics that can't be linked back to the medical staff would be interesting. I think we should talk to the consultant and maybe some of the other medical staff to make sure we've got the story straight. I don't think it's worth pushing it too far until we've had the post-mortem findings, but if it does turn out there's something in this we don't want to have screwed up these early stages.'

'I'm happy to get over there and have a chat with him. Fancy a trip, Gin?'

To his slight surprise, Ginny hesitated. 'I've a load of admin to plough through. Why not take Josh?'

McKay was on the point of offering a retort, but something in her expression made him bite back the words.

'Fair enough. You up for a hospital visit, Josh?'

'Sounds perfect to me,' Helena Grant said. 'From what I

hear, Josh's the one with the inside track.' She grinned at Carlisle. 'Don't be surprised, Josh. You're not the only one who keeps their ear to the ground.'

CHAPTER ELEVEN

'You're okay with Indian?' Craig Fairlie asked. 'It tends to be my default at lunchtime.'

'Always happy with a good curry,' Gordon Rennie said. 'Barbara's not keen on the spicy stuff. Nice to get the chance.'

'It's a decent wee place,' Fairlie said. 'Better than average food.'

Rennie looked around the basement dining room, his expression showing scepticism. 'You seem to have a knack of finding places where you can hide yourself away.'

'I'd never really thought about it. I don't like working at home. I've found a few places where I can work without attracting too much attention.'

They fell silent as the waiter approached to take their order. Fairlie ordered his usual lamb bhuna and waited patiently while Rennie dithered over the menu before selecting a chicken biryani.

As the waiter departed, Fairlie said, 'Are you happy to carrying on talking about the O'Donnell case?'

'I was surprised by how much emotion it brought back. It's affected me more than I'd realised.'

'It was a shocking business.'

'We tried to keep it low-key at first. Didn't say much about what had been done to O'Donnell. But we couldn't keep a lid on it. For a start, there were public safety concerns. We had a brutal murderer out there. You remember the impact the story had?'

'Very clearly.' Fairlie had covered the story for the local press. He remembered the reactions of the people he'd interviewed. The horror at the savagery of the killing. The contrast between that and the rural setting and O'Donnell's own middle-class respectability. The fact he had worked for the police.

Above all, the killer was still at large. There was no obvious motive for the murder, and no knowing if, when or where the killer might strike again. Communities that had hardly bothered to lock their doors were now bolting them firmly and not just at night. People were looking twice or three times at unfamiliar faces in their neighbourhoods. The fear had grown, day by day, week by week, as long as the murder remained unsolved.

'The breakthrough was a while coming, I remember?'

'You can say that again,' Rennie said. 'We were tearing our hair out. O'Donnell had been a colleague. There was a genuine sense of panic among the public. The media were piling the pressure on. But we weren't getting anywhere.'

'Why was it so difficult?'

'We didn't expect it to be at first. It was a horrific, almost inexplicable murder, but we thought that would make the investigation easier. Someone prepared to commit that level of violence would be on our radar already, surely? That was the way we were thinking.'

'But it didn't pan out that way?' Fairlie recalled the frustration expressed by the detectives he'd spoken to at the time, though most had been cagey about the inquiry itself.

'We found traces of DNA in the room and at the point of entry that didn't match O'Donnell's, but they didn't match anything on the database either. The house was sufficiently remote that we couldn't identify any witnesses who'd seen anything unusual on that Sunday. CCTV coverage was limited in those days. There were no traceable fingerprints that didn't match either the O'Donnells or the small number of other people – a cleaner, a couple of recent visitors – who'd had good reason to be there.'

'And no suspects?'

'No suspects. There was no obvious motive for the murder other than a break-in gone horribly wrong. We identified nothing in O'Donnell's personal life that might have provided a reason for the killing. There was no evidence that he was anything other than he appeared.'

Fairlie was jotting down occasional notes in his old-fashioned shorthand. He usually recorded interviews these days, but he'd thought Rennie would talk more openly without a microphone in front of him. 'What about his role in the police? Could that have provided a motive?'

It was a moment before Rennie raised his head. 'We did look closely at that. Any evidence of corruption, backhanders, any signs that O'Donnell might have got mixed up with the wrong crowd. Even at the time it felt like a long-shot, but sometimes you can't tell. There was nothing. O'Donnell was just a backroom boy. There was nothing incongruous in his lifestyle. He seemed to be exactly what everyone had told us he was. A competent manager, well regarded by his colleagues, liked by his team. Straight as a die. So no leads there. Every avenue we explored turned out to be a dead end.'

'What eventually led you to Kevin Clark?'

'We were getting more and more desperate. The media were ramping up the pressure – well, you'd remember that as well as anyone – and the higher-ups were pushing it all on to the investigation team. We were lucky we had Rory Grant as SIO.'

'I remember Rory. Decent man.'

'Very decent man. And a fine cop. But he was something much rarer in the force. He was a good manager. He knew how to motivate people. He could be forceful when he needed to be, but he respected the team and knew when to listen to them. Above all, he knew how to shield us from the shite coming down from above. Don't get me wrong. He didn't mollycoddle us, and he made sure we knew what the senior ranks were saying. But he saw his role as taking that flak so the rest of us could get on with our jobs.'

'He's a sad loss.'

'He was that. It was probably only because Rory kept calm that we finally made a breakthrough. He kept telling us there was no alternative. We had to keep on keeping on, doing the right things, and eventually we'd get there. The important thing was not to panic, not to lose faith. Some of us had almost reached that point. It's the way with investigations. In most cases, the story's obvious and the challenge is to make sure you've enough evidence to convince the Fiscal and make it stand up in court. Even where it isn't, you usually make the breakthrough quickly – within the first forty-eight hours or so. The longer it drags on, the less chance you have of resolving it. You reach the point where you've exhausted all the direct lines of inquiry, and you're depending on pure dumb luck.'

'That's what happened here?'

'More or less. We'd had an ongoing appeal to the public right from the start of the investigation. It's a time-consuming process, and it brings out all the green-ink brigade and the time-wasters and the comedians who think it's funny to wind up some harassed call-handler in a murder inquiry. But every now and then you get a small gem – a witness who saw something useful, a relative of the perpetrator who's noticed them acting oddly, that kind of thing. In this case, it was an anonymous caller who claimed to be a relative of a young man called Kevin Clark, a supermarket worker living in Inverness. The caller reported that Clark had seemed uncharacteristically anxious and depressed in the days following the murder, and had been seen leaving his home on the Sunday evening carrying a bin bag.'

Rennie paused while the waiter removed their used plates. Fairlie ordered them both coffees, and then prompted. 'Clark had learning difficulties, didn't he?'

'He did. Still living with his mum and dad along with a couple of younger siblings. We never identified the caller, but we were fairly sure it wasn't any member of the immediate family. To be honest, we didn't take it too seriously at first. Clark had no criminal record and, on first sight, didn't seem like someone capable of a brutal murder. He was a vulnerable adult so we interviewed him initially in the presence of his mother and father.'

'Tricky interview, I imagine,' Fairlie said.

'From what I heard, he seemed terrified and confused. His parents were adamant their son wouldn't have been capable of anything like O'Donnell's killing. But they admitted that Kevin had fallen in with some bad types – I think that was actually the phrase they used. People took advantage of him, sometimes for a laugh, sometimes for more questionable motives. They agreed Kevin had been uncharacteristically quiet around the time of the killing, although they reckoned they couldn't be sure of the exact timing. They'd no memory of the supposed bin-bag incident, and we never found any evidence it had happened. Clark himself denied any knowledge of the murder or the break-in. At first we were inclined to believe him, if only because we didn't think he had the ability to come up with a convincing lie.'

'He cut a pretty pathetic figure in court,' Fairlie said. 'In other circumstances you'd have been inclined to feel sorry for him.'

'I did at first. I was sure one of his so-called mates had set him up. We persuaded him to give us the names of some of the people he'd been associating with. A couple had records, mainly for housebreaking and petty theft. For the first time, we thought we might have a lead. I still didn't see Clark as the killer, but it was possible he'd been involved. Cut a long story short, we interviewed a load of the supposed mates. They were a motley bunch, but they didn't seem any more likely as killers than Clark. Just teenagers he'd been at school with. One or two were the kind of small-time chancers who end up bouncing in and out of prison because they're not capable of much more. But most were just kids. We were running out of road. We were close to giving up on that line of inquiry.'

'What about DNA matches?'

'You need to remember this was the early days of the DNA database. That side of things was all a bit primitive. And we couldn't take matches without consent unless we had grounds to arrest someone. But then we struck lucky. Further checks were carried out on some of the items from O'Donnell's bedroom – the bedclothes, his pyjamas, some of his clothes that had been on a chair. I can't even remember why we had them done. Probably just Rory Grant making sure we'd double-checked everything. But finally we struck lucky. We found a match. With Clark himself.'

Rennie took a mouthful of coffee. 'We still didn't know for sure whether he was the killer. But there was no doubt now that he'd been in the room. He'd been there when O'Donnell was murdered.'

CHAPTER TWELVE

'No Jock?' McKay asked.

'Would you believe he's got a day off?' Pete Carrick, one of the crime scene examiner team, was standing in the doorway of the room where Brian Renton had died. 'I drew the short straw.'

'What the hell does Jock do with a day off? Doesn't he have to stay out of the sunshine in case he crumbles to ash?'

'Wedding anniversary, apparently. Taking his wife out to lunch.'

'The least she deserves if she's put up with Jock for all these years.' McKay peered past Carrick. 'Body's been removed, I take it.'

'We did what we had to do then let them take it.'

'Convenient for the mortuary anyway.'

'About the only part of this that is convenient,' a voice said from behind McKay, 'or so my colleagues keep telling me.'

McKay turned to see who had spoken. A tall, slim man, probably early forties, with a shock of greying ginger hair. He peered at McKay through glasses that gave him a permanent look of surprise, and held out his hand. 'Robin Callaghan. I'm the consultant who's made himself deeply unpopular by declining to sign the death certificate. I take it you're the police officer who's no doubt going to make me even more unpopular.'

'It's a gift I have.' McKay shook the proffered hand. 'DI Alec McKay.' He gestured to Josh. 'DC Josh Carlisle. Is there somewhere we can talk?'

'Probably simplest to stay on the ward. There's a room at the far end the nursing staff use. There's no one around now, as you can see.' He gestured at the rows of empty beds.

'Hence your unpopularity?'

'Exactly. We had to empty the whole ward, find alternative accommodation for the patients. Quite a task given how busy we are. It's not as if the staff here don't have enough on their plates.'

McKay and Carlisle followed Callaghan back down the ward to the nurses' station. The room to its rear was clearly intended as a staffroom, with a couple of tables surrounded by dining chairs. There was a sink, a kettle, and a selection of tea and coffees on a worktop by the far wall.

'Coffee?' Callaghan asked.

'Aren't you at risk of making yourself even less popular with the nursing staff?' McKay asked.

'Should be okay. I dutifully pay my subs into the coffee fund every month, though I hardly ever use it. They'll let me live as long as I wash the mugs afterwards.' He was already filling the kettle. 'To be honest, I could do with a caffeine hit. It's been one of those days.'

'Why not, then?' McKay said. 'Just black's fine for me. Josh?'

'Same, please.' Carlisle had seated himself awkwardly at one of the tables. McKay wandered around the room in his usual restless manner. It was a featureless space, the only decoration a couple of official posters with hygiene reminders.

There was a bookshelf behind the door which contained a few tattered paperbacks and a stack of old magazines. He seated himself beside Carlisle and waited for Callaghan to bring the coffees over.

When they were settled, McKay said, 'You could have had a quiet life if you'd just signed the death certificate.'

'Don't remind me. But my conscience would have nagged at me. I wasn't comfortable.'

'In what way?'

'It's partly an instinct thing. Something just doesn't feel quite right. You must get that in your line of work too?'

'What set your instincts tingling?'

'First, the death was unexpected. We'd initially placed Mr Renton in the ICU because we weren't sure about the extent of his injuries. The initial tests indicated they were relatively minor. He'd lost consciousness in the collision, but there were no signs of any brain injury beyond mild concussion. He'd recovered consciousness a while before his death. He still seemed confused about the accident itself, but that was most likely due to shock rather than any physical cause. There were no signs of his condition deteriorating.'

'Presumably it's still possible something was missed in the diagnosis?'

'We're only human, and tests were continuing. We'd have kept him in for several more days to be sure he really was out of the woods. The post-mortem will confirm if something was missed.'

'But you suggested asphyxiation might have been the cause of death?'

'I'm probably being melodramatic. There were red blotches in his eyes and on his skin which can be indicative of death by suffocation. They're not exclusive to asphyxiation so it's no more than a possibility. I felt I ought to mention it so you and the pathologist were aware. I've probably made a complete fool of myself – it's not my area of expertise – but I'd rather that than ignore it.'

'Would it be feasible, though? To kill someone that way.'

'Perfectly feasible in theory,' Callaghan said. 'If the killer was single-minded enough, it would only take a few minutes. Whether it would be possible to do it in this environment, I'm not so sure.'

'Presumably Renton would have been closely monitored?' Carlisle said.

'Very. But it was a busy time on the ward. There'd been a couple of new admissions, so no one had checked on him physically for a while. He was being monitored electronically but by the time the nurses reacted to the alarm, he was already dead.'

'Hypothetically, is it possible someone could have entered the ward, killed Renton and left without being spotted?' McKay asked.

'I've been thinking about that. I'd say – if only hypothetically, as you put it – the answer's yes. That room's secluded. We put Renton in there for precisely that reason. We thought if your people wanted to interview him, it was better to do that discreetly without disturbing the other patients. It's away from the main ward and accessible through an entrance at the far end.'

'Could an unauthorised visitor enter that way?'

'In theory, no. In practice, the security's compromised all the time. If you look as though you've the right to be there, you probably won't get challenged. There are no restrictions on visiting times so visitors come and go. The wards are locked but if you come in as someone's going out, probably no one will stop you.'

'But it would be tricky to get in without being seen?'

'I'd have thought so. Whether your presence would be registered is another question. People are very focused on their jobs.' Callaghan paused. 'But to come in here with the express intention of killing a patient, well, let's say you'd need nerves of steel.'

The last phrase had stirred a memory in McKay's mind. Before he could register what it might be, the door opened, thrown back on its hinges.

'So this is where you're hiding.' The speaker was a short, slightly portly man in a well-tailored suit. He had an expensive-looking haircut seemingly designed to conceal his growing baldness. His expression suggested the opposite of Callaghan's quiet amiability.

Callaghan looked up in mild amusement, as if he'd been expecting the interruption. 'Afternoon, Shaun. What can we do for you?'

The man glowered down at them. 'What you can do for me is tell me what's going on and why I haven't been consulted about it.'

Callaghan smiled. 'Grab a seat, Shaun. I'll make you a coffee and we can tell you.'

The man looked from McKay to Callaghan and then back again, and finally pulled out a chair, his expression suggesting that someone – most likely some unlucky subordinate not in the room – would suffer for this.

'Milk? Sugar?' Callaghan said.

The man clearly recognised when he was beaten. 'Just milk.'

McKay offered his own bland smile. 'And you are, sir?'

'Shaun Sanderson. Deputy Chief Executive.'

'Good to meet you. Albeit in rather difficult circumstances. DI Alec McKay. DC Josh Carlisle.'

Callaghan slid a cup of coffee in front of Sanderson. 'There you go.'

'So what exactly's going on here?' Sanderson said.

'We have a potentially suspicious death.' Callaghan sipped at his own coffee. 'As I reported to your office a couple of hours ago. You and the chief were off-site and I was told your meeting couldn't be interrupted. I felt I had no alternative but to use my own initiative and speak to the police.'

'You should have spoken to the Communications Department.'

'I did. As a courtesy. So they were aware of what was going on if there should be any media inquiries.'

'I don't like the idea of police crawling over the hospital.'

McKay nodded. 'At the moment, other than myself and DC Carlisle, there's one uniformed officer ensuring that the potential crime scene remains secure and a couple of police examiners collecting evidence from the room in question. I'm sorry we've had to interrupt the hospital's routine temporarily, but there's really no alternative.'

'Are you seriously suggesting one of our patient's might have been murdered?'

'We're suggesting that one of your patients died in circumstances that are currently unexplained and which may be suspicious. So far, nothing more than that. We understand a post-mortem has been requested which may well confirm the death was the result of natural causes.'

'So why not wait for the post-mortem?'

McKay reflected, not for the first time, that an unexpectedly high proportion of the world's numpties ended up occupying senior management roles in all kinds of organisations, the police service certainly not excepted. 'If the post-mortem concludes the death wasn't the result of natural causes, we need to ensure that all available forensic and other evidence has been collected before there's any risk of the scene being compromised. The alternative would have been to have kept the room and this ward closed until the post-mortem.'

'Sorry, Shaun,' Callaghan added. 'I'm sure I'm just being over-cautious. But that's my job. I couldn't let it go.'

Sanderson shifted awkwardly, obviously recognising that the moral high ground had already crumbled beneath him. 'I just don't like being out of the loop on something like this.'

McKay gave an emollient smile. 'If there should be a need for a further investigation, we'll of course co-operate fully with the hospital authorities and management. Would you be the most appropriate contact, Mr Sanderson?' Smarm wasn't McKay's natural register, but he could turn it on when needed.

'I suppose so.' Sanderson reached into his pocket and produced a business card. 'If I'm not available, my PA should be able to get a message to me.' He glared at Callaghan who continued to smile amiably. 'I'll make sure to tell her this matter takes priority over all other meetings.'

'That would be helpful.' McKay pocketed the card and slid one of his own across to Sanderson. 'Let's hope this comes to nothing. I'm assuming your communications team will help keep it under wraps until we have the post-mortem results, but if there should be any queries from the media, let me know.' McKay turned back to Callaghan. 'You say Renton regained consciousness before his death?'

'For a while. He was drifting in and out of sleep. He still seemed very confused.'

'Is it possible for us to talk to any of the nurses who were attending to him?'

'I don't imagine the nurses will be able to tell you anything more than Dr Callaghan has already told you,' Sanderson said. 'They're very busy people.'

'I've no intention of taking up any more of their time than I need to. But I'd like to talk to whoever was there when Renton initially recovered consciousness. I'm interested in anything he might have said. I assume you didn't hear him say anything significant, Dr Callaghan?'

'Not really. I was called to check on him when he first woke up. At that point, he was confused about what had happened and where he was. The nurse was trying to explain that to him, though I don't know how much he was taking in. I left them to it as I was in the middle of a ward round. But I can track down the nurse who was with him, assuming she's still on duty. I'm assuming you don't need her for long?'

'Just a few minutes at this stage.' McKay smiled blandly at Sanderson. 'Then we can leave you to get on with your busy lives.'

CHAPTER THIRTEEN

They'd returned to the bar. Rennie rang the changes on his soft drink by ordering a lime and soda. Fairlie bought a second pint which he'd eke out until the bar began to fill up at the end of the working day. He generally took that as his cue to leave. He'd half-expected Rennie to head back home once they'd finished eating, but he'd seemed happy to follow Fairlie back to the pub.

They settled themselves back at the corner table. Fairlie took a tiny sip of his beer and said, 'So that was the big breakthrough?'

'Almost the only breakthrough, to be honest. After that, it was more a question of gathering the evidence to make it hold up. The forensics were persuasive – there was no way Kevin Clark couldn't have been in the room – but the Fiscal wanted more. Our initial assumption was that Clark hadn't acted alone. He had no record and there was no evidence he'd previously been involved in any burglaries, even if some of his associates had been. I didn't think he had the wit or the gumption to carry out a break-in by himself.'

'What did he say?'

'We had to interview him very carefully. We wanted to ensure anything that emerged from the interviews would be admissible evidence. We didn't want any suggestion he'd been coerced into a confession. His solicitor and his parents were rightly protective of his well-being. We were trying to do it all by the book. So it took us a while to prise anything from him.'

'Even when you presented him with the DNA evidence?'

'I'm not sure he really understood its significance. His solicitor was trying to muddy the waters by asking if there were other ways the DNA could have been present on the materials, whether there was any possibility the evidence had been compromised, that kind of stuff.'

'And was there?' Fairlie thought back to the hints Hugh Preston, the podcaster, had dropped about corners being cut, evidence being fabricated.

'I can't see it. Rory Grant ran a tight ship. If there'd been anything, it wouldn't have escaped Rory's eagle-eye.'

Fairlie had only met Grant a few times – partly because, unlike some of his colleagues, Grant hadn't been keen to hobnob with the media – but he was inclined to accept Rennie's word on this. Grant's reputation remained untarnished. If there'd been any dirt, someone would have leaked it by now.

'When we asked about the break-in and the killing, at first Clark refused to say anything. Then he claimed not to understand what we were talking about. When we told him we had evidence he'd been at the murder scene he seemed baffled. If it hadn't been for the DNA, we might have started to doubt ourselves.

'But eventually, very slowly, he began to break down. He admitted he'd been involved in some break-ins, going along with a couple of his dodgy mates. I suspect they probably did it as much for the *craic* as anything else. They weren't going to get rich stealing mobile phone or a few quid and some bank cards.

A couple of Clark's mates had been egging him on to carry out a break-in on his own. I reckon they were having a laugh, knowing Clark would screw it up. Unfortunately, it turned out that the screw-up was much greater than they'd bargained for.' Rennie fell silent for a moment, staring into the depths of his untouched drink. 'Little bastards. In his way, Clark was as much a victim as O'Donnell. Clark's story, as it eventually emerged, was that he'd finally plucked up the courage to have a go. One of his mates had told him O'Donnell's house was going to be empty for the weekend, so he decided to have a shot at that. He got a couple of his mates to drop him off nearby and pick him up afterwards. That's how half-arsed the whole thing was. Clark goes to the house, breaks in by copying what he'd seen his mates do, and gets inside.'

'All by himself?'

'So he maintained. We couldn't shake him on that part of the story. We couldn't even persuade him to shop the friends who'd given him the lift. Reckoned they hadn't known what Clark was up to. If you believe that, I've a few bridges to sell you, but we couldn't shift him on it.'

'So why kill O'Donnell? And why kill him so brutally?'

'Sheer panic, he claimed. Once he was in the house, he didn't know what to do. I'm not sure he'd even gone with the aim of taking anything, except maybe a souvenir of the escapade. He was just wandering about the house, and he ended up in the bedroom.'

'Where he encountered O'Donnell.'

'O'Donnell had heard someone moving about and was getting up to investigate when Clark entered the room. Clark panicked and struck out with the knife.'

'How come he was carrying a knife in the first place?'

'Another one of his bloody mates. Told him if he was going to do this, he ought to be properly armed. Not that any of his mates would have been stupid enough to go housebreaking with a bloody great knife.'

'Who needs enemies when you've got mates like that?' Fairlie said.

'Exactly. He reckoned he stabbed out at O'Donnell who fell back onto the bed. Clark didn't know what to do, so carried on stabbing, wanting to make sure O'Donnell was really dead.'

'What about the ransacking of the house?'

'He was never able to tell us what happened after the killing. My guess – well, the view of the psychologist at the time – is that he was in shock. Couldn't believe what he'd done, and then didn't know what he was doing.'

'What about his clothes?' Fairlie asked. 'They must have been bloodstained.'

'We never found the clothes. Clark couldn't tell us what had happened after the murder. He reckoned he hadn't got the intended lift with his mates, though he couldn't tell us what he'd done instead. It's conceivable he got a train from Beauly to Inverness – though if his clothing was bloodstained, you'd have thought he'd have been conspicuous. No witnesses ever came forward. His mum and dad were out when he got back home. At church, would you believe?'

'Sounds like a big gap in the narrative.'

'It was. The biggest weakness in our case, but there wasn't a lot we could do about it. Clark claimed not to remember anything, and nothing we did ever persuaded him to change his story. We tried hard to find any witness who might have been able to give us an insight into what actually happened, but no success. We interviewed Clark's associates and checked out their vehicles but again nothing.'

'You think O'Donnell was protecting one of his so-called mates?'

'I still think it's likely. But we could never persuade him to admit it.'

'So it's possible Clark wasn't the killer or at least not the only killer.'

'It's possible, though for me that part of the story does ring true. I could imagine Clark panicking like that. Anyone with more nous would have made themselves scarce when they ran into O'Donnell. Even if a second person was present, I don't find it difficult to believe Clark was the killer.'

'Do you think Clark was telling the truth about not being able to remember?'

'Who knows? The psychs thought it was likely. I'm a cynical cop so I'm inclined to think the worst.' He shrugged. 'I suspect the reality may be somewhere in the middle.'

'What about the knife? You didn't find that at the scene?'

'No. That was the final piece of the jigsaw. We'd searched the immediate vicinity, but the knife was eventually found in the garden of a house nearer the village. The location did reinforce the idea that Clark might have headed to the railway station after the killing, and had simply tossed it over a hedge as he'd passed.'

Fairlie raised an eyebrow. 'Lucky.'

'We might have made the case stick without it, but it would have been tricky. It was the final bit of corroboration we needed. We had a confession but there were doubts about that because of the gaps in Clark's memory. We had the DNA on the clothing which placed Clark at the scene of the crime. But we didn't have conclusive evidence that he'd actually committed the murder.'

'The delights of Scottish law.'

'Aye. Fortunately, given we're talking about the Highlands, the weather had remained dry since the murder. O'Donnell's blood was on the knife, confirming it was the murder weapon.

More importantly we found Clark's DNA and his fingerprints on the handle. In other words, evidence that he'd not only been present at the crime scene, but had actually held the knife.'

'Someone else could have committed the murder and handed him the knife,' Fairlie pointed out.

'The defence tried that line. Despite his confession, Clark pleaded not guilty on grounds of diminished responsibility. The defence case was that, given his learning difficulties, the confession was unreliable. If Clark was covering up for some associate, there wasn't definitive evidence he'd wielded the knife. But, whatever we might have suspected, there was no actual evidence anyone else had been present. Clark denied it. There was no clear forensic evidence of another person. Given Clark's fingerprints were on the knife, it was a stretch. The jury certainly gave the idea short shrift.' He took another mouthful of his drink. 'So how does all that fit with what this podcaster's been saying?'

'Hard to say. He's playing it close to his chest. There were parts of your account that didn't come through strongly in the media at the time.'

'The stuff about Clark claiming not to know what happened after the killing, you mean? We weren't happy with that. We pushed him as hard as we could, but we had to tread carefully given Clark's vulnerability. You reckon that's where this podcaster's going to focus?'

'I honestly don't know. All that's in the public domain if you go looking for it. He might just be tugging on that particular thread in the hope something more will emerge.'

'We thought the defence might make more of it at the trial,' Rennie said. 'But it was potentially a double-edged sword. The prosecution could use it to cast doubt on our version of events, but it was also a confirmation of Clark's traumatised state after the killing. The jury clearly weren't convinced by the diminished responsibility argument. Clark's learning difficulties weren't so severe he couldn't be held accountable for his actions. In the end, the jury was only out for about half an hour before they returned a unanimous verdict.'

Fairlie took a second minuscule sip of his beer. 'That's really helpful, Gordon. It'll be interesting to see what, if anything, our podcasting chum comes up with. I don't know if he's got some insider source, but it sounds as if you had everything covered.'

'That was Rory Grant. He was punctilious. Wanted to ensure the case was as watertight as possible.'

'At the moment, my guess is that all we'll get from the podcast is a summary of the gaps in the case along with a bucket-load of innuendo about manufactured evidence. All pitched just this side of defamation.' Fairlie paused. 'Of course, you can't defame the dead.'

'You think this guy will target Rory Grant?'

'No idea. But he'd be the safest target. I assume the rest of the team are still with us?'

'As far as I'm aware. Some retired, like me. Some still serving.' Rennie swallowed the last of his water. 'I hope you're wrong, though. Rory Grant deserved better than that.'

'I've no special insights into what this guy's up to. I don't know if he's got anything substantive or if he's kite-flying.'

'You'll keep me up to speed, won't you? If someone's trying to shaft us, I'd like to be forewarned.'

'You'll be the first to know. And if you pick up anything on the grapevine, you've got my number. Or you can generally find me in here.'

Rennie looked round at the gloomy interior of the bar, still empty apart from the two of them. 'It's been quite an experience. But I reckon I'll phone.'

CHAPTER FOURTEEN

M cKay rose as the nurse entered, and gestured for her to take a seat. She looked very young – although these days most people looked young to McKay – and very nervous. The poor lass probably thought she was going to be quizzed about the circumstances of Brian Renton's death. There might well come a time for that, depending on the findings of the post-mortem, but for the moment McKay had other interests.

He'd persuaded Shaun Sanderson not to sit in on the meeting. Callaghan had brought the nurse up from the ward and made his own discreet exit.

'Would you like a tea or coffee?' McKay asked. 'Josh here's a dab hand with a kettle.'

'I don't want to put you to any trouble.'

'No trouble,' McKay said. 'Not for me, anyway. And I'm sure Josh can cope. I'm having a tea anyway so you might as well have a drink while we're about it.'

'I'll have a coffee then. Thank you. Just milk.'

'I'll make sure Josh puts a contribution in the kitty.' McKay smiled and, after a moment, she offered an anxious smile in return. 'I'm DI Alec McKay. My kettle-wielding colleague is DC Josh Carlisle.'

'Rosie McColl,' she said. 'Dr Callaghan said you wanted to talk to me.'

'Don't worry, you're not in any kind of trouble. I just wanted to have a chat about Mr Renton, the patient who died this morning.'

McKay could see his words hadn't reassured her. 'I've still not quite got used to it. Patients passing away on the ward. But of course it happens. Mr Renton was a shock, though. We thought he was past the worst.'

'It must be difficult to be sure,' McKay said. 'I understand there'll be a post-mortem so that'll no doubt confirm the cause of death. At the moment, I'm more interested in the collision itself.'

'The collision? I don't really know anything about the collision. I heard it was another one on the A9. We see too many of those.'

'So do we. This was a nasty one. Two fatalities, and now we can probably add Mr Renton to the list. We treat all accidents as potential crimes – everything from driving without due care and attention up to potential manslaughter or even murder depending on the circumstances – and we investigate on that basis.'

'Yes, of course. That makes sense.'

Carlisle brought the drinks over to the table, and sat himself down beside McKay. His amiable presence seemed to be helping McColl relax. McKay took a sip of his own tea and continued. 'It was a nasty crash and a fairly baffling one, to be honest.'

'Baffling?'

'A head-on collision between the truck Renton was driving and a car. We're still waiting on the collision inspector's report but on the face of it there were just the two cars involved. Renton doesn't seem to have been at fault. He was driving on the right side of the road within the speed limit. Dr Callaghan has confirmed there were no signs of alcohol or drugs. So at the moment it looks as if the car driver was to blame. He seems to have driven on the wrong side of the road directly into the oncoming truck. We're trying to understand why he might have done that. It was a straight road, daylight, perfect driving conditions. We were hoping Brian Renton would be a key witness, assuming he had a clear recollection of what happened. I understand you were with him when he first recovered consciousness.'

McColl still hadn't touched her coffee. 'Immediately afterwards, anyway. We'd seen from the monitors that there'd been a change in his condition. So a couple of us went to check. He was stirring as we went in, and then he opened his eyes.'

'How did he seem?'

'Confused, mainly. But that wasn't surprising. He'd suffered from concussion and was on a cocktail of drugs. He had no real idea of where he was or what had happened to him. But he seemed responsive, so we tried to explain to him why he was in hospital. I'm not sure how much he understood at first, but he gradually seemed to take it in.'

'Did he say anything about the collision?'

'Not at first. He just seemed uncertain, as if he still didn't understand how he'd ended up in hospital. Then he asked what had happened to the people in the other cars—'

'Cars? Plural?'

'I'm pretty sure that's what he said. I didn't know anything about the accident except that he was the only survivor, so I didn't really think about it.'

'If there was a second car involved, they didn't wait around.

That's why it's important. Think carefully. You're sure that's what he said?'

'It wasn't just that. He was definitely talking about two cars. He was most concerned about the car that had hit his truck. I didn't want to distress him and I didn't know the details anyway, so I just said I'd find out for him. Then he said he was less concerned about what had happened to the mad bastard. Those were his words.' She paused, looking mildly embarrassed.

'Don't worry, lass,' McKay said. 'I've heard worse language than that. Usually from DC Carlisle here. What do you think he meant?'

'I think he was talking about another driver. The one he blamed for the accident.'

'Maybe not so much of an accident if it was caused by some mad bastard,' McKay observed. 'Did he say anything else?'

'I'm trying to remember,' she said. 'There was something about a black car. Driving like a maniac. He was already drifting back to sleep so it wasn't very coherent. I don't think there was anything else.'

'That's plenty,' McKay says. 'If nothing else, it tells us there's another witness out there somewhere. Quite possibly more than just a witness. That's been very helpful.'

'What about Mr Renton?' she said. 'Do you really think his death's suspicious?'

'At the moment, it's nothing more than unexplained. We're going through a routine. There's no point in speculating ahead of the post-mortem.'

'I suppose not.' She swallowed the last of her coffee. 'Do you need anything else? I ought to be getting back to the ward. We're stretched to the limit.'

'We won't take up any more of your time. That's been invaluable.'

McKay waited until she'd closed the door behind her before

turning back to Carlisle. 'More useful than I expected. So we have the beginnings of an explanation for the collision.'

'A mad bastard?'

'The next question is what exactly the mad bastard did that caused someone to drive head on into a bloody great truck.'

'Pity Renton isn't still around to tell us.'

'Yes,' McKay said. 'That is a pity. And very convenient for whoever our mad bastard turns out to be.'

CHAPTER FIFTEEN

I t felt like a comedown after their past triumphs, but Ben Vaughn accepted they had to take it step by step. That was what Iain Pennycook kept telling him. Pennycook had done this before, from a much lower starting point, and he could do it again. Small acorns, and all that. Vaughn had been working as one of Pennycook's assistants for a year or two now, and he'd learnt a lot from the man. For the moment, Vaughn was prepared to trust his judgement.

They'd been a receptive crowd. That was the important point. Pennycook's speech had gone down well, ending with a standing ovation. The subsequent questions from the audience had mostly been supportive. There were one or two of the usual rent-a-gob lefties harping back to the usual topics, but Pennycook had quashed those easily enough, earning himself a further smattering of applause.

He'd mostly steered away from politics on this occasion. The whole point, as he'd emphasised repeatedly today, was that this should be a cross-party campaign. This was bigger than petty divisions. Everyone should be in favour of saving lives, regardless of where they sat on the political spectrum. Who could argue with that?

Of course, that hadn't stopped him getting in a few digs at the mainstream political parties in Holyrood who'd failed to get a grip on this issue. The delays, the broken promises. The failure to allocate the necessary resources to the Highlands. It was all smartly done, Vaughn was forced to admit.

Vaughn found Pennycook sitting in the small kitchen at the back of the community hall that had been used to prepare refreshments for those who'd attended the meeting. He'd hung around for a while in the main hall, being back-slapped by members of the departing crowd, but had clearly decided he needed a few minutes to himself, leaving his small team to deal with any remaining questions. That was another of his techniques, Vaughn had noticed. You made yourself available, but not too much so. Maintain some distance, leave them wanting more. These were skills he'd honed over his career.

'So this is where you are,' Vaughn said. 'I was wondering where you'd got to.'

Pennycook looked around the small room. 'There weren't too many options. Shut the door behind you. I don't want to encourage the great unwashed to come wandering in.'

Vaughn closed the door behind him. 'Thought those were your people?'

'They are. Doesn't mean I have to mix with them any more than I can help.'

Vaughn pulled out a chair and sat at the table opposite Pennycook. 'You're still sure this is the right way forward? I mean, we're not exactly playing Carnegie Hall here.'

'Don't despise the little people, Ben.'

'You generally do.'

Pennycook laughed. 'Not if there's any risk of being

overheard. These people need us. They need what we can offer.'

'And we need what they can donate. I get it. But you're sure about this?'

'It's a calculated risk. We were getting diminishing returns in Edinburgh. The old causes are fading away. Brexit's done and dusted, and nobody wants to talk about it. The independence debate rumbles on without getting anywhere. There's plenty for people to grumble about, but no real focus for it beyond a general sense the whole country's screwed and nobody knows what to do. We need to find another way in, another cause to back.'

'And you came up with road safety on the A9?'

'Now, now, Ben. Stick to the script. The A9's a symptom, not a cause. It's an important symptom because people are literally being killed, but it's simply another way in which the people of the Highlands and Islands are neglected and undervalued. There are countless more: the state of the ferries, the general condition of the roads, even trivial things like the cost of getting items delivered to these parts.'

'You don't need to lecture me about any of this, Iain. I've read the script a thousand times and can recite it from memory. I often do when I'm out raising funds for you. But when we're having to hold events in a two-bit hole on the outskirts of Inverness, I sometimes wonder if this is the way forward.'

'It's the only way. It's the way I built up my profile before.'

'As long as nobody suggests you're a has-been.'

'That's the whole point. It's not that my star has waned – or, if it has, the people out there don't know that – but that I've actively chosen to leave the big city behind to return to my own folk in their hour of need.'

'Aye. You're William Wallace reincarnated. I get it.'

'Bugger off, Ben. You know what I mean. I'm the champion

they need. The voice of the Highlands. We start like this. Then we build the profile. I'm already doing plenty of radio and TV interviews. We're getting into the press. We've got the A9 campaign going in that rag. It's all coming together.'

'I can't deny that. The newspaper campaign seems to be getting up a head of steam now.'

'I know which buttons to press,' Pennycook said. 'And I'm pretty shameless about how often I press them.'

'It's a pity it's competing with this O'Donnell thing. But I think you're coming out on top.'

'O'Donnell thing?' For all his skills in attracting publicity, Pennycook rarely looked at the media. As far as he was concerned, Vaughn thought, newspapers were for appearing in, not for reading. He had people, including Ben, to do that for him.

'Long before my time. Some bloke who was brutally killed in an apparent break-in. Young guy was convicted for the killing, but there are suggestions it might have been a miscarriage of justice. It's the twentieth anniversary, and a podcaster's covered the story. One of the other papers is running a campaign to get the case reopened.'

'Sounds like the usual half-baked nonsense. But keep an eye on it. Let me know if this podcast comes up with anything.'

'Really? I wouldn't have thought it was your kind of thing.'

'It isn't,' Pennycook said. 'But I don't want the bugger stealing any of our fucking thunder.'

CHAPTER SIXTEEN

On his way back to the office, McKay called in to the workshop where the collision investigators worked. A couple of investigators were working on cars, but Adam Sutherland was in the office at the rear, sitting at his computer. 'Afternoon, Alec. We seem to be seeing a lot of you at the moment.'

'You're not going to complain, though, are you, Adam? You don't like dealing with the admin any more than I do.'

Sutherland glanced at the monitor. 'You're not wrong there. Forms about forms. Not my happy place. I'd much rather be under a car bonnet.'

'Wondered if you'd made any progress with this morning's smash yet?'

'Give me a break. I've been out all morning. Do you know how many collisions we've had on the A9 just this week?'

'That's one reason I'm interested.'

'Not your killer on the road idea again? I've told you, it's a non-starter. Hope you're not getting obsessive in your old age.'

'I've always been obsessive. It's what's kept me young. No, I was wondering because I've just come from the hospital. Sadly, our truck driver didn't make it.'

'Shit. I'd heard his injuries didn't look serious.'

'That's what they thought. We'll have to see what the post-mortem says. For the moment we're treating it as a suspicious death.'

'Suspicious? Not just unexplained?'

'Don't blame me. It was the consultant's judgement. It'll probably go nowhere, more's the pity. I could do with a nice juicy murder.'

'Aye, I've got that impression.'

'Thing is,' McKay said, 'it seems our truck driver recovered consciousness briefly before he died. He was still chock-full of drugs and not very coherent, but he said something about a "mad bastard in a black car".'

'Did he now?'

'As I recall, the only other car at the scene was red.'

'A red Kia. The couple who died.'

'So where's the mad bastard in the black car?'

'If he and the car ever existed. You said yourself the truck driver wasn't very coherent. People's memories of serious crashes are unreliable. It might fit in with what the collision analysts are finding, though. There's some evidence of a third vehicle at the scene. We're trying to make sense of the tyre marks. It's not easy because the marks are faint and patchy, and it's not clear what's new and what's old. There are also some interesting marks on the hard shoulder.'

'Hard shoulder?'

'And the grass beyond it. The ground's solid at present because we've had so little rain. It's possible there was a vehicle on the wrong side of the road which veered onto the hard shoulder to avoid hitting the Kia. We're checking if there are any paint marks on the Kia that aren't consistent with it hitting the lorry. Again, not easy because, frankly, there's not much left of the front half of the Kia. The poor buggers must have died more or less instantly.'

'Probably thankfully, given the likely alternatives.'

'Amen to that. So we're thinking there could have been a third car involved. Makes the most sense, anyway.'

McKay closed his eyes, trying to envisage the scene. 'You're saying someone overtook the lorry, heading directly for the Kia coming in the opposite direction, and then avoided the collision by driving off the far side of the road. Whereas the Kia pulled over into the path of the lorry.'

'That's about it. Most likely the Kia driver panicked and tried to avoid the oncoming car. Either that or the oncoming vehicle winged the Kia and forced it into the lorry's path.'

'You think the third vehicle was most likely a car?'

'From the tyre marks we've found, yes. Maybe a biggish car, but not a large van or truck.'

'Then this bugger just drove off?'

'Maybe just a panicked reaction. Question is whether they'll hand themselves in subsequently. You never know.'

'You never do,' McKay agreed. 'The question I'm left with is why anyone would overtake in the face of an oncoming car at that point. It's a straight stretch of road, visibility should have been good. Why do it?'

'We've been through this, Alec. And I've been through it countless times over the years. Mostly, the only conclusion you can come to is that people are idiots. Some people don't realise they're driving a lethal weapon.'

'Who's leading the collision inquiry from our side?'

'Charlie Farrow's the SIO. Assume you know him?'

McKay laughed. 'Oh, aye. I know him all right. We go way, way back. Some history there.'

'Not good history, I'm guessing.'

'Charlie boy's all right as long as you don't take him as seriously as he takes himself. But we're not exactly bosom buddies. Still, I suppose I'd better let him know what the truck driver said.'

'He won't be happy you discovered that before he did.'

'No, he won't, will he?' McKay smiled. 'That's probably why I'll really enjoy telling him.'

CHAPTER SEVENTEEN

McKay arrived back at the office to find Helena Grant and Ginny Horton talking earnestly at Horton's desk. The room was empty apart from the two of them, but they were speaking in whispers. Grant gave him a look that he took as a warning. He hesitated, wondering what was going on, and considered making a discreet exit. He could always pretend he was going to make a coffee.

He half turned, but Horton was already gesturing for him to join them. 'I want to let Alec know now. It's only fair. I don't know how it's going to pan out yet.'

'How what's going to pan out?'

Helena Grant was still wearing her warning expression, but now it was clear she was signalling that he shouldn't speak without engaging his brain.

'Ginny's had some bad news,' Grant said.

'It's about Isla. You know she was having some hospital tests.'

McKay nodded. Horton had mentioned it when she'd booked her recent day's leave, but hadn't given the impression anything serious was involved.

'The tests were to check out whether she has Hodgkin's lymphoma. A form of cancer. She's just had the results through.'

Horton had always seemed a calm and resilient character, capable of maintaining her cool in the face of almost any provocation. She'd initially struck McKay as quintessentially English, stiff upper lip and all, though it had turned out she was at least half-Scottish.

'It's not good news,' she went on. 'It could be worse, but it's not good. The tests were positive. They hope they've caught it in time, but they're not sure. It's readily treatable, but also very aggressive. They didn't quite put it in so many words, but my impression is it may be touch and go.'

'Shit. I'm sorry, Gin. How is she?'

'Fine for the moment. She says it's surreal that she doesn't feel ill.'

'When did you find out?'

'Literally just a few minutes ago. We weren't expecting the results for another day or two. But they phoned to let her know. They want to start treatment as soon as possible.'

'What's the treatment?' McKay asked.

'Regime of chemotherapy and radiotherapy, I think. Whatever it is, it won't be pleasant.'

'Take whatever time you need, Ginny,' Grant said. 'I'll square it all with HR.'

'I've no idea yet what it's going to be like, but I appreciate that. Thanks.'

'Is Isla at home? You should get back to her.'

'She got the call at work, would you believe? Right in the middle of a client meeting. Had to interrupt the meeting and then, after she'd taken the call, continue the discussion as if nothing had happened.' Horton gave a thin smile. 'The delights of the private sector.'

'They'll help her out, though, surely?' Grant said.

'She's a partner there, so I'd hope her fellow partners would be sympathetic. But it's a cut-throat world. You can never tell. Anyway, she's heading home as soon as she can. I'd like to be there to greet her.'

'You get yourself off,' Grant said. 'Are you up to driving?'

'I'm fine. It's just been a shock. We knew this might be the outcome, but you keep persuading yourself it won't happen.'

'What's the next step?' McKay asked.

'Meeting with the consultant. Talk through the implications and options. Then we work through it.'

'We're here for you,' Grant said. 'For both of you. Let us know if you need anything.'

'Aye, seconded,' McKay said gruffly. 'Now bugger off home before Isla gets back.'

'If you're sure—'

'Don't be daft, Gin. Just bugger off. All the best to both of you. Stay strong.'

'I'll keep you both posted.'

McKay waited until the office door had closed behind Horton. 'Poor wee lass. Imagine having to deal with that. No wonder she wasn't keen to come to the hospital.'

'It's the not knowing that must be the worst. The only blessing about Rory's death was that it was quick and painless. That didn't help me at the time, but it helps me now. Speaking of which, I notice there hasn't been much on the O'Donnell case in the paper over the last few days.'

'Probably exhausted whatever material they had. Told you it would all fizzle out. There's nothing for them to find.'

'Hope you're right. What about the hospital? Anything there?'

'Potentially. It depends on the post-mortem findings. Renton did say something before he died, though.'

'Something interesting?'

'About the collision. Was asking what had happened to the – and I quote – "mad bastard in the black car"?'

'So there was a second car?'

'Looks like it. Popped in to see Adam Sutherland on my way back. It's consistent with what the analysts are finding.'

'I know you're desperate to get your teeth into something, Alec, but the collision isn't our investigation.'

'It might become ours if Brian Renton was unlawfully killed.'

'I'm not seriously expecting that, though, are you? I'm struggling with the idea of someone being killed in cold blood in a hospital.'

'Stranger things have happened.'

'Not many. Even in our line of business. For the moment it's not our case.'

'I ought to share this nugget of information with the SIO.'

'Of course. It's a potentially important piece of evidence...' She caught his expression. 'All right. Break it to me. Who's the SIO?'

'My good friend Charlie Farrow.'

'Oh, for goodness' sake, Alec. You're not going to go stirring up trouble?'

'When do I ever stir up trouble?'

'Do you seriously want me to answer that? I know what you think of Farrow.'

'It was a privilege to work under his inspired leadership.'

'You lasted a day, drove him nearly insane, and engineered your removal from his team.'

'It was a very productive day.' This had been a very brief period, a year or two before, when McKay had briefly been seconded to Farrow's team to avoid a potential conflict of interest. It hadn't gone well, at least from Farrow's perspective. 'I'll simply break the news that I've come across some potentially significant evidence that's not been picked up by his inquiry team.'

'He'll be furious you visited the hospital in the first place.'

'You asked me to. In connection with a potentially suspicious death. Nothing to do with the collision.'

'I know that and you know that. It won't be what Farrow chooses to believe.'

'I'm just trying to be helpful.'

'Of course you are. You're bored, Alec, and when you're bored you end up making mischief. I know you.'

'I've got to take my small pleasures where I can.'

'Just don't expect me to back you up if Farrow's on the warpath.'

'Ach, I've made worse enemies than Charlie Farrow.'

'I know, and so far you and your career have somehow come through unscathed. But one day your luck'll run out. Our new Area Commander's looking to steady the ship. He seems a decent guy but he's not going to tolerate—'

'Mutineers? I've always fancied the idea of carrying a dagger between my teeth as I shimmy up the rigging. Or whatever it is that mutineers do.'

'I was going to say troublemakers.'

'Much less exciting. But, okay, message received and understood. I promise I won't wind up Charlie Farrow any more than I can help.'

Grant shook her head. 'Funnily enough, Alec, for some reason I still don't find that promise entirely reassuring.'

CHAPTER EIGHTEEN

Charlie Farrow had so far held on to his own office in an increasingly open-plan environment. Of course he had, McKay thought. What was more impressive was that, since the last time McKay had had serious dealings with the man, he'd secured one of the most impressive offices in the building outside the chief officers' suite. A corner room on the second floor with expansive views out over the city to the hills and mountains beyond.

Farrow had never encouraged an open-door policy. His door remained firmly shut, and McKay had been warned by one of Farrow's team that any uninvited intrusion would be far from welcome. As far as McKay was concerned, that was simply an incentive.

Luckily, even Farrow hadn't managed to have the glass office dividers replaced by anything more opaque. Farrow was sitting alone, tapping away on his keyboard. McKay didn't bother to knock but opened the door and stuck his head inside.

'Afternoon, Charlie? Busy?'

'Too busy to waste time on the likes of you.'

'Not here to waste your time, Charlie. You know me.'

'Aye, too well.'

'I've come with some potentially valuable information.'

'Your potential retirement date, Alec? I can't think of much else you could tell me that would be of interest.'

'You're much closer to that than I am. You'll be a great loss to the force, Charlie.' McKay glanced at his watch. 'I won't keep you any longer than I need to. Must be nearly time for the golf course.'

'I'm certainly looking forward to the time when I don't have to sit here listening to your shite. If you've got something to say, say it and we can all get on with our lives.'

'I've just been visiting the hospital.'

'Sorry to hear that, Alec. Nothing trivial, I trust.'

'I was there on business.'

For the first time since McKay had entered the room, Farrow stopped pretending to type and looked him full in the face. 'Business?'

'Aye, you remember. Policing. What we do between rounds of golf.'

'What kind of business?'

'Unexplained and potentially suspicious death.'

'I'm sorry, Alec. You've lost me.'

'No, I'm the one who should apologise, Charlie. I'll use shorter words. Someone died. I was asked to check it out.'

'What does this have to do with me?'

'The deceased – sorry, dead person – was one Brian Renton. A lorry driver.'

It took Farrow a few moments to place the name. Which was probably indicative of how much interest he had in the investigation, McKay thought. McKay had always seen Farrow as a glory hunter, someone mostly interested in cases that might attract the attention of the chief officers, at least once he'd brought them to a satisfactory conclusion. If an inquiry showed signs of going off the rails, Farrow was adept at making himself scarce. A probably routine RTC, even one involving fatalities, wouldn't be high on his agenda. 'The guy from the A9 crash?'

'That's the one.'

'You're telling me he's dead?'

'It's always a struggle to keep up with your lightning intellect, Charlie. Yes, he's dead. This afternoon.'

'But how?'

'You know that word "unexplained"? Well, what that means—'

'Anyone told you you're a pain in the arse, Alec?'

'Usually because I've stopped them talking out of it. The consultant contacted us because he wasn't comfortable signing the death certificate. The death was unexpected. Renton's condition had been improving. They'd taken him out of the ICU. The most likely explanation is that he died from something they'd initially missed, maybe some undetected internal injury.'

Farrow was still eyeing McKay through narrowed eyes, clearly suspecting that there was more to come. 'So why suspicious?'

'Because the consultant reckoned there were symptoms that might be consistent with asphyxiation. Possibly suffocation.'

'Oh, for fuck's sake. Who'd want to kill a lorry driver?'

'I've come close once or twice. Especially on the A9. But the consultant's got to play it by the book. That's not the main point. There's something else.'

'There always is with you, Alec. Go on.'

'Renton briefly recovered consciousness before he died. And he said some things.'

Farrow jabbed his finger towards McKay. 'This is out of order. Renton was my witness.'

'With respect, Charlie, he's no one's witness now. Except maybe the pathologist's.'

'Why didn't anyone even tell me he'd died?'

'What can I say? You just can't get the staff. For what it's worth, I just went over there because I was told to. They wanted someone over there quickly while the examiners were still doing their thing. I didn't realise it was a territorial matter. If you fancy coming to piss in our offices as compensation, I'm sure Helena wouldn't object.'

Farrow closed his eyes as if hoping that McKay might disappear. 'Okay,' he said wearily. 'What did he say?'

'I spoke to one of the nurses who'd been with him for those few moments. Young woman called Rosie McColl. He spoke about a second vehicle. He talked about the red car – the one he hit – but then he asked what had happened to the "mad bastard in the black car". I quote. Roughly.'

'Anything else?'

'Not according to the nurse. He slipped back into unconsciousness so she left him to rest. He was all monitored up and they didn't think there was any risk.'

'Well, thanks for letting me know. It's a potentially useful piece of information.' McKay could tell Farrow was speaking through gritted teeth. 'I'll see if it ties in with what the collision team are coming up with.'

McKay restrained himself from mentioning he'd already spoken to Adam Sutherland. 'They're usually good at identifying that kind of thing,' he said neutrally.

'I want to make this crystal clear. I'm grateful for this little nugget of information, but this is my case, my investigation. I don't take kindly to anyone else sticking their nose into it.'

'You know me, I just do what I'm told.'

'Aye, that'll be the day.'

'Anyway, I've taken up more than enough of your time. The

fairways will be beckoning. You don't want to be wasting a fine afternoon like this.'

'Oh, fuck off, Alec.'

McKay pushed himself to his feet. 'I assume you'll be wanting to take a formal statement from the nurse I spoke to. I'd make sure you clear any visits with Shaun Sanderson, the Deputy Chief Executive. Charming man but he doesn't like people coming into his hospital without his permission.'

'I don't care what he likes. This is a police investigation. I don't need the permission of some petty bureaucrat.'

'That's the spirit, Charlie. You do it your way. Win friends and influence people. It's always been your main talent. One day you might be as good at it as I am.'

CHAPTER NINETEEN

There were days when Craig Fairlie felt like using Ally's bar for its intended purpose rather than as a makeshift office. Not that Ally seemed to care much why he was there. Fairlie's presence provided a touch of additional character in a place already rich in its own distinctive quirks. 'Aye, that's our resident newspaper hack,' Fairlie had once heard him tell an American tourist. 'We keep him in captivity for visitors to gawp at.'

Today was one of those days when Fairlie could easily be tempted to knock back a few pints instead of working. It had started with a phone call to Hugh Preston, the podcaster investigating the case. It had been over a month since the first podcast had appeared.

Fairlie's understanding had been that Preston was preparing a follow-up as part of a continuing true crime series. Over the last couple of weeks, though, Preston had gone disturbingly quiet. In the period before and immediately after the first podcast and the article, Preston had been in constant contact, wanting to know what else the newspaper had in mind, and promising Fairlie first sightings of what would be in the follow-up.

Then, suddenly, Preston had gone to ground. At first he'd answered Fairlie's calls, but had seemed uncharacteristically cagey. Then Preston had ceased taking Fairlie's calls at all. The number had rung out to voicemail, Preston promising to get back if the caller left a number. Fairlie had left repeated messages, but Preston had never fulfilled his promise. He'd been preparing to leave the same message that morning. Instead, to his surprise, the phone was answered almost immediately.

'Craig.' Preston's one word response provided no clue to his state of mind.

'Hugh, good to talk to you at last. Hope all's well at your end?'

'Not bad. You know.'

In their initial conversations, Preston had been voluble, full of thoughts and ideas and only too keen to share them. Even when he'd seemed more cagey, he'd still talked fluently and at length. Fairlie had never heard him as taciturn as he seemed now. 'How's the follow-up coming along?' Fairlie asked.

'I'm not sure there's going to be one. Not at the moment anyway.'

'What do you mean?'

'What I say. I've lost faith in the whole thing.'

'Are you saying the evidence wasn't as strong as you thought?'

'Let's just say there are issues.'

'What kind of issues?'

'Just issues. Look, I don't want to go ahead with it, that's all.'

'If you're not sure about it, why not pass whatever you've got to me and I'll let you know whether I think it stands up. You can't just let this go.' Colin Wishaw wouldn't be best pleased if Fairlie allowed this to slip through his fingers.

'I can't do that.'

'But surely—'

'Sorry if I've strung you along. My fault. But there's no point in talking further. Don't bother phoning again.'

Fairlie had tried to call him back but the phone had cut straight to voicemail. Fairlie couldn't leave it there. Partly because of his own professional pride, but mainly because he needed something to give to Colin Wishaw. He couldn't tell Wishaw the whole story had gone tits up. He had to provide some alternative. The problem was that, other than his conversation with Gordon Rennie, he didn't have anything.

He was musing on this when the phone buzzed on the table in front of him. For a moment, Fairlie thought it might be Preston calling back to say he'd changed his mind or been winding Fairlie up. But the number on the screen was unfamiliar. Fairlie answered cautiously. 'Hello?'

'Is that Mr Craig Fairlie?'

'Speaking.'

'You don't know me, Mr Fairlie. My name's Edward Lawrence. I'm a member of a law firm, Harvie and Lawrence, based in Inverness. I represent a man called Kevin Clark.'

'Kevin Clark?'

'I've been reading your newspaper articles with some interest, as you can imagine. I wondered if it would be possible for us to talk.'

'We seem to be talking already.'

'I was thinking face to face. At your convenience, of course. When would suit you?'

'Whenever you like. Now, if you want. I'm in town, presumably not far from where you're based.'

'I could do that. Do you want to come here?'

'Just let me know where.'

Lawrence's office address was a business park on the edge of town, a short taxi ride away.

'I look forward to meeting you, Mr Lawrence.'

'I hope you'll find it to your advantage.'

Fairlie ended the call and sat back to think. What was it they said? One door closes, another one opens. In Fairlie's experience, the second door often just slammed in your face as well. But it wasn't as if he had any other options. If there was a possibility Lawrence could offer him something new on the O'Donnell case, it was worth a try. It might at least deflect Colin Wishaw from subjecting him to the mother of all bollockings when he broke the news about Preston.

Okay, Mr Lawrence, he said to himself, let's see what you've got to offer.

CHAPTER TWENTY

The offices were less upmarket than Fairlie had expected. Better than a gloomy corner in a backstreet bar, maybe, but functional rather than luxurious. Perhaps that reflected the firm's clientele. An environment designed not to intimidate those facing a brush with the law.

Edward Lawrence turned out to be a man probably in his early sixties. He had a slightly patrician air, with a barely detectable educated Edinburgh accent. He was informally dressed – although clearly more expensively than Fairlie – and looked like someone who made an effort to keep in shape. He led Fairlie through to a meeting room, where a tray of coffee and biscuits was already waiting.

'I read your articles with great interest, Mr Fairlie.'

'I hope you found them accurate?'

'I thought, for the most part, they were extremely fair and balanced.'

Which, Fairlie noted, didn't entirely answer his question. And 'for the most part' wasn't exactly a ringing endorsement.

'I note you've been working with a podcaster called Hugh Preston.'

'He's the one who's reinvigorated interest in the case. I was only reporting on his podcast.'

'Do you know what Mr Preston's intentions are now? My impression was that he was planning a follow-up on the case.'

'That was my understanding. But you'd have to ask Mr Preston, I'm afraid.'

'You're not in contact with him?'

'Not at present.'

'I see. So you can't help me get in touch with him?'

'I do have a phone number. May I ask why you want to talk to him?'

'I have a proposition to put to him. I already have a number for him and I've attempted to contact him. He doesn't seem to be taking calls.'

'I take it you've left messages for him.'

'Repeatedly. And explained the nature of my proposition.'

'Which, with respect, perhaps suggests he's not interested in your proposition.'

'That may be. But I must confess I'm surprised.'

'Look, Mr Lawrence, can I be absolutely straight with you?'

'Please do.'

'As it happens, I spoke to Hugh Preston this morning myself, for the first time in weeks. I've been in exactly the same position you are. I was expecting the follow-up podcast to be published shortly. I'd assumed we'd give it the same coverage we gave the first. But, like you, I've been leaving repeated messages with no response.'

'But you have spoken to him this morning?'

'He finally took my call. But only to inform me there wouldn't be a follow-up.'

'You're sure about that?'

'He seemed unequivocal. He wasn't intending to continue.'

'But why?'

'Your guess is as good as mine. He told me he'd lost faith in the project. There were – to use his words – issues with the material.'

'I see. Do I take that to indicate his supposed new evidence has turned out to be less compelling than he expected?'

'That may be one way of putting it,' Fairlie said. 'My own conclusion was that he'd probably been bullshitting us all along.'

To his credit, Lawrence laughed. 'I appreciate your candour, Mr Fairlie. I imagine you develop a carapace of cynicism in your job.'

'Aye, something like that,' Fairlie agreed. 'All I know is that it's left us – and by us I mainly mean me because I can't imagine anyone else will take the rap – with egg on our face.'

Lawrence looked thoughtful. 'It's possible I may be able to help you with that.'

'If you've anything to offer, I'm all ears.'

'If Mr Preston's chosen not to continue his work, I'm happy to offer the opportunity to you.'

'Opportunity?'

'As I said, I represent Mr Clark. I represented him in the original trial. I've continued to do so on a pro bono basis ever since.'

'That's very public spirited of you.'

'I'm not sure my partners entirely approve. The trial divided opinion, as you may recall.'

'So why your continued involvement?'

'I feel I owe him something.'

'Why's that?'

'We did as much as we could for Kevin,' Lawrence said. 'We felt there were significant gaps in the prosecution's account—'

'Such as what happened to Kevin after the killing?'

'Exactly so. I note you didn't make reference to that in your original article.'

'I've been researching the case in more depth recently. I hadn't realised how little evidence there was about the period after the murder.'

'It was the single biggest weakness in the prosecution case. We chipped away at it as much as we could to try to undermine their narrative.'

'But you were unsuccessful?'

'Ultimately, as I'm sure you're aware, we were hamstrung by two factors. First, Kevin's own confession. Second, what appeared to be definitive forensic evidence. That, along with various other factors, provided sufficient corroboration to persuade the jury.'

'Unanimously.'

'Unanimously and very quickly. Our strategy was to cast doubt on whether Kevin was alone at the scene and whether he was actually capable of committing that kind of act. In other words, to suggest that some third-party could have been involved and was potentially responsible for the murder. That Kevin's confession had been intended to protect a third party.'

'What was your own view? Did you think Clark was guilty?'

'I had sufficient doubts about the case to take that possibility seriously. Kevin had – and has – significant learning difficulties. He wasn't incapable of understanding the situation he was in, but he had problems appreciating its seriousness. My impression was that he was scared of something or someone. I was never convinced by his supposed confession, even though he resolutely stuck by it through the trial.'

'Does he still stick by it?'

'He's never changed his story. Didn't want to appeal the verdict. I've not challenged him in recent years. There didn't seem any point.'

'You still see him?'

'I visit him in prison periodically.'

'That's good of you.'

'There's no one else. His parents are deceased. There are two brothers, but they've more or less disowned him.'

'How's he coped in prison? If he has the kind of learning disabilities you've described.'

'Surprisingly well. I thought he'd struggle, that he'd be bullied, particularly given the nature of his crime. But prisons can be strange places, and Kevin's an unusual personality. He comes across as a gentle, likeable person. That's one reason I found it hard to believe he could be guilty of that kind of murder.'

'It doesn't always work like that, though, does it?'

'I know that better than most, Mr Fairlie. I've seen all kinds come through these offices. Sometimes the worst crimes are committed by the least likely individuals. I'm just describing how Kevin struck me when I first met him. He seemed less like a threat to public safety than someone who'd need protection himself. That's worked to his advantage in prison. He was bullied at first by some of his fellow prisoners, but others protected him. The routine of prison life suits him. In some ways, he seems more content in prison than he ever was outside.'

'From what I know of prison life, that's a bleak thought.'

'The whole case was bleak. It destroyed so many lives. O'Donnell himself, of course, and no doubt other members of his family. Kevin and his mother and father. Probably even his brothers. All essentially for nothing.'

'You said you felt you owed Clark something?'

'As I said, we did what we could for him. I think we did a decent job in the circumstances. But personally I'm not fully convinced of his guilt. I've spent twenty years searching for something that might fill the gaps. Either to confirm Kevin was guilty or help prove the opposite. That's why your articles were of interest to me. I thought some new evidence might finally emerge.'

'I'm sorry I can't help you further.'

'Perhaps you can. I last visited Kevin a week or so back. I'd told him about the podcast and your articles in case he found out from another source. I wasn't sure how he'd react. I thought he might be unhappy at the whole affair being raked over again. But he surprised me. He said he was pleased someone was looking at the case after all these years. He said he wished he could talk to someone about it.'

'Are you suggesting he's changing his story?'

'Not so far. But as I was leaving, he said again that he wanted to talk about it. Tell someone the full story.'

'The *full* story?'

'Those were his words.'

'That does imply he has something new to say.'

'It seems like it. Whether that'll change anything, or if he just wants to add more detail to what we already know, I can't say.'

'I can't imagine the Prison Service would agree for me to interview him,' Fairlie said. 'Even if he was prepared to do that. He doesn't fall into any of the public interest categories that might justify talking to the media. He's not claiming a miscarriage of justice.'

'I appreciate that. And it may be that he wants to talk as some form of therapy. I did ask him if I should consult one of the prison psychologists. He insisted it wasn't about that. He just wanted to tell the story. As best he remembered it.'

'Do you think it's likely he's got something new to say?'

'I don't know. If he has, I've no idea why he'd want to say it now. Except that it seemed to be the podcast and your articles that prompted it.'

'So what are you suggesting? I don't imagine there's any prospect of the authorities allowing me in there.'

'I have to play this carefully. I can't do anything that might risk damaging the reputation of the practice, and I've no desire to do anything underhand.'

'But?'

'But if Kevin does have something new to say, I think it deserves to be heard. I've arranged an interview session with him later this week – an extended interview as his lawyer – and I'm hoping he'll be prepared to talk to me openly. My proposition is that, if he tells me anything new and significant – and obviously subject to his agreement and other relevant considerations of client confidentiality – I'll be prepared to share the details with you.'

'What would you want from me in return?'

'Nothing more than fair treatment. Accurate representation of anything that Kevin says.'

'That sounds reasonable. I'm happy with that.'

'Thank you, Mr Fairlie. I'll be in touch once I've met with Kevin. Thank you for your time.'

'And thank you for contacting me,' Fairlie said, as he followed Lawrence out of the room. 'I look forward to hearing what Kevin has to say.'

CHAPTER TWENTY-ONE

'You're not supposed to look so delighted,' Helena Grant said.

'My natural cheery disposition,' McKay said. 'Obviously, I'm shocked and horrified by the news. What's the world coming to?'

'Aye. Very convincing, Alec.'

'He's sure, though? The pathologist, I mean.'

'I wouldn't raise your hopes without good reason. I mean, it was couched with the usual caveats. But it was as unambiguous as you ever get. Cause of death asphyxiation caused by suffocation. Most likely a pillow being used to block the airways.'

'So an unlawful killing?'

'Has anyone told you a permanent grin doesn't suit you?'

'Oddly enough, it's never come up before.'

'But, yes, an unlawful killing.'

As if no longer able to contain his pent-up energy, McKay stood and began to walk around the room, finally stopping to stare out of the window at the Inverness skyline. 'I take it this one's coming to us.'

'Unless someone down south decides to take it on. But after their last couple of experiences up here, I'm guessing they'll be wary of getting their fingers burned again.'

'That's what happens when they treat us like a bunch of uncouth *teuchters*,' McKay said.

'You're not a Highlander, Alec. You're from Dundee.'

'I ought to have citizenship by now.' McKay turned back from the window, still smiling. 'What about Charlie Farrow?'

'What about him?'

'He wasn't best pleased about me looking into Brian Renton's death. Told me it was his case and I should butt out.'

'The traffic collision is his case. This is Major Investigations. Farrow's no longer Major Investigations. It was his choice.'

'He was looking for a quiet life up to retirement.'

'Well, he's got it. Investigating RTCs. Not murders. This comes to us.'

'What if they're connected?'

'What if what are connected?'

'Renton's death and the RTC.'

'Is this your mad killer on the road idea again, Alex?'

'Do you mean "mad killer" or "mad idea"?'

'Both, probably. I can't see how anything like that would work.'

'Me neither, if I'm honest. All the more so after talking to Adam Sutherland. It was just a thought.'

'It was an attempt to avoid doing admin, Alec. We both know that. Now it looks as if we've got something we can legitimately get our teeth into.'

'But why would anyone kill Renton?'

'We don't know much about him yet, so that'll be one of our first tasks. We've got some initial background information on him through his employers. Lived in Stirling. Wife and two youngish children. Wife was informed about the accident and

Renton's subsequent death. Took it pretty badly, I understand.'

'Not surprising,' McKay said. 'Especially with two kiddies to bring up.'

'Beyond that, we don't have much. Employer was a haulage company on the outskirts of Stirling. Renton mostly covered the Highlands. Well regarded. Reliable, good with customers.'

'Spare me that kind of obituary when I'm gone.'

'Trust me, Alec, no one will describe you as reliable or good with customers.'

'No skeletons in Renton's closet?'

'You never know till you look. But so far no suggestion of anything out of the ordinary.'

'So we're left with the question of whether he was actually a target or just happened to be in the wrong hospital bed at the wrong time.'

'If it's the latter, we've a potential nightmare on our hands,' Grant pointed out.

'I've got the picture,' McKay said. 'It's where we have to start, though. We have to assume there's a potential risk to public safety, and take action accordingly. Shaun Sanderson's not going to be happy.'

'Who's Shaun Sanderson?'

'Deputy CEO. Chief prick.'

'Another one who didn't fall for your mesmerising charm?'

'Baffling, isn't it? He was just annoyed someone had stepped into his territory without his express permission. You know the type. He's not going to be keen at having coppers traipsing all over his hospital.'

'He may have no choice if there really is a threat to patient and public safety.'

'I take it there've been no other recent suspicious deaths?'

'We're going to have to double-check. If there's a pattern of similar deaths, we'll know where we stand.'

'Well and truly in the shite, you mean?'

'Something like that.' Grant sighed. 'Sounds like there's plenty for us to get on with. I'll make sure we've got the green light. I'm assuming I'll be appointed as SIO unless they decide to send someone up here.'

'If they suggest that, just let them know how much I'm looking forward to working with whoever they send.'

'That should discourage them right enough. In the meantime, we can start putting a team together. Suspect we may need a fair few feet on the ground. What about Ginny?'

'What about her?'

'Do you think she's up to being part of this? It's likely to be a big one.'

'She'll be pissed off if she isn't.'

'Just don't want to pile too much on her. She'll have a lot on her plate over the coming weeks.'

'I reckon we play it by ear. She's a much tougher nut than she appears.'

'I don't doubt that for a second.'

McKay had finally returned to his seat. He reminded her of an eager dog, straining at the leash to get going. 'The bad news is you might need to put that admin on the back-burner.'

'That right? In that case, I'd better get back to my desk and get as much of it out of the way as I can.'

'You're kidding?'

'Ach, of course I fucking am.' He pushed himself to his feet. 'But I might make myself a celebratory cup of coffee. After that, I'll mostly be imagining the look on Charlie Farrow's face when he finds out about this.'

CHAPTER TWENTY-TWO

I t looked set to be another fine day.

This was Gary's favourite time of year. The end of summer. The weather often improved as August drifted into September. The most intense part of the tourist season was coming to an end; the roads were a little quieter. If he set off early enough, he was unlikely to encounter much other traffic on his way into the city.

The nights were already growing noticeably longer, and he'd left the house before sunrise. As he drove north towards Inverness, the morning grew steadily lighter, the sky turning from a bruised purple to a clear blue. It was a daily commute he never tired of. The surrounding landscape was largely hills and thick woodland until he reached the outskirts of the city. Even now, he was oddly thrilled by the first glimpse of the Kessock Bridge and the blue expanse of the Moray Firth as the road dipped down towards Inverness.

The road seemed particularly quiet today. He'd passed a few lorries, but almost no other cars. He was generally in the office just after 7am, giving him an hour or more before the rest of the team began to arrive. It was time he found restful and often inspiring. He spent much of it catching up on administration and correspondence, getting the mundane stuff out of the way. But he also spent time sipping espressos and gazing out of the window at the river, his mind drifting nowhere in particular.

It was the time when he came up with his most creative ideas. You needed that space, a period when you weren't under the cosh, trying to come up with ideas within a ridiculous and usually arbitrary deadline.

He was lost in these thoughts when he first noticed the car behind him. There'd been a slight morning mist in the air as they'd come over the summit, and he hadn't registered the car in the distance behind him. It was only when he realised how quickly it was gaining on him that he paid it serious attention. 'Some daft bugger in a hurry,' he muttered to himself.

It was a kind of SUV, one of those massive semi-trucks that take up two spaces in the car park. They weren't necessarily as ridiculous in this part of the world as they were in a London suburb, but this one didn't look like a working car.

It was right up behind him now, inches from his rear end. 'For fuck's sake, man,' Gary said. 'You can't overtake here. At least wait till the road straightens before you kill us both.'

As if in response to Gary's mutterings, the car pulled out as if to overtake. They were on a single-carriage stretch of the road, with sharp twists and turns every few hundred yards. It was an idiotic place to overtake.

Gary pressed his brakes, allowing the car sufficient time to pass. To Gary's surprise, the car slowed to match Gary's speed, then gently bumped the front of his BMW. Gary slowed again, hoping to avoid a further collision.

The second bump left him little doubt about the other driver's intention. This was a deliberate act. The bastard was trying to force him off the road. Gary slammed on his brakes, reasoning that even that monstrosity would find it difficult to push a stationary car off the carriageway.

It was already too late. One final harder bump forced the still moving car off the road, sending it sliding down a grassy bank. Fortunately, Gary's attempts to stop his car had resulted in it leaving the carriageway at a relatively safe point. Another forty or fifty yards, and the drop would have been much steeper. Gary was already bringing the car under control. He bumped further down the slope and finally came to a halt.

Gary pulled on the handbrake and took a breath, his heart pounding. He closed his eyes, forcing himself to relax. He had no idea what that stupid fucker had been playing at, but it didn't matter now. He was unscathed. He could get the car back up the slope to the road. The other bastard had no doubt already made themselves scarce, buggering off to find another potential victim.

He'd have to call the police, he thought. Stop the maniac before he did this to someone else. Gary could only half-remember the registration but that and a description of the vehicle ought to be enough for the police to track down the owner.

He took another deep breath and reached forward to restart the car. Then he stopped, frozen, as someone tapped softly at the driver's side window.

CHAPTER TWENTY-THREE

The phone call provided Helena Grant and Alec McKay an excuse to extract themselves from an increasingly turgid liaison meeting with Shaun Sanderson at the hospital. The meeting had been needed to kick off the investigation into Renton's death, but Sanderson's grudging responses to their various requests had become increasingly tiresome. As it was, they'd left him with a written list of what was needed. He could grumble about the content in his own time, McKay thought.

Helena Grant was already back on her phone as they walked down the corridor towards the lifts. 'When was it spotted? Do we know how long it had been there? I'm at the hospital with Alec. Probably best if we drive down there. I take it the examiners are already on site?' She listened for a few more seconds before ending the call.

'Down where?' McKay said.

'The A9. We've another one.'

'RTC?'

'Sort of. But it's an odd one. I'll tell you as we're driving.'

It took them another five minutes to retrieve their car from the distant reaches of the hospital car park. Once McKay had navigated the series of roundabouts back on to the A9, he said, 'Odd one?'

'Car spotted somewhere off the carriage, down a slope on the northbound side. Not clear why it left the road. Fairly gentle slope and no obvious damage to the car.'

'And the driver?'

'Dead. No obvious cause of death. Doesn't appear to be from the collision itself.'

'Heart attack or stroke then,' McKay said. 'Cause rather than effect.'

'Maybe. Driver wasn't old, though. Male, mid-30s. Had his driving licence and various cards in his wallet so we've identified him as a Gary Donaldson. That's all I know so far. But there seem to be some other oddities.'

'What sort of oddities?'

'Driver's door was open, but there was no sign the driver had tried to leave the car. Positioning and posture of the body seemed wrong for the victim of a fatal heart attack. No apparent symptoms of a stroke.'

'None of that proves anything,' McKay said. 'As far as I'm aware, there's no approved way of having a heart attack or stroke.'

'The other thing is that the car seemed to have been brought under control by the driver. The handbrake was on.'

'So the driver stayed alive long enough to bring the car under control before shuffling off this mortal coil.'

'There's one more thing.'

'Aye, I thought there might be. You wouldn't have brought us out here for nothing while we've a murder investigation going on.'

'It looks as if there was an attempt to torch the car.'

'Thanks for saving that till the end. I might have lost interest if you'd mentioned it at the beginning.'

'I've learned at the feet of the master,' Grant said. 'But, yes, petrol poured into the footwell on the driver's side. Too much to be there by accident or from some past spillage.'

'And no chance it was a result of whatever caused the car to leave the road?'

'No damage to the car at all. There's no sign of a petrol can in the car or in the boot.'

'Someone planned to set fire to the car but didn't go through with it?'

'It looks exactly like that.' Grant gestured ahead of them. 'There's a road closed and a diversion sign at the next junction. Must be just beyond that.'

Sure enough, a patrol car was parked across the carriageway at the next junction directing cars off on to an alternative route. 'Poor buggers,' McKay commented. 'An additional fifty miles on to their journey south. The joys of living in the Highlands.' He pulled up by the marked car and waved his warrant card out of the window. 'DI McKay and DCI Grant.'

'They've sent out the big guns for this one, then.'

'Only the very best for you, son,' McKay said. He recognised the officer, though he didn't know his name. 'Where's the car?'

'About half a mile ahead. We've cordoned off the immediate areas for the collision analysts and examiners to do their stuff, but you'll be able to get fairly close.'

'Always good to hear at my age, son. Thanks.'

The officer cleared a couple of cones so McKay could manoeuvre his way past the barrier. There was an array of marked cars, a fire engine, an ambulance and a couple of white vans. McKay parked as close as he could, and greeted a middle-aged PC striding purposefully towards them. 'Morning, Andy. It's only us. Couple of detectives here to help.'

'First time for everything.' Andy Gilmour was well known

to them both, a long-serving and well-regarded officer. 'It's an odd one, this.' He led them to the edge of the road and pointed down to a silver BMW 5 Series on the grassy slope.

'What's happened to the body?' Grant asked.

'Been moved to the ambulance prior to being shipped back to the mortuary. Not a mark on it, apparently, so identifying the cause of death should be interesting.'

'And you think someone tried to set fire to the car?' McKay asked.

'Looks that way. I can't think of any other reason why you'd pour petrol over the interior.'

'No possibility it got there by accident?'

'We've found no sign of a container. If it was spilled accidentally someone must have removed that.'

McKay was scanning the landscape. 'Could it have fallen further down the hill?'

'Only if it was thrown, I reckon. We can get it checked out properly, just in case.'

'So it looks as if there was a second person on the scene, whether a passenger in the car or another driver,' Grant said. 'But why would they have wanted to torch the car?'

'And if they wanted to, why didn't they?' McKay added.

'Might have been worried about being spotted,' Gilmour said. 'We don't know exactly what time the car went off the road but must have been early. Reported about 7.15. Car was visible from the road. Traffic starts to build up around seven.'

'Do we know anything more about the driver?'

'You'd have to ask the examiners,' Gilmour said. 'We got a name and address but we didn't want to risk compromising the scene so we didn't delve around.'

'That's the thing with examiners,' McKay said. 'Just by mentioning their name, you can summon them from the vasty deep.' He gestured to the angular figure of Jock

THE LOW ROAD

Henderson striding awkwardly up the hillside. McKay waved cheerfully, and Henderson changed direction to head towards them.

'Should have known you'd join the party,' he said to McKay. He nodded a greeting to Grant. 'Morning, Helena. I'd have thought this was a bit below your pay grade.'

'It doesn't sound like your bog-standard RTC.'

'Not remotely. No collision for a start, or at least no evidence of anything significant. There are a couple of minor dings on the driver's side front wing, but we don't know if they're significant or existing damage.'

'Any evidence of a second vehicle being involved?' Grant said.

'Too early to say. Some tyre marks but I'll let the collision analysts decide what they might mean.'

'What about the petrol?' McKay asked. 'Any thoughts on that?'

'That's a baffler. Kids might do it if the car was abandoned, but not with a bloody body in it.'

'Might depend on the cause of death,' McKay said. 'Or if someone wanted to muddy the waters about the nature of the accident.'

'It's possible. If it had gone up, we'd have a lot less to work with, certainly.'

'What about the driver?' Grant said. 'Any more on him?'

'There were some business cards in his wallet. MD of a graphic design company in Inverness. We've got business and domestic addresses which I've passed on to our uniformed friends to follow up.' He leaned forward and peered at Grant and McKay. 'I'm still wondering why you're both here. Is there something I should be aware of?'

'We were at the hospital kicking off the investigation into Brian Renton's death,' Grant said.

Henderson looked down at the car. 'You think there might be a link?'

'I've no idea, Jock,' Grant said. 'It's just the kind of coincidence that makes me uneasy.'

'Been a hell of a lot of RTCs here in recent weeks,' McKay added.

'Bloody road's a deathtrap. Not as bad as it used to be, but still a deathtrap. But it's been worse than usual this summer. Serious RTCs are an examiner's worst nightmare. You see stuff you don't want to see again. Ordinary folk. Holidaymakers, tourists, commuters. Wee bairns.' He turned away from them.

McKay hadn't seen Jock show this level of emotion since they'd both attended a multiple killing a year or so previously. That had been a grotesque one-off. Now, he was talking about something that must almost be part of his daily life. 'It's a hidden massacre. One we never talk about.'

'Aye,' Henderson said. 'All people do is complain about the speed limits and the cameras, and the fact that it's taking them ten minutes longer to get to Perth. We need to improve the road, sure, but we also need to stop the fuckwits driving like lunatics.'

'Speaking of which,' McKay asked, 'did you see our old friend Iain Pennycook's launched a campaign on that topic?'

'That wee gobshite? I thought we'd seen the last of him up here.'

'The prodigal son's returned.'

'Aye, because his career down there's tanked. Bugger like that won't come back with his tail between his legs, though. He'll be as bumptious as ever, making out he's honouring us with his presence.'

'You're not a fan?' Helena Grant said.

'He's a two-bit grifter. The only thing Pennycook cares about is lining his own pocket.' Henderson shook his head, seemingly mourning all the iniquities of the world. 'I best get back down there.' He looked at McKay. 'You'll notice I've not lit up?'

'I thought you were worried about blowing us to kingdom come.'

'Aye, that too. But I've given up. Or at least I'm trying to.'

'Just when I thought I was past being surprised by anything ever again,' McKay said. 'So what's brought this on?'

'Wedding anniversary. Thirtieth. I said we ought to do something special to celebrate.'

'Too right. Especially your poor wife. You can get less than that for murder.'

'I had in mind something like a cruise or an exotic holiday. I made the mistake of saying I'd do whatever Aggie wanted. She said what she really wanted – I mean, she's nagged me about it for the last thirty-odd years so I should have known – was for me to give up smoking.'

'Does she realise that's likely to make you live longer *and* be even more of a cantankerous old bastard?'

'I did point that out to her. She seemed adamant.'

'Good luck with it, Jock,' Grant said. 'You were the last of a dying breed.'

'With the emphasis on dying,' McKay added. 'But, yes, good luck with it.' He pulled a packet of chewing gum from his pocket, holding it out for Henderson. 'There you go, Jock. Welcome to the club.'

CHAPTER TWENTY-FOUR

Iain Pennycook stopped in the entrance and looked around. This was a bit more like it. He'd spent the last few weeks roughing it in community halls and centres around the Highlands, spreading the word among those who depended on the A9. They'd been good-natured if occasionally boisterous gatherings, fully behind his cause.

Pennycook knew exactly how to play those crowds, toying with them in the early stages of his speech, gradually building the enthusiasm to end on a high point that guaranteed a standing ovation. In another, possibly better world, he might have used this gift for a gentler purpose – stand-up comedy, perhaps – rather than for rabble-rousing. But he told himself he was doing it in the aid of good causes rather than simply to line his own pockets.

It had been an enjoyable enough few weeks, and he'd visited some areas he'd never been to before. The local organisers had been hospitable and welcoming, and he'd succeeded in building support for the cause. But there was only so much weak coffee and home-made cake a man could eat, and he was looking forward to some more upmarket dining.

It took him a moment to spot Vic Farrell at the bar. 'Good to see you again, Vic. Business must be doing okay if you can take me to a place like this.'

'Business is shite,' Farrell said bluntly. 'You know that. Newspapers are dying on their arse. I'm screwing as much as I can on expenses before they finally dispense with my services.'

'They couldn't manage without you, Vic. Not a man of your experience.'

'I'll be replaced by some eighteen-year-old who can operate an AI system. Whatever that might be. What can I get you?'

'G and T would be good. Anyway, I'm delighted you're splashing some of your expense account on me.'

'Nothing personal. I'll splash it anywhere if it gets me a decent meal. But I reckon I do owe you one.' He raised a hand to the bar tender and ordered a gin and tonic for Pennycook and a beer for himself.

'Not a sentence I've often heard from you,' Pennycook said.

'I've never thought it wise to acknowledge any debt if you can help it. But your work on the A9 campaign's really boosted our sales up in this neck of the woods. And nicely timed, given our rival's focus on the Kevin Clark case.'

'Another story that sells papers up here?'

'Any true crime story's flavour of the month at the moment. But unless they've something sensational up their sleeves – and I've seen no sign of that so far – it's ancient history. Whereas our campaign's relevant now.'

Pennycook waited while the bar tender set out the drinks, replacing the bowl of complimentary peanuts. 'I'm not doing this just to sell newspapers.'

'Heaven forfend, Iain. You're a serious man. You care about people. Nobody could ever accuse you of being a two-bit grifter looking to line your own pockets.'

'Fuck off, Vic.' The two men had known each other long

enough not to take this kind of banter too seriously, even though both knew there was some truth in it. 'I've spent three or four weeks traipsing round every bloody community hall in striking distance of the A9. I've more than paid my dues.'

Farrell gave a mock shudder. 'I don't doubt it. Anyway, good to see you. Almost makes it worth a trip to the benighted far north.'

'What brings you up here anyway? I take it you've not come all this way just to buy me dinner.'

'Not even you're that good company. I felt it was time for one of my increasingly infrequent visits to our office up here. Missionary work among the heathens.'

'To be honest, I'm surprised you still have an office here.'

'I don't know how long it'll survive. We've always tried to keep a presence, even if it's a a token one. Otherwise, the locals might gain the entirely accurate impression that we've no idea what goes on north of Perth. But it's not much more than an address and a couple of administrators who could be based anywhere. Only a matter of time before the senior team decide the overhead can't be justified.'

'You do realise this is exactly the mood I'm tapping into up here. The sense of a community ignored by the metropolitan elite down south – Holyrood as well as Westminster.'

'Lucky they've got a sincere champion like you to represent their interests then.'

'That's what I keep telling them. And they seem to be listening.'

'A man of your talents is wasted here, Iain. I'd have thought you'd have seen a future for yourself down south, rather than this return to your roots.'

'If you lose touch with your roots, what's left?' Pennycook intoned.

'Aye, I remember you using that line in your anti-immigration spiel. You seem to have left that behind at least.'

'Old hat, isn't it? Every bugger's jumped on that bandwagon. I try to be ahead of the crowd.'

'That right?' Farrell raised a cynical eyebrow. 'And it's definitely not that you've fallen off the bandwagon. Or that it's left without you?' He took a large mouthful of beer. 'Or maybe you prefer to be a big fish in a much smaller pond.'

'I'll admit there's some truth in that, Vic. That's definitely part of my thinking. Down south, I'm just one voice among many, and they're getting more shrill by the day. But there aren't many up here with my talents. It's easier to stand out from the crowd.'

'You've proved that already. You've certainly made a splash since you arrived back in this neck of the woods.'

'It's early days yet. I'm just starting to think what we do next.'

'I've one or two suggestions,' Farrell said. 'That's partly why I wanted to take you for dinner. That and the sheer pleasure of your company, of course.'

'Aye, they say there's no such thing as a free lunch, so I'm guessing there's no such thing as a free dinner. Not in a place like this anyway.'

'That's where you might be wrong,' Farrell said. 'You might find this is not just a free dinner, but a potentially lucrative one from your perspective.'

'I'm all ears.'

Farrell glanced at his watch. 'Shall we go through? Our table should be ready.'

Pennycook followed Farrell into the restaurant. They were seated in a discreet corner with riverside views. 'Been here before?' Farrell said once they were seated.

'Once or twice,' Pennycook lied, 'but not in recent years.'

'Always been reliable enough,' Farrell said, 'but the food's really come on in recent years. Owner's got Michelin star aspirations, by all accounts.'

'Sounds perfect.' Pennycook picked up the menu, perused it briefly and decided what he wanted. He was more interested in getting on to the business at hand. 'You said you had some suggestions?'

'Just a few thoughts. But if you're interested we can work them up. You're a larger-than-life figure, Iain. People may love you or hate you, but it's hard to ignore you. You're a dedicated and very skilled self-publicist.'

'It's not about me. It's about the cause,' Pennycook said.

'Whatever the cause might be this week. My point is that there's something in this for both of us. We can give you a platform to help raise your profile up here—'

'And I can help you sell papers and advertising.'

'Exactly so.'

'You've said I'm a skilled self-publicist,' Pennycook pointed out. 'So why do I need you?'

'Maybe you don't. But we could save you some time.'

'Save me some time?'

'We can give you a platform. You can use it to highlight the issues you think will have most impact. You've many talents and one of them is an unerring ability to tap into the zeitgeist.'

'I always thought zeitgeist was some kind of spot remover. But flattery will get you everywhere. When you say give me a platform, what do you have in mind?'

'We can work up the details once we know you're interested. But I was thinking a column, once or twice a week. The voice from the north, or something less corny.'

'I don't know that writing a column is necessarily my strength.'

Farrell laughed. 'You wouldn't actually have to write it,

obviously. Just come up with ideas or topics you want to vent about, then chat to one of our staff reporters. They'll turn your thoughts into sparkling prose. We could link that to ongoing campaigning – on the A9, the state of the roads up here generally, the railways, whatever you wanted.'

'I won't deny it's an attractive idea. I've been mulling over how to create a platform here.'

'This would give you one ready built.'

'I'd be free to write and talk about whatever I wanted?'

'Of course. Within the limits of the law, obviously.'

'What about the limits of your paper's politics?'

'I don't think there's much danger of you coming into conflict with that, Iain. Not unless you've shifted ground quite radically.'

'I'm a free thinker. I don't stick to party lines. People don't always like that.'

'The whole point of our columnists is they offer a diversity of opinion.'

'Not as diverse as they'd like to pretend,' Pennycook said. 'But I take your point. I can't imagine wanting to say anything your editors and proprietors wouldn't be broadly happy with. So in principle I like the idea.'

'That's great, Iain. Perhaps I should order some bubbly to celebrate.'

'I'm happy to stick with that rather decent red you ordered.'

'Either way, it's a celebration. I'll get our people to work up some initial ideas for the format and then we can make it happen. In the meantime, let's press on with the A9 campaign. That really does seem to be a hot topic at the moment. Been more fatalities over the last couple of months than in years.'

'I'm keeping an eye on the numbers. It may just be fluke, but it does seem to be getting worse. Improving that road needs to be a priority. The people up here deserve it.'

'Save the soapbox for the column, Iain. But it's an emotive topic. We need to find a way of capturing people's imaginations. That's the advantage of the Kevin Clark story. The whole background grabs readers' attention – the nature of the killing itself, Clark's own backstory, the possibility of a miscarriage of justice—'

'You're beginning to depress me,' Pennycook said. 'If that's what we're competing with.'

'It's sensationalist nonsense. Sure, our campaign is more mundane, but it's more pertinent to people's lives. We need to find a way to communicate that, and you're the perfect man for the job.'

'I'll do my best.'

'And your best will be brilliant. I don't believe the Clark story's going anywhere anyway. There's no evidence of a mistrial. There are no grounds for the case to be reopened. You watch. Over the next few days, it'll just quietly fade away.'

Pennycook was silent for a moment. 'I hope so,' he said. 'I really hope you're right.'

CHAPTER TWENTY-FIVE

Edward Lawrence waited while the prison officer locked the gate behind them. They were standing in a small yard, the walls of the prison buildings looming over them. The mid-afternoon sun was excluded from this space, and it felt as if autumn had already arrived.

Lawrence found these visits discomforting. As he'd joked to the officer on the main gate, he'd spent too much of his life inside. He still harboured irrational fears that he might accidentally find himself locked in here himself. It wouldn't ever happen, of course. For a start, he was barely ever left by himself, partly for his own protection and partly because the system was designed to discourage trust in everyone, including lawyers. Perhaps especially lawyers, Lawrence added to himself.

He followed the prison officer across the yard to one of the older buildings. It was mostly used now as an administrative unit, but there were rooms here for formal meetings with prisoners. Lawrence again waited while the officer unlocked the door, led him inside and locked the door behind them.

'Assume you've been here before?' the officer asked.

'A few times,' Lawrence said. 'Are we in the room upstairs?'

'That's the one. I'll settle you in there, then go to get Clark.'

'Thanks.' Lawrence followed the officer up to the first floor, where he was ushered into a bleak-looking room. There was a table and a couple of high-backed chairs but no other furniture. The walls were painted a grey that might or might not have once been white, and the barred window looked out on to the yard. Not a hospitable environment, but it wasn't designed to be.

While he waited, Lawrence extracted his notes on the case, along with a notebook and pen. There were copious files on Clark back at the office. Lawrence had re-read the material, reminding himself of the details. Most of it remained firmly imprinted in his mind even after more than two decades, but there were points he'd forgotten or misremembered. He'd prepared a few pages of hand-written notes for his meeting with Clark.

After a few minutes, the door opened to reveal Clark, followed by the prison officer. 'In you go, lad.'

Lawrence rose to his feet to greet Clark. He'd be in his late thirties now, but still looked largely unchanged from the young man Lawrence had represented all those years before. It was telling that the officer, probably himself no more than a year or two older than Clark, had addressed him as 'lad'. 'Good afternoon, Kevin,' Lawrence said. 'Good to see you again. Sit yourself down.'

'I'll leave you to talk in private,' the officer said. 'I'll be just outside if you need anything. Not that this one's likely to give you any trouble. I understand you asked for an hour.'

'I don't know if we'll need all of it. We'll see how it goes.'

Once the officer had left, Lawrence turned to Clark. 'How are you, Kevin?'

Clark considered before responding. Lawrence knew from

experience that Clark took every question equally seriously. He seemed incapable of any kind of small talk. 'I'm okay, Mr Lawrence, thank you. I thought I might have a cold coming, but it seems to have gone away now. But not too bad. How are you, Mr Lawrence?'

'I'm fine, thanks. When I last visited you said you were keen to talk at greater length?'

Clark momentarily looked puzzled. 'About why I'm in here?'

'I assumed that was what you wanted to talk about, yes.' Lawrence knew this wouldn't be a quick process. It was better to allow Clark to proceed at his own preferred pace.

'You said there'd been a story in the newspapers.'

'One of the nationals has run a couple of pieces about the case. There's nothing new in them so far, but they've attracted a lot of interest.'

'Are people still interested?'

'They must be.'

There was another long silence before Clark said, 'Are they saying I didn't do it?'

'Not exactly. They're suggesting there might have been problems with the prosecution case. They're implying that the prosecution didn't have the full story. And that perhaps they manipulated some of the evidence against you.'

'Manipulated?' Clark looked blank.

'They found your DNA on the murder weapon and on various items from O'Donnell's bedroom. They claimed that proved you must have been present in the room.'

'Well, it did, didn't it?'

'It appeared to,' Lawrence said. 'But the DNA might have got onto those items in some other way. We tried to argue that at the time.'

'How could it have got on there?'

'There might have been various ways, Kevin. That was what the newspaper report was looking at. But you said you wanted to talk to me. What did you want to talk about?'

'I hadn't thought about it for a long time. What happened, I mean. I didn't want to think about it. It made my head spin.'

Lawrence recalled how Clark had responded to the intense questioning he'd faced in court. The judge had had to intervene on several occasions when the young man had become too confused to respond.

'But you do understand why you're in here, Kevin?' Lawrence asked now.

'Yes, because I killed him. That man.'

'O'Donnell.'

'Yes, that man. I killed him.'

'Did you kill him, Kevin?' Lawrence had asked the same question repeatedly over the years, and never received an entirely satisfactory answer. Clark's initial confession to the police had emerged step by painful step under police questioning, and had seemed unequivocal. But in subsequent discussions with Lawrence and others, Clark had never seemed quite so certain.

'I must have done, mustn't I?'

'Why's that, Kevin?'

'Because that's why I'm here, isn't it?'

'So what is it you want to tell me?'

'Since you told me about the newspaper, I've been trying to think about it.'

'About what?'

'About what happened. About why I'm here. About how I killed him.'

'And how did you kill him?'

'I'm not sure.'

'Do you remember what you told the police?'

'I think I told them I stabbed him?' It was a question, not a statement.

'That's what you said, Kevin. Is that what you did?'

'Well, I must have. If that's what I told them.'

'But you've been thinking about it?'

'I was trying to remember.'

'Do you remember stabbing O'Donnell.'

'I don't really. That seems strange. You'd think you'd remember something like that.'

'You'd think so.' This was the most definitive response Lawrence had received from Clark. He seemed genuinely baffled by this lacuna in his memory, as if he'd only just realised it was there.

'So what do you remember?' Lawrence prompted.

'I remember being in the house. That house. Where it happened. Going through the cupboards, pulling everything out. It was a mess.'

'Was this before or after Simon O'Donnell was killed?'

'I don't know. I was just there. In the house. Emptying the cupboards.'

There was nothing new here. Clark had always claimed to remember being in the house, emptying out the cupboards and drawers. Lawrence had never been sure if these were genuine memories or if Clark had been regurgitating details the police had conveniently dropped for him. 'Why did you do that, Kevin? Why did you empty out the cupboards?'

'I suppose I wanted to steal something. That was why I was there, wasn't it? That was why I was in the house.'

'Do you remember going into the bedroom?'

'I must have done. Or I couldn't have stabbed him.'

'But you don't remember stabbing him?'

'I don't know.'

'What else do you remember? Do you remember going to the house?'

'I think so. Someone dropped me there.'

'You don't know who?'

'I didn't know them. I mean, I recognised their faces but I didn't know their names.'

'Why did they give you a lift?' They'd been through these questions a thousand times, and never got any closer to a clear answer.

'They'd told me the house would be empty.'

'Who'd told you?'

'Mates. I don't know who. Mates in the pub. They said someone would take me.'

It had always been infuriatingly vague, but Lawrence had always been inclined to believe Clark's account. It was quite possible Clark had been set up by people he barely knew, maybe for nothing much more than a laugh.

'You said you wanted to talk about all this, Kevin. What was it you wanted to say?'

'I was just thinking about it. Trying to remember as much as I could. That's all.'

'What else do you remember?'

'I was trying to think about afterwards. I mean, about what happened after I stabbed the man. Because you kept asking me about that and I couldn't remember anything.'

'And do you remember something now?'

Clark nodded, his expression that of an eager schoolboy offering his homework for marking. 'Yes,' he said. 'I think I do.'

CHAPTER TWENTY-SIX

'So what do you remember, Kevin? Talk me through it. Take your time.' Edward Lawrence smiled at the young man sitting opposite him. It was crucial he allowed Kevin to tell his story in his own way, no matter how disjointed the account might seem.

'I was thinking about what happened after... well, you know, after I did the stabbing. I remember being outside the house. I don't remember coming downstairs or going outside but I was somehow there. I don't know if that was when I was emptying the cupboards or if that was before...' He trailed off, as if he'd already confused himself.

'It doesn't matter, Kevin. Just tell me what you remember.'

'I was outside. I just felt... scared. I don't know what I was scared of but I was scared. And sick. I felt sick. I thought I was going to be sick, but I wasn't. I didn't know what to do or where to go. I went down the path to the road, but I was too scared to go through the gate.'

'What happened after that?'

'I don't know.' He stopped. 'There was a car. I was in the back of a car.'

'Can you remember who was driving the car? Was it someone you knew?'

'I think it must have been the people who'd dropped me off. I'm not sure.'

'You said you were in the back of the car,' Lawrence said. 'Was there someone else in the front seat? In the passenger seat, I mean.'

Clark had closed his eyes, as if trying to summon up an image of that moment. 'There was someone else there.'

'Someone you knew?'

'I don't know. It might have been. I can't remember who.'

'Do you remember anything else?'

'We were driving somewhere. I don't know where. I had something in my hand.'

'Can you remember what you were holding?'

There was a further silence. Clark still had his eyes closed. 'I think it was the knife. The knife I did the stabbing with. I think it was that.'

'Are you sure? That you were holding the knife used to kill Simon O'Donnell?'

'I think that's what it was.'

'Was it your knife, Kevin? Did it belong to you?'

'I didn't have a knife. Not of my own.'

'Who gave it to you?' They'd explored this question countless times while preparing for the trial, and Clark had never been able to answer it.

'I still don't know.' Clark sounded almost despairing, as he wanted to offer Lawrence something more. 'I'm sorry.'

'It doesn't matter, Kevin. Can you recall what happened to the knife after that?'

'I think someone took it from me.'

'One of the people in the car?'

'It must have been.'

'Did you see what they did with it?'

'I just remember not having it.'

'Do you know where you went in the car?'

'The next thing I remember is being at home. I don't know if they took me there or if we'd been somewhere else first.'

'Can you remember what you were wearing? Was it the same as you were wearing in the car?'

'I think they were the same. But they were just clothes, you know. Just stuff you wear. I've never understood why people care about clothes.'

'Is there anything else you remember, Kevin?'

'That's all, I think. It was just the bit about being outside the house and then in the car. I'm sorry. It's all a bit foggy.'

'Don't be sorry. This could be important.'

'Could it?'

'It's the first time we've had any evidence that someone else was involved in the break-in. We've still no evidence they were in the house, but it's a step forward.'

For the moment, this changed nothing. Without some corroboration, no one was likely to believe Clark's revised story. But it was something, a new thread to pull on. With any luck, Clark's memory of that day might continue to improve.

'Okay,' Lawrence said. 'I know how difficult and stressful this is for you. I won't press you any further today unless there's anything else you want to say.'

'I don't think so. I think that's all I can tell you. Was that helpful?' He had the air of an eager dog who'd returned a thrown stick and was seeking its owner's approval.

'Very helpful, Kevin. A big step forward for us. But keep thinking. See if you can remember anything else.'

'I will.' Clark looked around him at the bleak featureless room. 'If I keep remembering things, will that mean I can't stay in here?'

'We're a very long way from the day when you leave here. All I want is for you to keep telling me the truth as best you remember it.'

'I've been thinking about it a lot lately, ever since you told me about the newspaper. It feels as if every time I think about it, I remember something new.'

It was quite possible, Lawrence thought. Sometimes this kind of trauma-induced amnesia was permanent. But he'd come across cases where the memories had eventually returned, often gradually at first, then increasingly quickly as one recollection triggered another. 'I'll come and see you again, Kevin. In a couple of weeks' time. Keep thinking and you can tell me what else you've remembered.'

'I'll do that,' Clark said cheerfully. 'I want to have more to tell you next time.'

'Well, let's hope you have, Kevin. Let's hope you have.'

CHAPTER TWENTY-SEVEN

C raig Fairlie looked up to see Iain Pennycook looming over his table. Pennycook wrinkled his nose in distaste. 'You really use this place as an office?'

'Well, workspace, let's say. And usually only in the daytime. It's much quieter then.'

Pennycook seemed unconvinced. 'I can imagine.' He gestured towards Fairlie's half-drunk pint. 'Same again?'

'Aye, why not, if you're paying.'

'I'm paying for this round anyway.'

Fairlie didn't know Pennycook well, and he didn't much like the man, but he had to acknowledge there was something impressive about him. At the very least, he was unignorable. Even in this backstreet boozer, he seemed to have made an impact already. It wasn't clear whether anyone in here actually recognised Pennycook or if he simply carried himself with the air of someone who mattered. Either way, heads were turning in their direction. As Pennycook approached the bar, the small cluster of drinkers parted as if in recognition of his importance. Pennycook nodded to a couple of the regulars as if he knew them well, and chatted amiably with them while he waited for his pints to be poured.

He returned a few moments later carrying the drinks. 'Decent clientele, anyway.'

'More converts to the cause?'

'Sowed a few seeds anyway. Couple of them even knew who I was. Saw me being interviewed on the news a few nights ago.'

'This the A9 thing?' Fairlie took his pint with a nod of thanks.

'Important to everyone in these parts, Craig.'

'I don't doubt it, Iain. You don't need to persuade me.'

'Force of habit. Anyway, good of you to see me at short notice.'

Fairlie had been surprised to receive the call that afternoon. He'd crossed paths with Pennycook once or twice in the old days, but they'd lost touch when Pennycook had moved south. Fairlie had heard nothing from him since Pennycook's return to the Highlands but Pennycook had talked as if they'd never lost contact. 'Just a couple of things I want to chat to you about. Wondered if you fancied meeting for a drink? Don't suppose tonight's any good?'

Fairlie wasn't keen to spend much time in Pennycook's company, but there was no harm in maintaining him as a contact, especially if his star was back in the ascendant. He'd accepted the invitation, suggesting Ally's bar so he'd feel on home territory.

'Good to see you again, Iain. Been a while. Though I take it this isn't just a social chat.' Fairlie took a sip of his beer, watching Pennycook's expression.

'Always good to catch up. It's been too long. But there are a couple of specific things I wanted to talk to you about.'

'Always happy to talk.' Fairlie felt as if they were dancing round each other like a couple of wary boxers, each waiting for the other to throw a punch.

'You'll have seen the press campaign about the A9?'

'I assumed you were behind that.'

'I wasn't, actually. Not initially. We both happened to focus on the same topic at the same time. Probably not surprising given its importance to the Highlands.'

Even less surprising if you just jumped on the bandwagon they'd already started rolling, Fairlie thought. 'Their campaigning seems to have gained some traction, just as yours has.'

'That's the point,' Pennycook said. 'We've both had an impact. But they know this kind of campaign is my forte, so they've proposed we join forces. They can give me a public platform, and I can push the case for better facilities in the Highlands.'

'Not just the A9 issue?'

'The A9's a perfect focus for our initial campaign, but it's only a symptom of the issues we're wrestling with.' This seemed like a suspiciously well-honed line, but it was an effective one. Fairlie had heard Pennycook use variants of it in a number of media interviews.

'If you've got the newspaper on board, I don't see how I can help.'

'Look, Craig, I want this to have as much impact as possible. The paper has promised they'll give me visibility. They've said they'll cover the events I organise, and they've offered me a regular column. They've even said they'll do the legwork for me in terms of actually writing it.'

'Sounds like you're well set up. I don't see what I can add to that.'

Pennycook took a large swallow of his beer before responding. 'There are a couple of things. First, and most importantly, I only want to work with the best. I don't want to cut corners. And the best, at least in these parts, is you.'

'Flattery'll get you anywhere, obviously. But I'm just a hack.'

'You're a very good one. And you're based up here.'

'If the paper's already offered you a ghostwriter, they're not going to want me butting in.'

'You've done work for them in the past?'

Pennycook had clearly done his research. 'I have, yes. Quite a bit over the years.'

'And you know Vic Farrell. He's got a lot of time for you.'

'Have you asked him that?'

'I have, actually. He sang your praises. Well, as much as he ever sings anyone's praises.'

'Which isn't much at all, in my experience.'

'It's like this, Craig. If I'm going to collaborate with someone on these columns, I'd much rather it was someone based up here. Partly that's just practical. I'd rather be able to sit and discuss ideas like this, over a pint or two, rather than talking over the phone or exchanging emails. And partly it's about understanding the context. You live here. You understand the issues. You appreciate how they affect people's lives. You and I are on the same wavelength.'

Fairlie doubted that but it wasn't the moment to challenge Pennycook. Like any freelancer, he had to take opportunities for work wherever he could find them. 'How does Vic Farrell feel about that?'

'I've floated the idea with him. I said it would make more sense to work with someone based here. He wasn't keen on paying a freelancer if there was someone on the staff who could do the job.'

'I bet he wasn't.'

'But they've cut the staff to the bone anyway. And he knows that, while we might be engaged in mutual backscratching, he probably needs me more than I need him. The local press up here would jump at the chance to have me on board. I'm making it clear to Farrell that if I'm going to do this, I want to do it on my terms.'

Fairlie couldn't imagine Vic Farrell would respond well to any direct ultimatum. But he knew enough about Pennycook to understand he could be very persuasive. He'd probably get his way without Farrell even realising. 'This is all very flattering,' he said. 'But I'm still not entirely clear why you're so keen to involve me.'

'I've given you the reasons, Craig. If you're not interested, that's fine. I appreciate a man of your talents won't be short of work. If that's the case I'm happy to look elsewhere.'

'No, don't get me wrong,' Fairlie said hurriedly. 'I'd be delighted to be part of it. I'm fully behind what you're trying to do, and I'd enjoy the work.' For all his reservations about collaborating with Pennycook, work was work and Fairlie still had a mortgage to pay. 'I'd be delighted to be involved.'

'I'm delighted to hear that. It'll be a privilege to have you on board. I'll clear the details with Vic, but I'm sure it won't be a problem.'

'Thanks for thinking of me.'

'Like I say, I prefer to work with the best. Speaking of which, I thought your articles on the Simon O'Donnell case were excellent.'

'You read them?'

'I like to keep up with anything that's of local relevance. And that case was a big deal for those of us of a certain age. Really shocking story.'

'It had an impact on anyone living in these parts at the time.'

'The articles implied there might be some new revelations to come. Is that right?'

'To be honest, it's not really my story. The groundwork's

been done by a podcaster. Guy called Hugh Preston. I've just been helping him get the story out there, but he's playing the detail very close to his chest. I don't really know any more than I wrote in the article.'

'Could be some red faces if there are questions about the conviction,' Pennycook observed. 'You've presumably got more articles planned?'

'That's up to Preston.' Fairlie already felt he'd said too much about the O'Donnell case. If it turned out there really was a story there, he didn't want to find it had leaked back to the likes of Vic Farrell.

'Strikes me Preston may not be the only one playing his cards close to his chest. Fair enough. It's your story. If you're going to be working for me, I'd expect the same kind of confidentiality.'

'That's taken as read,' Fairlie said. He gestured towards Pennycook's nearly empty glass. 'Another?'

'Aye, why not? Let's seal the deal with a pint.'

Fairlie swallowed the last of his own drink, then rose to make his way to the bar. He wasn't sure quite what was going on here, and why Pennycook had been so keen to secure his services. There was little point in speculating. Assuming the deal worked out, he'd no doubt find out soon enough.

For the moment, all he knew was that, even as a regular, it was likely to take him much longer to get served than it had taken Iain Pennycook.

CHAPTER TWENTY-EIGHT

Hugh Preston cut the call and swore loudly. He'd blown it. There was no doubt about that now. He'd suspected that was the case, but he'd hoped he might still be able to talk Viper round. Now it was crystal clear that wasn't going to happen.

His own stupid fault. He should have trusted his instincts from the start, or at least taken more seriously what Viper had said to him. He certainly shouldn't have trusted Craig Fairlie. The journalist had talked a good game, blethering on about journalistic integrity and the public interest. But Preston should have known a hack was always just a hack.

The first article had been fine. They'd more or less written that together. Preston had provided the content, and Fairlie had worked it into a form that suited the newspaper's readership. Fairlie had consulted him throughout, and Preston had ensured Viper was comfortable with the material.

The problems had arisen with the subsequent articles. Preston could understand why Fairlie had produced them. He'd wanted to keep the story alive while they waited for the follow-up podcast. The first couple of pieces hadn't been too bad, revisiting the details of the original case, building expectations about the potential content of the follow-up. Even then, though, Viper had been unhappy. He'd made it clear he wanted to be fully in control of the material, releasing it on his own terms and to his own timescales. He'd felt that control slowly slipping out of his hands.

Preston had been growing uneasy for some weeks. He'd always had to take Viper's account and promises on trust. He'd assured Preston he had substantive evidence of police wrongdoing in the original investigation. He'd handed over some titbits, most of which had been included in the first podcast.

Everything changed when the newspaper launched its campaign to reopen the case. Viper had called him immediately, demanding to know how the hell this had been allowed to happen. Preston had been slightly baffled by Viper's reaction. Preston hadn't been particularly happy about the campaign himself – he'd thought it tacky and sensationalist, out of keeping with the measured tone he'd been striving for in the podcast – but he couldn't see it changed much. But, for whatever reason, Viper had felt differently.

Preston had done his best to be conciliatory, promising to speak to Fairlie to try to have the campaign discontinued. But Viper wasn't placated. He'd told Preston he needed time to think, and said he'd be back in touch once he'd made a decision.

Preston had no idea who Viper really was – Viper wasn't his real name, of course – and the only means Preston had of contacting him was a mobile phone number, without voicemail, which Viper left switched off most of the time. Preston had tried the number several times over the last few weeks, but each time had received the message that the number was unobtainable.

Preston hadn't revealed to Craig Fairlie that his 'research' into the O'Donnell case was largely based on one source. The first episode had been structured around historical interviews, with contributions from various commentators who had examined the case over the years, including a legal expert to explain the niceties of the Scottish legal system. Preston had expected the follow-up to include a contribution from Viper himself – probably with his voice appropriately disguised. Preston had also hoped that, by then, he'd have enough material to approach others who'd been involved in the investigation or the trial.

Unable to contact Viper, Preston had strung Fairlie along, not answering his calls, maintaining radio silence. He hadn't been sure how long he could keep this up, especially with the supposed launch date of the follow-up approaching. He'd been steeling himself to speak to Fairlie, intending to say that there'd been a delay for some unspecified technical reason. Fairlie might have decided not to continue, but that wouldn't have been a great loss. By now, Preston had persuaded himself that he could promote the podcast just as effectively by himself.

In the event, the question was academic. Before Preston could phone Fairlie, Viper had finally phoned back. The call had been short but far from sweet. Viper had accused Preston of betraying him and said he was pulling the plug on the whole thing. 'I'm just going to keep my head down now,' he'd said. 'And I'd advise you to do the same. Or, better still, fuck off back to England. You might be safe there.'

Preston hadn't known what to make of that, except that he was screwed. That was when he'd called Fairlie to say he wasn't intending to continue with the follow-up.

The whole thing was a monumental balls-up and there didn't seem any way of salvaging it. He'd tried Viper's number once more, and this time the message had changed: 'This number is not recognised.'

The only question now was whether he could salvage something from the mess, maybe investigate the case himself without relying on Viper. He wasn't inclined to take Viper's warnings about his safety too seriously. That had just been Viper's melodramatic way of slamming the door in Preston's face. The more pertinent question was whether Preston could find a way to make this work without Viper's involvement.

A moment later, as if in response to his internal question, Preston's phone buzzed on the table.

CHAPTER TWENTY-NINE

'Apparently there's a route through to Narnia at the back somewhere,' McKay said.

'There's a what?' Josh Carlisle looked up from his laptop.

'Never mind.' The tiny room was even smaller than McKay remembered, but someone had managed to fit in two chairs and a narrow table. McKay had spent the last hour with Shaun Sanderson, who was still promising to come up with more suitable accommodation. McKay wasn't holding his breath for that to happen. It probably didn't matter now. The small team was rapidly working through the interviews with potential witnesses, and they'd probably be finished with the bulk of them in the next day or so.

The interviewees mainly comprised of staff working on the relevant ward, some staff from adjacent wards, and some more itinerant employees – doctors, porters, catering staff – who might have had reason to visit the relevant wards at the time in question.

Carlisle was sitting behind the desk gazing up at McKay with the air of an errant schoolboy expecting a dressing down. It was characteristic of Carlisle that, despite being the oldest and most experienced DC on the team, he was occupying the least comfortable of the available interview rooms.

'Sorry about the accommodation, Josh,' McKay said. 'Shaun Sanderson reckoned it was the best he could come up with. The best he could come up with without putting his arse into any kind of gear, anyway. He didn't put it like that, you understand.'

'It's okay, though I'm a bit stir crazy. Wouldn't be so bad if it had a window.'

'You can't expect miracles, son. At least he's had the brooms removed. How's it going so far?'

'No real breakthroughs. I've mainly been interviewing nurses and other staff from the ward where Renton died. No one's been able to add much to what we've already got. Everyone was busy on the main ward, with no reason to go into Renton's room.'

'Other than the person who killed him,' McKay pointed out. 'We have to consider the ward staff as potential suspects.'

'I know,' Carlisle said. 'If only on the basis of opportunity. It would have been easier and less suspicious for any of them to enter Renton's room than anyone else. I've asked them to account for their movements around the time Renton was killed. They were all able to give me a decent account as far as they could remember, but it's going to be tricky to corroborate. We're getting the CCTV checked out, but there's nothing on the wards and not much on the corridors. Patient privacy. The only places with good coverage are the public areas, and they're too busy to be useful.'

'Why don't you go and get yourself a coffee?' McKay said. 'You need a break if you've spent the morning in this place.'

'I've not long before the next one. But just about time for a coffee and a breath of air.'

'I can hold the fort here for a few minutes. Make sure no

one walks off with your laptop. I need to make a phone call anyway. Just one thing, Josh.'

'Boss?'

'I wouldn't go out the back way. It's perpetual winter out there.'

'Boss?'

'Go and get your coffee. You deserve it for spending a morning in this place.'

McKay pulled out his phone and dialled Helena Grant's number. She answered almost immediately. 'Morning, Alec. Assume you're over at the hospital?'

'Aye. Sitting in one of Shaun Sanderson's cupboards. Just relieved Josh for a few minutes so he can reacquaint himself with fresh air and daylight.'

'How's it going over there?'

'Pretty much as you'd expect. Not much new so far.'

'I was about to call you. Couple of new developments I thought might be of interest. First, I've just been talking to the pathologist about Gary Donaldson.'

'The guy who was found in his car?'

'They've just finished the post-mortem.'

'And?'

'It's confirmed his initial suspicion. The cause of death was suffocation. Same as Renton.'

'Harder to suffocate someone who's not up to their eyeballs on sedatives, I'd have thought.'

'Donaldson might already have been unconscious. But the pathologist reckons there's no sign of any head injury or any medical condition that might have caused him to lose control. If he was conscious, it would have taken some physical strength. He still had his seat belt on and didn't seem to have made any attempt to leave the car.'

'So he was taken by surprise?'

'It could have been over quite quickly if the killer knew what they were doing. But it means you're right, at least up to a point. We do have a killer on the road. Whether that ties in with any of the road collisions is another matter.'

'I've been as sceptical as you are, Hel. I was really just playing around with an idea. But every bit of evidence changes the picture, and the news about Donaldson is a hefty piece of evidence. Then there's the fact that someone presumably wanted to torch Donaldson's car. Why would you want to do that, unless you were looking to muddy the waters and destroy evidence?'

'We'd have identified the fire as arson. It would still have been a suspicious death.'

'But if Donaldson's body had been badly damaged in a fire, it would have been much more difficult to confirm the cause of death. And if the car had been badly damaged, it would have been harder to assess what made it leave the road.'

'If there's even half a possibility you're right about this, it opens up one hell of a can of worms. I don't know if we can even issue any public warning about this without either looking stupid or panicking people.'

'Can we increase the number of patrols on the road at least?'

'I can look at it. At least that would only make me look stupid internally.'

'Join the club. We could couch it as a potentially dangerous driver we're trying to identify rather than a mad killer on the road, if that helps.'

'Leaves a lot of questions hanging. But I'll see what I can do. We need to trawl back through other RTCs from the last six months or so. See if we can find any similar characteristics. We should give the relevant CCTV footage another going over. We might be able to spot something new if we've a better idea what we're looking for.'

'Or this could all be a monumental waste of time?'

'There's enough here now, particularly with Donaldson's killing, to make it worth pursuing.' She was silent for a moment, and McKay could tell she was thinking through the implications of what they'd been discussing.

'Go on,' he said.

'What I'm mainly thinking, just at the moment, is that I'm never going to forgive you if you were right about this all along.'

CHAPTER THIRTY

H ugh Preston looked at the screen of his phone. Number withheld. He took the call and cautiously said, 'Hello?'

'Is that Hugh Preston?'

'Speaking.'

'I wondered if I might have a word.'

'Go ahead.'

'I was thinking in person. It's about your podcast.'

Preston hesitated. There was something about the caller's tone that was making him feel uneasy. 'I'm sorry. You're...?'

'Former DS Marty Coleman. Retired now. I was involved in the O'Donnell inquiry.'

'I see.'

'I was interested by your podcast. Assume the follow-up's due any time?'

'Anytime,' Preston agreed vaguely. 'Can I ask what this is all about?'

'I just thought it might be useful to talk about the podcast. I found the first episode very interesting. I suppose there's no point in asking who your sources might have been?'

'I'm afraid not—'

'No, obviously. You've got to protect your sources. However unreliable.'

'I've no reason to believe they're unreliable.' Preston realised as he said the words that he'd had no real reason to trust Viper. At the very least, he'd not delivered what he'd promised. At worst, he'd been bullshitting all along.

'Aye, well. Believe what you like, son. There was a lot of mealy-mouthed innuendo about that investigation, but it was as straight as they come.'

'I'm sorry. I still don't understand why you're calling.'

'I thought it might be useful for you to have the real story. Before you damage anybody's reputation any further.'

'I've not damaged anyone's reputation.'

'Maybe not yet, Except by implication. That first episode, along with the newspaper articles, implied that anyone on that investigation was a suspect.'

'I wasn't responsible for the newspaper articles. I didn't approve them or necessarily agree with their content.'

'You just stirred the shit in the first place. Aye, I understand.'

'Look, I'm not sure there's any point in continuing this conversation. I've just been trying to take another look at the case. See if anything might have been done differently.'

'With the benefit of hindsight?' Coleman was silent for a moment. 'Look, I'm sorry. This has started off on the wrong foot. It's just that I know how hard we all worked on that case. Rory Grant handled it scrupulously. We did everything we could to ensure it was watertight. It's not easy to hear someone questioning it, ten years after the event.'

'I understand that. I just want to be fair and objective.'

'That was why I wanted to talk. I was uncomfortable with the implications raised in that first episode. You said you wanted to explore the whole story in detail. I don't know who you've been speaking to so far but I'd like the opportunity to talk to you about it. There are some aspects of the case you need to understand.'

'You don't think we can do it over the phone?'

'I think it would be easier to talk face to face. It was a lengthy investigation so there's a lot to talk about. I'm more than happy to come to you.'

'Would you be willing to let me interview you? For the podcast, I mean. On the record.'

'I've nothing to hide. Happy to tell it like it was.'

'If you come here, we can have an initial chat, then do a formal interview if there's material we'd like to include in the podcast.' He gave Coleman his address. 'Not too far for you?'

'No, that's fine. No distance at all. Whenever suits you. Assume you'd want to do it fairly quickly if the follow-up is imminent?'

'It would be useful to do it as soon as possible. I don't suppose you're available tomorrow.'

'I'm a retired police officer,' Coleman said. 'It's you or golf.'

'Tomorrow then.' One door closes and all that, Preston thought. This might give him an opportunity to revive the follow-up podcast. Even if he couldn't come up with the revelations he hoped for, it was an interesting story. Coleman's call offered him a new way forward.

But it was only now that it occurred to Preston to wonder how Coleman had obtained his number. Or why his manner had shifted so suddenly from belligerent to conciliatory. Or indeed what positive information Coleman might have to tell him that wasn't already in the public domain.

Or, for that matter why, having ended the call, Preston was left feeling quite so uneasy.

CHAPTER THIRTY-ONE

Craig Fairlie watched Edward Lawrence gaze bemusedly around the bar. He looked more comfortable than Fairlie might have expected, but still had the air of an astronomer reviewing a barely habitable alien environment. 'This is your office?'

'The place I use when I'm not working from home,' Fairlie said. 'It's convenient for meeting people in town.'

'It's certainly characterful.'

'I did offer to come to your offices,' Fairlie pointed out.

'I'm more than happy to come here. I'd rather keep this as separate as possible from my professional practice. At least for the moment.'

'Your choice. At least allow me to buy you a drink for your trouble. What can I get you?'

'It's more or less lunchtime, isn't it? Maybe a beer then. Whatever you're drinking but just a half. Otherwise, I'll be asleep by mid-afternoon.'

'I'm adept at making a pint last most of the day,' Fairlie said. 'Just enough to keep Ally behind the bar happy.'

'He doesn't mind you spending the day in here?'

'It's not as if my presence is keeping out the big spenders. Ally makes his money in the evening.'

By the time Fairlie had returned from the bar with the beer, Lawrence had already extracted a file from his briefcase and placed it on the table. 'Kevin Clark's file,' he said. 'Or part of it. I've added my latest set of notes.'

'You went to see him again?'

'A couple of days ago. Spent the best part of an hour talking to him.'

'And?'

'He seems to have remembered something more about what happened after the killing. He recalls being in a car with other people and holding something he thinks was the murder weapon. And he remembers handing it over to someone else.'

'Can he identify who was in the car?'

'He says not. He just remembers that there were others. The driver and someone in the passenger seat. Probably but not definitely the same people who dropped him off at the site.'

'Do you believe him?'

'I've always felt that Kevin's told the truth as best he can.'

'You don't think he was leaned on to keep quiet, for example?'

'The honest answer is I don't know. I'm also not sure the two possibilities are mutually incompatible.'

'How do you mean?'

'I think it's more than possible that someone threatened Kevin at the time of the killing. Made him take the rap on his own. But I also think it's conceivable Kevin has no recollection of that.'

'Really?'

'When the police first interviewed Kevin, he was in a genuinely confused state. He claimed to remember nothing at all. I think he was telling the truth, even if the police didn't believe him. They thought I was naive for taking him at his word. But I've seen no evidence of cunning in Kevin. He's just not capable of it. I don't know what happened in that bedroom, or if Kevin was or wasn't party to it, but I do believe his brain initially blocked out his memory of what happened. In that state of mind, immediately after the killing, he'd have been impressionable enough to accept whatever anyone told him. Especially someone he looked up to.'

'Like these so-called mates of his?'

'I'm not sure they'd even have needed to threaten him in the conventional sense. Just insist to him he was there by himself. He'd have been in no state to work out what was or wasn't true.'

'But now he claims to remember being in a car with someone?' Fairlie was aware that he sounded sceptical. 'But he doesn't know who.'

'I'm more inclined to trust Kevin than you are. That's understandable. I've spent years talking and listening to him. I honestly don't think he's capable of lying – not in the sense that you or I understand it. That doesn't mean he necessarily always tells the truth. He tries to please the people he's talking to, particularly if he likes them or they've treated him well. I saw it sometimes even in the police interviews. If the interviewer was aggressive, he'd clam up. But if the interviewer was gentler with him, he'd try to please, sometimes to his own disadvantage. But I think I can tell when he's doing that. And this isn't that.'

'So what is it? His memory coming back?'

'At least some of the clouds slowly lifting. It's not uncommon in this kind of case. As the trauma of the original event becomes more distant, people start to remember. Sometimes the whole memory, sometimes just parts of it. Sometimes it's a quick process and sometimes it takes years.'

Fairlie had no real idea how much to believe this. Lawrence

wouldn't be the first lawyer to be hoodwinked by his client. Perhaps Clark was more canny than he appeared.

But none of that really mattered. The simple fact was that this was a new development in the O'Donnell case. The first new development in many years. It wasn't enough to suggest the verdict might be unsafe, and nothing like enough to justify reopening the case. But it was enough to sell a few more newspapers and give the campaign a boost. Above all, it was something he could sell to Colin Wishaw as an alternative to the podcast material.

Fairlie took a sip of his pint, which had been sitting largely untouched for the past hour. 'I suppose it's time for me to ask the obvious question. Why are you telling me this? Or, to put it another way, what do you want me to do with it?'

'When I first read about the podcast, I thought it might be useful to get in touch. I could help ensure that Kevin's side of the story was reported accurately. I didn't envisage Kevin would say anything new.'

'And now?'

'This is definitely new. In itself, it doesn't change anything, other than indicating that Kevin must have had some kind of accomplices. It doesn't prove anyone else was involved in the murder. It doesn't prove anyone else was present in that bedroom.'

'It indicates that someone else must have been involved after the fact,' Fairlie pointed out. 'And the presence of the murder weapon suggests they must have known what Kevin had done. If that's true, it suggests someone literally got away with murder, if only indirectly.'

'If it's true,' Lawrence said. 'The problem is that we've really only Kevin's word for any of this. The obvious explanation for these new revelations is that Kevin's concocting them to throw doubt on his conviction.'

'Isn't that a possibility?'

'It could be, but why wait all this time? And there's another consideration.'

'Which is?'

'I'm not sure Kevin even wants to overturn the original verdict. I think he's... not happy exactly, but comfortable in prison. He's institutionalised. He couldn't cope with life outside. That's why I'm not sure what to do with this. I want to do what's in Kevin's best interests. My instinct has always been to keep chasing the truth. But I don't know if it's better just to let sleeping dogs lie.'

'You didn't specify that any of this should be off the record. I'm a journalist. You've given me a story.'

'You're a decent man, Craig. If I ask you not to run with this in Kevin's interest, you won't.'

'I'd much rather be working on this with your approval and goodwill. Let's put it that way.'

'I appreciate that. My feeling is we should run with it. But I need to be careful. That's one reason I preferred to meet here rather than at the office. My professional role here is... well, let's say blurred. There's the whole issue of client confidentiality, for example. For what it's worth, Kevin's confirmed he's happy for me to speak to the media. But I honestly don't know if Kevin really understands the significance of that. If you are going to cover this, I'd prefer my name wasn't mentioned.'

'I'm not sure that's possible. If we want this story to have any credibility, it needs to be more than tittle-tattle. I can anonymise the source of the story. Just say that "sources close to Kevin" have revealed he's been talking about his returning memories. We could then include a bland comment from you, as Kevin's lawyer, refusing to confirm or deny what Kevin's been saying, but confirming you've been in discussion with Kevin. That would distance you from the actual revelation, but indicate to readers that there might well be something of substance in them.'

'I thought lawyers were cunning.'

'Journalists are rattlesnakes. Cunning and venomous.'

'You're being disarmingly honest.'

'It's my saving grace. One of the few things that distinguishes me from my less scrupulous colleagues. I can't help myself.'

'You're an interesting man, Mr Fairlie. But I'm happy to proceed on the basis you describe.'

'I'm still not sure what you're hoping to achieve with this.'

'I'm not sure myself. I'm just not convinced that Kevin is guilty. If we publish this story, it might help stimulate Kevin's own memories, or it might prompt a new witness to come forward, even after all these years. I want to try anything I can that might provide a chance to prove Kevin's innocence.'

'Even if that's not necessarily in his own best interests?'

'I'll need to think about the implications of that if more evidence should emerge.'

'That wasn't what I meant,' Fairlie said. 'Or not all I meant.'

'What else?'

'If someone did put pressure on Kevin to keep his mouth shut all those years ago – whatever type of psychological persuasion they might have used – they might not be best pleased if Kevin starts talking again.'

'You don't think Kevin's safe in prison?'

'It depends who these supposed associates were, and what they might have become. Most likely they were teenagers like Kevin who managed to avoid his fate. But it's possible some of them might have become more influential in the intervening years. If so, Kevin might not be safe. Not even in prison.'

'I find it hard to believe that any of Kevin's young associates would ever have acquired that kind of power.'

'I just want to be sure you've thought through the implications. It has to be your decision. Yours and Kevin's. If you're happy to go ahead, I'll do whatever I can to help.'

CHAPTER THIRTY-TWO

'What do you think?'

Craig Fairlie scanned the half-empty rows of seats. 'Is this typical?'

Iain Pennycook did at least have the grace to look embarrassed. 'Not the best turnout. Not even for an afternoon meeting. Too nice a day.'

Fairlie could believe that, at least. It was another fine late summer's day, the skies clear, the sun as hot as it was likely to get in these climes. Not a day likely to entice many people into a gloomy village hall in the wilds of Caithness. The small group of people were mostly elderly, treating the event more as a social get-together than a campaign rally.

'I thought it better if you saw the extremes,' Pennycook said. 'So you can see how the campaign's developing. Obviously, we do a lot better with evening events in the bigger towns.'

'So why bother with events like this?' The room was no more than a third full, though inevitably the audience had spread itself out across the available seats.

'That's the question Ben keeps asking.' Pennycook gestured towards Ben Vaughn, his young assistant who was at the door, welcoming the last few late-comers. 'He thinks we should focus our efforts on the areas of greatest return.'

'He might be right,' Fairlie pointed out. 'There's a danger of spreading yourself too thinly.'

'There might be, if you were a typical grifting politician, just interested in maximising your vote.'

'But that's not you?' Fairlie tried to keep any note of irony out of his voice.

'I'm not a politician at all. Not in the conventional sense,' Pennycook said. 'I'm a campaigner. I represent people's views, whoever they are. That's why we're here.'

In all honesty, Fairlie had no real idea why he was there, other than to keep Pennycook happy. Pennycook had persuaded the newspaper to employ Fairlie to ghost his column. Fairlie had been more than content with the payment terms offered. It was hard to get any regular gigs these days, let alone one that was well remunerated. Whatever Pennycook's other qualities, he was clearly a smart negotiator. Fairlie wondered how much Pennycook might be receiving for a column he'd never actually write.

Pennycook gestured to Vaughn, who ushered the last of the arrivals to their seats and closed the external doors. Vaughn took a seat at the rear, from where he could deal with late-comers. Fairlie slipped into a seat near the front, and watched as Pennycook bounded up onto the raised platform.

'Good afternoon, folks,' he began with the air of a funfair barker. 'First of all, thanks to you all for taking the trouble to come here on a fine day like today. I imagine you've all got plenty to say, and I'm here to listen. I want to make sure that your voices are heard.' He looked around, as if registering every individual in the room. 'I'm not here to spout my own opinions, though as many of you will know, I'm not afraid to express my views when I need to.'

Fairlie conceded that Pennycook was very good at this stuff. It wasn't anything he said. He was fluent and sounded as if he was speaking off the cuff, but the content was mostly banal. It was all in the delivery. There was nothing demagogic about the way Pennycook spoke. His intonation was that of a kindly teacher, eager to educate and communicate. He made you feel as though he wasn't talking to an audience. He was talking to you individually. It was a trick, but it was a good one and it was working very effectively on this particular group. They looked utterly rapt, as if Pennycook was the most impressive orator they'd ever heard.

Fairlie didn't bother to listen closely to what Pennycook was saying. It was the usual stuff, initially focused on the failings of the A9 but broadening the argument to encompass the neglect of the northern Highlands. Pennycook's language was subtly different even from that he might have used in Inverness. There was the possibility of stoking distinct and additional grievances here, and even more so as Pennycook progressed further west and north or over to the Islands.

With this audience, Pennycook's schtick was going down well. Fairlie had allowed the content to wash over him, but Pennycook was clearly reaching the climax of his presentation. His tone became less amiable and conversational, taking on a more rhetorical edge. He still sounded as if he was speaking off the cuff, but Fairlie had little doubt this part of the speech had been crafted and honed for maximum impact. He finished with a verbal and physical flourish that brought the sparse audience to its feet in a standing ovation. Fairlie climbed wearily to his feet and joined the applause, not wanting to suggest any lack of enthusiasm.

For a few moments, Pennycook basked in the warmth of the audience's response. Then he gestured for everyone to retake their seats. 'Thank you, everyone. That means a lot to me. It tells me we're speaking the same language, that we're on the same wavelength. I've told you what I think, and we're clearly in agreement. But now I'd like to hear what you have to say. The floor is yours. Please raise anything you want. If you want to ask questions, I'll do my best to answer them. If I can't answer them myself, I'll seek answers from those who can. If you have comments, I'm here to listen. Most importantly, if you have needs or demands, I'll campaign to deliver the change we need. Ladies and gentlemen, the floor is yours.'

The question and answer session was as lacklustre as Fairlie had expected. It wasn't long before Pennycook began drawing things to a close, taking the opportunity to re-emphasise the themes from his earlier speech and prepare himself for a final peroration. 'We've just a few more minutes,' he said. 'Any final questions?'

An elderly man sitting at the far end of the front row nervously raised a hand. Pennycook nodded to him. 'Yes, you, sir?'

The man climbed slowly to his feet. He looked around, as if slightly bewildered to find himself in this position. Finally, he returned his attention to Pennycook. 'I've listened very carefully to what you've had to say. I can see that the rest of this audience have listened with similarly rapt attention. It was an extremely compelling presentation.'

'Well, thank you, but—'

'I'm just wondering how many of us gathered here today know who you really are.'

There was a moment's silence. 'I'm sorry? Look, I think—'

'I wonder how many people here know you started out as a small-time crook, a petty thief, a fraudster?'

'I've never concealed my background,' Pennycook said. 'I made mistakes as a young man, and I deeply regret that. But I served my time and rebuilt my life. One of the reasons I'm here today is because I understand what life is like for those who are disadvantaged. I can offer a perspective that perhaps isn't available to others.'

Ben Vaughn had made his way to the front of the room, waiting to see how matters would turn out before physically intervening. If Pennycook kept the audience onside, it would be counterproductive for Vaughn to involve himself in a physical struggle with an elderly man.

But the man clearly hadn't finished. He was becoming more animated, shouting over Pennycook's smooth justifications. 'You've trotted out that bilge for years. Saying you paid the price. It's shite and it always has been. Sure, you served time for your petty theft and your fraud. But, if there was any justice, you'd still be inside, instead of leaving some poor kid to languish in prison in your place.' The man jabbed his finger in Pennycook's direction. 'You've got blood on your fucking hands, son. Blood on your fucking hands!'

Vaughn moved to take the man by the arm. For a moment Fairlie thought the man was going to resist Vaughn's attempts to remove him. Instead, he forced his way past Vaughn and strode out of the room, not looking back.

'I'm sorry, folks.' Pennycook's voice remained calm, but his body language suggested he'd been more shaken by the unexpected intervention than he wanted to reveal. 'I really don't know what that was all about. I've always been transparent about my past, and I stand by what I said a few moments ago. I'm sorry that that unfortunate contribution disrupted what I think has otherwise been a very useful and productive meeting. Thank you all for coming this afternoon.'

It was clear the heckler had little support among the wider group. Pennycook left the stage to a standing ovation, and was immediately surrounded by people wanting to talk to him.

Fairlie stood up to allow a man and woman to exit from the

row. 'Good speech,' the man said to Fairlie as he passed. 'The sort of man we need in politics. Someone who represents ordinary people like us.'

'Pity about the disruption at the end,' Fairlie said.

'Mouthy old bugger. Not sure he's still got all his marbles.'

'You know him?'

'I know who he is. Everyone round here knows who he is. Daft old bastard with a shed full of axes to grind.'

'Plenty of them around. What's his name?'

The man gave him a curious look. 'Why do you want to know?'

'I'm working with Iain. Useful to be forewarned if our friend tries to interrupt any future sessions.'

'I take your point. His name's Clark. Alasdair Clark. But I wouldn't worry. He's all mouth.'

Fairlie's eyes were fixed on Pennycook on the far side of the room. 'Aye. He certainly seemed to have plenty to say.'

CHAPTER THIRTY-THREE

'Nice set-up you've got here.'

Hugh Preston nodded. 'It's only a small place. I've not been here long, but I'm gradually getting it how I want it.'

Marty Coleman was sitting in one of the armchairs, a mug of coffee cradled on his knee. 'Nice location too. Good to see an incomer buying a place to live in, rather than as a second home or holiday let. Place needs new blood.'

'I'm trying to do my bit to support the local economy. I can do this work anywhere so I might as well be somewhere that's pleasant to live.'

'The podcast?'

'That's part of it. I also do voice-over work and audiobooks and suchlike. I'm gradually building it up.'

'What led you to the true crime material?'

This was turning into something closer to a job interview than Preston had expected. But that was fair enough. If Coleman intended to share sensitive information, he'd want to ensure he could trust the man he was speaking to.

'I'm happy to admit I was jumping on a bandwagon. It's

much more common in the US, of course, but there are some good examples in the UK.'

'What drew you to the Kevin Clark case?'

'I'd been researching various cases potentially involving some miscarriage of justice. Some of them had already received extensive coverage so I whittled it down to a few cases that were less well known. I used to be a radio presenter and I had some decent contacts down south, so that was where I started. The one thing I managed to cultivate during my time in broadcasting was sheer brass neck. If you don't ask, you don't get. If you do ask, you get what you want more often than you might think. Most of the time I just call people and ask if they want to take part. If they say no, they say no. Most don't.'

'Even ex-cops?'

'They're warier. But, for one reason or another, most are prepared to say yes, even if they insist on anonymity.'

'Why do they do it? Talk to you, I mean.'

'Sometimes they feel the record needs setting straight. Often because they think some aspect of the investigation has been misrepresented in the media.'

'Tell me about it. Bloody hacks usually haven't a clue. No offence.'

'None taken. I'm not a hack. Not in that sense.'

'What led you to the O'Donnell case?'

'I'd put the podcast on hold while I completed the move up here. Long and dull story but I'd split with a long-term partner. I'd come across the O'Donnell case when I was carrying out my initial research. Now I was living down the road from where the killing took place, I thought it might be worth giving it a closer look. I made some calls to contacts within Police Scotland, trying to identify anyone prepared to take part in a podcast. To be honest, I didn't have a lot of success. Everyone seemed cagey. Many had retired. Some of them talked about the emotions stirred up by the original investigation, and felt it would be insensitive to revisit the story without good reason. Basically I found the door repeatedly slammed in my face.'

'I can't say any of that surprises me.'

'I hadn't realised how much the case shocked the community in these parts.'

'It did that, all right. Why did you carry on?'

'I'd almost given up when I had a phone call out of the blue. Number withheld and the caller refused to give his name. Said he was an officer who'd worked on the O'Donnell case. He reckoned he could tell me the truth about what had happened during the investigation. He implied there'd been a miscarriage of justice.'

'And you believed him?'

'He gave me enough background information to convince me he was a cop or an ex-cop and that he'd worked on the investigation. I was prepared to keep an open mind.'

'Did this contact tell you anything useful?'

'He gave me some material.'

'The material you used in your first episode and in that newspaper article?'

'That was the start. There was more.'

'I suppose you wouldn't be prepared to tell me how much more?'

'Not at this point, no. I know nothing about you. Other than that you claim to be a retired DC.' Since receiving the original call from Coleman, Preston had made some efforts to find out more about the man sitting opposite. He'd confirmed that a DC Marty Coleman had worked in the local Division of Police Scotland until a few years before, but had been unable to obtain any more detail. There were various Martin Colemans living in the area, but Preston had been unable to confirm whether any was an ex-police officer.

'You're quite right to be cautious. But at least I've given you my name.'

'I have to protect my sources,' Preston said again. 'If you were to have any dealings with me, I'm sure you'd expect the same.'

'I've nothing to hide,' Coleman said.

'You believe others have?'

'I'm not saying that. I just wanted to talk to you about the investigation. Set the record straight.'

'I'm very open to any input,' Preston said. 'That's the point. To give all sides of the story and allow listeners to make up their own minds.'

'Or to scattergun a whole load of innuendo, and leave the listener to jump to unfounded conclusions?'

'That's not my intention.'

'It's all sensationalism, isn't it? You're not really interested in the plain and boring truth.'

'I'm interested in the truth,' Preston said. 'If you have something to tell me, I'll be delighted to listen.'

'And include it in the podcast?'

'That depends on what you have to say. I'm not starting out from the assumption that the investigation was flawed. I know how much work went into it, and how rigorous the inquiry was. I'm also aware the jury reached a quick and unanimous verdict.'

'So why open the can of worms again after all these years?'

'It was a high-profile case. It had a huge impact on this community. There've been repeated suggestions that Kevin Clark might have been a fall guy.'

'Clark went down fair and square.'

'So tell me about the investigation. Tell me how you carried it out. Reassure our listeners that you didn't cut corners. That the conviction was the right one. People are interested in understanding the whole picture. They want to know how the police work, how an investigation's carried out. A straight account of the process will attract as many listeners as one trying to come up with dramatic revelations.'

'You reckon?' Coleman sounded sceptical.

'I don't see why not,' Preston said. 'If you and others are prepared to talk openly to me.'

'I don't know why we should trust someone like you. How do we know you won't edit the material to twist what we say. I know from experience how easy it is to misrepresent something that's been said in good faith.'

'I can't make you trust me. But I'd allow you an opportunity to listen to the edited version prior to broadcast so you can correct any factual errors and respond to any views that you think are unfair or unreasonable.'

Coleman was looking thoughtful. 'I might be prepared to give it a go on that basis. But I'd want to define my terms. I wouldn't want you to use my name or my material without my express permission. I reserve the right to walk away if I'm not happy. There are ex-colleagues of mine who are just as keen to set the record straight, and who'd be willing to take part if I vouched for you. That depends on you not screwing me over.'

'I'm not interested in screwing anyone over,' Preston said. 'Look, let me show you the recording studio. It's nothing grand, but it's got everything that's needed. We could record an introductory chat – nothing controversial, just a general introduction. I can edit that in the way I normally would, and you can see if you're happy with the outcome. It'll give you a feel for the way I operate.'

'Aye, why not?' Coleman said. 'This is all new to me. I'd like to see how it works.' He placed his coffee mug down on the table beside him. 'Lead the way.'

Preston climbed to his feet. 'Just down here.'

He led Coleman down the hallway, opening the door of

what would have once been a second bedroom in the cottage. 'This is where the magic happens.' He stepped back to allow Coleman to see past him into the room.

It was only then he realised what a big a mistake he'd made. He was thrown back against the wall by the considerable weight of Coleman's body. He struggled for a moment, trying to break away. Then he felt something soft pressed against his face, blocking his mouth and nose. He tried to struggle, but already the grip was tightening. It was some moments before consciousness slipped away.

CHAPTER THIRTY-FOUR

Ginny Horton was in the kitchen when she heard Isla's car pull into the driveway of their cottage in Ardersier. The kettle had boiled ready for coffee, if that was what Isla preferred, but there was an opened bottle of red wine on the kitchen table. Ginny had no idea how this would play out. When she'd spoken to Isla on the phone earlier, her partner simply sounded flat. Another day, yet another meeting with the consultant to discuss next steps. There'd been no trace of emotion in Isla's tone, as if she were dealing with another business matter, some legal complication that needed untangling.

Ginny waited until Isla had retrieved her briefcase from the rear of the car, then walked out to fling her arms around her. Isla pressed her face into Ginny's shoulder, saying nothing.

Back in the house, Isla threw herself onto the sofa in the living room. 'I'm hoping there's alcohol?'

'As much as you need.'

'I doubt that. But I hope there's as much as I can cope with.'

'Wine?'

'Perfect.'

Ginny returned to the kitchen and poured two glasses, carrying them back into the living room. 'How are you feeling?'

Isla helped herself to a large mouthful of the wine before responding. 'Physically, fine. Emotionally, well, better than I might have feared.'

'What did they say?'

'Not much new. They reckon they've very likely caught it in time, though they can't be certain until they've done more tests. It's likely to require some combination of radio- and chemotherapy which will be pretty debilitating. I've spent part of the afternoon talking to the other partners about the implications.'

'I assume they were sympathetic?'

'They were great. As good as I could have hoped. But it'll put a lot of additional pressure on them. I've said I'll do as much as I can for as long as I can.'

'As long as you don't do too much.'

'You know me.'

'That's why I'm saying it. What happens next?'

'Another appointment. First just to talk through the implications. Some more tests.'

'I can come with you for that.'

'You don't need to. I can look after myself. And you've a job too.'

'Don't be daft. That's what I'm here for, and Helena's made it clear I should treat this as a priority.'

'What about Alec? He's never struck me as the touchy-feely type.'

'You might be surprised. No, he's the same. We're a team. That's the point.'

'If you say so. I'm not going to pretend I can cope with this by myself. I just feel numb at the moment. It'll hit me at some point, I guess.'

'That's usually how it works. I'll be here.'

Isla was silent for a moment. 'Then there's the question of my mum.'

'I thought you weren't on speaking terms?'

'We're not. Or only barely.'

Ginny had never really enquired too much about Isla's background. Ginny had had plenty of family issues of her own, some of which had intruded into their life a few years before. She knew Isla had faced similar childhood traumas, mostly involving her alcoholic father. Isla had seen her mother, Carole, as overly complicit in covering for her husband's failings. Ginny didn't know enough to assess whether that was a fair judgement or whether Isla had failed to appreciate the challenges her mother had faced. When Ginny first met Isla in London, Isla's parents had been separated and she still maintained a mostly cordial if strained relationship with Carole. Then Isla's mother had apparently reconciled with her husband, and the couple moved back in together. That, exacerbated by Isla's decision to move to the Highlands with Ginny, had resulted in a further falling out. The two had still been at loggerheads at the time of her father's death a few years before. Now, daughter and mother spoke occasionally on the phone, but only when there was some practical issue to deal with.

'Do you need to tell her?'

'I've been mulling that over since I got the call. I think I do, don't you? I mean, she's my mother.'

'So what's the problem?'

'I don't know how she'll take it. I mean, it's lose–lose when I speak to her. If I don't tell her and she finds out, she'll be offended. If I do tell her, she'll behave as if I'm dumping my problems on her.'

'It isn't about her,' Ginny pointed out.

'You have met her, haven't you.'

Ginny had met Carole a few times during the early stages of their relationship. They hadn't warmed to one another, although they'd maintained a frosty politeness. Ginny had assumed this was largely because Carole disapproved of the same-sex relationship, but Isla had assured her that the tensions would have been the same in any circumstances. 'I think because she's had so little happiness in her own life, she can't help begrudging it in others.'

'If that's the case, you should feel sorry for her,' Ginny had said.

'She doesn't make it easy even to do that.'

'You're probably right,' Ginny said now. 'You do need to tell her.'

'That's not what worries me, though.'

'So what does worry you?'

'That she'll want to come up here. To help.'

'Is she likely to do that?'

'She's a great one for duty. That's what kept her with my dad all those years. She felt she had an obligation to look after him even though it was destroying her and me. She might feel the same now. I'm not sure I could face that on top of everything else.'

'So tell her you don't need her help. You can do it politely but still be firm.'

Isla smiled. 'I ask you again: you have met her, haven't you. If she gets an idea into her head, she's not easy to dissuade.'

'Another bridge we'll have to cross when we come to it,' Ginny said.

'I've a feeling there'll be more than enough of those bridges over the coming months,' Isla said. 'Let's hope we've got the energy to keep crossing them.'

Ginny nodded. 'And there aren't too many trolls living underneath.'

CHAPTER THIRTY-FIVE

The weather was bound to break soon, Craig Fairlie thought. In these parts, any extended stretch of decent weather felt unnatural. Fairlie was sure there must have been previous warm summers, but he couldn't recall any that had been sustained as long as this one.

Not that Fairlie cared too much. He was divorced, his ex-wife and kids now down south, and not currently in a relationship. He spent most of his time sitting in the gloom of Ally's bar with no real idea what the weather outside might be doing. He wasn't one for beaches or, really, for holidays of any kind. If it had rained solidly all summer, he wouldn't have noticed.

But it made a difference on a day like today when he was yet again heading up the coast to Caithness. Driving up the A9 was a pleasure in the warm afternoon sunshine, a pleasant change from the times he'd struggled up here in the rain, mist or snow. The road was narrow and winding, potentially treacherous in poor conditions, but today an enjoyable, picturesque drive.

Even so, he'd have preferred to have stayed up here after yesterday's meeting with Iain Pennycook, rather than making the journey twice. Pennycook had been keen for Fairlie to join them at a larger evening meeting back in town. There'd probably still have been time for Fairlie to make it back for the meeting, but he hadn't wanted to give Pennycook any reason to suspect his actions or intentions.

From Fairlie's point of view, the second meeting had been a waste of time. It had demonstrated Pennycook's ability to work a room and a larger crowd than the one he'd faced in the afternoon. But it had essentially been more of the same, and the final question and answer session was even more anodyne than the earlier one.

It hadn't taken long for Fairlie to track down an A. Clark living in the village they'd visited the previous day. Whoever he was, Clark was making no effort to conceal his identity. He was on the electoral roll and his details were available through online directory enquiries.

There was no guarantee Clark would be prepared to speak to Fairlie, or indeed that he had anything of value to say, but it was worth a shot. Fairlie assumed Alasdair Clark was a relative of Kevin, but the man had looked too old to be one of the brothers.

Fairlie turned off the A9 and followed the road into the village. He passed the community hall where they'd held the previous day's meeting. There wasn't much more to the village, not even a convenience store or pub. Fairlie turned right onto a single-track road. The house he was looking for was on the left, a small bungalow close to the road. He found it without difficulty, although there was barely enough space for him to park his car by the gate. There was no other vehicle visible. This wasn't a place accustomed to receiving guests.

The bungalow didn't exactly look neglected, but it didn't appear to have received much recent maintenance. The garden was slightly overgrown, and the house looked as if it could do with a coat of paint. Fairlie opened the gate and made his way up the garden path to the front door.

He pressed the doorbell, hearing the sound of its ringing inside. After a few moments, he heard shuffling footsteps. The door opened a crack and a face peered out followed by a hand. 'Thanks.'

Fairlie was unsure how to respond. 'I'm sorry. For what?'

'For whatever crap you're delivering today. Presumably something you can't just stick through the letterbox, if you've dragged me to the door.'

'I'm sorry...'

The door opened wider. 'You're not the postman, are you? What are you, some kind of courier?'

'No,' Fairlie said. 'I'm looking for Alasdair Clark.'

'That right? And who the hell are you?'

If he told Clark he was a journalist, Fairlie suspected the door would be slammed in his face. 'I'm doing some work with Edward Lawrence, Kevin Clark's solicitor.'

The door opened a little wider. 'What kind of work?'

That answered at least one of Fairlie's questions. 'Would it be possible to come inside?'

'I'm not accustomed to letting people into my house without having a clue who they are.'

'I understand that. I'll be straight with you. I'm a journalist. Freelance. But I am working with Edward Lawrence. He approached me because he wanted advice about how to bring Kevin Clark's case back to public attention.'

'Why would anyone want to do that?' The words sounded sceptical, but Fairlie could sense he'd already engaged Alasdair Clark's interest.

'Kevin claims to be remembering more about what happened on the day of the O'Donnell murder. Nothing of major significance. But there's the possibility it might ultimately shed some new light on Kevin's conviction.'

'Why would that be of interest to me?'

'I was present at Iain Pennycook's meeting yesterday. You made an intervention.'

'Why were you at the meeting?'

Fairlie was beginning to suspect Alasdair Clark was not a man to underestimate. 'As I said, I'm a journalist. I'm interested in Pennycook's return up here. I thought there might be a story in it.'

'In a sparsely attended meeting in the wilds of Caithness?'

'That's partly why I think there might be a story. Why is a high-profile figure like Iain Pennycook spending his time talking to a few dozen people?'

Fairlie had clearly pressed the right button. 'Because Pennycook's a washed-up has-been who never should have been anything in the first place. You'd best come in.' Clark opened the door wider and ushered Fairlie inside.

The house was tidier than Fairlie had expected. He'd assumed, without really thinking about it, that Clark would be living alone. But as he followed Clark into the small living room, he was greeted by an elderly woman rising from one of the armchairs.

'We've got a visitor, Fiona.'

'I can see that. Are you going to introduce us?'

'Take a seat, Mr...?'

'Fairlie. Craig Fairlie.'

'Fiona, meet Mr Fairlie. He's a journalist, apparently.'

'Oh, aye? Are we newsworthy?'

'We'll have to see, won't we? He's working with Kevin's solicitor.'

Fiona Clark sighed. 'I should have known it would be that.

Is this something you've organised behind my back?' The question was addressed to her husband.

'Not at all,' Clark said. 'He just turned up on our doorstep.'

'I'm afraid that's true, Mrs Clark. I hope I'm not intruding.'

'It's not like we've much else to spend our time on. That's Alasdair's trouble these days. Too much time on his hands. Can I get you a tea or coffee? We were just about to have one.' The change in tone was noticeable. Fiona Clark had made her position clear, but was happy to be hospitable. She reminded Fairlie of his own mother.

'Coffee would be good, thank you. But don't go to any trouble.'

'I can cope with sticking on a kettle. It'll give you a chance to chat to Alasdair.'

'She worries about me,' Clark said. 'Probably with good reason. So what's this all about? What's brought you to this benighted spot? Two days in a row, as well.'

'As I said, I'm working with Edward Lawrence. The reason he approached me was because I'd written a newspaper article about the O'Donnell case.'

'I wouldn't have seen it because I never look at any of that shite. With all due respect.'

'You're not shy about expressing your opinions, Mr Clark.'

'Too outspoken for my own good sometimes. What was the focus of this article of yours?'

'It wasn't exclusively my article. It was based on material provided by the producer of a podcast—'

'Podcast?' Clark's expression suggested he'd never heard the word before.

'A chap called Hugh Preston was producing a broadcast on the case. He approached me to get some newspaper coverage of the series.'

'Like a radio broadcast?'

'Something like that, yes. But designed for downloading on to your computer.'

'I've heard mention of the idea. So this Preston had been working on the O'Donnell case?'

'I can't tell you much about what he was working on. He played his cards very close to his chest. He clearly had at least one contact in the police feeding information to him. The podcast contained some interesting revelations about police practices which potentially raised questions about the integrity of the investigation. That was the material we covered in the article.'

'And there's more to come?'

'That's what I don't know. For whatever reason, Preston seems to have gone to ground. He'd promised a follow-up podcast but it hasn't appeared so far. Preston seems to have stopped taking my calls.'

'So what's your interest in the case now?'

Clark paused as his wife reappeared bearing a tray with a teapot, mugs and a plate of biscuits. 'Sorry the biscuits are just plain ones. Best we had in the house, I'm afraid.'

Fairlie smiled at her. 'You shouldn't have. Not that I can ever refuse a biscuit.'

'We don't get many visitors,' she said. 'I make the most of it when we do.' She sat down in the armchair. 'You don't mind me sitting in?'

'I've no secrets from you, Fi,' Clark said. 'Mr Fairlie was just explaining why he was here. He's working with Edward Lawrence and he's written an article on the O'Donnell case. He was at Iain Pennycook's meeting yesterday.'

'So you saw Alasdair make a fool of himself. I told him not to go.'

'I didn't mention the O'Donnell case,' Clark pointed out.

'You didn't. But I noted your surname, and wondered if you might be a relative of Kevin Clark. Is that right?'

'I'm his uncle. His dad's brother.'

'I see.'

Clark was looking at his wife, and Fairlie could sense that there was some unspoken communication between them. 'You need to understand that what happened with Kevin has dominated much of our lives.'

'And destroyed them too,' Fiona Clark added.

'Maybe. Though not as badly as it destroyed Kevin's.' Clark held up his hand before his wife could respond. 'And, yes, I know how that sounds. If Kevin really did commit that murder, he deserves everything he's got.'

'But you question whether he did?' Fairlie asked.

'The evidence presented in court was very persuasive. I wasn't surprised by the verdict. But I know Kevin. I don't know if he's capable of an act like that. I felt there were still too many unanswered questions about the police account.'

'But you've not campaigned to get the case reopened?'

'Not recently, no.'

'Not recently?'

'It was all a real shock at the time. We weren't the sort of family to get involved in anything like that. Respectable working class, that was us. My brother Donald, Kevin's dad, was a tradesman, a plumber. Poor but honest.' There was a touch of bitterness in his tone. 'Donald had known Kevin was mixed up with some questionable people. People took advantage of him.'

'You think that's what happened with O'Donnell?'

'I'm sure of it. I can't be sure whether Kevin was capable of committing the murder. But I'm damned sure he'd never have been in that house if someone hadn't set him up. And they might have done it just for a laugh. Kevin was a plaything to them. He was bound to get into some sort of trouble eventually. We just never expected it to be anything so serious.'

'You said it affected all your lives?'

'Donald was convinced of Kevin's innocence and spent the rest of his life campaigning for the case to be reopened. Some of the media had portrayed Kevin as little more than a monster.'

'That wasn't universal,' Fairlie pointed out. 'His father wasn't the only one who campaigned for his innocence.'

'Most people reserved their sympathy for O'Donnell and his family. No one challenged that Kevin had been present at the crime scene. The only question was whether he'd wielded the knife himself. Even among those who believed there'd been a miscarriage of justice, no one had much time for Kevin. Kevin's brothers bailed out of the campaign early on, and have kept their heads down ever since. Donald was angry about that, but I can't say I blamed them. They didn't deserve to be saddled with that burden for the rest of their lives.' Clark fell silent for a few moments. 'Donald and his wife received hate mail and worse. Fiona and I did our best to support them—'

'Financially as well as everything else,' Fiona Clark added.

'Aye, well, we maybe didn't do as much as we should have, but we did what we could. Looking back, I don't think we did enough. Donald gave his life to this. We didn't come anywhere near that.'

'So what caused you to make that intervention yesterday?'

'Just that,' Clark said. 'I feel guilty. I feel I should have done more. I should at least have done *something*. When I saw that guy turn up virtually on my doorstep, I didn't think I had a choice.'

'That's what I don't understand. What does Iain Pennycook have to do with any of this?'

'It's one of the things that infuriates me about that bastard.

I've watched him on TV, pontificating about this, that and the other. When he's just a petty thief, a cheap fraudster.'

'He's never concealed his past,' Fairlie pointed out.

'He's exploited it. He uses it to suggest he's dragged himself up by his bootstraps. It's like a badge of honour. But some of us remember him from the old days. We know what he was like.'

'What was he like?'

'I only saw it from a distance and second hand from what Donald told me. He was an obnoxious, sadistic little bastard. He was a few years older than Kevin, and he brought Kevin into what passed for his gang. It was so they could toy with him, laugh at him, play with him. They'd already got him into trouble, even before the O'Donnell case. He'd been caught shoplifting. Something they'd put him up to. Pennycook was the tinpot leader of all that.'

'You think Pennycook was involved in the O'Donnell killing?'

'My guess is he wasn't directly involved. Pennycook tried not to get his hands dirty. He was the kingpin. Nothing would have happened in that group without him being aware of it.'

'Including the O'Donnell murder?'

'Including the O'Donnell murder. After that Pennycook distanced himself from the group. He went up in the world, because the likes of Pennycook always do. Next thing we heard he'd been convicted for some kind of white-collar fraud.'

'I'm not sure I follow,' Fairlie said.

'What I'm saying is that Pennycook *knows*. He knows what happened in that house. He knows who killed O'Donnell. And he knows what happened afterwards.'

CHAPTER THIRTY-SIX

'I'm not one to say I told you so,' Alec McKay said.

'You know what, Alec. You've always struck me as exactly the type to say I told you so. Probably with considerable glee.'

'Only when I'm right. But then...'

'Aye, I get it. But I still can't say for certain you're right about this.'

'It's looking more likely, though, isn't it?'

'It pains me to say it, but it may do.' Adam Sutherland flicked aimlessly through the file in front of him, as if hoping it might provide some greater elucidation. 'Though it's partly a matter of perspective.'

'How do you mean?' Helena Grant asked.

They were gathered in one of the meeting rooms on the top floor of the building. The rooms were popular because they offered a more attractive view of the city than most of the offices. From where McKay was sitting, the view was even more striking because over the top of the Tesco supermarket he could see the subject of their discussion: the A9 trunk road. It was mid-morning, and the traffic was relatively light.

Sutherland was spreading out the files on the table. 'It's a question of how you look at these cases. Unless there's an obvious link, we treat each investigation on its own merits. We've a rigorous procedure to ensure nothing's overlooked. We look at the forensic evidence, tyre marks and suchlike. We look at evidence gathered by Jock's team.' He gestured towards the fourth member of the meeting, Jock Henderson, who was sitting slouched in a chair at the end of the table, morosely chewing on a piece of gum. 'My team look at the state of the car, because that's the specific expertise we bring to the party. Sometimes we identify a fault in the vehicle that's responsible for the crash. Sometimes the nature of the damage gives a good idea of what happened. Quite often the physical evidence contradicts what witnesses remember—'

'Is this going somewhere?' Jock Henderson said through a mouthful of gum. 'I've an urgent appointment with a cigarette.'

'Thought you'd given up?' McKay said.

'I've given up *officially*,' Henderson said. 'By which I mean I don't smoke when Aggie's around.'

'Can I gently remind you two we're conducting a murder inquiry?' Helena Grant said. 'Carry on, Adam. Ignore the kids in the back row.'

'Most of the cases are easily resolved,' Sutherland said. 'The cause is either blindingly obvious or quickly becomes so. Every now and then we get one that can't be straightforwardly explained. But those are uncommon, and we can usually make a reasonable assumption about the cause even if we can't evidence it.'

He waved his hand towards the array of files in front of him. 'This year, we've had an unusual spate of cases that don't have an obvious explanation. Cars that seem to have left the road for no good reason, usually in good driving conditions. We've also had several cases where we're pretty sure another vehicle was involved, but not been able to track it down.'

'Is that unusual?' Grant said.

'We've usually got something. Genuine hit-and-run cases are rare in serious collisions, not least because the responsible driver's often not in a condition to drive away. When they do, we can usually identify them through CCTV or witnesses. One way or another, we tend to catch up with them. But not in these cases.'

'What does that tell us?' Grant said.

'At first, I thought we were just going through an unlucky patch. It happens.' Sutherland gestured at the window towards the A9. 'Especially on that bloody road. It's nothing like as bad as it used to be, but the single-carriageway stretches still attract more than their share of numpties.'

'You've changed your mind?' McKay asked.

'Not yet. But the sites of the collisions are interesting. Away from any CCTV or other cameras. Most of the road has crash barriers to prevent vehicles leaving the road. In several of these cases, the collision happened at the only spot in the area where a vehicle could actually leave the carriageway.'

'If someone is doing this deliberately, that would need real driving skills, presumably?'

'I'd have said so. And careful planning.'

McKay had finally succumbed to the temptation to leave his seat, and had wandered over to the window. He was staring at the sunlit strip of the A9 as if hoping to catch the killer at work. 'But this doesn't make any sense. We've got a very skilled driver, seemingly planning each incident meticulously. But surely the victims can only be random?'

'Unless the killer deliberately tracks them with the aim of taking them out,' Grant said. 'Which is a chilling thought. I take it we've identified no links between any of the victims?'

'Nothing so far. They're just ordinary people. No criminal records, no high profile. No other kind of notoriety that we've found. Just a bunch of folk who picked the wrong time to drive on that road.'

'Okay, so perhaps these are people picked at random. Is that different from most multiple killers?'

McKay turned back from the window. 'Maybe not. Otherwise, you're in Agatha Christie territory. So it may not matter who the victims are. The killer's interested only in the act. The thrill lies in the risk. A high stakes gamble.'

'With their own life?'

'This can't be someone who cares much about their own life. If they lose, they lose. Though so far, they seem to have won every time.'

'That can't go on forever,' Sutherland said.

'I don't suppose the killer much cares,' McKay said. 'Might even be consciously upping the stakes. Hence the involvement of Renton's truck.'

'Must care about being caught, though,' Grant said. 'If they killed Renton because he was a potential witness.'

'I'd imagine getting caught is the last thing they want,' McKay said. 'They want to go down in a blaze of glory. Not sentenced to thirty years inside. Killing Renton the way they did just upped the risk.'

'None of this is exactly cheering me up,' Grant said. 'The question is what happens next? How do we prevent more deaths?'

'There are some things in our favour,' Sutherland said.

'Go on.'

'If there is a killer, there are relatively few spots on the A9 where they can operate the way they want. Some targeted temporary cameras and increased patrols might limit what the killer can do.'

'The A9's a bloody long road, though,' McKay said.

'On the basis of the cases we've looked at, the killer's so far limited their actions to a small geographical area,' Grant said. 'So it would be the place to start. But there's nothing to stop them expanding that further south. Or north, for that matter. The road's less busy north of Inverness but it's single carriageway and there are some potentially treacherous parts.'

'And there are other roads,' McKay added. 'Have you checked out incidents on other routes in the area?'

'Not in the same depth,' Sutherland said. 'But there's nothing comparable. Virtually all the other recent RTCs have straightforward explanations. So far, our killer seems to have limited their actions to the A9.'

'So far,' Grant echoed. 'What really worries me is what Alec said.'

'It's not the first time you've uttered those words over the years,' McKay said. 'But which bit exactly?'

'About the killer wanting to go down in a blaze of glory. If we're right about this, that makes a lot of sense. But, given what's happened so far and what we think our killer might be capable of, that thought scares the hell out of me.'

CHAPTER THIRTY-SEVEN

'I'm sorry,' Craig Fairlie said. 'You're saying Iain Pennycook actually knew Kevin? I didn't come across any reference to him when I was researching the case.'

'That doesn't surprise me,' Alasdair Clark said. 'Pennycook's thoroughly sanitised his background. There were aspects of it he couldn't conceal. The fact that he's been inside is a matter of public record. He exploits that. Makes a big play of how he's paid the price, learnt his lesson. First became a gob on a stick pontificating about criminal justice issues.'

'I remember,' Fairlie said. 'His first big thing before his next big thing.'

'That's Pennycook all over. Another grifter looking for a bandwagon to jump on.'

'You're saying it wasn't true?'

'I'm saying it wasn't the whole truth. Pennycook might have been lucky to get sent down when he did. He had his fingers in countless pies. The fraud stuff he was convicted for was only a small part of it. Some of it was much nastier.'

'What kind of things?'

'Pennycook was cock of the walk in his part of Inverness at

the time. He was only mid-twenties, but he wasn't much less than a fully-fledged gangster. Big fish in a tiny pond, of course, only getting away with it because he was too small-time to trouble the big players. But he had the lot. Drug dealing, protection rackets, loan sharking, you name it.'

'I've never heard mention of this.'

'He's whitewashed it very successfully. You'd imagine at worst he was a white-collar criminal rather than the sort of bastard who might slit your throat for a few quid. He'd done worse things than ripping off some poor bugger's credit card.'

'You can't be sure of all that, Alasdair,' Fiona Clark said. 'A lot of it was just rumour.'

'Aye, and at the time Pennycook was happy to encourage the rumours. But there was enough.'

'But he was sent down for fraud?'

'I don't know the detail of that,' Clark said. 'Word was that some big players were getting irritated by Pennycook's activities, so someone shopped him. He already had a record. Only for relatively minor stuff but enough to put him inside. I reckon Pennycook was warned off at that point. From what I heard, there was enough in Pennycook's past to get him sent down for a very long time.'

'I've never heard any of this,' Fairlie said.

'There's no reason why you should, is there? Pennycook's not likely to publicise it. Anyone involved with him at the time is going to keep quiet.'

'Hence your intervention yesterday?'

'I just felt that, if he was going to turn up on my doorstep, I owed it to Kevin to do something. Took me a couple of drams to build up the Dutch courage, I can tell you.'

'A couple?' Fiona snorted. 'And the rest.'

'Aye, well, unaccustomed as I am to public speaking and all that. Don't even know what I achieved. I just wanted

Pennycook to know not everyone had forgotten what he used to be. I don't imagine Pennycook's the type to feel any guilt. It was more about assuaging mine. I'm not sorry I did it.'

'You're not afraid of reprisals from Pennycook?'

'What's he going to do? I'm a nobody from the arse-end of nowhere. The real question is why you're interested.'

'I've spent a lot of time looking at the O'Donnell killing. I don't have any opinion on Kevin's guilt or otherwise. The prosecution case was strong, but there were unanswered questions. What you've told me adds another dimension to that.'

'I've been very honest with you, Mr Fairlie, even though I've no particular reason to trust you. It's time for you to put your cards on the table. You said you're working with Edward Lawrence but you haven't told me what Lawrence's interest might be.'

'Are you aware Lawrence is still representing Kevin?'

'If he is, I don't know who's paying.'

'My impression is he's doing it pro bono. He visits Kevin periodically.'

'Really? Then he's the only one who does since Kevin's mum and dad died. His brothers never have. Fiona and I keep saying we ought to go, but I honestly can't bring myself to do it. I'm not proud of that. So why is Lawrence still visiting?'

'You'd have to ask him. My sense was that he felt he'd let Kevin down at the trial. Didn't do enough for him.'

'He's being hard on himself then,' Clark said. 'He pushed the prosecution as hard as he could. Exposed some weaknesses in their account. But the odds were always stacked against Kevin. There was too much evidence against him, including his own confession.'

'The biggest gap seems to be what happened after the killing. What if I told you Kevin's memory might be coming back? The last time Lawrence visited him, he claimed to have some memory of events after the murder. He was in the rear seat of a car, with a driver and someone in the front passenger seat. He had a memory of holding something. He thinks it was probably the murder weapon.'

'That's a big deal, surely? It shows Kevin must have been acting with accomplices.'

'I'm not sure it would cut much ice in court. And even if someone else was involved, there's no evidence they were involved in the actual killing.'

'Especially if Kevin recalls handling the knife. Aye, I take your point.'

'Unless someone handed the knife to Kevin to ensure his prints and DNA were on it,' Fairlie said. 'But there's not enough there to get the case reopened. Not yet.'

'I'm still not entirely clear why you're here, Mr Fairlie. Or what your role is in all this.'

'I'm a hack. My instinct is to follow a story, even if I'm not sure what it is or why I'm chasing it. And I've a living to earn. Hugh Preston's left me high and dry, so I've been digging around to see if I could add anything myself. Lawrence gave me one angle. But what you've told me might provide another way into the story.'

'You don't care that there are real people involved in all this?' Clark said.

'Very much so. But I also want to know the truth, or as close to the truth as I can get.'

'Sometimes it may be better not to,' Clark said.

'You could be right. But something made you confront Pennycook yesterday.'

'I'm not even sure what that was. Or if it was a smart thing to do.'

'That's very much the position I'm in at the moment. Look,

I've taken up enough of your time. I'm grateful for what you've told me, even if I decide to do nothing with it.'

'No problem, son. If any of this can help Kevin, then it's all to the good.' Clark eased himself up from his armchair. 'I'll show you out.'

Fairlie said goodbye to Fiona and followed her husband to the front door.

'Good luck with it all,' Clark said. 'I've no idea whether it's wise for you to be prodding this particular hornet's nest. I've a feeling there's more behind this than any of us realise. Kevin was a convenient scapegoat but I don't know for who or what. I'd just repeat what I said in there. Iain Pennycook's your man. He's the one who *knows*.'

CHAPTER THIRTY-EIGHT

'It's not gone away,' Helena Grant said. 'I never really thought it was going to.'

When she'd asked Alec McKay to pop in for a word, she hadn't been planning to mention this. She'd been intending only to inform him that the additional road patrols and cameras were now in place. She'd even folded the newspaper away and stuck it back in her desk drawer, where even McKay was unlikely to find it. But somehow she found herself blurting it out as soon as he entered the room.

'What hasn't?'

'This.' She opened the drawer and pulled out the newspaper, flinging it onto the desk in front of her. She'd folded it back to the page with the article.

McKay sat down and turned the paper towards him. 'Oh, Christ. More of that bollocks. I thought they'd given up on it.'

'So did I. It's been a couple of weeks since the last one, and the follow-up edition of that podcast doesn't seem to have appeared. I thought they'd run out of steam.'

'They probably have,' McKay said. 'This is just a last dying billow.'

'It doesn't read like it. It reads like the start of a new phase.'

'What are they saying?'

'They seem to have changed tack, for what that's worth. There's no mention of the podcast in this one—'

'That's interesting in itself.'

'Maybe. But this one is supposedly based on some sort of contact with Kevin Clark himself.' She leaned over the desk and pointed to a spot halfway down the first column of the article. 'There.'

'"Sources close to Clark indicate that his memory of the day of Simon O'Donnell's murder may be beginning to return". Who the hell are "sources close to Clark"? One of the screws?'

'Isn't it usually a euphemism for the person themselves?'

'It is when it's "sources close to the prime minister". I'm not sure it's the same when it's some lifer inside for committing a brutal murder. In this case, it probably means: "we plucked this out of our arse". It's the same old bollocks. Some crappy innuendo masquerading as a news story. Ignore it.'

'There's plenty of innuendo in there, right enough.'

McKay had been scanning through the article. 'There's not much else. The bit about Clark regaining his memory is the only vaguely substantive element. If his memory really is returning, you'd have thought he might have remembered something specific, rather than just having "growing recollections of what happened after the killing". There's bugger all in this.'

'They quote his lawyer, saying he's been in contact with Kevin.'

'Who refuses to confirm the bit about Kevin's memory returning.'

'He refuses to deny it as well.'

'Doesn't seem to want to say much, does he? Almost as if it's all a load of shite.'

'It's still out there.'

'What is?' McKay pushed the paper back towards her. 'There's nothing there but a load of hot air. They're obviously trying to squeeze some life out of the story while they still can. It's dying on its already skinny arse.'

'But what if Clark's memory is coming back?'

'What if it is? Look, Hel, you know as well as I do that Rory was a good cop. He did things by the book. He'd have managed that investigation as well as anyone could have. If Clark does eventually recover some of his memory, that'll just help confirm the police case. The only weakness in it was the lack of evidence about what happened after the murder, but there was no reason to think anything there would undermine the existing evidence.'

'Unless someone else was involved in the killing.'

'I'm only telling you what you already know. The police did a superb job with the evidence they had. Yes, of course, it's conceivable some further evidence might emerge. It's not likely but it's possible. But that doesn't mean the police, or for that matter Rory, did anything wrong. Most likely any new evidence would simply confirm the prosecution case.'

'And if it doesn't?'

'Then we, and the Fiscal, need to respond to the new evidence. It doesn't undermine the original investigation.'

'But what if it does? What if Rory missed something?'

'Then he was only human. This isn't like you, Hel. You're normally the level-headed one who keeps the rest of us on the straight and narrow. This is just tomorrow's fish and chip paper. Confected crap to sell a few more papers. Don't get it out of proportion.'

'Aye, of course you're right. It's just a bit too close to the bone. The O'Donnell case was pretty much Rory's last major inquiry before he died – not that either of us knew it at the time, of course. It was a big one, high profile, and it took a lot out of him. They were under a hell of a lot of pressure to get a result, especially as it was police family and all that. I sometimes wonder if the stress contributed to his death.'

'I doubt it, Hel. Just the luck of the draw.'

'Probably. But when something like that happens, you can't help looking for reasons. And all this nonsense just seems to be casting a further shadow over his memory.'

'You need to be less hard on yourself,' McKay said. 'You've been through a hell of a lot in the last year or two. Don't start looking for ghosts where none exist.' He pulled the newspaper back towards him. 'What really intrigues me is who's stirring up all this crap and why. Who wrote this bollocks, anyway?' He picked up the newspaper and peered at the byline. 'Ah, Interesting.'

'What is?'

'The author of this piece. Craig Fairlie.'

'Name rings a vague bell. Who is he?'

'We go way back. We were at university together. We've done a bit of mutual backscratching from time to time—'

'I'm not sure I want to know.'

'Nothing inappropriate. Just a bit of shared intel when it's suited us both. I had him down as one of the good guys. Or at least one of the less bad guys.'

'I'm not sure this is entirely reassuring me,' Grant said.

'What I mean is that he's pretty straight. I've had various dealings with him over the years, and he's never tried to screw me over, as far as I'm aware. But I suppose a man's got to eat. And he's got a divorce to pay for, if I recall correctly. I wonder if the previous articles about the O'Donnell case were also by Fairlie?'

'Hang on. I assume they're available online.' Grant tapped at her keyboard. 'Here's the last one. Yes, also by Fairlie. And there are links to the others.' She tapped again. 'All by Fairlie.

Though the first one's jointly credited to the guy who was supposedly producing the podcast.'

'So young Craig's made something of a cottage industry out of the O'Donnell case then. Even beyond the podcast.'

'I've been keeping an eye on that podcast,' Grant said. 'I downloaded the first one, out of curiosity. There wasn't much to it. The whole thing seemed to be based around a single source. Some supposed ex-member of the investigation team who was only prepared to speak anonymously.'

'And did our anonymous friend have anything of interest to say?'

'Enough to convince me that he really was an ex-cop. And maybe enough to persuade me he'd been involved in the O'Donnell team—'

'Lots of people were,' McKay said.

'Well, yes, exactly. As far as I could judge, he didn't come up with anything that wasn't in the public domain already. Just a lot of unverified stuff about how he supposedly saw corners being cut to get the result the police wanted.'

'So the kind of thing any bugger could say then? What about the promised follow-up?'

'Second edition should have been out a week or two back. But no sign of anything so far.'

'So maybe our friend's source wasn't quite all he was cracked up to be. Which might explain why young Craig here's reduced to regurgitating the same old content-free nonsense.'

'What about the stuff about Clark's memory coming back?'

'There might be something in it, I guess. Fairlie's a decent journalist. He'll have his sources. Might even have a few among the screws looking after Clark. Whether or not there's anything in it, it strikes me as the kind of story you plant if you want to stir up some responses.'

'How do you mean?'

'Well, we're fairly sure Clark couldn't have acted entirely alone in the O'Donnell killing, aren't we? Someone took him to that house in Beauly. Someone encouraged him to break in. Most likely, someone helped him get away afterwards. None of that means there was anything wrong with the police investigation. My guess is that one of Rory's frustrations was that he couldn't fill in all the gaps.'

'That's true enough,' Grant said. 'Obviously, his priority was to put together a case that would stand up in court, but that was never enough for Rory. He wanted a narrative that made sense. He wanted to be sure he'd not overlooked anything. Even though they had enough to convict Clark, there was too much left unexplained.'

'My guess is that there are a few people out there who might be nervous at the prospect of Kevin regaining his memory. People who might have been accessories before and after the fact. I suspect Fairlie might be throwing a few pebbles into the pond. See what he stirs up.'

'I hope you're right.' Grant was looking past McKay at the open office door. 'Morning, Josh. What can we do for you?'

McKay turned to see Josh Carlisle peering round the office door. There'd come a day when Carlisle wouldn't look like a nervous cadet in McKay's presence, but that time hadn't arrived yet.

'Come and join the party, Josh,' McKay said. 'The fun's just getting going.'

'I wasn't sure whether to interrupt,' Carlisle said. 'But I thought you'd want to know.'

'Know what?'

'That we seem to have another one. An RTC, I mean.' Carlisle sounded slightly breathless. He'd obviously hurried to break the news.

'On the A9?'

Carlisle paused to catch his breath. 'Yes. Well, sort of. Off the A9. It's another strange one.'

'I had the feeling it might be,' McKay said. 'Go on.'

'It's a different location from the others, for a start. Further north. North of Inverness, in fact, a little way south of the Tore roundabout. It's not even clear that it's a collision. Just a car driven off the road and set on fire.'

'More likely to be joyriders than our supposed killer then,' Grant said.

'Well, yes, except—'

'Except what?'

'Except that there was someone inside. Well, a body, that is. A dead body.'

CHAPTER THIRTY-NINE

'All the way over there?' McKay said.

'Where you can see the smoke in the air.' The uniformed officer pointed across the field towards a clump of trees. The smoke in question formed a dense-looking cloud, slowly dissipating in the rising wind. 'The car was on fire.'

'I'd worked that out, son. There's not much gets past me, even at my advanced age. There's no way to get closer without walking?'

'You could take a vehicle down that side road, but the walk's about the same.'

'So how did the car get there?' McKay asked.

'Someone drove it, I'm guessing.'

McKay was beginning to suspect the young uniform might be taking the piss. If so, he was either brave or he'd never heard about Alec McKay. 'That's what you're guessing, is it?'

'I don't see any other explanation.'

'Have you thought about a transfer to CID? Becoming a detective?'

'Now you come to mention it—'

'We can always use incisive brains like yours. Compensates for the brain-dead buffoons we usually get.'

'I wouldn't say that—'

'Most of our lot would never have worked out the best way to get a car somewhere is to drive it. Can you offer any more insights of that calibre or is that you done?'

'I didn't mean—'

'I didn't mean to waste my breath talking to you, but here we are.' McKay sighed. 'I'm not trying to be difficult. I realise it's no fun for you to be stuck out here doing bugger all except chase away rubberneckers. So let's start again, eh? When I asked how the car got there, I meant which route did it take. It's obviously been driven off the road, so did it come from this direction?'

'Sorry, sir. It's just—'

'Which way?' McKay said wearily. 'Or don't you know?'

'Looks like it came this way.' The officer gestured to their left. 'There's no gate into the field up here, but the fence is down.' He pointed into the field. 'You can see the tyre marks in the grass.'

'Next question – and trust me, son, you really need to get this one right – is how muddy is it over there?'

'Hardly at all. The field's dry and solid. There's the odd puddle but they're easily avoided.'

'Bless this Highland weather,' McKay said. 'I'm going to leave the car here, and I'll trust you to keep an eye on it. Some thieving bastards on this road. I'll ask you one more time, just in case you're inclined to change your mind now you've got to know me. You're sure this is the quickest way to get to where this car's been dumped?'

'There's honestly not much in it. You're as well starting from here.'

'Good to hear, son.'

Smiling, McKay set off, stepping carefully over the broken fence into the field. The A9 was behind him, the Tore roundabout to the north. He followed the trail of flattened grass without difficulty. The question – or at least one question – was why the driver had taken the trouble to drive so far from the road. There was no possibility of this being mistaken for any kind of accident. That in turn suggested this was a different kind of killing from the previous incidents. Either they had a second killer on their hands – which even McKay acknowledged was unlikely – or the killings had entered a new phase.

He had no doubt, even from the little they'd been told already, that this was a murder. There hadn't been much detail in the original report. The vehicle had been torched and the victim had been secured in the car. It would have been a nasty way to die.

There was another fence at the far end of the field. It took McKay a moment to spot the gap the driver had used to manoeuvre the car into the thicket of trees. He pushed his way through to the cordon of police tape. It was only then that he finally saw the burned-out car. 'Bloody hell.'

'Especially for the poor bugger trapped inside,' a voice responded from among the trees. 'Well, maybe not bloody, but hell, right enough.'

McKay stepped cautiously over the police tape and made his way to where the ungainly figure of Jock Henderson was propped against a tree, a cigarette between his fingers.

'Anybody ever tell you you've no willpower?'

'I'm an addict, Alec. If it was heroin, people would take it seriously. But I've cut back. Now I only have one when I'm witnessing the aftermath of a gruesome death.'

'So a couple a day in your line of work?'

'At least.'

'What's the story with this one?'

'Doesn't fit the pattern. Some bugger drove it over here deliberately.'

'I take it the bugger in question isn't the one in the car?'

'What do you think? The bugger in the car is in the passenger seat, firmly fastened to the inside of the door with a couple of those plastic ties.'

'So murder?'

'I'd have said so. Not that I've had chance to look inside the car yet. I've just been waiting for the water fairies to finish.' Henderson gestured towards the fire officers still watching the burnt-out car.

'How long are they going to be?'

'They're checking the car's safe to approach. Fine by me. I don't want to go near if it isn't.'

McKay was looking around him, taking in the location. As the uniformed officer had said, there was another single-track lane passing the rear of the trees.

'The vehicle was doused with petrol and then ignited,' Henderson said. 'Quite spectacular, I imagine. Not that there's anyone round here to witness it.'

'What time are we talking?'

'Couple of hours ago. Morning, but sun well up so less conspicuous than it would have been at night.'

'Would have been even less conspicuous if the driver had brought the car over from that back road,' McKay pointed out.

'I was wondering about that myself.' Henderson gestured across the open field. 'Easier entry, too. Open gate over there.'

'Maybe the killer didn't know about the back road. Or perhaps they were signalling to us that, even though it's away from the road, this is still another A9 murder.'

'Methodology's different from the previous ones. No collision. And we don't know that the victim was asphyxiated.

Why would you secure the victim to the car if they were already dead?'

'Maybe as a security measure, just in case they weren't. I imagine being burned alive might bring you to your senses pretty quickly. But I take your point. Does feel different. That might explain why the killer was keen to ensure it was linked to the A9.'

Henderson nodded towards the car. 'Water fairies are done, by the looks of things. We can get the site properly secured now.'

'Priority's to identify the victim,' McKay said.

'That so? I sometimes wonder what my lot would do without your sage advice. But we won't have a lot to work with. Car's burnt out, so whatever's inside will be burnt out as well. No fingerprints. No distinguishing features. Teeth, DNA and whatever forensics can glean from the remaining clothing.'

'You paint an attractive picture, Jock.'

'Come and have a look if you like.'

'I might give that a miss just for now.'

'Good to have the choice. I'll let you know what we find.'

McKay watched Henderson make his ungainly way across the field towards the car. He had little doubt this killing was linked to the previous ones. The question was why the killer had so radically changed their approach.

That was one key question. The other, which might help answer the first, was who the poor bastard who'd died in that inferno actually was.

CHAPTER FORTY

The only good news, Lawrence thought, was that he'd got out of the city before the worst of the rush hour. For the rest of it – well, at best he'd wasted a day. At worst, he might have lost whatever relationship he'd had with Kevin Clark.

Lawrence had known straightaway something had changed. It had been hard to pin down at first. Kevin had seemed slightly more reluctant to enter the room, hanging back behind the officer who'd escorted him. He'd looked at Lawrence almost as if he was afraid of him. Lawrence had never felt that before. Kevin had always seemed, if not exactly pleased to see him, at least comfortable in his company.

'I'll wait outside,' the officer said. 'Give me a knock when you're finished.'

With the door locked behind him, Kevin had looked more anxious. But, finally and seemingly reluctantly, Kevin had taken the seat opposite him.

'Good afternoon, Kevin.'

'Afternoon.' The word was mumbled, almost indecipherable, in a way that had been characteristic of Kevin's early days inside.

'How are you doing?'

'All right.'

Kevin had kept his head down throughout the meeting, staring blankly at the floor.

'Don't you feel like talking today, Kevin? We don't have to if you don't feel up to it.'

'Nothing to say.'

'If you don't want to talk today—'

'Not today. Ever. That's what I mean. I don't want to talk to you ever again.'

'But I thought—'

'Don't want to talk. Nothing to say. Nothing to talk about.'

'But I thought you were beginning to remember—'

'Don't remember anything. Nothing at all. It's all the same. Nothing to remember.' His voice sounded clearer than before, but he'd recited the words monotonously as if he'd rehearsed them before the meeting. 'Nothing to talk about.' He muttered the words in a steady stream, as though afraid Lawrence might interrupt.

'I'd probably better leave you for today...'

'Don't want to talk to you.'

'I'm here to help you, Kevin, that's all.'

There had been a moment's silence, as if Kevin had been trying to absorb what Lawrence had said. Finally, he replied, 'I know. But I don't want to talk any more.'

'We can't stop talking now. We're starting to make some progress.'

Kevin had looked confused. 'I don't care. It doesn't matter.'

Lawrence had regretted his next words as soon as he'd spoken them. 'But what about the newspaper article?' Fairlie's article had appeared the previous day. Lawrence had been intending to discuss it with Kevin in the hope of prompting further recollections.

To Lawrence's shock, Kevin's response had been almost screamed. 'I don't want that! I don't want anything. I just want you to leave me alone.'

Lawrence heard the rattling of the keys in the meeting room door and knew it was over. The prison officer peered into the room. 'Everything okay?'

Kevin had slumped back into silence, his head down, breathing heavily.

'Everything's okay,' Lawrence said. 'But I think it's time for me to go.'

Fifteen minutes later, he'd been allowed back out through the main gate. He suspected it might be his last visit, unless Kevin changed his mind. Lawrence couldn't see any way of resuming his visits unless Kevin specifically requested it.

He'd have a word with Craig Fairlie, suggest they forget any further articles. If Fairlie wanted to proceed without him, there wasn't much Lawrence could do about that, except insist he wasn't quoted. It probably wouldn't matter much either way. Kevin would almost certainly never see it, and nobody else was likely to take much notice.

Lawrence's mind had been focused on these issues as he followed the road north, finally turning back on to the A9 towards Inverness. It had remained a fine late summer afternoon, the traffic relatively light, allowing him to make good time. He turned on Radio 3, and tried to lose himself in the music, his eyes focused on the straight road ahead. The piece playing was something he recognised, though he couldn't immediately identify the composer.

It was shortly after he'd passed the junction for Aviemore that he registered the vehicle behind him. A large black SUV. Its presence felt oddly familiar, as if it had been there for a while without him consciously registering it.

The vehicle was getting closer. They were on one of the

stretches of dual carriageway, so Lawrence assumed the driver was intending to overtake.

That didn't happen, though. The black car was now sitting a little way behind him. The dual carriageway came to an end, and the road narrowed back to two lanes. The car drew closer still.

Bloody typical, Lawrence thought. A long stretch when he could have passed and he waits until now. Luckily, the road ahead was relatively straight and clear of traffic. Lawrence himself was in no particular hurry. He slowed to allow the other car to pull past him. The car drew closer, then pulled out.

It was only as the car drew level that Lawrence sensed something was wrong. The SUV was a little too close, showing no sign of pulling past. The road ahead was still clear, though a bend reduced visibility in the distance. The car remained level with Lawrence's.

Instinctively, Lawrence slowed, hoping to encourage the SUV to move past. Instead, the vehicle pulled to the left, its front wing heading towards Lawrence's car. Lawrence hit his brakes, but the wing of the SUV had already made contact.

'Bugger. That stupid bastard—' Lawrence twisted the steering wheel and braked, trying to find space on the road. The other vehicle struck again, this time more forcibly, and Lawrence was forced off the carriageway.

The slope beyond was relatively gentle and in other circumstances wouldn't have caused Lawrence much problem. But he was already losing control and moving too fast. As he slammed on the brakes, the front of his car struck something on the hillside. The car tipped, thrown onto its side by the force of the collision. Lawrence closed his eyes, felt the car turning over. It had left the farm track and toppled down a short but steeper drop to the fields below.

It finally came to a halt upside down in the rough grassland.

Lawrence opened his eyes. He was pressed against the side of the car, held in place only by his seat belt. He felt bruised and battered, but not seriously harmed. Fumbling by his side, he managed to unfasten the seat belt, and twisted round to try to force open the door.

The roof had been partly crushed in the collision, but had remained sufficiently intact to prevent Lawrence being seriously injured. The driver's door was jammed firmly shut. The passenger door looked less damaged, if he could struggle over to it he might be able to get it open.

Lawrence took a breath, trying to calm himself long enough to identify an escape route. Even if he couldn't force his way out himself, he had his phone and could call the emergency services. All he had to do was take it slowly and avoid panic.

His legs were wedged in the footwell, but he succeeded in wriggling free and eased himself towards the passenger door. He reached out his hand to try the handle.

It was then that he heard the gentle knock on the window.

CHAPTER FORTY-ONE

McKay looked up to see Josh Carlisle standing beside his desk. McKay had been uncharacteristically engrossed in the file he was examining, and hadn't noticed the DC's arrival. 'Have you been standing there long?'

Carlisle shifted awkwardly from one foot to the other. 'Couple of minutes.'

'You're allowed to clear your throat to alert me to your presence, you know. Or you could even say something.'

'Sorry, boss.'

'Take the weight off your brains, son. You look as if you might have something to say.'

'I think we might have something...'

McKay pushed aside the file, which had been waiting for him on his return to the office. He'd requested it from the archive after his discussion with Helena Grant the previous day. 'What sort of something?'

'We've been going back through all the CCTV footage relating to the various A9 RTCs.'

'Go on.'

'I've been working with the video technicians and one of the analysts on it. We've identified a vehicle that seems to have been in the vicinity of three of the incidents. We didn't actually capture it on the A9 itself, but on adjoining routes before or after the incident, with timings that work.'

'What sort of vehicle?'

'A black BMW SUV. Looks like it's been customised. Reinforced bumpers at the front and rear.'

'I take it you've got the registration?'

'It's a ringer. Fake plates. It took us a while to check that out because the number's related to a similar vehicle.'

'You're sure it's not the same vehicle?'

'It's a black BMW SUV, looks like a similar age. Registered in the Borders, but we've checked out the car and the registered keeper. Vehicle doesn't have the adaptations of the one we filmed, and the keeper was able to prove he hadn't left his own neighbourhood this summer. All watertight.'

'That's good work, Josh, given the short amount of time you've had this case.'

Carlisle had been holding a stash of papers. He fumbled through them and pulled out some printouts of footage which he slid across the desk to McKay. 'These are the images.'

By the standards of CCTV, the images were relatively clear. There was no doubt all three pictures showed the same vehicle. The adaptations weren't obvious at first glance but McKay could see that the bumpers were larger than usual. 'Have you circulated these to operational teams?'

'I wanted to run them past you first.'

'We need to get these out to the operational patrol teams. It's the first solid lead we've had.'

'Will do, boss.' Carlisle's eyes had drifted, with undisguised curiosity, to the file on McKay's desk. 'Something interesting?' he asked casually.

'Refreshing my memory. You remember the O'Donnell killing?'

'The murder? That was a long time ago. I was still at primary school.'

'Oh, do fuck off. You can't be that young.'

'I remember it well enough, though,' Carlisle said. 'It was a huge deal at the time. That kind of thing just doesn't happen in these parts. My mum and dad were really shocked by it. Everybody thought there was some mad knife killer at large. They used to double-lock the doors every night. We loved it at school.'

'I bet you did. You know Rory Grant was the SIO?'

'Rory...?'

'Helena's late husband.'

'No, I didn't know that.' Carlisle glanced back at the folder. 'Is that why you're interested?'

'Not really,' McKay lied. 'I just came across a mention of it and thought I'd refresh my memory.'

'There've been a couple of press things about it recently, haven't there? Saw the headlines but didn't look at the stories.'

'You didn't miss much,' McKay said. 'Usual attempt to dig up some shite from the past. Anyway, haven't you got work to be getting on with? You need to tell the operational teams what you've found.'

'Well, it wasn't just me...'

'Bit of advice, Josh. When someone – especially me – gives you credit for a piece of work, grab it with both hands. It won't happen often. You've done a good job.'

'Thanks, boss.'

'Now, if you don't mind, I'd appreciate you going off to do another good job anywhere else but here. I've got an old file to look at.'

CHAPTER FORTY-TWO

'You look uncomfortable,' Iain Pennycook said.

'I feel uncomfortable.' Craig Fairlie looked around. 'Not my sort of place. Apart from anything else, I must be the oldest person in the room. I could be granddad to most of them.'

'In that case, I must be the second oldest person in the room. Makes me feel young.'

Fairlie had little doubt Pennycook had brought him here on purpose. Fairlie had sent over the draft of the newspaper column the previous afternoon. Pennycook had called back mid-morning to suggest they meet for a chat about it. He'd been adamant he wouldn't patronise Ally's bar, and had suggested this as an alternative venue for lunch.

There was nothing wrong with the place, Fairlie supposed, or at least nothing that couldn't be addressed by a thorough demolition job, with priority given to destroying the bloody sound system. Even that would leave the baying crowd of customers untouched. Fairlie hadn't realised there were people like that in Inverness: young, affluent, unjustifiably self-assured, and just plain annoying.

'Do you mind if we sit outside? Can't hear myself think in here.'

'That's the kind of thing my dad used to say,' Pennycook said.

'Comes to us all in the end.'

He followed Pennycook through the crowded bar and out into the courtyard at the rear. In fairness, this was an attractive space, something of a sun trap on a warm summer afternoon, at least by Highland standards. There were high brick walls shutting out the bustle of the city, and the music was reduced to a distant murmur. The crowd here looked different, too. More tourists, fewer local bright young things.

'Delighted with the article, Craig. First-rate stuff. Captured exactly what I intended to say, and you probably said it even better than I could.' He laughed. 'Seriously, it would have taken me days to produce something like that. I can do it up there on the platform, but put a screen and keyboard in front of me and the words disappear.'

'Glad you liked it.' Fairlie took a sip of his beer. A fancy Spanish lager. Not his sort of thing, but refreshing enough.

'I've a couple of minor suggestions but I can email those back to you. Then we're good to go.' He paused to take a mouthful if his own beer. 'Thought we might as well strike while the iron's hot and think about the next one.'

'I'm not sure I can afford to plan every article in a place like this,' Fairlie said.

'My treat, obviously. Chance to take advantage of the sunshine. Don't get many summers like this.' He paused while the waiter arrived with the first of their small plates. Grilled chorizo and a blue cheese salad. Pennycook helped himself to each before pushing the dishes towards Fairlie. 'How's your work on the O'Donnell case going? Saw your article the other day. Intriguing.'

The question was asked casually but it confirmed Fairlie's suspicions about why Pennycook had really organised this meeting. 'There wasn't a lot in that one, to be honest, but hoping for more. Waiting for an update.'

'I take it Clark's happy for this to appear in the press. He always seemed a shy and retiring character. For a brutal knife killer, anyway.'

'That's my understanding.'

'Can't believe he's really got a lot to tell you. Always seemed an open-and-shut case to me. Not much to be gained from poking about in it.'

'There's still a lot of interest out there.'

'I'm sure there is. I just don't think there's anything new. Probably somebody taking advantage of Clark again. Stirring up trouble.'

'If so, it's not me. I just report what I've been told as long as it's from a reputable source.'

'And you've a reputable source, have you?'

'That's the only type I use.'

'Aye, I can believe that.' Pennycook fell silent while more food arrived. Corn ribs. Fritto misto. Slow-cooked lamb. Fairlie had barely touched any of the food so far.

'I wonder how reliable this one might turn out to be, though. I've a feeling you might find this ends up going nowhere.'

'If it does, it does,' Fairlie said. 'I've got a few articles out of it. That's all I care about. Surprised you're interested.'

'Just part of my youth, wasn't it? That whole case. You remember what an impact it had.'

'I always felt there was a sense of unfinished business,' Fairlie prompted.

'It all seemed pretty cut and dried at the trial.'

'There were a lot of gaps in the story. Especially about what happened after the murder.'

'I don't suppose we'll ever know. If Clark can't tell us, no one else is likely to.'

'You didn't hear any rumours at the time?'

Pennycook looked up. 'Me? Why the fuck would I have heard any rumours?'

'Was just thinking you'd have been about the right age. You said yourself, it was the time when you were still mixing with some dodgy types. Just wondered if there'd been some word on the street? No offence.'

'None taken. I've always been open about that period of my life. But, to answer your question, no, there was no word on the street or anywhere else as far as I'm aware. Most of the people I knew were glad the murderous little bastard got what he deserved. You're just fishing for another story, aren't you?'

'It's what I do.'

Pennycook smiled and reached for the corn ribs. 'If you want my advice, you'd be better off concentrating on my column if you're looking to hitch yourself to a rising star.'

Fairlie nodded. 'That's what we're here for, isn't it? We'd better get started. What are your ideas for the next one?'

CHAPTER FORTY-THREE

'This is getting scary.' For once McKay was driving, Ginny Horton sitting in the passenger seat staring out at the passing landscape.

'It's just that you're out of practice. I think your driving's okay, to be fair,' she said.

'Aye, very funny. I thought I was doing you a favour. Alleviating the pressure. That sort of thing.'

'You do realise I'm not actually ill myself, Alec?'

'Some gratitude would be nice. One of the few benefits of making Inspector is that I can delegate driving duties. I voluntarily forego that privilege and all I get is you taking the piss.'

'You didn't have to come,' Horton pointed out. 'One of us would have been enough.'

'Another killing. Another burnt-out car. Like I say, it's getting scary.'

'We don't know if it is a killing. We only know it's an RTC and a burnt-out car—'

'With a body inside.'

'With a body inside. But those things happen. It doesn't mean it's a killing.'

'Just a coincidence? Really?'

'It's further south than any of the previous murders.'

'And so outside the scope of our new patrols and cameras. We did say the killer might expand their field of operations.'

'They can't have known we'd put the new measures in place.'

'Not difficult to guess we might. And this is well south. Right in the Cairngorm National Park. If you wanted to play safe, isn't that where you'd do it?'

'I don't have your finely honed criminal mind.' Horton was silent for a moment. 'Thanks, anyway.'

'For what?'

'For taking on the driving. For taking over various tasks over the last couple of weeks. Don't think I haven't noticed. You and Helena.'

'I've been trying to pile as much as I can on to you. Must be losing my touch.'

'If you say so. I hate this phoney war period. Waiting for it start. I'm hoping it'll be better once we've kicked off the treatment. It won't, of course. It'll just be a different kind of hell.'

'We're all here for you.'

'I know.' She pointed at one of the roadside message boards. *Road closed after next junction. Follow diversion.* 'Looks like we're nearly there.'

McKay could see a row of flashing blue lights, the line of marked vehicles. He pulled onto the roadside and the two of them climbed out of the car. A harassed-looking uniformed officer walked over to greet them. McKay waved his warrant card. 'What's the latest?'

'Fire's been extinguished now. There's not a lot left of the car.'

'What about the driver?'

'Even less, apparently. Can't say I've been to take a look.'

'Don't blame you, son. Examiners on site?'

'Just beginning to look at the scene now, I think. Not sure how much there is to see.'

'They'll find something,' McKay said. 'They usually do.'

McKay left the officer and walked up the road, Horton following behind. They were inside the boundaries of the national park, the imposing peaks surrounding them. In the summer afternoon, the landscape looked idyllic: green grassland, the glittering trail of the River Spey, the darker hillside beyond. In the foreground there were fluttering lines of police tape, the blackened shell of an upturned burnt-out car. Any smoke had been dissipated by the brisk breeze, but the smell of burnt rubber hung in the air. Two white-suited figures were examining the remaining shell of the car.

McKay walked to the edge of the protected area and waved. After a moment, one of the figures waved back, tapping his wrist to indicate he'd be over in a few minutes. McKay offered a thumb up in return.

'Pete Carrick?' Horton asked.

'Looks like it. Jock must be swinging the lead again.'

Horton was looking past him at the car. 'I don't even know how the driver managed to do that,' she said. 'The slope's not that steep.'

'If you're going too fast and you lose control, anything can happen,' McKay said. 'But I can't see what would have made the driver leave the carriageway. Straight, dry road. Good visibility. I'm also wondering why the car caught fire.'

He felt his phone buzzing in his pocket. He glanced at the

screen before taking the call. Helena Grant. 'Helena? We've just arrived at the RTC. Waiting for a chat with Pete Carrick.'

'Lucky you. How does it look?'

'Suspicious. Unless Pete tells me different.'

'I think we might have a candidate for our other recent A9 death. Report of recent suspicious behaviour over in Avoch on the Black Isle.'

'I'm surprised there's any other kind of behaviour over that way.'

'Very droll, Alec. The person who called us saw someone dragging something large out to a car in front of their neighbour's house, late on the night before the burnt-out car was reported. The person involved wasn't the neighbour, and there's been no sign of the actual neighbour since.'

'Could just be away.'

'That's why nobody took much notice of the report at first. But the caller was insistent. Eventually control got one of the uniforms to pop over there and check it out.'

'And?'

'Neighbour's door's unlocked. No sign of anyone inside. Place was tidy enough. No obvious sign he'd left in a hurry. Nothing particularly suspicious. Except that there was a dog.'

'You mean the dog had been left in the house?'

'By itself. Just wandering round. There was a water bowl and a food bowl the dog had emptied. It seemed fairly desperate to get outside for the obvious reasons. Clearly hadn't been walked that morning.'

'So a negligent dog owner?'

'A negligent dog owner who's not there. But whose car still is.'

'Fair enough. What links this to the car we found?'

'We're trying to find any evidence of DNA matches. Neighbour seems the right sort of age, male, white. We don't have any other local mispers that would fit the bill. But that's not the most interesting thing.'

McKay looked up at Horton, who'd been listening to the exchange. Behind her, he could see Pete Carrick heading up the bank towards them.

'The most interesting thing is the man's identity. Meant nothing till I noticed the incident report mentioned a home recording studio in the cottage. Professional-looking set-up.'

'I'm not sure I follow.'

'The missing neighbour is one Hugh Preston. The producer of the podcast on the O'Donnell case.'

'Ah.'

'So there's at least a possibility that the charred corpse in that car is Preston. And if that proves to be the case, I'd say it raises a lot of interesting questions, wouldn't you?'

CHAPTER FORTY-FOUR

'At least we know what we're dealing with now,' Ginny Horton said.

'Pete seemed pretty confident.' McKay started the car and U-turned back onto the northbound carriageway.

'The fire wasn't caused by the collision,' Pete Carrick had told them. 'The vehicle examiners will be able to confirm but I reckon that's what they'll say. The car's been drenched with petrol and torched after the event.'

'So we're talking murder?'

'Looks like it. And a deeply nasty one. The driver was trapped inside the car. He'd have been literally burnt alive. I won't be too graphic but I think he'd have been well aware of what was happening to him.'

'Any idea of the victim's identity?'

'The registered keeper's a guy called Edward Lawrence. Address in Inverness. We don't have any other information yet.'

The name had seemed familiar to McKay. It was only now, as they headed back up the A9 to Inverness, that he recalled why. 'He's a lawyer. A criminal lawyer.'

'Who is?'

'Was, I suppose, if he really is that poor bastard back there in the car. Edward Lawrence.'

'A criminal lawyer?'

'I've come across him a few times over the years. Always struck me as one of the decent ones. I've remembered why his name rang a bell. He acted for Kevin Clark in the O'Donnell case.'

'Really?'

'Really. So it looks like we've two victims linked to the O'Donnell case.'

McKay had told Helena Grant they'd head up to Avoch on the Black Isle to have a look at Hugh Preston's cottage. Grant had asked for the cottage to be secured and examined as a potential crime scene. 'Bloody ridiculous,' he said as they descended the main road towards the village. 'They can't even pronounce the name of the place sensibly.'

'Beautiful place on a day like this,' Horton said diplomatically, gesturing towards the waters of the Moray Firth glittering in the afternoon sunshine.

'Aye, I'll give it that. We can probably see your house from here.' Horton lived on the opposite side of the firth. 'You could give Isla a wave.'

'She's not there. At the moment, Isla's still going into work. Just like she'll carry on doing till the last possible minute.'

'Aye, well,' McKay said, 'maybe that's for the best.'

Hugh Preston's cottage was on a side street off the main road, one of a series of former fisherman's cottages that comprised much of the village. There was a marked car parked outside, along with the examiners' white van. McKay pulled in behind it.

A bored-looking officer was sitting in the marked car, his gaze fixed on the entrance to the cottage. McKay walked along the passenger side and tapped gently on the front window. The officer gave a start then looked up quizzically at McKay before lowering the window. 'Oh, it's you, Alec. You made me jump.'

'Vigilant at all times. That's what I like to see.'

'I was doing my job. Watching the front door,' the officer said. 'Laser-like attention.'

'What's going on?'

'Examiners are in there at the moment.'

'They're having a busy day. Assume you've had no other visitors?'

The officer jerked his thumb over his shoulder. 'Neighbour that way's popped out here a few times. She was the one who reported the incident in the first place. You know the type.'

'Aye, concerned member of the public. Useful source of intelligence. That kind of thing.'

'If you say so. Probably worth talking to, anyway.'

'I'll have a word. And I'll leave you to keep watching that door.'

'It's the adrenaline keeps me going,' the officer said.

'That's the spirit.'

He pressed the doorbell to Preston's cottage. After a moment, the door opened and a masked face peered out. 'Oh, Christ. Will no one rid me of this turbulent bloody priest?'

'Afternoon, Jock. Thought I'd missed the pleasure of your company today.'

Jock Henderson pulled back the mask. 'I shouldn't be here, you know.'

'That's why you should give them up, Jock. Aggie's got a point.'

'I'm supposed to be on leave. Lunch with Aggie, as it happens. I had to cancel to come up here.'

'At least here you can sneak out for a crafty smoke. But I'm sure that thought hadn't occurred to you.'

'I don't even know why you're here, Alec.' Henderson

glanced at Ginny Horton. 'Let alone why you've come mob-handed. There's nothing to tell you yet.'

'We were on our way from another incident. Another burnt-out car on the A9, as it happens.'

'Becoming quite the thing, isn't it?'

'Seems to be. What's the story here?'

'Like I say, not much to tell so far. The abandoned dog's being taken care of by one of the neighbours. By the way, the other neighbour – the one who called in the original incident – is keen to give a statement so if you're here looking for work, I'm sure she'll keep you busy. Missing owner of this place is a guy called Hugh Preston, as I assume you know. Seems to be some kind of broadcaster, voice-over artist—'

'Podcaster.'

'Aye, that too, whatever one of those might be.'

'He's the guy who made the podcast on the O'Donnell case.'

'Is that right? Interesting.'

'He presumably had background material on the case. We'll have to go through that once you're finished with the house.'

'You'll be welcome to it, for what it's worth. My guess is that there's stuff missing. The filing cabinets in the studio and in the area that's clearly been used as an office are both empty. We've not found a laptop or computer. No phone either. Won't leave you a lot to work with.'

'Story of my life,' McKay said. 'Any signs of anything else missing?'

'Not obviously. The whole place is pretty tidy. It's not been ransacked, so it doesn't feel like an opportunistic burglary. If stuff's been cleared out, it's been done methodically.'

'So someone with time on their hands.'

'Looks that way.'

'Anything else?'

'One set of fingerprints predominates throughout the house,

so my assumption is that those are Preston's. There are a couple of other sets, as yet unidentified. We should be able to get traces of DNA that will help us to determine if Preston is that individual in the car. One small point. The dishwasher had been set to run with only a few items in it – a couple of mugs, some plates, a bit of cutlery. Either Preston cleaning up before he left, or someone cleaned up for him. Whole place looks as if it's been cleaned, actually. Not in depth, but tidied and all the surfaces wiped down.'

'Either Preston being houseproud, or someone trying to minimise the risk of leaving any traces.'

'Exactly.'

'I'm sure your mighty talents won't be defeated, Jock.'

'If there's anything to find, we'll get it.'

'I'm sure you will. We'll go and have a chat with our friendly neighbour.'

'Aye, you do that,' Henderson said. 'She'll be glad to spend time with someone her own age.'

Before McKay could respond, Henderson had closed the cottage door on them. Horton said, 'Don't even think of ringing the doorbell so you can get the last word.'

'Never crossed my mind. Let's go see what our friend next door has to say.'

As Henderson had predicted, the neighbour greeted them with enthusiasm. She peered at his warrant card, initially with suspicion and then with delight. 'An Inspector? I'm glad to see you're taking this seriously.' The woman led them into a homely if cluttered room full of a lifetime's memorabilia, with a dominant fishing theme.

'We won't keep you any longer than we need to, Mrs...?'

'Nairn,' the woman said. 'Moira Nairn.'

'You live alone here, Mrs Nairn?'

'I'm a widow. Jack was a fisherman. That industry's mostly

all gone now.' She spoke in a slow, almost singsong voice, with the air of someone telling a story. 'It's been a good few years I've lived alone.'

'You know your neighbour, Mr Preston?'

'I wouldn't say I know him. He's not been here very long. It's all incomers these days. Not that I've anything against that. They bring new blood into the village, which seems like a good thing to me.' She fell into silence.

'But you've spoken to him?' Horton prompted.

'Oh, aye. Seems a pleasant young man. Helped me out with one or two things when I needed it. Running messages and the like. He told me he'd been on the radio, you know.'

'We understand he's some kind of broadcaster.'

'You haven't found him yet?'

'We're still looking into that. He may have just gone away.'

'He wouldn't have just left Archie though, would he? Poor wee thing.'

'Archie? Oh, the dog.'

'I would have offered to take him in, but I couldn't cope these days. But Hugh loved him. He wouldn't have just left him behind.'

'We don't know, do we?' McKay said. 'There might have been all kinds of reasons why he had to leave quickly. Perhaps he wasn't expecting to be away so long.'

'He didn't leave, though. That's the point,' Mrs Nairn said.

'What do you mean by that, Mrs Nairn?' Horton asked.

'I saw that man arrive in the afternoon. Hugh greeted him. They seemed amiable enough, though I had the impression they didn't know each other.'

'Did you see them again after that?'

'I didn't see Hugh again after that. Only the other man.'

'What time of day was this?' McKay asked. 'When the guest arrived, I mean.'

'It must have been mid-afternoon. About three. When I sit here, I can see out of that window.'

The window in question looked out over the street with Preston's front door clearly visible. From here, it was possible to see all the way down to the harbour.

'I spend most of my days sitting here,' Mrs Nairn went on. 'I like looking out at the street. It's more interesting than what's on TV.'

'You see the comings and goings?'

'I enjoy it. I see what the neighbours are up to. Most of them know I'm watching and give me a wave.'

'So what else did you see during the rest of that day?'

'Not much. Not of Hugh, anyway. Or of his visitor. I was a bit surprised, to be honest.'

'Where had the visitor parked? Outside Mr Preston's house?'

'No. He must have parked down by the harbour and then walked up here.'

'You saw something later in the evening?'

'I usually go to bed around eight. I don't have the stamina for much after that. But I usually get up a couple of times in the night – well, you know. That takes me past the window upstairs. I happened to glance out and I saw a second car parked next to Hugh's house. One of those big vehicles people have nowadays. It was the first time I'd seen anything out there other than Hugh's. It had reversed into the drive, the boot next to Hugh's back door. I couldn't see what was happening exactly, but someone was carrying packages out of the house. The first couple were boxes. The last one was something much bigger. The light down there wasn't good, and I couldn't see what it was.'

'What did you think you might be seeing, Mrs Nairn?'

She was silent for a moment. 'You'll think I'm daft.'

'I'm just interested in how it struck you.'

'It looked like a body. A human body, I mean. It was wrapped up in something, but that's what it looked like.'

'Then what happened?'

'He finished loading whatever it was. And that was it really. He closed the boot, pulled shut the rear door of Hugh's cottage behind him. Then climbed into the car and drove off towards the main road.'

'You're sure this wasn't Mr Preston himself?'

'Hugh's quite a slim man. A slight wee thing. This was someone much bigger, more heavily built. Muscular type. I'm pretty sure it was the same man who arrived at the front door earlier.'

'Is it possible that Mr Preston was already in the car?' Horton asked. 'He might have already come out?'

'I suppose so. But why would he have left the visitor to bring all that stuff out and close the door behind him? Anyway, that's what I saw.'

'Why were you concerned about this? I mean, concerned enough to call the police.'

'I didn't call the police immediately. But there was something about the whole thing that didn't feel right. The next morning, I went round to Hugh's to check he was okay. There was no answer. I didn't worry too much, because if he's working in his studio, he doesn't like to be disturbed. But I went back later and there was still no answer. I tried phoning him. He'd given me his mobile number in case I needed anything. I left a message but he didn't call back. I went back again in the afternoon. There was still no answer, and I could hear Archie barking inside. He sounded distressed so that's when I called the police.'

'I don't suppose you were able to see the registration plate on the vehicle at all? It would obviously help if we could track it down.'

'I didn't think about it till too late. I'm sorry.' She sounded genuinely apologetic.

'What about the visitor?' he said. 'You said he was heavily built. Is there anything else you can tell us?'

'I saw more of him when he arrived. I couldn't make out a lot of his face from here because he was wearing a scarf. He was older than Hugh. Perhaps in his forties or fifties. A lot younger than me, at any rate. Dark-haired.'

'When you say he was heavily built,' McKay said, 'do you mean overweight?'

'Just a big man. A lot taller than Hugh. Broad shouldered. But not fat.'

'Do you think you'd recognise him again?'

'I'm not sure. I might be able to.'

'Thank you, Mrs Nairn. That's been very helpful. We may need to talk to you again in due course.'

'Something's happened to him, hasn't it?' Mrs Nairn said. 'Something bad.'

'We can't assume that yet,' Horton said. 'There may be some perfectly straightforward reason for his absence. But you did the right thing in calling us.'

Mrs Nairn followed them to the front door, clearly keen to extract the last dregs of companionship from their brief visit. Even after she'd closed the door behind them, McKay could see her watching through the window.

'What did you make of her story?' Horton said.

'I reckon she's right to be worried. For one thing, who the hell would wear a scarf in weather like this? Especially when it's weather like this in the bloody Highlands. I'd say only someone who's keen not to be identified.'

CHAPTER FORTY-FIVE

Craig Fairlie glanced back as he entered the car park at the rear of the block. He'd been feeling nervous most of the evening, and he'd not entirely been able to pin down why. He wasn't used to staying out so late these days. He was normally back at the flat no later than six, and quite often in bed by ten. It wasn't as if he'd much to stay up for.

Tonight had been a rare exception. He'd met up with one of his old newspaper chums, a guy he hadn't seen for several years. Danny was based in Edinburgh these days, and had left journalism to work for a political lobbying company. He was back in Inverness for a day or two to visit his mother, and had suggested meeting for a pint.

They'd discussed work at first, but the conversation had rapidly moved on to more congenial topics like football and gossip about former colleagues. The evening had started with a pint in Ally's, then progressed to various other hostelries, taking in a burger in some bar on the way. They'd ended up shooting the breeze in a pub near the river.

In the last throes of the evening, tongues loosened by the booze, they'd reverted to talking shop, Danny regaling Fairlie with scurrilous anecdotes about various Holyrood politicians and staff.

'Have you had any dealings with Iain Pennycook?' Fairlie asked.

'Christ, that gobshite. Not many, but more than enough. I hear he's exiled himself back up here.'

'Seems to have. Banging on about getting a fair deal for the Highlands and Islands.'

'The only deal Pennycook's interested in is what's in his own best interests. He doesn't give a shit about anything else.'

'He's asked me to do some work with him.'

'Has he now? Well, make sure he pays you upfront.'

'Fortunately, it's not him paying. It's one of the nationals, wanting me to ghost a column for him.'

'Knock yourself out, then. But keep your own name off it.'

'His reputation that bad?'

'There's a lingering bad smell about him. I reckon that's why he decided his heart was in the Highlands. He knew something was going to come out eventually, so he left while the going was good.'

'What sort of something?'

'I've heard all kinds of mutterings. He's a nasty piece of work. He reckons he's put all the bad stuff long behind him, but I've heard rumours that suggest otherwise. He's shafted a few people. There are questions about how he funds his campaigns, and how much of that funding finds its way into his own pocket. I don't know much more than that. He's made some enemies over the years.'

'Thanks for the heads up,' Fairlie said. 'None of that seems to have percolated through to the public.'

'Well, it wouldn't, would it? Too much dirty linen to risk opening the airing cupboard. But if I was Pennycook, I'd be keeping my head down.'

'He's definitely not doing that. Made a big splash up here. Admittedly in a shallow pool.'

'You don't want or need my advice,' Danny said. 'But I'd steer clear of him. He may not even realise it himself, but he's damaged goods.'

After they'd said goodbye, Fairlie had made the short walk back to his flat just off the Clacknaharry Road. It was still a fine night, though there was a faint chill from the breeze off the firth, perhaps the first intimation autumn wasn't far away. He wasn't particularly fond of the flat, but it was what he'd been able to afford once the divorce had gone through. The positives were that it was close to the centre of town, and offered a decent view of the water and the landscape beyond. The downside was that the place was bleak and soulless, a functional box for living in. That was why he'd decided, after only a few weeks of living there, that he'd find somewhere else to work. The prospect of spending whole days cooped up in that place, with only a laptop for company, had seemed intolerable. He'd tried a few cafés in town, but they were too busy and noisy, especially in the tourist season, so he'd ended up finding a berth in Ally's, an old haunt of his.

On a night like this, though, the flat's location was perfect. He didn't need to worry that he had a few pints inside him. The weather was fine enough that he could walk back without having to hunt down a taxi. It was after ten, but the sky to the west still carried a translucent glow. The street lights seemed almost redundant.

During the walk back, he'd been thinking about the latest article on the O'Donnell case, due to go to press in the next couple of days. He was conscious that so far it was little more than a rehash of what he'd already written about the possibility of Clark's memory returning. They'd held up finalising it pending Lawrence's visit to Kevin Clark earlier today, in the hope there might be something more to add.

Fairlie had been half expecting Lawrence to call him with an update during the day, but there'd been nothing. He'd phoned Lawrence a couple of times late in the afternoon, but the calls had cut to voicemail. Fairlie assumed this was bad news, at least as far as the article was concerned.

There were a few residents' cars in the car park, but no sign of movement. Most of the block was in darkness. Fairlie made sure the main door was firmly shut and locked behind him, then took the lift to the third floor where his flat was located.

It was only when he reached the door of his flat, fumbling in his pocket for his keys, that he realised something was wrong.

The door was ajar, the flat beyond still in darkness. Fairlie cautiously pushed it open, listening for any movement from within. The lock on the front door had been broken, prised open with a crowbar or similar. The break-in would have been noisy, but most of Fairlie's neighbours would have been out during the day. This could have been done at any point since he'd left that morning.

He stepped inside, turning on the hallway light as he did so. To his left was the small bathroom, ahead the living room and kitchen. He checked out the bathroom and kitchen first. Both appeared undisturbed. Finally he pushed open the door of the living room and switched on the light.

The room had been ransacked. Drawers had been pulled out and emptied. The contents of the cupboards by the wall had been scattered across the carpet. The desk and filing cabinet in the small alcove he used as an office were standing open and empty.

It was impossible to know if anything was missing. Even if he carried out a full inventory of the contents of the drawers and cupboards, he'd never know for sure if a given document had been removed. As far as he could recall, there had been nothing there likely to be of use or interest to anyone else.

He'd had his laptop and phone with him, so those were both safe. Similarly, his passport, bank cards and other ID documents were in his pocket. The question was why anyone would want to break in here in the first place. It was a nondescript flat in an equally nondescript block. The only items of value in here were the TV and an old gaming console, and those would fetch peanuts on the black market even if the intruder had bothered to take them.

Why had they ransacked the drawers, cupboards and filing cabinet? The contents would mostly have been junk – old papers and bills he hadn't got round to throwing out. The filing cabinet had contained his work files. It was conceivable there might have been something sensitive in there, though Fairlie was careful on that front, shredding anything significant as soon as it was no longer needed. These days he rarely kept hard copies in any case. Anything important he kept securely on his laptop.

Fairlie pulled out his phone, intending to report the break-in to the police. He didn't imagine they'd do much, whatever the motives behind this, but he'd need a crime number for insurance purposes. Then he hesitated, and dialled a different number.

The call was answered almost immediately. 'You do know what bloody time it is?'

'Aye, sorry. Bit later than I'd realised. Hope I didn't wake you.'

'Lucky for you I'm a nightbird. I was reading. We might be disturbing Chrissie, though. Hang on.' Fairlie heard McKay say something to his wife, the phone muffled by his hand. 'That's better. Sorry, Chrissie was asleep. Didn't want to disturb her, though it's probably too late. But don't you worry about that, Craig. I imagine she'll allow me to live.'

'I hadn't realised how late it was.'

'I'm assuming this isn't just a social call.'

'I've had a break-in. Someone's broken into my flat.'

'You know you can just phone 101?'

'I was about to do that. But then I decided I should talk to you.'

'Very thoughtful of you. Although, frankly, Chrissie was quite company enough. Even asleep.'

'The thing is, Alec. They didn't just break in. They've ransacked my whole bloody flat. Emptied all the drawers and cupboards. Broken into my filing cabinet. As if they were looking for something.'

'Do you have something worth looking for?'

'Not to my knowledge. But I'm wondering if someone thinks I do.'

'This is a bit cryptic for me, Craig. Can we get to the point?'

'I've been writing about the O'Donnell case.'

'Aye, I saw. Are you looking for reviews?'

'I've been working on another piece. About what happened after the murder. The word is that Kevin Clark's memory might be coming back.'

'Is that right? And how would you know that, I'm wondering?'

'I have my sources.'

'I'm sure you do. What does any of this have to do with your break-in?'

'The story seems to be attracting a lot of interest. From Iain Pennycook, for example.'

The uncharacteristic silence at the other end of the line confirmed he'd hit the right button. Finally, McKay said, 'Pennycook's expressed interest in the O'Donnell case?'

'It's not just that.' Fairlie recounted the conversation he'd had with Alasdair Clark, and Clark's claim that Pennycook must have known what happened in the O'Donnell case. 'Clark said Pennycook had blood on his hands.'

'I wouldn't ask you to reveal your sources, but have you had any dealings with Edward Lawrence?'

'Kevin's solicitor. I've spoken to him at various points. Why?'

'I shouldn't be telling you this,' McKay said. 'The body hasn't been identified yet, but we've reason to believe Lawrence was killed in an RTC early this afternoon.'

'An RTC?'

'For want of a better term. His car had left the road, and it looks as if there might have been a second vehicle involved.'

'You said he hadn't been formally identified.'

'I didn't say formally. It's not really a matter of formalities.'

'I don't understand.'

'The car was burnt out. We think it was torched deliberately, after the collision. We know it was Lawrence's car. We assume he was driving it. But identification will be a matter for DNA matching.'

Fairlie could feel the clutch of fear in his stomach. 'I see. For what it's worth, I'm pretty sure it would have been him driving. Where was this?'

'Off the A9. A little way north of Perth.'

'He was visiting Kevin today. He'd have been coming back from meeting Kevin Clark.'

'There's something else. Hugh Preston.'

'What about him?'

'Another RTC on the A9. Or probably not an RTC and not exactly on the A9. But another torched car. Looked as if the car had been deliberately driven off the road and set on fire.'

'Preston?'

'Again, we don't know. This time the victim looks to have been a passenger rather than the driver. The car wasn't

Preston's. It was just one stolen from a local drive. But the victim wasn't there by choice. He was firmly strapped in when the car was torched.'

'My God.'

'Maybe unconscious. Maybe not. Not nice either way.'

'Why do you think it might be Preston?'

'Preston's missing. Neighbour saw someone turn up at his house the day before the car was discovered. She saw nothing more of Preston, but saw the visitor loading something heavy into the back of a car later that night. Preston disappeared leaving his dog behind.'

'Why are you telling me all this?'

'I'm not. If anyone asks, I'll deny everything. But no copper likes coincidences. We now have at least three incidents connected to Kevin Clark and the O'Donnell case.'

'I don't like the sound of this, Alec,' Fairlie said. 'Some bastard's broken into my flat. Two people I've had recent dealings with are dead. Where does that leave me?'

'I haven't a clue, pal. What state's your flat in?'

'Fine in itself. Just a mess. But the front door's been smashed in.'

'Can you secure it? For tonight, I mean. If you can't, I'd suggest calling out an emergency locksmith.'

'It's after eleven.'

'Even so.'

Fairlie walked over to the door. 'I reckon I can secure it. There's a reasonably heavy bolt on the inside. I can jam it shut, pull the bolt, maybe stick a chair under the handle. It won't stop someone who's really determined to get in, but it should be safe enough.'

'I don't think there's much chance of anyone coming back tonight,' McKay said. 'Or maybe at all, for that matter. But do that. If there's any sign of trouble, call 999 and then call me, and

I'll make sure any response is expedited. I don't want to take any chances.'

'I'd like to say that's reassuring, but it really isn't.'

'I'm not going to sugarcoat it, Craig. I don't think you're in any immediate danger, but I can't say you're in no danger at all. I'll do what I can to keep you safe while we try to work out what's going on.'

'Thanks, Alec. Appreciated. You're a pal.'

'That's as maybe. But I also want to keep you safe because I reckon you're one of the few buggers who might be able to help me work out what this is about. Fix the front door and get yourself off to bed. Don't disturb the living room any more than you need to, and I'll get an examiner to come out and check it over in the morning. Chances are we'll get nothing, particularly if it's a pro job, but you never know.'

'Understood.'

'We can have a chat tomorrow. Between us, we might know more than we think. In the meantime, try to get as good a night's sleep as you can.'

'Thanks, Alec. Sorry again for disturbing you.'

'No worries, pal. Just don't make a habit of it, okay?' McKay paused and then, with untypical warmth, added, 'Seriously, though, take care. Call if you need to.'

'I will.' Fairlie ended the call, still staring the front door. He'd do what McKay had suggested and then get himself off to bed. But he knew sleep would be a long time coming.

CHAPTER FORTY-SIX

'Weather's finally broken.' Helena Grant was standing at the window of the main Major Investigations Team office, gazing out at the messy cityscape. It was still early, but there was a queue of traffic at the main roundabout leading into the centre. The bulk of the hospital in the distance was almost lost in the haze of rain.

For once, McKay was settled at his desk. 'Can't say I'm sorry. Too much decent weather makes me twitchy.'

'Shame, though. We've had a half-decent summer.'

'The autumn'll make up for it,' McKay said. 'Highland karma.'

She finally turned back from the window. 'Okay, tell me about Craig Fairlie and his break-in.'

'You know Craig. Enthusiastic hack of this parish.'

'Oh, I know Fairlie. Not least because he was behind those bloody articles on the O'Donnell case.'

'He's a hack. It's what they do. Craig's better than most. He generally plays it straight.'

'If you say so.'

'Fairlie's been working on more articles about the O'Donnell case.'

'More bullshit?'

'Who knows? It certainly didn't strike me as much in itself. The word is that Clark's memory is beginning to come back.'

'Aye, I saw the last piece he produced. This is about what happened after the killing?'

'Exactly that. Fairlie reckoned nothing significant had emerged yet, though.'

'But he was planning more articles on it anyway?'

'That's the way it works, isn't it? I reckon it's partly a fishing expedition. Fairlie's hoping it might stir up other people's memories.'

'People worried about what Kevin might remember?'

'Something like that.'

'Who's Fairlie's source for this?'

'I'm guessing it's Clark himself. Filtered through his lawyer.'

'His lawyer? Ah, right...'

'The same Edward Lawrence who we think died in the torched car yesterday. Fairlie says he was on his way back from a meeting with Clark. So what have we got? Lawrence probably dead, presumed murdered. Hugh Preston missing, also presumed murdered. Now we've a break-in at the flat of someone who links the two of them, with the place ransacked as if the intruder's looking for something. And Fairlie in turn reckons there may be a link with our friend, Iain Pennycook.'

'Do we have any grounds to bring in Pennycook? It sounds as if he might have some answers.'

'I can't see we have. There's nothing yet to link Pennycook to any of it, other than Fairlie's gut feeling and some heckling from Clark's uncle. We can talk to the uncle, but it doesn't sound as if he's got anything of substance either. If it was anyone else, I might just say bugger it and bring Pennycook in anyway.

But imagine how much mileage he'd get out of being brought in by the police to discuss his possible involvement in a decades-old murder on the basis of no evidence whatsoever.'

'So what then?'

'First thing is to confirm the identities of those bodies in the cars. If we know for sure they're Lawrence and Preston, then we've got a definite link with the O'Donnell case. If it's true that Kevin Clark's memory is returning, that could give us a reason to interview Clark again.'

'Reopen the case, you mean?'

'I'll leave you to finesse that with your consummate political skills—'

'Bugger off, Alec. I'm wise to your soft soap.'

'It doesn't need that, anyway. Lawrence's death gives us a good reason to interview Clark. Clark would have been one of the last people to see him alive. It's reasonable for us to talk to him as a witness to Lawrence's state of mind.'

'Fair enough. What about the O'Donnell case itself? Maybe we ought to be taking another look at it.'

'I've been doing that—'

'Of course you have.' She gestured to the stack of files on the floor by his desk. 'So that's what this is all about. Do you ever bother telling me anything?'

'I'm telling you now. I've dug out the files from the archives and been working through them.'

'And?'

'It was a complex case. Hell of a lot of material. Countless officers involved.'

'I remember. I only avoided being dragged in because HR had decreed Rory and I should be kept at arm's length. Surprised you weren't part of the circus?'

'I was on secondment down south,' McKay said. 'Personal development. That is, I'd already put a few too many noses out of joint. I was dragged back in the end because they were so short-handed but by then the O'Donnell show was over. From what I've read so far, the investigation seems to have been carried out by the book.'

'Rory was always adamant that his evidence should be as watertight as possible. He didn't like having stuff bounced back by the Fiscal, and he didn't like losing a case in court.'

'The case against Clark seems sound enough in its own terms,' McKay said. 'The only uncertainty is whether he acted alone or whether he had an accomplice. And, if so, whether he or the accomplice actually committed the murder. But there's no evidence anyone else was there. In other words, there was no need to fake any evidence to prove Clark's involvement. The question is whether there's any missing evidence that might have placed anyone else at the scene.'

'You can't prove a negative,' Grant pointed out. 'The chances of finding anything new must be pretty much non-existent.'

'So why is someone seemingly so exercised about the possibility that they've been prepared to commit murder?'

'Maybe we're barking up the wrong tree. Maybe this has nothing to do with the O'Donnell case. And where do the other A9 killings come in? They seem to have been random. The whole thing just seems to have shifted gear somehow.'

'You're right about shifting gears,' McKay said. 'That's exactly what it feels like. A very skilled driver.'

'So what about the O'Donnell case? What have you found so far?'

'It's a fascinating read,' McKay said. 'Though I don't know how much it's telling me, other than that Rory did a sound job.'

'You're not just saying that to reassure me?'

'I'm not one to sugarcoat. If I'd found something concerning,

243

I'd tell you. But I was right about everyone working on the case. I keep coming across familiar names.'

'Such as?'

'Charlie Farrow, for example. Just a lowly detective constable in those days. Seems to have done a lot of the legwork on the case.'

'Rory would have kept him on a short leash. Nothing wrong with Farrow, but he was always a bit of a loose cannon.'

'If he was less of a lazy bugger, he might have done a lot of damage over the years. But I think you're right. It doesn't look as if they trusted him with anything that might have involved contact with the public. He was mainly focused on looking at O'Donnell's role in the force. Checking if there was anything that might have provided a motive for the killing.'

'I assume he found nothing.'

'Seems not. It's a fairly perfunctory set of notes, but that's what I'd expect from our friend Charlie. O'Donnell had been managing various financial accounts which, in theory, might have provided opportunities for fraud and backhanders but there was no sign of anything that looked questionable. According to Charlie Farrow, anyway.'

'You think he could have missed something?'

'Farrow could miss the Loch Ness monster if it climbed into his rowing boat,' McKay said. 'But I presume he wouldn't have been looking at this on his own.'

'I can't imagine Rory would have trusted Farrow to handle it by himself. I'm surprised he gave Farrow the job in the first place.'

'Farrow's always talked a good game. That's how he made DCI. Not much to do with competence or work ethic. He's got a knack for taking credit for other people's work. He might have bamboozled Rory into believing he was up to the job.'

'Rory wasn't easily bamboozled. But Farrow's a past-master

at that. From what I remember, that line of investigation wasn't taken too seriously. There were conspiracy theories but there always are. O'Donnell was just a boring middle manager. His lifestyle was entirely in line with his salary. It was much more likely that he was just the victim of an opportunistic burglary.'

'There was also the whole police family thing,' McKay said. 'Everyone closed ranks around O'Donnell. He wasn't an officer but he was one of us, that was the line. It usually is the line, even in the instances when it shouldn't be. But in his case it was probably well-motivated.'

'But you still think it's worth ploughing through these files?'

'I can't help thinking that's where the answer lies. I just hope I'll know it when I see it.'

That was the rub. He still had no real idea what he was looking for. Some anomaly or resonance. The answer might lie in his knowledge of the individuals involved, the larger-than-life characters like Rory Grant, Charlie Farrow and the countless other names McKay recognised from his years in the force. He'd known them all at various points, and had worked with most of them. Some were retired, a few were dead, a handful, like Charlie Farrow, still hanging around. McKay couldn't imagine that any young DC with a few years' service under his or her belt, would have any chance of spotting whatever it was they were looking for.

'If you're sure.'

'I'm sure,' McKay said. 'In the meantime, I think the next step is to set up a meeting with our friend Kevin Clark.'

CHAPTER FORTY-SEVEN

Coppers were never popular in prison, McKay thought. Even when they were only visiting.

He'd occasionally wondered what it would be like to be sent down as a police officer. Years before, he'd had a recurring nightmare in which he'd been accused of some unspecified disciplinary offence. It always started as something trivial, but each defence he offered seemed only to compound the transgression to the point where he found himself dragged out of court to a prison cell. None of it had made much sense, but he vividly remembered the feeling of dread that accompanied the closing of the cell door in the moments before he woke up.

'You okay, boss?' Carlisle said.

'I'm fine, son. Just remembering something. How long have we been here?'

'About five minutes.'

'That all? Seems longer.'

They were in the waiting room behind reception at the main gate. Finally, they heard a key turning in the solid door behind them. It opened to reveal a smartly dressed woman who carefully relocked the door behind her.

'DI McKay?'

'That's me. And DC Carlisle here.'

'I'm Bridget Delany, the governor.'

'Good to meet you.'

'Let's head upstairs. We might have more to talk about than I'd expected when you set this up.'

They followed her into the interior of the prison, re-locking each door and gate they passed through. Delany finally led them into her office. 'We don't often have the privilege of a Detective Inspector on site,' she said.

'We're not usually good news.'

'You certainly don't seem to be on this occasion.'

'Is that so?'

'You were due to see Kevin Clark this morning,' she said. 'I'm afraid that won't be possible.'

'It's important we speak to him.'

Delany paused while the PA brought in a tray of tea and coffee. As she handed out the cups, she said, 'He's in hospital.'

'Hospital?'

'Intensive care. He was attacked during association period this morning. The assailant had some kind of home-made knife. Managed to slice Clark's throat among other serious injuries. Clark might have died if it hadn't been for the quick work of a couple of the officers. As it is, I understand it's touch and go.'

'Who was the assailant?'

Delany glanced down at the notes in front of her. 'Prisoner called Tommy McCarthy. He'd already had a minor altercation with Clark. Yesterday morning, in fact, before Edward Lawrence's visit here. I'll be honest with you. We screwed up. McCarthy is a newbie in here, bit of a loudmouth. We thought he was just trying to stake out his territory.'

'So what happened today?'

'It was only a minute or two before he was dragged away by

the officers, but that was all he needed. We managed to get the knife off him without anyone else being harmed, but it was too late for Clark.'

'Has he said why he attacked Clark? I mean, Clark in particular.'

'He's clammed up since the incident.'

'This will need a police investigation.'

'I'm well aware of that. I've done everything by the book. I also told them that you had a scheduled visit here this afternoon.'

There was probably a message waiting on the phone McKay had been obliged to leave in the locker by the main gate. 'Do you have any idea why he might have attacked Clark?'

'None at all. There's no link between the two of them that I'm aware of. They probably wouldn't have encountered each other in here before the incident yesterday. If there is something between them, it's from outside or from another establishment. But he probably just saw Clark as vulnerable.'

'Unless he'd been set up to do this.'

'How do you mean?'

'I take it you've not seen the news today.'

'I was listening to the radio on my way in, but not since then. Had rather a lot of other things on my plate. Why?'

'There was a fatal collision on the A9 just north of Perth yesterday. We've now been able to confirm the identity of the driver killed in the incident. Edward Lawrence.'

'My God. That's dreadful.'

'It's worse than that. We've reason to believe Lawrence's death was an unlawful killing.'

'You mean not an accident?'

'We tend to avoid the word accident,' McKay said. 'But in this case, I think we can safely say there was nothing accidental about what happened to Lawrence. It's early days so I can't say any more and I'd ask you to treat even that information as confidential. But that's the way it's looking.'

'So Clark being attacked this morning—'

'Isn't likely to be coincidental? We can't be certain, but I think we have to assume a link.'

'I see. So this Tommy McCarthy...?'

'We need to find out as much as we can about him. We can check his past record, but it would be useful to know why he's inside, how he came to be in this establishment, anything else you can tell us about him. I imagine you can get hold of that information more quickly than we'll be able to. I'm not in a position to share details of any ongoing inquiries, as you'll appreciate, but we've reason to believe what's happened to Lawrence and Clark may be linked to a number of other recent deaths. We need to treat this as a matter of urgency.'

'Understood.' Delany rose to her feet. 'I'll ask my PA to track down the relevant files.'

She left the office and McKay heard a muttered exchange from the outer office. 'That'll be the gossip all round the prison.'

'You don't seem too concerned about that,' Carlisle said.

'If it helps to stir things up some more, it might be useful to us.' McKay looked up with a bland smile as Delany re-entered the room.

'All in hand,' she said. 'We should have the basics up here before you leave. How else can we help?'

'We've heard a suggestion Clark might be recovering his memory of what happened after O'Donnell's murder. Were you aware of that?'

'I wasn't. Presumably that was what Lawrence was talking to Clark about?'

'It's possible,' McKay said. He swallowed the last of his

coffee. 'Now, if you've no objections, it would be the perfect time for us to find out what this Tommy McCarthy might have to tell us.'

CHAPTER FORTY-EIGHT

Tommy McCarthy's prison file was waiting for them in the outer office. It was a slim document. McCarthy was little more than a petty criminal. He'd been convicted of a series of minor offences in his late teens and early twenties, culminating in a short custodial sentence for drugs offences. As was so often the way, that first sentence had proved to be a gateway to more serious offences, culminating in his current conviction for housebreaking.

'Not the brightest,' McKay commented as he flicked through the file. 'Caught three times on CCTV, face clearly visible.'

'If he was older, I'd have said he wanted to get caught,' Delany said. 'A lot of them are institutionalised. There's nothing for them outside, so they try to get themselves back inside as quickly as possible. But this is McCarthy's first serious sentence.'

McKay handed the file to Carlisle. 'Have a quick read, Josh.'

Carlisle followed McKay's example and skimmed through the scant pages in the file. 'He's from Inverness,' he said finally. 'Same area as Clark.'

'Luck of the draw,' Delany said. 'We get prisoners from all over Scotland. It's a mixed bunch.'

'He's ten years younger than Clark so it's unlikely they knew each other,' McKay said. 'He'd have only been early teens when Clark was sent down. But it's conceivable they might have mutual friends. Presumably there's no way he could have arranged to be sent here rather than another establishment?'

Delany shook her head. 'To be honest, the system's so full we're juggling what space we've got across the overall estate. Often gets changed late in the day.'

'How long's McCarthy been in here?'

'It'll say in the file. Three or four weeks?'

Carlisle flicked back through the pages. 'Nearly four.'

'So unlikely he was placed here to attack Clark, but it's conceivable he was set up while he was inside.'

'I suppose so.' Delany sounded sceptical. 'Anything's possible in a place like this.'

'Perhaps we should ask him.'

'He's in the isolation unit at the moment. We can arrange a meeting room for you over there with an escort for McCarthy. Can you set that up, Louise?' she added to the PA. 'Tell them we want to see him immediately. I'll take you down to the isolation unit.'

They followed her down to the ground floor. She led them across a patch of outside space towards the rear of the prison then into another building. This area seemed more austere, and they were greeted by a principal officer, a solidly built man who looked firmly of the old school.

'We've put McCarthy in the meeting room.' He turned to McKay. 'Do you want an officer in the room with you?'

'I'm happy for us to deal with him alone as long as you've taken that bloody knife off him.'

'Knife already bagged up as evidence. Ready for your people to take.'

'Thanks. I'll check on how we're handling this one when I get back. We may need to treat it as part of a wider inquiry but that's not my call. McCarthy may have to be interviewed further after this. Just so you're aware.'

'Good luck in getting anything out of him. He's barely said a word since it all kicked off. Come through.'

The meeting room was as bleak as McKay had expected, containing nothing but a table and four chairs, all firmly fixed to the ground. A skinny young man sat hunched on one of the chairs, his eyes firmly fixed on the ground.

'Two police officers to see you, Tommy,' the officer said. 'They want to talk about what happened this morning.'

McCarthy offered no response as McKay and Carlisle took the seats opposite him. The officer left the room, advising them he'd be waiting outside. Delany had remained in the corridor.

'Good afternoon,' McKay said. 'I'm Detective Inspector McKay and this is Detective Constable Carlisle.'

McCarthy still showed no reaction, his head lowered, his arms wrapped round his body.

'How did you come to know Kevin Clark, son?'

McCarthy looked up briefly, but long enough for McKay to detect the fear in his eyes. 'Didn't know him.'

'We've been told differently.'

'Never seen him till I came in here.'

'But you knew who he was. What he'd done.' McKay allowed a minute or two to pass, then said, 'Who told you that, son? Who told you what he'd done?'

'No one told me anything.'

'Who told you what he'd done?'

'No one told me about any of that.'

'Any of what?'

There was another prolonged silence, which McKay was happy to extend. Finally, he said again, 'Any of what?'

'Nothing.'

'You surely didn't remember it yourself. You were only a bairn when it happened. Someone must have told you.'

'I don't know what you're talking about. I've nothing to say.'

'Nothing to say about what, son?'

'Nothing to say about anything.'

'You must have something to say about something. You like football?'

'What do you mean?'

'Simple enough question. Do you like football? You know, that game where they kick a ball about till one of them manages to kick it in the goal. Do you follow that at all?'

'Aye, I mean, I suppose.'

'You have a team? A team you follow, I mean.'

McCarthy blinked. 'Not really, my dad used to follow the Staggies. But they're crap. Scottish football's shite, mainly. I watch Rangers, these days.' It was as if someone had pressed a switch and allowed him to speak.

'Aye, it's a point of view, all right,' McKay said blandly. 'You made any friends inside? People who share your love of football?'

'Aye, Glen Carty. He reckoned he'd look after me.'

'That's good to hear. Always good to have a friend. Glen'll take care of you, I'm sure.'

'He said he would. Said he'd get me out of trouble if I needed it.' McCarthy stopped suddenly. 'He said I wasn't to tell anyone.'

'That's all right, son. I'm just glad you've got someone to take care of you. Look, we've taken up enough of your time. We'll leave you to it for now.' He walked over to the door, calling to the officer that they were done.

A moment later, the officer unlocked it and led them out into the corridor. 'You stay there,' he said to McCarthy. 'I'll be back for you in a minute.' As he locked the door, he turned to the two police officers. 'Short and sweet, gents. I thought you'd need longer than that.'

'He'll be interviewed at greater length. But he told me what I needed to know for the moment.' McKay turned to Bridget Delany, who was watching him in evident bemusement. 'What can you tell me about a prisoner called Glen Carty?'

CHAPTER FORTY-NINE

It was early evening before they left the prison. It was still light, but the weather hadn't improved since the morning. It was pouring down with rain, and the sky was heavy with cloud.

They'd spent another hour or so with Bridget Delany discussing Glen Carty. Carty was one of the bigger fish among the prisoner population, one of the small number of influential inmates who unofficially run the show. 'We try to keep them in their place,' she said. 'But to be honest we turn a blind eye much of the time. The good ones are smart. They make the rules and help us keep order. They run their own little empires but they know how far to push things. They do right by us, and we mostly do right by them.' She sighed. 'Sounds awful, doesn't it?'

'Sounds like realpolitik, I suppose,' McKay said. 'So Carty rules the roost?'

'Actually Kevin Clark's a good example of how it works. Clark's the opposite of Carty. Vulnerable prisoner who can easily become the recurrent victim, the fall guy. He was bullied a lot during his early days inside – long before my time, but it's all in the file – till he was transferred here. Then, for whatever reason, Carty took him under his wing. Another way of exerting power, I guess. But it meant Clark was taken care of. And that was one less hassle for us.'

'And now – again, for whatever reason – he's decided to "look after" Tommy McCarthy,' McKay said. 'All heart, Glen Carty.'

Delany had asked if they wanted to interview Carty. McKay had declined, saying he didn't want to risk treading on the toes of the incoming SIO. Carlisle had blinked at that, given McKay generally showed little hesitation when it came to toe-stepping. But McKay was happy to allow Carty to wait. It wasn't as if he was going anywhere.

When he'd collected his phone at the main gate, McKay had found a message and a missed call from Helena Grant. He'd waited until they were away from the prison and back in the car before responding.

'They've finally let you out, then,' she said.

'Time off for good behaviour.'

'That'll be a first. Shocking news about Kevin Clark.'

'Lengths some people will go to to avoid talking to me.'

'They've already set up an investigation out of Forth Valley,' she said. 'I called to let them know there might be links with our ongoing investigation.'

'They're not handing it over?'

'It's firmly in their jurisdiction. To be frank, we've enough on our plates up here. I'm happy for them run with it for the moment, as long as they keep us in the loop. I know the SIO a little.' She paused. 'I'm assuming you've done nothing to queer the pitch?'

'Not my style, Hel. You know that.' He ignored the cynical grunt from the other end of the line. 'I had a brief chat with the guy who assaulted Clark. Seemed only fair since he'd stopped me seeing the person I really wanted to.'

'As long as you stayed out of trouble.'

'We didn't talk about much. Football mainly.'

'Why do I have a bad feeling about this?'

'You've never shown much interest in football,' McKay said. 'Maybe that's it.'

'Did you get anything useful from this discussion about the beautiful game?'

'Maybe. But I cut my losses at that point and decided to leave. Let Forth Valley get on with it.'

'You heading back now?'

'Soon as I've finished talking to you.'

'I've one more bit of news. Confirmation that the body in the first burned-out car was indeed Hugh Preston, the podcast guy. DNA match with traces from his house proved positive. We've not tracked down any next of kin yet.'

'So two murders definitely linked to the O'Donnell case.'

'Looks that way.'

'And a killer who seems to be making their intentions increasingly clear.'

'Seems clear as mud to me.'

'Me too. Except that every road, including the A9, leads back to O'Donnell. If you can squeeze some extra resources to help me work through the O'Donnell files, that might not be a bad idea.'

'Might be something for Ginny. She's adamant on continuing working but I'd like to keep her relatively desk-bound while she's handling all the stuff with Isla. She's more than enough on her plate.'

'Perfect. Just don't tell her that's the reason.'

'I want her to apply her sharp analytical brain. Is that better?'

'Much. And also true, though don't tell her I said so.'

'When are you likely to get back?'

'Not sure. Weather's looking pretty murky. By which I mean, it's pissing down.'

'Making up for that nice summer, I guess. Okay, take care. See you later.'

Since then, they'd made slow progress back across the country towards the A9. The roads had been heavy with traffic, and the traffic had been moving slowly. It was only as they approached Perth that the roads cleared, enabling them to make better speed.

Even so, the driving conditions were awful. The heavy rain had reduced visibility to a few hundred yards, the wipers struggling to cope with the torrent of water. McKay peered into the murk, his eyes alert for the vehicles in front. Every passing lorry threw up a tidal wave which briefly reduced visibility still further.

They eventually reached Perth, turning off the roundabout onto the A9 heading north to Inverness. McKay didn't know exactly where Edward Lawrence's car had been found but it was somewhere off this stretch of road. He tried to avoid being distracted and focused on the route ahead.

The A9 itself was relatively quiet, but the road conditions worsened as it ascended towards the mountains. The pouring rain thickened into mist and then fog, forcing McKay to lower his speed still further.

It was after they entered the stretch of open moorland north of Dalwhinnie that he first noticed the headlights in the mirror. 'Some bugger's got his headlights on full beam,' he said to Carlisle. 'Not that it matters much in these conditions.'

Carlisle had been half asleep. He shifted in his seat and peered into the wing mirror. 'See what you mean. Bit close too.'

McKay glanced in the rear-view mirror. Carlisle had a point, he thought. The vehicle behind them was getting too close for comfort, particularly in these conditions. 'Stupid bampot.'

They were on one of the stretches of dual carriageway, so McKay assumed the vehicle was preparing to overtake. If some numpty was determined to exceed the speed limit in weather like this, he was more than happy to let them. He slowed slightly to encourage the other driver to pass.

The vehicle stayed firmly on his tail, its headlights just yards behind them, dazzling even in the fog. Finally, it pulled out to overtake. It drew level with McKay's car and then slowed to match his speed. McKay glanced across. The car was a large SUV. From here, he could make out nothing of the driver beyond a silhouette.

McKay's hands tightened on the wheel. He felt the first bump against the wing of the car.

'What the hell's he up to?' Carlisle said.

'I think,' McKay said, 'that he's trying to kill us.' He slammed on his brakes, hoping to drop behind the SUV, trying to avoid further contact. But it was already too late. There was another, much harder bump against the front of the car. McKay felt himself losing control. There was nowhere to go. He couldn't slow down sharply enough to avoid another collision.

The final blow from the SUV forced him off the road. There was no barrier, and the land beyond the carriageway was still relatively steep. McKay struggled to straighten the car. It was sliding on the grass and mud, and McKay could feel it beginning to tip. 'Here we go,' he said to Carlisle, trying to keep his voice calm. 'Close your eyes, say your prayers, stick your head between your knees and kiss your arse goodbye.'

CHAPTER FIFTY

For a moment, McKay was sure the car was going to tip fully over, but then it regained its equilibrium. He could see through the dense fog that a track lay across the slope, offering a gentler route down into the valley. The change in gradient had partially broken their fall.

Luckily, the engine hadn't stalled. McKay pressed the accelerator, and scrambled the car back onto the track. He drew to a halt, closing his eyes for a moment as he finally exhaled.

He killed the engine, pulled on the brake and pushed open the door. The fog rolled around them as if they were inside a cloud. Above, on the edge of the road, the SUV had paused, the driver presumably waiting to check the outcome of his actions. As McKay emerged from the fog, he heard the engine of the car above him start and the SUV pulled away. By the time he reached the edge of the carriageway, it had already disappeared.

Carlisle was standing in the fog and rain waiting for McKay's return.

'Get back in the car, Josh. You'll catch your death.'

'Any luck?'

Murrain shook his head. 'He'd buggered off, heading north.

I'm pretty sure it was our friend from the CCTV. We seem to have narrowly escaped being his latest victim.'

Carlisle released a breath he might have been holding since the first collision. 'I wasn't expecting that. Well done, boss.'

'I'd love to claim it was my consummate driving skills, but it was mainly dumb luck.'

The track was too narrow for McKay to turn the car around. He reversed back up it, peering into the fog to ensure the A9 was clear before pulling out on to the main road.

'That can't have been coincidental,' Carlisle commented.

'I wouldn't have said so. We were targeted.'

'How could anyone know we were here. How could anyone know we were in this car?'

'Because the driver knew we were at the prison. Because they were there waiting for us. Because they'd followed us. Because they were behind us for the entire journey. That's the only way they could have worked this.'

'But how—?'

'I don't know, Josh,' McKay said patiently. Josh's question was a good one, though. Plenty of people would have been aware of their presence at the prison – prison officers, prisoners, administrative staff, probably some of the governors. Any of them might be on someone's dodgy payroll. Someone like Glen Carty might well have one or two prison officers in his pocket.

The rest of the drive north passed without incident. The fog dissipated as they descended towards Inverness, the rain lessening by the time they reached the southern edges of the city.

It was after five, and the car park at HQ was emptying, allowing McKay to park the pool car near the entrance. There were minor dents in the wing where the SUV had collided with it. 'Best get the examiners to look at that,' McKay said to Carlisle. 'On the off chance there are fragments of paint or anything else that might be useful. We'll need to report the damage as well, but I want the car checked over first.'

Upstairs, the Major Investigations Team offices were as empty as the car park, just a couple of people tapping away at keyboards. Ginny Horton was behind her desk, surrounded by stacks of files.

'Everyone buggered off but you?' McKay asked her. 'You being the one person who really ought to be home by now.'

'I'm assuming you've not had a good day?'

'Not the best. Traipsed all the way down south only to discover our interviewee is in intensive care.'

'So I heard.'

'Lucky to be alive, assuming he still is.'

'I've not heard anything to the contrary. Long way to drive for nothing.'

'Especially when someone makes an attempt on your life on the way back.'

'I hope you're joking.'

'I'm deadly serious. With the emphasis on deadly. Someone tried to run us off the road. Just north of Perth. Or, more accurately, someone succeeded in running us off the road. Luckily, we were saved by my matchless driving skills. That right, Josh?'

Carlisle had been heading back towards his own desk. 'Something like that, boss.'

'Serious attempt, though. Looked like our friend in the black SUV, but I didn't get chance to catch the number.'

'Whoever this is, they're not even trying to conceal it any more, are they?' Horton said. 'They want us to know what's happening.'

'I don't think there's any doubt about that now.' McKay gestured at Horton's cluttered desk. 'I take it you drew the short straw with the O'Donnell files.'

'Helena thought it would be a suitably undemanding task given the other pressures on me.'

'She didn't actually say that—' McKay caught Horton's expression. 'You're taking the piss?'

'You don't have a monopoly on it. She told me about your conversation. She's probably right that I need to be careful. It's tempting to throw myself into the work.'

'All the more reason why you really should be getting home.'

She began to gather up the files, but McKay put a hand on her arm. 'Leave them. I can sort them out. I'll probably spend a bit longer looking through them before I finish. I don't suppose you've found anything?'

'Only just started, really. And I've no idea what I'm looking for. Have you?'

'Not really. Just a hunch the answer's in there somewhere. Trouble is, that's a hell of a lot of somewhere.' He picked up a stack of files and carried them over to his own desk. 'I reckon I may have a long evening ahead of me.'

CHAPTER FIFTY-ONE

'Have you been here all night, Alec?'

'I'm pretty sure I went home at some point.'

Ginny Horton looked at him sceptically. 'I'll get you a coffee. You look like you need one. Or possibly two.'

'You're not wrong about that. But I have been home.' He was conscious he sounded like a child insisting he really had done his homework. He had been home, though. He hadn't got back till after nine, admittedly, and his evening had comprised little more than a plate of Chrissie's stovies followed by a dram before bed. Chrissie knew him well enough to recognise his mood, and had made no attempt to engage with him beyond the smallest of small talk. He'd slept fitfully and woken early, his brain still caught up in the endless array of files relating to the O'Donnell case. He'd left the house early, leaving Chrissie still asleep, and been back here before first light. Not that he was planning on telling Ginny any of that.

She returned bearing two mugs of coffee. 'Anything?'

'I'm not sure. I've mainly been jotting down names.' He tapped a pad on the desk in front of him.

'What kind of names?'

'Names I recognised. Or thought I recognised. It threw up a few surprises.'

'Go on.'

'For example, Sheila McGivern.'

'Rings a vague bell, but I can't place it.'

'One of our early RTC victims. One of the ones we hadn't initially treated as murder. Just another unfortunate victim of some numpty driver.'

'You're losing me. You're saying she's referenced in the O'Donnell file?'

'I can't be sure it's the same person, obviously. We'll have to get that checked out. But a Sheila McGivern was interviewed during the inquiry. She was a friend, or at least a schoolmate, of Kevin Clark. Lived in the same part of Inverness. They interviewed pretty much anyone who knew Clark in the hope of identifying possible accomplices. She hung around with some of the same dodgy types who'd palled up with Clark.'

'I know you've been up all night—'

'I haven't been up all night.'

'I'm joking. But this sounds like slim pickings for the hours you've put in.'

'I'm not finished yet, smartarse. The next name on my list is Gary Donaldson.'

'Donaldson? Wasn't he another RTC victim?'

'Now you see where I'm going with this. Yes, another victim.'

'And he's referenced in the files?'

'Another schoolmate of Clark's interviewed during the investigation. Again, can't be sure it's the same person till we check it out. Not much in the interview itself. Claimed to know Kevin Clark only distantly – just another kid at school.'

'Okay, so we have two coincidences.'

'Three, and counting. Gavin McCann.'

'No, this time you really have lost me. Who's Gavin McCann?'

'One half of the couple in the Kia that drove into Brian Renton's truck.'

'I'm not sure I ever registered their names.'

'Gavin and Brenda McCann. Married couple living up in Tain. We were so busy focusing on Renton's killing we lost sight of the original victims. Took me a few moments but I knew I'd come across the name somewhere recently.'

'And don't tell me, a Gavin McCann was interviewed in the O'Donnell investigation.'

'Lived in the same part of Inverness. Also at Clark's school. Same story as Gary Donaldson. Claimed only really to know Clark by sight. Never had any real dealings with him.'

'It's a bit far-fetched, though. Some lunatic driver decides to take out all Clark's schoolmates who were interviewed during the O'Donnell inquiry?'

'Countless schoolmates were interviewed but most aren't dead. Just a select few.'

'Selected for what?'

'Maybe they knew Clark better than they let on.'

'There's no way of checking with them now,' Horton pointed out.

'Which may be precisely why they're dead.'

'Because they knew something about the O'Donnell case?'

'Someone might have thought they did. Or that there was a risk they might.'

'It's a convoluted way of killing people.'

'Only if you haven't the skills to do it. If you have, it might be the perfect way to dispose of people unobtrusively. Who's going to notice another fatal RTC on the A9? If it's skilfully done we might not even see it as suspicious. There's no reason why we should make any link between these individuals. The connection lies way back in their past, and they've led very different lives ever since.'

'The perfect murder, then?'

'If it works.'

'Okay, so if you're right we've now got a link with the fatal RTCs...'

'And potentially with others. Might be worth doing a detailed correlation of those interviewed in the O'Donnell and A9 fatalities over the past year or so. We don't know how long this has been going on. We could easily have missed someone. I've just jotted down any names that sounded familiar, regardless of context. But some of them will just be coincidences.' He tapped the notebook. 'That one, for example.'

Horton peered at the name. 'I assume so. Not an uncommon name in these parts.'

'That's part of the difficulty. It's why we need to be systematic. But there are one or two other interesting names in there. We've talked about Charlie Farrow. But there's another name that rang a bell with me. Charlie Farrow was reporting to him on the inquiry. Guy called Gordon Rennie.'

'Gordon Rennie? There's a blast from the past.'

McKay looked up to see Helena Grant standing in the office doorway. 'Your tone suggests not necessarily a pleasant one,' he said.

'You might say that. Not that I've any personal reason to dislike him.'

'But?'

'Rory didn't rate him. Or, more accurately, rated him badly.'

'I've a vague memory of him,' McKay said. 'Always struck me as a supercilious git.'

'That's another way of putting it. Smarmy type, always keen to suck up to his superiors and put the fear of God into anyone junior.'

'Sounds like Farrow adopted him as a role model.'

'There's something in that, all right. Rennie was smarter and less lazy than Farrow. Made DCI before retirement. He certainly looked the part. Not one of your dishevelled hard-drinking coppers. Happily married, or apparently so. Couple of kids, presumably now long grown up. Good track record. Maybe suspiciously good, some said, but that was probably just sour grapes. All fine. Except Rory didn't trust him, and frankly Rennie gave me the creeps. Why's his name come up?'

'The O'Donnell inquiry.' McKay briefly outlined what he'd discussed with Ginny Horton. 'He was a DS at the time, running the internal aspects of the investigation. Looking at O'Donnell's police role, and whether that might have provided a motive for his killing. Charlie Farrow was his gopher, pulling together any relevant evidence.'

'You gave me the impression Farrow had done a pretty half-arsed job.'

'I'd put that down to Farrow's characteristic indolence. You reckon Rennie was less of a lazy bugger?'

'If he was trying to impress. He'd have wanted to look good on a case like that.'

'Surprised he accepted what Farrow produced then. Which makes me wonder. Did you ever get any sense that Rennie was bent?'

'Maybe. Not at that point, probably. But Rory had some concerns later on. You're suggesting he might have been up to something on the O'Donnell inquiry?'

'I'm just wondering. If only a sin of omission, as the religious types say. It's not difficult to commit a sin of omission if you've Charlie Farrow on the case. If there's half a chance not to do something, he'll be the first not doing it.'

'And that would mean?'

'Not delving too deeply into anything O'Donnell might

have been involved in. He might have just been going with the flow. I imagine there'd have been one or two at senior levels who wouldn't want to risk airing any dirty linen outside the police family.' McKay placed an ironic emphasis on the last two words.

'Not Rory,' Helena Grant said. 'He wouldn't have tolerated turning a blind eye.'

'I wasn't suggesting that. But if Rennie had looked into O'Donnell's affairs and said "nothing to see here", Rory wouldn't have had any reason to challenge that.'

'He'd have challenged a half-arsed job.'

'Those were my words, largely based on my experience and opinion of Charlie Farrow. The conclusions were presented persuasively enough. Gordon Rennie might have added the surface polish. Rory would have been run off his feet. He'd have challenged anything that looked wrong or dodgy. But he might easily have not spotted that something simply wasn't there.'

'What sort of something?'

'I don't know. Evidence of O'Donnell's wrongdoing. Something indicative of corruption.'

'With respect, Alec, this is just speculation. I'm not keen to see Rory's name dragged through the mud for the sake of one of your hunches.'

'Aye, I understand that, Hel. I'm just telling you what I've found and thinking out loud. I've not had time to absorb any of this yet.' He paused. 'There are a few other names in the files that struck a chord. But there's one in particular that keeps doing the bad penny thing.'

'I don't think this is going to be much of a surprise. Iain Pennycook?'

'The one and only. There was clearly something in what Alasdair Clark said. Pennycook was interviewed several times. He was a few years older than Kevin Clark. Already had a record, though this was before he was sent down. Very much on the police radar as a wrong 'un. We had him down as the brains behind recurrent spates of housebreaking around Inverness. He'd managed not to be directly involved – he found other mugs who'd actually do the deed – and we couldn't muster enough evidence to make any charges stick. One of those where we all know the truth, but can't do much about it.'

'Had plenty of those over the years,' Grant said. 'I imagine Pennycook's smarter than most.'

'Not smart enough in the end, but yes. Other than the small matter of the murder, the O'Donnell break-in had Pennycook's fingerprints all over it. Sadly not literally. Prosperous house in a prosperous neighbourhood. Simple break in through a rear window, then ransack the place for whatever they could find.'

'Ideally not leaving a dead body behind.'

'Exactly. But Pennycook was in the frame from early on. Long before Clark in fact. Not necessarily as the killer or even as one of the housebreakers, but as the organiser of the whole debacle. He was seen repeatedly during the inquiry but the interviews went nowhere. He had a watertight alibi for the day of the killing, and there was nothing beyond circumstantial evidence to indicate any kind of link to it.'

'I'm sure he complained he was being harassed,' Grant said.

'Even went to the local papers to complain about how he was being treated. The first public appearance of his massive brass neck and self-promotional skills. Of course, the media lapped it up and that just added to the pressure on the inquiry.'

'Little shit.'

'The thing is, what emerges from the interview notes is a pretty damning picture, even if they couldn't pin this one on him. He was a big name in the area, running a network of small-time crime – housebreaking and other theft, his own various scams, some dealing. All low level but adding up to something sizeable. It's maybe a good thing he was sent down – and perhaps not entirely coincidental. If he'd pushed it much further, he'd have started treading on the toes of the big players.'

'But he walked away scot-free at the time?'

'Until he got sent down for fraud. Looks as if we were determined to get him for something so the effort focused on the fraud allegations. Something with documentary proof, even if all the witnesses melted away.'

'And the O'Donnell case?'

'Very much his trademark style. He pulled the strings in that part of the city at the time. He knew Clark and anyone else who was dodgy. A lot of them just teenagers, admittedly.'

'Where does that get us?' Grant said.

'Assuming that the deceased really are the same people who were interviewed back then, it links the A9 deaths firmly to the O'Donnell case. The question is why those individuals have been picked out.'

'Because they were involved?'

'Difficult to believe they were all directly involved,' McKay said. 'They might have known something, I guess. But why would someone want to silence them after all these years?'

'Why would any of this happen after all these years?'

'Because someone was afraid of Clark's memory coming back?'

'Possibly. But why not just take Clark out? They seem to have tried to do that in the end anyway.'

'Maybe Clark's not the only one who knows the story. Or different individuals know different parts of the story.'

'So where now?'

'We need to confirm the A9 victims are the same people who were interviewed in the inquiry. I'll get someone looking into that. Beyond that, maybe it's time for another chat with Charlie Farrow?'

'Is that wise? I mean, until we've got something more definite.'

'It might be fun to rattle Charlie's cage. If he's got something to hide, I imagine Charlie's eminently rattleable.'

'Don't expect me to protect you if Farrow cuts up rough.'

'Charlie's a pussycat. You just need to know how to handle him.'

'I've seen you handling him. It's not a pretty sight. Okay, I'll leave you to it.' Grant gestured to the pile of papers. 'I should say – and I do so only very grudgingly, you understand – that you've done a good job here. Early days, but it might be the breakthrough we've been needing.'

'Not bad for a night's work,' Ginny Horton added.

'I really did go home, you know.'

'Barely, I'm betting,' Grant said. 'Just enough time to hone your brain for a battle of wits with Charlie Farrow.'

McKay smiled. 'No, I was definitely home for a lot longer than that.'

CHAPTER FIFTY-TWO

M cKay didn't bother to knock. Charlie Farrow was in the middle of a phone call, and he scowled at McKay in a manner unambiguously instructing him to fuck off, preferably forever. Any other sentient human being would have taken the hint, but McKay ambled in and dumped himself on the chair in front of Farrow's desk.

McKay could tell Farrow was torn between ignoring him and continuing the call, or ending it so he could tell McKay to fuck off even more explicitly. In the end, he continued, though it was clear McKay's presence was cramping his style. Charlie Farrow rarely sounded so monosyllabic. 'Aye. Of course. You do that. Yeah. Call whenever.' McKay guessed the call related to one of Farrow's many side-hustles. McKay didn't much care.

Farrow ended the call, slammed his phone on the desk and said, 'The original unflushable turd.'

'You were talking to a plumber?'

'What the fuck do you want?'

'Just a quick chat before you leave for the day.'

'It's ten thirty in the morning,' Farrow pointed out.

'Aye, and not the weather for golf. That's why I thought I might catch you.'

'You needn't have bothered, you know that?'

'I'm always looking for a stimulating conversation. Failing that, a chat with you, Charlie.'

'Tell me what you want and fuck off.'

'Like I say, a chat.'

'There are phone lines you can call for that sort of thing.'

'I doubt it. I fancied a chat about the O'Donnell case.'

Farrow rubbed his face in a way McKay suspected was intended to hide his expression. 'The what?'

'You can't have forgotten. The Simon O'Donnell murder. It was a big deal at the time. You must have noticed. You were working on the case.'

'It's a long time ago. Why do you want to chat about it now?'

'It's the twentieth anniversary. Everybody's talking about it.'

'That right? I'm not.'

'Why not, Charlie? Don't you want to talk about it?'

'Why would I want to talk about a twenty-year-old case?'

'It's been all over the papers. There's even a campaign to get the case reopened.'

'I don't read the papers. Why would anyone want to get the case reopened? That little bastard went down bang to rights.'

'There was some controversy at the time, I remember.'

'Not much. It didn't take long for the jury to return a unanimous verdict.'

'Your memory seems to be coming back. A bit like Kevin Clark's.'

'What are you talking about?'

'That's the word on the street. That Clark might be regaining his memory.'

'So what?'

'So he might remember more about the background to

O'Donnell's murder, I guess. Or about what happened afterwards.'

'So what if he does? Where's this going, Alec?'

'You tell me. I understand you were the officer looking into O'Donnell's police role?'

'What?'

'In the inquiry. I heard that was your job. Looking into O'Donnell's background.'

'Been delving in the archives, have you? Why the hell would you want to do that?'

'Man needs a hobby. That's right, though, isn't it? That was your role?'

'For what it's worth, yes, that was my job. I remember you weren't involved at all because you'd been stuck on the naughty step.'

'Something like that. Did you find anything?'

'What?'

'I wondered if you found anything dodgy about O'Donnell?'

'You've been looking at the files, Alec. Did it look as if we found anything?'

'Sometimes things don't get recorded.'

'What are you insinuating? That I covered something up?'

'What was it like working for Gordon Rennie?'

'What?'

'Gordon Rennie. I wondered how you found it to work with him. I worked with him later and formed my own opinions.'

'He was fine. Why are you wasting my time with this bollocks?'

'It's still raining. You don't need to rush down to the golf course yet.'

'Look, I've been very patient with you. But if you don't fuck off, I'm sorely tempted to get my lads to throw you out physically.'

'I wouldn't want to end this conversation on an acrimonious note, Charlie. Just curious about Gordon Rennie's management style. Was he a hands-on boss? Did he tell you where to look, or where not to look?'

'What the hell is this all about?'

McKay rose to his feet. 'I wondered if you might have overlooked something. Whether O'Donnell was as clean-cut as he appeared to be.'

Farrow's expression had hardened. 'I don't know what this is all about. But don't push this too far. O'Donnell was one of us. No one likes people being bad-mouthed after they're dead. You could make enemies, spreading rumours like that.'

McKay held up his hands. 'I'm spreading nothing. Just asking a few questions.' He looked past Farrow through the window. 'Looks like it might be clearing up a bit. You might get a round in, after all. I'll leave you to it.'

He left the room before Farrow could respond. Once McKay had closed the door behind him, he glanced back. Through the glass wall of the office, he could see Farrow behind his desk, his eyes fixed on McKay.

McKay took the trouble to acknowledge Farrow's gaze with a friendly wave, then continued along the corridor.

CHAPTER FIFTY-THREE

'What's this crap?' Iain Pennycook leant over the table, brandishing that morning's newspaper. Craig Fairlie looked up from his laptop.

'There's a masthead at the top,' Fairlie said. 'National tabloid. Scottish edition. Today's date. What else can I tell you?'

'You can stop taking the piss for a start.'

Since the break-in, Fairlie had been having second thoughts about his dealings with Pennycook. Work was work, but sometimes the price was too high. 'What's the problem, Iain?'

'This article of yours.' Pennycook sat down at Fairlie's table. He glanced over his shoulder at Ally who was watching cautiously behind the bar. Ally wouldn't stand for any trouble, even if the perpetrator was Iain Pennycook.

'I told you it was going to be appearing.'

'You didn't tell me what you'd be saying.'

'I told you I had information that Clark's memory could be returning.'

'That was all you told me. And you put that in the first article. This goes a lot further.'

'You still haven't told me what the problem is.'

'It's a pile of bullshit.'

'I've got that bit. But what exactly's the problem? Just to warn you, Ally doesn't like people shouting. If you're not careful, you'll be out on your ear.'

'I'd like to see him try.'

'Trust me, you really wouldn't. Calm down and tell me what you're bothered about.'

'I'm bothered about all of it. The bloody hints and rumours.'

The tone of the article hadn't been Fairlie's decision. His original submission had been straighter, presenting the facts – reports of Clark's memory returning, Lawrence's death on the A9 – and allowing readers to draw their own conclusions. Colin Wishaw had felt they were underselling the story. A rewrite had introduced the innuendo that had apparently offended Pennycook, implying a conspiracy to silence Clark. At the last minute, just hours before the article had gone to press, Fairlie had called the prison to try to check a couple of details and had been told – by some receptionist who'd probably said more than she was supposed to – about Clark being in intensive care. Fairlie's story was bumped up to the front-page lead, with a couple of hastily cobbled together background articles on the inner pages.

'That's newspapers, Iain. The assault on Clark made it a front-page story.'

'That's not the real problem, though, is it?'

'So what's the real problem?'

'You've dragged me into this farrago of bollocks. Referencing what that bampot shouted at my rally the other day. That must have come from you.'

'It was a public event, Iain. There were lots of people there.'

'But only one fucking reporter. The guy with his byline on this pile of shite.'

'I thought it was pertinent.'

'Pertinent? You've strung together some crap about the O'Donnell case, and then implied a connection with me because some senile old bastard heckled me.'

'We said the O'Donnell case had a major impact on the local community, and that there's evidence of that even today. I used your meeting as an example. We made it clear there was no suggestion you had any involvement in the case.'

'I don't like my name being taken in vain, however smart the wording. I'll be talking to my lawyers.'

'That's your prerogative, Iain.'

'You're a smug git, aren't you, Fairlie? I assume you realise this is the end of any working relationship between us. I hope whatever you got paid for this shite makes that worthwhile.'

'Again, your choice. I'm sorry about that.'

Pennycook pointed a finger at Fairlie. 'Just don't try to be too much of a smartarse. I don't like making enemies, but my enemies like it even less. Fuck around and find out, as they say. That's a warning, pal.'

'Duly noted,' Fairlie said.

Pennycook rose to his feet. As he leant to pick up the newspaper, he lowered his head close to Fairlie's. 'A fucking warning,' he repeated.

CHAPTER FIFTY-FOUR

McKay pressed the doorbell and stepped back. He was outside a well-appointed bungalow in a decent part of Nairn. Exactly where and how he'd have expected Gordon Rennie to retire. Nothing too flash, and certainly nothing inconsistent with Rennie's likely pension. A newish car in the drive. Again, nothing too ostentatious.

Whatever his failings, Rennie was a smart man and a fairly cautious one. If there were ill-gotten gains, he'd have stashed them away discreetly where nothing short of a major investigation would find them.

McKay heard movement from inside the house, and he plastered his best unthreatening smile on his face. The door opened and a woman peered nervously at him. 'Yes?'

'Mrs Rennie?'

'Can I help you?' She presumably assumed he was about to try to sell her something.

He produced his warrant card. 'DI McKay. I was a colleague of your husband's. I was wondering if he could spare me a few moments?'

'Is this something official?'

'I'm involved in a case which might have a link to a past investigation. I was looking at the files, and I thought it would be useful to pick your husband's brains. That's one of the problems when people retire. We lose valuable knowledge.'

'You should have called,' she said. 'I'm afraid he's out at the moment.'

'Oh, that's a pity. I was intending to call but was passing through Nairn so thought I'd try my hand. It's a pity I missed him.'

'He's at the golf club.' She looked at her watch. 'He's probably finished playing by now. They usually have a pint or two in the bar afterwards.'

'I'll head down there,' McKay said. 'Buy him a pint for old times' sake. Sorry to have troubled you, Mrs Rennie.'

The golf club was less than a mile away, down by the shore, and he parked without difficulty in the spacious car park. Golf had always been a mystery to McKay. He couldn't see the attraction of the sport itself, and he wasn't keen on many of the people who played it, though they were generally a more eclectic bunch here than south of the border.

The young woman behind the reception desk smiled up at him.

'I'm looking for Gordon Rennie,' he said. 'We'd arranged to meet in the bar.'

'The bar's through there. I think Mr Rennie's still in there. I saw him earlier.'

'Thanks. I'll see if I can find him.'

It was midweek and it wasn't particularly busy, a couple of clusters of middle-aged men by the bar. McKay recognised Rennie immediately, a little greyer and stouter than the man he remembered as a colleague. Rennie had clearly been warned of his impending arrival. He detached himself from his associates and strode over to greet McKay by the door.

'Long time, no see, Gordon.' McKay beamed. 'How are things?'

'Relaxed, Alec. That's what retirement does for you. You should try it.'

'One day. Are you okay to spare me a few minutes?'

'What's this all about?' He gestured behind him. 'I'm with some mates here.'

'I won't keep you long. Just wanted to pick your brains about a couple of things.'

'Aye, so Barbara said. What kind of things?'

'The O'Donnell case.'

'Everybody seems to be obsessing about that at the moment.'

'It's the anniversary,' McKay said. 'Bound to generate some interest.'

'Let's go outside,' Rennie said. 'I'm not keen on talking shop in here.'

McKay had always assumed that talking a certain kind of shop was the primary reason golf existed. But he was more than happy to go outside if it meant he could talk more openly to Rennie.

The weather had brightened, although it was still more changeable than in the preceding weeks. For the moment the sun was out, and the benches at the front of the club had dried sufficiently to be useable. From here, they enjoyed an uninterrupted view of the golf course, the waters of the Moray Firth glittering beyond.

'What's this about, Alec? You've not driven out here for a nostalgic chat.'

'Like you said, there's a lot of interest in the O'Donnell case. It's not just the anniversary.'

'What then?'

'Various things.'

'Such as?'

'Kevin Clark's lawyer being killed in an RTC. A death we're treating as suspicious.'

'You're suggesting someone killed him because of his links to a trial twenty years ago?'

'It's a line of inquiry. The producer of a podcast on the O'Donnell case has also been found dead in suspicious circumstances. And we're investigating other deaths which seem to have potential links with the case.'

'Is this a joke?'

'Do I look a bundle of laughs? The final bit of news, which hit the headlines this morning, is that Kevin Clark himself has been attacked in prison. He's in intensive care.'

'Things happen in prison,' Rennie said.

'One of the claims is that Clark was regaining his memory of what happened during the O'Donnell break-in and afterwards. Perhaps someone wanted to make sure those memories stayed buried.'

'I've no idea why you've come to me, Alec. It's a long while since I've been in the loop for anything.'

'It's the long ago stuff I'm interested in,' McKay said. 'The original inquiry.'

'What about it?'

'I understand you were looking into O'Donnell's police role.'

'I can't remember the details now. It's all a long time ago.'

'That's what the file shows. That you were focused on O'Donnell, with support from Charlie Farrow. If support's the right word.'

'You never got on with Charlie, did you? Mind you, I'm not sure you got on with me much either.'

'You were okay, Gordon. Smarter than Farrow, anyway. Tell me about O'Donnell.'

'I don't know there's much to tell you. We only looked into him because we couldn't afford to leave any stone unturned. Nobody seriously thought there was a motive there.'

'Finance guy, wasn't he?'

'Aye, civilian role. Senior accounts manager or some such. Well respected.'

'No suggestions of any wrongdoing?'

'We found nothing to suggest any. No anomalies in his own finances. No sense he was living beyond his means. Is there a reason you're pursuing this line?'

'Just revisiting the whole thing, really,' McKay said vaguely. 'See if there's anything we might have missed.'

'We did a bloody good job on that case. I won't have anyone suggesting different. We got the result we needed.'

'What about you, Gordon? Did you do a good job in difficult circumstances?'

'We all bloody did.'

'I was looking through your notes on the case. They seemed a little scant. Charlie Farrow's even more so.'

'Are you suggesting I didn't do my job properly?'

'I was wondering if there were any factors that prevented you doing the job as rigorously as you'd have liked. We all know how it can be sometimes.'

'We did the job to the best of our abilities,' Rennie said.

'Have you come across a guy called Iain Pennycook?'

Rennie seemed thrown by the apparent non-sequitur. 'The mouthy one? Everyone knows him. Was never off the telly at one point.'

'I was thinking before that. Back in the day. At the time of the O'Donnell killing. Whether you remember him being around then.'

'He was around right enough. Already a wee gobshite. Saw himself as a big shot. What's this got to do with O'Donnell?'

'One of the big questions was whether Clark had an accomplice. Wondered if Pennycook might have been in the frame?'

Rennie stared out across the fairway. The breeze was blowing in from the sea more strongly now, and he was hunched against the cold. 'Not directly. Pennycook was already too much of a big deal by then. Saw himself as some kind of operator. He was running all kinds of scams.'

'You think he might have had a hand in the break-in, though?'

Rennie sat in silence for a moment, his eyes fixed on the distant water. 'Why don't you just bugger off, Alec? Stop being a pain in the arse. This was all a long time ago. I've nothing to tell you.'

'It's a murder inquiry, Gordon. A multiple murder inquiry. Someone's lost the plot, even after all these years. If you know anything that might cast light on this, you should tell me.'

'I'm a company man,' Rennie said. 'Simon O'Donnell was a member of the police family, and we all bust a gut to make sure his killer ended up behind bars. End of story. Justice was served. That's all anyone needs to know.'

'But what if it's not the truth? What if justice wasn't served? What if O'Donnell's killer is still walking free? What if O'Donnell himself wasn't the good company man everyone wanted to believe? What if people are being killed to keep that pretence alive? Would you be happy to live with that?'

'Just fuck off, Alec. Leave me and Barbara alone. I'm long retired. I've put all this behind me, and I don't want anything more to do with it.'

'I think it's too late for that. Think about it.' He took a

business card from his pocket and placed it in Rennie's hand. 'If anything occurs to you, give me a call.'

He left Rennie sitting there and made his way back around the building to the car park. At the corner, he looked back. Rennie was already pulling his phone from his pocket, ready to make a call.

CHAPTER FIFTY-FIVE

McKay watched as people filed in. From where he was standing, the whole event had a 'how are the mighty fallen' vibe, but he knew that would never be acknowledged. This wasn't the end of something, but the beginning of something else. A brief retrenchment before the next and decisive advance. The germ of a new empire.

Not just a sparsely attended meeting in a shabby village hall.

McKay wasn't sure why he was even there. He was in the middle of a multiple murder investigation. His colleagues were busting a gut doing all the routine stuff that should bring a result. Meanwhile, McKay was skiving off to an Inverness suburb he'd hardly known existed to watch this clown show. Prodding around in the hope something would be stirred up.

McKay guessed most of the sparse crowd knew each other. They were neighbours or friends or people who chatted in the local pub. The gathering looked more like a social event than a political rally. They were mostly elderly couples, presumably retired and free to attend an event like this in the middle of the afternoon.

The meeting was due to kick off at three, and it was now quarter to. Perfect timing. Early enough to have a decent chat with Pennycook, but late enough that Pennycook would be keen to get rid of him. McKay eased his way through those knots of people towards the front of the room.

Pennycook was standing near the small raised stage, chatting to a young man McKay assumed to be some kind of aide. He had the kind of earnest enthusiasm McKay associated with over-serious political kinds. He wouldn't exactly be the brains behind Pennycook – unlike many politicians Pennycook was smart enough to bring his own – but he'd be the one capable of sticking Pennycook's ideas onto a spreadsheet.

'Afternoon, Iain,' McKay said as he approached.

He'd clearly caught Pennycook by surprise, although McKay could see he was doing his best to conceal it. 'Alec. It's been a while.'

'Far too long.'

'I wouldn't have thought this was your kind of thing.' He turned to the young man. 'Forgive me, Ben. I just need a brief chat with Detective Inspector McKay here.' The inclusion of McKay's rank was clearly intended as a warning.

The young man pointedly looked at his watch. 'We've only ten minutes or so.'

'I know. I can tell the time. You just make sure everything's ready.'

The young man reluctantly peeled away from them and made his way to the lectern. Still, McKay noted, within listening distance. 'Decent turnout,' he commented.

'We get a lot better, but this is about par for the afternoon sessions. Most people have jobs to do. Speaking of which, Alec, what are you doing here? I take it you're not here to join the cause.'

'You might tempt me yet. I'm developing an interest in fatalities on the A9.'

'One of our major concerns, as you're no doubt aware. Perhaps you should stay to listen.'

'I suspect I've heard it all before. With respect.'

'So why are you here?'

'You remember the O'Donnell case?'

'I do indeed, aged as I'm becoming. I also remember it was twenty years ago. I'm more concerned with the future.'

'You were interviewed by the police at the time, weren't you?'

'Is this your job now? What do they call it? Cold case reviews?'

'I'm spending my time on a very live investigation. A murder investigation.'

'Then you're talking to the wrong man. I've been many things in my time, but murderer isn't one of them.'

'What about small-time gang boss in the arse-end of Inverness?' McKay said. 'Was that once one of your roles?'

'I've done my time,' Pennycook said. 'And I've always been open about it. I've nothing to hide. Now, if you'll excuse me.'

'I won't keep you,' McKay said. 'I only really popped by to let you know I've been talking to people.'

Pennycook had been turning away. Now he stopped and looked at McKay. 'So I've heard.'

'Grapevine working well, then?'

'I make it my business to know what's going on, Alec. I don't like to hear that people are being pestered.' He glanced pointedly at the waiting lectern. 'I'm not sure I like being pestered myself.'

'That's a pity. Because I've barely got started. And you wouldn't believe what a pain in the arse I can be when I really get going.' He looked past Pennycook to where the young man was waiting impatiently on stage. 'But you'd better get on. You wouldn't want to leave your public waiting.'

CHAPTER FIFTY-SIX

McKay returned to the office to discover he'd already been summoned for what he assumed would be a bollocking, or at least a warning, friendly or otherwise.

'What are you up to, Alec?' Helena Grant said. She was warily watching McKay prowl around her office. The contents of her shelves hadn't changed in several years, but McKay always behaved as if he'd found something new.

'I was wondering how you decide which files to put on which shelves.'

'I meant more generally.'

'Oh, right, I see.' He sat back down at Grant's desk. 'Just doing my job.'

'Iain Pennycook's made a complaint.'

McKay looked at his watch. 'Already? Okay, that's impressive.'

'You know Pennycook. Called straight through to the chief constable's office. Complained about being harassed just as he was about to make a major speech.'

'Did he mention this was in a backstreet community hall?'

'I imagine he left that part vague. Why were you there?'

'Went along for a little chat. We go way back, you know.'

'All the way back to that first arrest. Aye, I know.'

'I like to keep in touch. Otherwise, people might think you've changed.'

'You'll never change, Alec.'

'I like to think so. I assume no one's taking this complaint seriously.'

'I'm not sure anyone takes Pennycook as seriously as he takes himself. But if he starts causing trouble, he could become a real nuisance. No one wants that.'

'Heaven forbid.'

'You think there's something there? With Pennycook, I mean.'

'Aye, I do. He's got something to hide.'

'You're not suggesting he's behind our killings?'

'No. Not directly, anyway. But it's like Alasdair Clark told Craig Fairlie. Pennycook knows something.'

'I hope you know what you're doing.'

'You know me, Hel.'

'That's what worries me. What's your next move?'

'Are you keeping an eye on me?'

'That is supposed to be my job. Even it shouldn't be such a large part of it.'

'I'm still digging into the O'Donnell case. That's where the answers are.'

'So far you've done a great job of increasing the number of victims. I'm still debating with Comms how to present that. We can't keep quiet about the fact we've a multiple killer literally on the road.'

'A multiple killer who's targeting their victims, though. We know now it isn't random.'

'That's not exactly reassuring. And there's the risk of

collateral damage. The truck driver, Brian Renton, for example. He was just in the wrong place at the wrong time.'

'And his truck used as the murder weapon. Aye, I know. We need some urgent progress on this.'

'You reckon the O'Donnell files are helping you do that?'

'Yes, but not quickly enough.'

'And that's why you're out and about stirring up trouble with the likes of Iain Pennycook?'

McKay shrugged. 'Passes the time.'

'Okay. But take care, Alec. Pennycook's a nasty piece of work.'

'I don't doubt it. I'm watching my back.'

After his meeting with Helena, McKay returned to the main Major Investigations office to find the room deserted except for Ginny Horton still working through the files. She looked up as he entered. 'Thought I was the only one left in the place.'

'You shouldn't be here,' McKay pointed out. 'Have you seen what the time is?'

'I'd lost track.'

'Any joy?'

'A few minor titbits, but nothing to get excited about. Though this might be interesting. I've taken a copy of the key sections.' She handed him a sheaf of folded sheets. 'See what you think. Taking account of the officer involved.'

'I'll do that, but only if you bugger off,' McKay said. 'You're making the place look untidy, as my mum used to say.'

'I'm taking the hint.' Horton grabbed her coat from the rack beside the office door, waving as she left the room.

McKay opened the sheets Ginny Horton had given him, initially reading them with a sense of bafflement. They were case notes relating to an incident on the A9 from the distant past. It took him a moment to realise the incident had been roughly contemporaneous with the O'Donnell killing.

A car had been found abandoned off the southbound carriageway of the A9 between the Tore roundabout and Inverness. The vehicle had left the road and ploughed through bushes and undergrowth before turning over and coming to a halt some hundred yards from the road. It had been invisible from the carriageway and had sat unnoticed for several days before the police had been notified by the owner of the land where the car had come to rest.

The driver was still inside. He'd been trapped by the car's crushed roof, and had been dead for several days. The vehicle itself proved to be stolen from a car park in Inverness. The driver was eventually identified as Sean McArthur, a seventeen-year-old male from Inverness, a very newly qualified driver with no previous police record. No traces of alcohol or drugs were found in the body. The time of death had been hard to ascertain because of the variable weather conditions over the preceding days.

The obvious question was whether this incident had any connection with the O'Donnell killing. Had this been the unknown vehicle used to transport Kevin Clark and any associates away from the scene of the crime? From a vantage point of twenty years, it seemed more than possible, but no one seemed to have paid the question much attention at the time.

In fairness, at that point, the police still had nobody in the frame as a potential culprit for the O'Donnell murder, and there was no evidence there'd been any passengers in the car. The police had found various unidentified fingerprints and traces of DNA, but nothing identifiable. Whatever the background to the incident, McKay thought, anyone not trapped in the car would most likely have legged it. Not the most honourable course of action, but unsurprising.

Another dead end. McKay tuned over the sheet and looked at the last page of the notes. Ginny had mentioned the identity of the investigating officer, and there was the name.

Detective Constable Charles Farrow.

The familiar bad penny. Not that it meant much in itself. Quite probably this had been before Farrow was attached to the O'Donnell inquiry. Farrow had probably picked this case up as a local incident. Appended to the document, though, was another familiar signature. DS Gordon Rennie. It looked as if the old team were already together by this point.

There was no way to tell how thorough Farrow's investigation had been. He'd gone through all the right motions. Forensics. Interviews with McArthur's parents who inevitably professed themselves utterly shocked by a supposedly uncharacteristic act. But, as always with Farrow, the detail seemed lacking. Resources had no doubt been thin on the ground as officers were transferred to the O'Donnell case. That, combined with Farrow's natural indolence, might have been enough to justify a rushed job, especially as the only victim was McArthur himself.

It might be worth a deeper delve into the McArthur case, McKay thought. That could wait till the morning, though. It was time to go home and get some rest before his worked-up brain dragged him even further into the past. He put the files back in the cupboard, turned off the lights and began to make his way downstairs.

As so often, he felt as if he was the last person working in this part of the building, but as he descended the stairs he could see lights showing on the first floor. On a whim, he walked along the corridor towards the lit offices.

The man sitting at the desk looked up in surprise as he tapped on the door. 'Jesus, Alec. What brings you down to these parts?'

'Curiosity. I thought Charlie Farrow might be working late.'

'You really are taking the piss, aren't you?' DS Johnny Wills gestured at the computer in front of him. 'It's muggins here who's been left completing all the admin Charlie hasn't quite got round to today. Par for the course.'

'Language Charlie would understand. You need a transfer, Johnny. Ever thought of coming upstairs?'

'Been weighing up the options lately, to be honest. I've had more than enough of this place. On the other hand, promotion might be on the cards and there could be a vacancy here fairly soon.'

'Charlie?'

'He's not far off retirement. The way he's been talking, I wouldn't be surprised if he was angling to go early.'

'He's talking that way, is he?'

'Let's be honest, Charlie's never exactly been one to set the world on fire. But he seems to have lost whatever bit of spark he had. I reckon he's had enough.'

'Maybe he's not well?'

'Maybe. He doesn't seem himself. Worried about something, I'd say. Could be some medical condition, I suppose. Not the sort of thing Charlie would share with his underlings.'

'I guess not. I need to have another chat with him about a couple of things. Want me to put in a word for you?'

Wills grinned. 'Aye, very funny. I really don't think that would help.'

'The offer's there, son. Don't blame me if you pass it by. Anyway, tell Charlie I called. I'll probably pop back tomorrow, so if you change your mind...'

'Bugger off, Alec. But I'll pass on your good wishes.'

CHAPTER FIFTY-SEVEN

He was going to be in trouble again.

Charlie Farrow glanced at the clock on the dashboard, while trying to keep his mind focused on the road ahead. If he'd had his way and they'd stayed in town, his journey back would be a good half an hour shorter. But of course Margot was never prepared to acknowledge that. All she ever did was complain that he was late home again, and tonight would be no exception.

She was right, of course. He was almost always late getting home. That was because he didn't much enjoy going there. They'd just spend another evening sniping at one another. Margot would criticise his drinking. He'd retaliate by attacking her for – well, for being Margot, he supposed. For not being someone he'd rather be spending his evening with.

He wasn't quite sure how they'd got to this point. Admittedly, there'd never really been any halcyon days. The early years of their marriage had been okay, but even then he'd generally hung around with the other lads after work, clustered round the bar in whatever hostelry they frequented at that time. Then there'd been the years when he'd had successive affairs with a couple of female colleagues. He'd always assumed Margot had known what was going on, just as he assumed she was having work-based affairs of her own.

Now they'd just settled into this familiar routine. He always came home late, though now the cause was generally a few pints in the golf club rather than a session in some dodgy city centre bar. Margot had long ago given up cooking anything that would just become dried-up in the bottom of the oven. By the time he returned, she'd already have eaten, leaving him to stick a ready-meal in the microwave. She'd be well into a bottle of wine, and quite soon he wouldn't be far behind her.

On top of that, retirement was beckoning. He'd no great desire to continue working, but he wasn't keen on spending more time with Margot either. There were only so many hours you could spend on the golf course, even if you included the nineteenth hole.

And there were other matters he had to resolve before then. Most people would have assumed Charlie Farrow was a man without much of a conscience. Maybe that was true, but his Catholic upbringing had left him with a well-developed sense of guilt. He wasn't sure he could face old age without at least trying to put right some of the wrongs he'd contributed to in the course of his career. The question was how he could do that without jeopardising his own future. He'd had one shot at it, but then got cold feet when he'd registered the names of the victims of the A9 incidents. Maybe it had just been coincidence – no one could have known he'd been talking out of turn – but it had felt more like a warning.

He forced himself to concentrate on the road. His route home was winding and single track, some parts lined with hedgerows, some parts open to woods or moorland. He was unlikely to encounter any other traffic up here at this time in the evening, but if he did they'd have to ease past each other in one of the infrequent passing places. Alcohol made Farrow drive more cautiously than usual, but most other local drivers made little concession to the nature of the road. They came bombing down the hillside, unduly confident in their knowledge of the twists and turns.

He found himself driving increasingly slowly, particularly on the last half mile or so of the route when it was difficult to see what might lie beyond the next bend.

Even so, he was taken by surprise. The large black SUV was sitting in the middle of the carriageway, unmoving. Farrow slammed on his brakes, stopping in time to avoid a collision.

What the bloody hell was the arsehole doing? If he'd stopped a few yards back, there'd have been space for another vehicle to squeeze past him. As it was, he'd pulled to a halt where the road was at its narrowest, with a relatively steep drop on the far side. It wasn't a spot to try any smart driving manoeuvres.

The last passing place had been a quarter of a mile back. The next was visible just a few yards past the SUV. It was clearly sensible for the SUV to pull back, rather than for Farrow to attempt to reverse down the winding road behind him. In any case, Charlie Farrow wasn't the type to make concessions to arsehole drivers. He hit the horn, holding it down, the noise disturbingly loud in the twilight.

The SUV showed no sign of moving. In the gloom, Farrow couldn't even see if there was anyone behind the wheel. He inched forward slightly, still sounding the horn. Finally, Farrow slammed on the handbrake and climbed out to remonstrate with the other driver.

There was someone in the SUV, he was sure. But even in the light from his own headlights, he could make out little more than a silhouette. He stepped up to the door of the car and knocked hard on the window.

'I don't know what the hell you're playing at,' Farrow said in a voice he hoped was loud enough to be heard inside the vehicle. 'Just back up so I can get past.'

To his slight surprise, the SUV started to reverse. Maybe the daft bastard had finally woken up. Farrow decided there was no point in not accepting the concession graciously. He gave the other driver a thumbs up and walked back to his own car. He started the engine, waiting for the SUV to finish reversing.

The SUV pulled back a few yards, then stopped.

'Oh, come on, you numpty. It's not that difficult.' Farrow tapped frustratedly on the steering wheel. 'If you don't know how to drive a car like that, don't bloody buy one.'

Then he froze, realising too late what was happening. The SUV jerked forward and slammed heavily into the front of Farrow's car, forcing him backwards down the road. Farrow slammed on his brakes, trying to prevent his car from being shunted back, but the SUV's forward progress was relentless.

Farrow felt his car tip sideways as one of the rear wheels slipped off the road. He realised, a moment too late, that he needed to extricate himself from the vehicle. He struggled with the door but the moment had already passed. The car slid backwards, slowly at first then faster as it was forced fully from the road. At first the slope was relatively gentle, and Farrow breathed out with relief. Then, quite suddenly, there was nothing beneath the car and he felt it dropping abruptly. He closed his eyes, hoping something would break the fall, but the car was turning over and over. There was a sudden sharp impact, and then nothing more.

CHAPTER FIFTY-EIGHT

A lec McKay wasn't a fanciful man. If he'd had a bad night's sleep, that was because the evening's lamb bhuna had sat heavily in his stomach. McKay had known it was going to be another late night, so he'd suggested ordering a takeout he could collect on his way home. The food from their favourite Indian had been excellent, but a little rich for digesting so late in the evening.

Whatever the reason, he'd woken around 4am. He'd felt restless, his head full of thoughts he couldn't articulate. He rolled over and tried to sleep some more, but his mind was racing, chasing ideas always just outside his grasp.

Around five, he dragged himself out of bed, wide awake. He might as well make best use of the day. Chrissie was well accustomed to him disappearing in the early hours, and wouldn't be worried by his absence. For the second day in succession, he was out of the house and heading into the city before five thirty.

Just as he'd been one of the last to leave the previous night, so he was the first to arrive in the office that morning. He made himself a coffee, logged on to his computer and pulled out the material he'd been reviewing the previous evening.

It was after eight before other members of the team began to drift into the room, the noise gradually building as jackets were roved off, coffees prepared, the first chat beginning to be exchanged. It was a sound and an atmosphere McKay normally found reassuring. Work was under way, tasks being undertaken, everything taking them another step towards their objectives. Even if some of the buggers were simply buggering about.

Today, though, he felt no reassurance. He felt they were wasting their time, any sense of progress illusory, their supposed killer already too far ahead of them. Around eight thirty, McKay's phone buzzed on the desk. He glanced at the screen as he picked it up. DS Johnny Wills, the man he'd been chatting to the previous evening.

'Johnny? Changed your mind about getting out of there?'

'Not yet. And, you never know, I may not need to.'

'If you want to stay under Charlie Farrow's considerable shadow—'

'That's why I'm calling. You obviously haven't heard. Charlie's gone missing.'

'Done a runner? I can't say I'm surprised.'

'Nobody knows what he's done. Only that he didn't go home last night.'

'He's probably drunkenly overslept in the arms of some floozy. Do we still have floozies? And do we still call them that?'

'I'm not the one to ask, Alec. But you're not the only one to express a view along those lines.'

'I'd have thought Charlie was getting a bit old for that sort of thing. What's the story?'

'Played golf yesterday afternoon, apparently. Last seen in the evening – not that late, around eightish – knocking back a pint or two with his mates in the clubroom. Very male crowd, apparently.'

'You surprise me.'

'He left sometime after that. Probably had a few pints more than was strictly wise for driving, according to his mates, but that was Charlie. Always thought he could talk his way out of trouble.'

'He's got away with it for a good few decades so far. How seriously are you taking this? I mean, is this just Charlie pulling a stunt, or are people genuinely concerned?'

'It's being taken seriously. In fairness, it's not really characteristic of Charlie. Not these days, anyway. There was a time when he'd go AWOL, but now he divides his time between the golf club, home and the office. Probably in that order. His wife's worried, anyway.'

'If he'd been drinking...'

'That thought's occurred. Especially given where he lives. Up some single-track road in the back of beyond.'

The sense of dread that had been lying leadenly in McKay's stomach felt heavier. 'I take it someone's checking the route.'

'We've sent a patrol car up there. Waiting for them to report back. Nothing's been reported. If there was a collision in that neck of the woods, you'd have thought it would be easy to spot.'

McKay had no particular affection for Charlie Farrow, but he'd never seriously wished the man dead. He was another name on the list, though. Someone who'd been involved in that original O'Donnell investigation. Witnesses, investigators, maybe some who'd had no serious connection with the inquiry. It was as if the killer was winnowing through them all. 'If you hear anything, let me know. I was serious about needing to talk to him.'

'I'll call you if there's any word.'

More than likely, Farrow was safe enough. There'd be some

explanation, innocent or not, for his absence. But the tension hadn't disappeared. If he was right about the link with the O'Donnell case, there was no knowing who else might be on their killer's list. Dozens if not hundreds of people had been involved in that investigation. Any of them could be at risk.

It would take weeks to review them all. For the moment, McKay had only one more name to check out. The last name he'd recognised from the list of interviewees in the O'Donnell case. Almost certainly not a useful lead, even if the name wasn't just coincidental, but it was one more box to tick.

That was good investigative practice, he'd always been told. Keep plugging away at the routine stuff, eliminating possibilities until you were left with the only available truth. Easy enough to say, McKay thought. But nothing like enough when you knew time was running out.

CHAPTER FIFTY-NINE

M cKay was halfway down the corridor when his phone rang again. Another call from Johnny Wills.

'Bad news,' Wills said. 'They've found Charlie's car. The patrol officers had driven the route twice without spotting anything. Then a dog walker phoned it in.'

'Always the bloody dog walkers.' McKay tried to keep his voice light. What had been a lead weight in his stomach had turned to ice. 'Where was it?'

'Bottom of a very steep drop. Car badly damaged. Charlie even more so. They've taken him into Raigmore but I'm told there's no chance. He'd presumably been lying there since last night.'

'Nasty way to go. Any clues as to how it might have happened?'

'I'm only getting this second hand, you understand, and it's just what the uniforms thought. But if he'd just managed to drive himself off the road, they think the car wouldn't have ended up where it did. Looked as if it had left the road backwards, they reckoned.'

'Backwards?'

'Narrow road with passing places. Charlie might have been trying to reverse for an oncoming vehicle.'

'An oncoming vehicle that didn't bother to stop or call it in when they saw him reverse off the road?'

'I suppose it's possible they didn't realise. Or maybe the uniforms have got it wrong. Will have to see what the vehicle forensic guys say.'

'I can't say Charlie and I were close,' McKay said. 'But I wouldn't have wished this on him. Keep me posted.'

'I will. It's a nasty business.'

McKay slipped the phone back into his pocket. He'd been heading for Helena Grant's office, intending to talk to her about the McArthur case. Now he had more immediate and serious news to share with her.

Her office door was closed and he could see through the glass that the room was empty. He opened the door and peered inside. She'd clearly been in here already. Her computer was on in hibernate mode; her light summer raincoat hanging behind the door. It looked as if she'd dashed in and out.

McKay tapped on the door of the neighbouring office, occupied by a couple of administrators. 'Anyone seen Helena this morning?'

The young man sitting nearest to him said, 'She's been in. I saw her when I went for a coffee.'

'I think I heard her go out,' the woman behind him said. 'About fifteen minutes ago.'

Somewhere in McKay's head, a cog turned another notch. 'Thanks. Can you let her know I was looking for her?'

The sense of dread, the cold weight in his stomach, was growing heavier with every passing second. Something felt wrong, though he couldn't put his finger on what it might be.

He returned to Grant's office and looked around. He'd spent enough time aimlessly prowling around this small space to know every detail. Not that there was much to see. Helena kept her office tidy. There was a filing cabinet in the corner that McKay knew would be firmly locked. There were shelves with a handful of textbooks she'd collected over the years, and a few souvenirs of her police career to date, mostly items presented to her on overseas trips.

McKay paused. He couldn't think why he hadn't noticed it before, except that the item in question had been the opposite of ostentatious. It had been tucked towards the back of the shelf, almost concealed by the surrounding objects. Now McKay had noticed, its absence was glaring, as if the distant summit of Ben Wyvis had suddenly vanished from the Inverness skyline.

For as long as Helena had been in this office, it had sat discreetly in the middle of the shelf. A simple head and shoulders portrait. Nothing formal. A random shot from among a batch of others taken for official purposes. But the grinning face had captured the spirit of the man.

The man being Rory Grant. Late husband of Helena Grant.

Now the photograph was missing. And so, McKay thought, was Helena.

CHAPTER SIXTY

McKay hurried back into the office, his phone in his hand. He ended the call he was making, cursing loudly.

'You okay, Alec?'

McKay looked at Ginny as if he'd only just realised she was there. 'You don't happen to know where Helena might be?'

'Funny you should say that. She was going out, just as I was coming in. Didn't seem her usual self, but that seems par for the course this morning. I was late getting in. Have I missed something?'

'I'm beginning to wonder if we all have. How do you mean not her usual self?'

'I thought it was because she was in a hurry. She seemed flustered. The weirdest thing was she called me Virginia.'

'Virginia? Nobody calls you Virginia.'

'Nobody who wants to live, no. I thought I must have misheard or that she was making some sort of joke. But she didn't seem in a humorous mood.'

'Did she give you any idea where she was going?'

'There wasn't time. But she wasn't on her own.'

'Who was with her?'

'Adam Sutherland. The vehicles guy. That was all a bit odd, too. They seemed to be in a real hurry. Sutherland was pushing right behind her—' She stopped. 'What is it?'

'Adam Sutherland,' he said. 'You're sure about that?'

'Of course I'm sure about it. I mean, I assumed they were together—'

'His name was on the list of interviewees from the O'Donnell case you showed me the other day.'

'I didn't take that seriously, though. It won't be the same one. It's not that uncommon a name.'

'We don't know it's not the same one. I was planning to check Sutherland out, but only because he was the only familiar name we had left.'

'I'm not sure I understand.'

'I'm not sure I do, either. But I don't like the feel of this. Helena's number went straight to voicemail. Let's see if we can find out where Sutherland's gone.' He scrolled down his phone's contact list until he found Sutherland's number.

The call rang out before finally being answered by a voice McKay didn't recognise. 'Vehicle examiners.'

'I was trying to contact Adam Sutherland,' McKay said. 'I thought this was his mobile.'

'He must have it turned off. If he's not available it transfers to the office phone. Can I take a message?'

'Do you know where he is? I need to get hold of him urgently. DI Alec McKay.'

'He's supposed to be up at the site of the Charlie Farrow crash. Adam said he thought he should give it his personal attention. You know, police family and all that.'

Police family. Aye, McKay thought, a bloody dysfunctional one. 'I'll see if I can track him down there.' He ended the call then dialled another number.

'An unexpected pleasure at this time in the morning, Alec.'

'Likewise, Jock. Do you know which examiners are dealing with the Charlie Farrow RTC?'

'Are you taking the piss?' Jock Henderson enquired. 'I'm the one standing here in this delightful mix of sun and passing showers trying to make sense of what our old friend Charlie managed to do with his car. Utter tragedy, by the way. I feel for his widow in her time of loss.' McKay had often thought that Henderson had the air of a stereotypical undertaker, though he hoped Henderson would be able to summon up more sincerity if he ever took on the job for real. 'Still, he deserves the best we can offer him. After all, he was—'

'Police family. Aye, so I hear. Is Adam Sutherland with you?'

'The car man? Not seen hide nor hair of him. But those buggers never turn up till they're sure any unpleasantness has been cleaned away.'

'You're sure he's not there?'

'I may be advancing in years, but I'd recognise Sutherland if he was here.'

'If he appears, let him know I'm looking for him.'

'I'm only too delighted to be your messaging service, Alec. Now, if there's nothing else, I'll get on.' Henderson unceremoniously ended the call.

'Not there?'

'No sign. Let's try Helena again.' He began to dial then paused, noticing that a text had appeared on his phone while he'd been making the previous calls. A message from Grant which said simply: *A9. S of Tore.* McKay showed the message to Horton, then dialled Helena Grant's number. The phone cut straight to voicemail again.

'Nothing. Looks as if the phone's been turned off.'

'What do you think?'

'I'm not sure what I'm thinking but it's nothing good. Let's get a patrol car up to Tore, see what they can find. I don't know what else that text could mean. But why send it and then immediately initiate radio silence. Unless she didn't send it.'

'How do you mean?'

'If she's with Adam Sutherland, he knows you saw them leaving. He might have had a call from the office by now telling him I'm looking for him. If he knows we're after him, the text might be intended to send us off on a wild goose chase. It just feels too easy. Why would he simply tell us where he's going?'

'I'll get a patrol car up there anyway,' Horton said. 'They'll get there quicker than we can, and we can follow them up if there's anything to report.'

She busied herself calling the control room, while McKay sat staring blankly into space. There was still a connection he wasn't making. He'd described Sutherland as the last meaningful name on their list. But he wasn't. There were two more still out there. Iain Pennycook and Gordon Rennie.

'Patrol car on its way,' Horton said. 'They obviously thought it was just typical CID nonsense, especially as I couldn't even tell them what to look for.'

'I think they might be wasting their time, though.'

'We could track Helena's phone?'

'We can try but I'm not sure we have time.' He was silent for a moment. 'Do we know where Iain Pennycook's living these days?'

'No idea. We can probably find out easily enough.'

'Companies House might be the quickest way. He's bound to be running a handful of businesses.'

Horton tapped away at her computer. 'Address in Beauly, apparently.'

McKay moved to stand behind her. 'Jesus Christ. I don't

know what's more impressive. The sheer brass neck or the bloody sense of irony.'

'Really?'

'Really. The house where Simon O'Donnell was murdered.'

'I'm surprised Pennycook buying that didn't make the newspapers.'

'Pennycook's not as big a fish as he might think, even up here. But if he's living in that house, he's cocking a very on-brand snook at the world, including us. It's not coincidence. And I'm wondering if Adam Sutherland's aware of it.'

'You think he might have taken Helena there?' There was a note of disbelief in Horton's voice.

'I don't have anything else,' McKay said. 'And I need to have something. For Helena's sake. I'm going to check it out.'

CHAPTER SIXTY-ONE

'I've no idea where you got that,' Helena Grant said. 'But you're not going to use it. You really aren't.'

'It's police issue,' Adam Sutherland said casually. 'And you're wrong about that, you know. I won't hesitate to use it if I need to. So it's better you just do what I say.'

Grant still had no idea why Sutherland had turned up unexpectedly in her office. She'd just heard the news about Charlie Farrow's death and assumed he wanted to talk about that. At first, that was what he did. He told her he needed to be at the scene to help the examiners. After a few minutes, she finally managed to ask the obvious question. 'Is there a reason you're here then, Adam?'

He looked surprised, as if he'd forgotten where he was. 'I want you to come with me.'

'I'm not sure there's any point me attending the scene just yet,' she said, baffled by the request. 'The examiners can deal with it. If there're any signs of foul play—'

'Not there. I've somewhere else to go first.'

'I'm sorry. You've lost me.'

He had a waterproof jacket with him, cradled on his knee,

and he moved it aside to reveal the pistol. 'Best if you come with me.'

'Adam, this really isn't—'

'A joke? No, it isn't. And this isn't a replica. It's real, it's loaded and I'm happy to use it. It'll bring things to an end sooner than I'd like, but I can live with that.' He smiled. 'Or not live with it.'

'Just put the gun down. Then we can talk about it.'

'I've heard enough talking. I want to bring it to an end.'

'Bring what to an end, Adam?'

'I want you to come with me.'

'Where?'

'Not far.'

'And then you'll hand back the gun?'

'By then, it won't much matter.'

It wasn't the most reassuring response but she found herself nodding. 'Okay. I'll humour you.'

'Walk in front of me. I'll have the gun under my coat.'

She did as he said. As they left her office, he paused momentarily and picked something up from one of the shelves. She glanced back, puzzled, unable to see what he'd taken.

As they walked through reception, she'd been convinced they must look conspicuous and waited for someone to challenge them. But no one gave them a second glance. Even when they'd encountered Ginny Horton coming in, Ginny had apparently suspected nothing. It had only been when she'd given Ginny an explicit clue something was wrong that she'd seen a flash of puzzlement in Ginny's eyes. But by then it was already too late. They were out in the car park, Sutherland leading her to his vehicle.

Sutherland had kept her covered while he ushered her into the passenger seat. Then he locked the doors while he climbed in the driver's side. She looked around frantically for the central locking button, but hadn't been quick enough.

Sutherland had his coat on his knee, the gun resting on it. 'Don't try anything,' he said. 'You won't have a chance. Do you have a mobile with you?'

She pulled the phone from her jacket pocket. 'Here.'

He took it without speaking, started the engine and drove them out of the car park, then onto the northbound A9. Somewhere on the way she heard her phone ringing on Sutherland's lap, but he ignored it.

Just before the Tore roundabout, he pulled into a lay-by, stopping behind a black SUV. A black SUV she'd seen previously on CCTV footage.

They changed cars, Sutherland exercising the same caution he had back in the car park. He asked for the security code on her phone. She gave it to him and watched as he entered a short text. He held the phone up for her to read. The message had been sent to McKay. *A9 S of Tore.*

'He called you while we were driving here,' he said.

She had no idea why he'd sent Alec their current location just as they were about to leave. But then she had no idea what any of this was about.

They continued on to the roundabout, taking the left turn towards Beauly. Somewhere distantly behind her she heard the sound of a police siren.

'Can I ask where we're going?' she said.

He took his hand briefly off the wheel and touched the gun on his lap. 'Please be quiet until we reach our destination.' His strange politeness was almost more unnerving than any sign of aggression would have been.

They continued for another ten minutes until they were approaching the outskirts of Beauly. Just before they entered the small town, Sutherland took a left turn onto a single-track road.

The landscape was relatively flat here, the road surrounded by fields. They passed a bungalow on the left, and then continued for another half mile until the road petered out.

It was only then that Grant recognised the location. Ahead of them was a house that had featured in countless newspaper photographs and TV news reports twenty years before. It looked different now. The front windows and front door had been replaced; the garden substantially changed.

Grant had never had reason to visit the murder scene, but Rory had described it to her on a couple of occasions, perhaps to help exorcise his own demons about the case. For all the changes, she'd recognised the place as soon as the house came into view.

'What's this about, Adam?' she asked. 'Why are we here?'

The house looked well-maintained and occupied. There were two cars outside – a newish BMW 7 Series and an older Kia Sportage. This would be marketed as a desirable family residence, Grant thought, but it felt like the bleakest place she had ever been to.

'Why are we here?' she asked again.

'To tie up the last loose ends,' Sutherland said. 'It looks as if the gang's all here.'

CHAPTER SIXTY-TWO

Iain Pennycook had still been in bed, half asleep, when the doorbell rang. He tried to ignore it, rolling over, hoping whoever it was would bugger off. It couldn't be anything important, not at this time of the day. If it was a delivery, they could come back or leave the parcel dumped in the bin like they usually did. If it was anyone else, he didn't want to know.

The doorbell rang again, this time held down for longer. Pennycook pulled the duvet around his head, trying to drown out the sound. Finally it stopped and he momentarily relaxed. Then it started again, this time for even longer.

'Oh, for fuck's sake.' Pennycook threw back the duvet and sat up, reaching for his dressing gown. The clock on his bedside table told him it was just after nine thirty. It was unusual for Pennycook to sleep so late, but he'd been out networking the night before. He normally tried to avoid drinking too much in those sessions, seeing advantage in remaining the most sober person in the room. But last night he'd been celebrating a sponsorship deal with a local company. Nothing major, but some decent funding and another name to add credibility. He'd ended up getting a ludicrously expensive cab back here in the small hours. He had no commitments today and had intended to sleep off his hangover. Some bastard seemed determined to put an end to that idea.

Dragging on his dressing gown, he stamped towards the front door. Even in his semi-comatose state, he was alert enough to peer through the spy-hole before opening the door. He swore loudly as he struggled with the lock. 'What the fuck?'

The man on the doorstep looked startled at the angry reaction. 'Iain?'

'What the fuck are you doing here at this time of day? No, scratch that. What the fuck are you doing here at all? You know what we agreed.'

'You asked me to come.'

'What?'

'You sent me a WhatsApp message. Telling me to come over. Said it was urgent.'

'When did I send this message?'

'About an hour ago. I came straight over like you said.'

'Gordon, an hour ago I was fast asleep in bed. Which is where I want to be now.'

'But how—?'

'I don't know. You'd better come in.'

Rennie followed Pennycook through into the kitchen. 'I need coffee,' Pennycook said. 'Do you want some?'

'Thanks,' Rennie said. 'You're saying you didn't message me?'

Pennycook was busying himself with a sophisticated-looking bean-to-coffee machine in the corner of the kitchen. 'Unless I've somehow learned to message in my sleep, that's exactly what I'm saying.'

'So who did?'

'If I knew that, I'd be on my way to wring their neck. But I'm going to find out. I don't like this.'

'It's not that early—'

'It's much earlier than I want it to be. That's not the point.'

Pennycook carried over two large espressos. 'Strong,' he said. 'We're going to need them.'

'There's only a few of us now who know.'

'And one of them's not likely to be talking again. The others I'd thought were under control. Until the last few days.'

'Clark's solicitor, you mean? I was surprised by that one.'

'It wasn't anything I'd asked for. And apparently there's been another killing. The guy who produced the podcast about the O'Donnell case. That one's not public yet.'

'How do you know these things?'

'Because I make it my business to know,' Pennycook snapped. 'And I want to know what's happening now. Someone's playing games. And we both know who.'

'What about Charlie?'

Pennycook laughed. 'You mean bloody Viper? He's not got the bottle. I don't know why he tried it on with that podcaster – maybe thought he could screw a few more quid out of me – but he got the message quickly enough. He won't open his mouth again. No, Charlie's not the problem.'

Leaving Rennie sitting at the kitchen table, Pennycook stamped back through to the bedroom. He returned a few minutes later fully dressed and holding his phone. He was scrolling through the phone as he walked. He sat back at the table, holding the phone to his ear. 'Going straight to voicemail. What's the silly bugger playing at?'

'You're sure it's him?'

'I'm bloody well hoping it's him. If it's someone else, then we really are in trouble. But I don't know what game this is.'

He was about to say something more when the doorbell rang

again. The bell was pressed just once, for a relatively short time, as if the visitor was much more tentative than Rennie had been.

But Pennycook had little doubt who was at the door. And he had a growing sense that, whatever was about to happen, it wouldn't be good.

CHAPTER SIXTY-THREE

McKay pulled into the lay-by behind the patrol car. There was another car parked in front of it, and the two uniformed officers were walking round it, peering into the windows as if hoping the vehicle might divulge its secrets if they stared at it long enough.

McKay walked towards them brandishing his warrant card. 'DI McKay.'

'Do you know why we're here?' one of the officers grumbled. 'Seems like a bloody wild goose chase.'

'That right, son?'

'Nobody's told us what we're looking for—'

'I'm telling you now. You're here because I called you out. What you're looking for is the bloody car sitting in front of you. So well done.'

'Yes, but—'

'Have you checked who it belongs to?'

'We'd only—'

'Rather than standing here whinging, maybe do that. If it's not too much trouble.'

The second officer was already on the radio. 'Registered

keeper's one Adam Patrick Sutherland. Address in Inverness. Is this stolen?'

'Not stolen. I want it taken back to HQ for the examiners to go over. If you arrange the transport and for it to be securely stored, I'll sort out the examiners later.'

'Are you sure?' one of the officers ventured.

'Aye, I'm sure, son. Feel like debating it?'

'Not as long as I've your authorisation.'

'That's right, always find someone more senior to take the blame. You've got my authorisation. Mention my name. It'll open doors for you.'

Ginny Horton had been standing watching this exchange. 'So he's not here,' she said to McKay. 'You think they'll find anything in the car?'

'Probably not. My guess is the SUV is the one we need to be looking at. But it'll stop him driving it away.'

'You think he's intending to return here?'

'I haven't a scooby what he's intending to do. But I've a feeling there's a reason he's drawn us to this spot.' He looked around. They were surrounded by woodland and fields. 'We found Hugh Preston in the car over there. That was the only killing other than Charlie Farrow's that didn't involve the victim being forced off the A9. I'm guessing Farrow was just picked off at a convenient place. But Preston was brought here. I'm wondering why. The priority now's to get to Beauly. Let's hope I'm guessing right.'

The journey to Beauly took another fifteen minutes. 'Long before my time,' Horton said as they approached the town, 'but I can see why the O'Donnell killing would have been so disturbing. Not the sort of place you expect that kind of murder. Isla and I come up to the town at weekends sometimes. Lunch at the deli on the square, walk to the ruined church. Idyllic.'

'Murder happens everywhere. But not that kind of killing. I

don't know if people ever really believed Kevin Clark was the killer. No, that's not right. Many did, particularly how clear-cut the trial seemed to be. But a lot of us felt it wasn't the full story.'

'You like to play the hard-bitten cynical cop, don't you, Alec? But your instinct's usually right.'

'I'm not saying the verdict was wrong. I'm sure Clark was present at the murder. He's probably got what he deserved. But I've always sensed it wasn't the whole story.' He fell silent as they entered the outskirts of the small town. 'I guess we may be about to find out. This is the place.'

He turned off the main road onto a winding single track. He continued past a bungalow on their right. 'There are only a couple of houses up here,' McKay said. 'I always wondered how the owners of that place felt about the killing. I'm guessing they've long moved on.'

McKay pulled to a halt just beyond the first bungalow, steering the car into a farm gateway. 'We'd better leave the car here. If we drive up, they'll spot us straight away.'

'Who'll spot us?'

'We can assume Pennycook's going to be there. The rest of it's just guesswork. Although...' He climbed out of the car and walked along the track, beckoning Horton to follow. 'That looks like the SUV to me.'

'Seems as if your hunch was right.'

'I'm going up there. You don't have to come.'

'I'm coming.'

'But—'

'If you say anything that involves Isla and the state of her health, I'll find ways of making sure you regret it. You know that's not an idle threat.'

'You might insist on taking me running?'

'I can do far worse than that. But the point is, this is my job.

I've chosen to do it. Isla knows that. It's part of the deal between us, even now. She'd never forgive me if I used her as an excuse.'

'Point taken. Anyway, I was only trying to be gallant.'

She raised an eyebrow. 'Really? Well, I suppose there's a first time for everything.'

CHAPTER SIXTY-FOUR

Iain Pennycook approached the front door and peered through the spy-hole at whoever was standing on the doorstep. There were two figures, both familiar to him, but he hadn't the faintest idea why they might be here together.

He opened the door, and stared at Adam Sutherland in feigned surprise. 'Adam. An unexpected visitor.' He peered past Sutherland, his frown of puzzlement more genuine. 'DCI Grant. What brings you here with Adam?'

She took a small step forward, and for the first time Pennycook realised Sutherland was holding a revolver.

'I was hoping that you – or both of you – might explain that to me,' Grant said.

'I think you'd both better come inside.'

Sutherland gestured with the pistol for Grant to enter first, and then he ushered her and Pennycook towards the living room. Rennie was standing in the kitchen doorway.

'Glad to see the gang all here,' Sutherland said. 'You'd better come and join us, Gordon.'

Rennie scurried ahead of them into the living room.

Sutherland waited till the others were seated, then lowered himself into the armchair nearest the door. He held the gun on his knees. 'Just as a warning, I know how to use this and I'll have no hesitation in doing so.'

'You don't need to be going to these lengths,' Pennycook said. 'We're friends here. Put your gun down and we can talk about whatever it is.'

'You're no friend of mine, Iain. You claimed you were, and I was stupid enough to believe you.'

Pennycook glanced at Helena Grant. 'I've done a lot for you over the years, Adam. You know that.'

Sutherland shook his head. 'I've done everything for you. For years. I've protected you. I've saved my own skin in the process, sure, but I don't feel good about that.'

'Look, there's no need—'

'To tell the story. I think there is. Though there's only one person here who doesn't know at least some of it. And it's probably time she did.' Sutherland reached into his jacket and pulled out the small photograph of Rory Grant he'd taken from Helena's office. 'I thought it might be appropriate to have this here. I'm sorry for taking it, Helena.'

'What's this about?' Grant said. 'If you've got a story to tell me, there are more suitable circumstances.'

'I can't think of anywhere more suitable than here. I was astonished to discover you were living here, Iain. You really do have some brass neck, don't you?'

'I'm not the superstitious type. The rent's cheap for obvious reasons.'

'You're hiding in plain sight,' Sutherland said. 'Do you actually sleep in that room?'

'As it happens, no. But only because I prefer the room at the back. Better views.'

'You're quite something,' Sutherland said. 'I'm not comfortable being here. I don't know how you can stand it.'

'But you've a reason not be comfortable, haven't you, Adam? You're the one person who knows exactly what went on in here.'

'You know.'

'I know what you told me. I know how you fucked it up.'

'You fucked it up, Iain. You used two kids who weren't up to the job. Because we were expendable. Because nobody would believe us if we tried to tell the real story.' He turned to Helena Grant. 'Would you like me to tell you?'

'There's no need for this, Adam,' she said.

'Simon O'Donnell was bent. He was taking backhanders from one of the local providers in exchange for contracts, and siphoning a cut for himself. We're not even talking big bucks. It was just another of Iain Pennycook's scams. He'd got O'Donnell hooked with a few petty bribes, and after that O'Donnell was too scared to say no. Got sucked further and further in. Part of Iain's little network, just like Gordon Rennie over there.'

'This is all a long time ago,' Rennie said.

'It doesn't feel so long ago to me,' Sutherland said. 'And Iain here hasn't changed much in the meantime. Still has fingers in countless pies. Still running the same kinds of grift.'

Helena Grant leaned forward. 'So what happened with O'Donnell?'

'He was going to blow the whistle. He realised how much shite he'd got himself into and he'd lost his bottle. But he made the mistake of telling Iain here first.'

'He's no idea what he's talking about,' Pennycook said. 'It's all bollocks.'

'It's not though, is it? There was nothing sophisticated in what you were doing in those days. You were involved in every grift going. Drug dealing. Extortion. Corruption. All petty stuff, and housebreaking was a part of it. You never did anything yourself, but you acted as a middle-man and took a cut from those who did. That was how you knew me, and a whole bunch of kids from our neck of the woods. It was you gave us the nod about a supposed valuable stash in this house.'

Pennycook glared at him, as if daring him to say any more.

'You told us the place would be empty. A piece of piss, you said. Get in, grab the stuff, get out and be gone. You didn't tell us O'Donnell would be in the house. You got me on board, because you knew what kind of kid I was in those days. You saddled me with Kevin Clark. Clark was always tagging along with us. Desperate to get involved. You persuaded me he'd be okay. When you knew full well he wouldn't.'

'So what happened?' Grant said.

'We got in easily enough. Kept quiet, though we assumed the house was empty. There was no sign of any of the stuff Iain had promised. We'd searched the lounge, then we moved on to the bedrooms. O'Donnell must have been using some kind of sleeping tablets, which is why he hadn't heard us. He was confused and panicked when he woke up, and charged at us off the bed. I didn't even know Clark was carrying a knife – another gift from Iain, I'm guessing. Clark was in an even more confused state than O'Donnell and lashed out at him. Cut him across the face, then the chest. O'Donnell was still alive, still okay at that point. But he'd seen our faces.' He stopped, staring at Pennycook. 'I knew I was going to have to do something. I wasn't thinking clearly. I grabbed the knife and lunged at O'Donnell.'

'You were the one who stabbed him?' Grant asked.

'It was easier than I'd expected. I'd hurt people before. Iain knew that. That was what I was, just a thug. But I'd never done anything like that. And it was easy. Not physically – it took a lot

329

more than I expected to kill him. But emotionally, psychologically. I was killing another human being in the most brutal way possible, and it was simple. Satisfying, almost. I made sure he was dead, then we left.'

'How did you get away?'

'We had some mates waiting in a car nearby. At first, they just wanted to leave us there. We eventually talked them into taking us back into town. Just because they were mates...' He looked up, gazing blankly into the air as if reliving those moments. 'There was something that didn't strike me till afterwards. Pennycook had set all this up. He'd advised Sean McArthur who was driving the car to cover the seats with plastic. He'd come up with some story about DNA traces, and Andy had bought it. It was only afterwards that I wondered if Pennycook had organised it that way for another reason.'

'You talk such shite,' Pennycook said. 'How could I know you'd lose your head and kill O'Donnell, if you're saying that's what happened.'

'Because you knew me. You knew me better than I knew myself. You'd spotted what I was. It takes one to know one.'

'I'm not a killer.'

'I don't know about that. But I know you easily could be. And you can read other people. I gave you the result you wanted, and more.'

'I've no idea what you're talking about.' Pennycook shook his head. 'I think you'd better stop this, before it's too late for you.'

'Let me finish the story. We didn't get away. Not fully. We were halfway down the A9, heading back towards Inverness, when Andy lost control. He should never have been driving. He was panicking, going too fast, the rest of us telling him to slow down. Kevin was still holding the murder weapon. I was trying to take it from him, thinking I'd find a way to dispose of it. Then suddenly we were off the road, turning over and over, until finally we crashed to a halt. I thought someone must have seen what happened, but no one appeared. Andy was badly injured, but somehow the rest of us seemed to be okay. I forced my way out of the rear door, and helped the other two out. We didn't know what do about Andy. In the end, we just fled. I had enough presence of mind to drag the plastic covers off the rear seats, but there wasn't much else we could do. We walked the rest of the way back into the city. Kevin and I lived near each other, so we both managed to change without being seen. I bundled up the soiled clothes, the seat covers and the knife into a bin bag. Then I called Iain.'

'This is a very impressive narrative,' Pennycook said. 'Pity it's all fluent bollocks.'

'Even then Iain didn't handle any of it himself. He sent round some associate who relieved me of the bag. I assume the clothes and the seat covers were burnt. Iain already had a plan in place, I'm guessing. Kevin was taken off, along with the murder weapon. I don't know exactly what happened. My guess is that the knife was cleaned but then given back to Kevin to get his fingerprints and DNA. He'd have been daft enough to play along. I don't know if he was telling the truth about not remembering what happened after the killing, or whether they just scared him into silence. I was told to keep my mouth shut and I'd be all right. That threat's hung over me ever since.'

Pennycook brought his hands together in fake applause. 'Great story. It might even be true. But I had nothing to do with any of it.'

'That was always your thing, wasn't it?' Sutherland said. 'Plausible deniability.'

'I'm assuming you've no evidence for any of this pile of nonsense?'

'After all these years, probably not. That's not what I'm interested in.'

'Why are you telling us this?' Helena Grant asked.

'Because I want to finish it,' Sutherland said. 'The funny thing is, Iain, that for a long while I was grateful to you. The shock of it all – not just the killing, but the car crash, the whole fear of being caught – shocked me into changing my ways. I was lucky. Not just because I'd literally got away with murder but because I had no criminal record. I managed to get myself a proper job. Apprentice car mechanic. My career's gone pretty well. I saw the police job advertised a few years ago. Got it, and made a career of it. It seemed the right thing to do.'

'So what changed?' Grant asked.

'Everything happened at once. The twenty-year anniversary of O'Donnell's death meant people were getting interested again. That podcaster was hinting he had the real story, with some whistleblower who'd been involved—'

'Charlie Farrow, I'm guessing?' Grant said.

'Aye, Farrow. Gordon's bag-carrier back in those days. He knew where the bodies were buried.'

Gordon Rennie had been sitting in silence listening to Sutherland's account. Now he said, 'You're full of shite, Sutherland. You know nothing.'

'You were in Iain's pocket, and Farrow did whatever you told him. I don't know what prompted him to blow the whistle or how much he really knew, but I'm guessing he was sick of the lies.' He paused and turned his attention back to Pennycook. 'But he made the same mistake O'Donnell did, all those years before. He told you what he was planning to do, wanted to give you fair warning. He didn't think it would trouble you too much, given you've always tried to keep your own hands clean. Farrow misjudged you. You were about to make your big comeback, and you couldn't afford to jeopardise that. And you had me on a string. You fed all your paranoia onto me, making me think the real story was about to come out. You'd heard talk that Clark's memory might be returning. Was the solicitor on your payroll too? Someone must have been paying him to maintain contact with Clark.'

There was still no response from Pennycook, who had closed his eyes as if trying to block out the scene in front of him.

'You knew exactly what you were doing. You told me there was a real danger the true story of O'Donnell's death might be exposed. You played on my paranoia. Tried to turn me back into a killer.'

Pennycook opened his eyes. 'I don't know what you did. And I didn't tell you to do it.'

'That's almost true. It wasn't directly at your bidding. But you knew what I was, what I was capable of. I'd spent years avoiding any temptation to repeat that act of twenty years ago. But I'd enjoyed it. I got a kick out of it. I wanted to do it again.' He paused. 'There's something else you don't know.'

'Adam—' Helena Grant said. But it was clear that nothing would prevent him speaking.

'I'm dying. Terminal cancer. Six months to a year, they reckon. You'd think they could be more precise, wouldn't you? But that changed the game. I've nothing to lose, and I can't see any reason why anyone else should live much longer if I'm about to die.'

'This is insane—' Rennie said. 'Just put the fucking gun down, son.'

'It is insane,' Sutherland said. 'I mean, I must be insane, I suppose. But that's the way it is. I wouldn't hesitate to put a bullet in any of your brains. Just for the hell of it. Even yours, Helena, and you've done nothing to deserve it.'

'You don't really believe this, Adam,' Grant said.

'Please don't try to test me.'

'I'm not. But—'

Sutherland turned towards her, the gun gripped firmly in his hand. 'I've told you, Helena. Please don't do this. Not yet.'

'Adam—'

She said nothing more because Sutherland, still shaking his head, raised the pistol and fired.

CHAPTER SIXTY-FIVE

'What the hell was that?' Ginny Horton said.

'Do cars still backfire these days? Haven't heard one in years. If not, I'd say that was a gunshot.' McKay's tone was light, but his expression was more serious than Ginny had ever seen.

'You reckon that was from inside the house?'

'Difficult to be sure with the acoustics out here. Could have been some Hooray Henry shooting grouse.' He stopped. 'But I think it was from inside the house.'

'We need to get in there.'

'I want to know what we're getting into before we go any further. You call for backup, and I'll try to get a closer look.'

'But—'

'Just do it, Gin.'

While Horton made the call, asking for armed backup and an ambulance, McKay approached the bungalow from the side, doing his best to remain unseen from inside. He edged along the wall towards the rear window of the house.

It was a few moments before he returned to join her.

'They're in the living room. I could see Pennycook and Sutherland. Sutherland was holding some sort of handgun.'

'Any casualties?'

'I couldn't see. And I couldn't see Helena, though that doesn't mean she's not in there.'

Horton gestured towards the front of the house. 'I've had the registration's checked out. The SUV is a ringer, almost certainly the same one we identified previously though the registration's been changed. The other car belongs to Gordon Rennie.'

'Quite a house party.'

'It's going to get livelier soon. Armed backup on its way. So do we try to get in there?'

'If he's shot someone already, we're not going to help anyone by putting ourselves in the firing line.' McKay sounded as if he was trying to convince himself. Left to his own devices, he might not be quite so cautious.

Within seconds, though, the question became academic. As they watched, three figures appeared from the front of the house. Sutherland was at the rear, the pistol still in his hand, shepherding the others towards the SUV.

CHAPTER SIXTY-SIX

'Shit.' For the first time, Pennycook's seemingly relaxed demeanour had disappeared. 'You really have shot him.'

Rennie was slumped in a blood-drenched armchair. There was a neat wound in the front of his head and a less elegant exit wound in the rear.

Sutherland was looking at the gun as if it had somehow acted of its own volition. 'I told you.' It wasn't clear who he was talking to.

Helena Grant had been holding her breath since the gun was fired. She'd thought Sutherland was going to shoot her. She still wasn't sure that hadn't been his initial intention. At the last moment, he'd turned the gun to Rennie and fired.

'What the fuck have you done, you fucking moron?' Pennycook said.

'Look, Adam,' Grant said, 'just put the gun down now. We can call for help. You don't need to take this any further.'

'It was what I wanted to do,' Sutherland said. 'I did it sooner than I'd intended. Before I'd told you the whole story. But we've time for that.' The photograph of Rory Grant was still on his lap. Holding the gun steady, he slipped the picture back into his pocket. 'Let's go for a drive.'

'A drive?' Pennycook said. 'Are you fucking insane?'

'I think the answer to that should be obvious,' Sutherland said. 'Come on.'

Waving the gun, he brought them to their feet and shepherded them out of the house on to the front drive. Grant was desperately hoping the sound of the gunshot might have alerted someone, but there was no sign of any movement. The nearest house was back along the track, and there was a car parked beside it, but nothing else she could see. Sutherland ushered them into the SUV, Pennycook in the passenger seat, her in the back. Sutherland started the engine and turned the car back out onto the track.

'Where are you taking us, Adam?'

'A little drive while I finish the story. It was about a year ago that Iain contacted me. He was subtle at first. A few drinks, a few thoughts casually dropped into my head. But behind it the threat of exposure if I didn't play ball. He'd bring down the whole life and career I'd built for myself since I'd known him. I didn't care about any of that. My first reaction was to tell him to fuck off. But then I got the cancer diagnosis. And everything changed.'

'In what way?' Grant asked, trying to keep her voice calm.

'After that, I felt it was a lottery. I felt the thrill of killing someone again. I made it a contest. Killings that were undetectable, but pitted my life against theirs. Iain had told me the people he was concerned about, so I worked from there.'

'I didn't want you to kill them,' Pennycook said. 'I just wanted you to find out if there was a risk they might betray us. Put the frighteners on them. Nothing more.'

'I knew exactly what you really wanted,' Sutherland said. 'I always know.'

'Some of them were hardly even involved. The other guy in the car with you and Kevin. The girl he was stupid enough to tell what had happened. Another mate who'd been in on the deal. Why the hell did you kill them?'

'Because you wanted me to. It was a warning to Charlie Farrow. He recognised the names of the victims of those RTCs. He must have realised it wasn't coincidence.'

'For Christ's sake, that wasn't—' Pennycook said.

'It doesn't matter, anyway. For me, it was a game. I was testing my skills. I put it in the lap of the gods. If I'd died in one of those collisions – well, no great loss to anyone. But I survived, and they died. Then there was you, with your bloody road safety campaign. You were taking the piss, weren't you?'

The expression on Pennycook's face told Grant that Sutherland was at least half right. It was typical Pennycook, the same brass neck that had led him to move into O'Donnell's house.

'What about Brian Renton, the truck driver?' she asked. 'Did you kill him?'

'I screwed up,' Sutherland admitted. 'I'd tried to kill Gavin McCann earlier, but messed it up. I didn't want to miss the chance. His wife and the truck driver were collateral damage. I killed Renton simply because I didn't want to be arrested. If it was going to end, I wanted it to end on my terms.'

'So you killed him in cold blood?'

'I enjoyed the risk. Getting onto the ward. Picking the right moment to act. But it was too easy in the end. Disappointing.'

They'd reached the roundabout at Tore. Barely pausing at the junction, Sutherland took the right turn on to the A9 towards Inverness. Somewhere behind them a horn blared.

Grant closed her eyes. They'd narrowly missed another vehicle on the roundabout, and Sutherland was accelerating. The road was quiet, but not enough for their speed not to be dangerous. Sutherland continued speaking, his voice toneless. 'After that I picked them off one by one. But it was too easy. I could have taken them all out without anyone being the wiser. So I started to make the foul play more obvious. I left clues to my involvement. I even left one of the victims in the place where Andy had crashed the car all those years before.' He glanced back casually at Grant. 'McKay was the only one to spot the pattern. He was a long way ahead of everyone else.'

'Why am I here? You made a point of bringing me. I was nothing to do with any of this,' Grant said.

'That's true, you weren't. But your husband was.'

'He wasn't involved in the corruption or the killings.'

'Is that what you think? He was the SIO on the investigation. By all accounts, he ran a tight ship. I doubt the work Rennie and Farrow did would have passed muster if he'd really scrutinised it. Evidence was conveniently found to corroborate Clark's story. I'm surprised your husband didn't question that.'

'Everything was solid. It stood up to the Fiscal, and it stood up in court.'

'I wonder how much pressure your husband was under to get a result. How much pressure he was under from senior officers not to implicate a good member of the "police family".' The contempt he injected into the last two words was almost palpable.

Grant wanted to tell him it wasn't true. Her eyes were fixed on the speedometer, the needle easing up the dial. At that speed, even the slightest misjudgement could be lethal, although Sutherland's driving skills were obvious.

She looked up. In the distance there was a flickering of blue lights. Something was happening.

One way or another, their journey might be coming to an end.

CHAPTER SIXTY-SEVEN

McKay and Horton had wasted precious seconds checking out the house, driving up there after the SUV had passed. If Sutherland had spotted them, he hadn't bothered to stop and chat.

The door to the bungalow had been left open. McKay had made his way cautiously to the living room. It only took him a moment to discover why Gordon Rennie hadn't accompanied the others into the car.

'The smell of blood,' Ginny said. 'There's no mistaking it, is there?'

'Not in this case, anyway,' McKay said.

'I've called in. Told them to try to intercept the SUV. Warned them that Sutherland's armed and dangerous. The ambulance is still heading up here.'

'No point staying here. Let's see if we can get after them ourselves.'

'What's this about?' Horton said, when they were back on the road. 'Where the hell's he taking them?'

'My guess is onto the A9 south of Tore,' McKay said. 'That's what he told us. Before he made his detour.'

'This is connected to the crash after the O'Donnell murder?'

'I'm guessing so. Sutherland's finishing the job.'

'So why's he taken Helena?'

'That's what I've been asking myself. There's only one answer that springs to mind.'

'Rory?'

'Rory.'

McKay increased his speed, skilfully overtaking a slow-moving van on the single carriageway road, driving as fast as he felt able. They were five minutes away from the Tore roundabout now, and there was no sign of Sutherland's SUV.

Horton was still talking to the control room. 'They're closing the A9 at the roundabout and at Kessock Bridge,' she said. 'Diverting existing traffic and then setting up a roadblock somewhere around the Munlochy junction.'

'That's something,' McKay said. 'Though I've a feeling that might be too far south.'

'You want me to try to get it moved?'

'It's all guesswork,' McKay said. 'But it's going to end the way Sutherland wants it, whatever we do.'

'That doesn't sound good.'

'I'm praying I'm wrong,' McKay said. 'But I really don't think I'm going to be.'

CHAPTER SIXTY-EIGHT

It was only now that Helena Grant realised how quiet the road around them was. The northbound carriageway opposite was empty, and there were no cars behind them. Blue lights twinkled in the distance, growing closer.

Sutherland seemed oblivious. His eyes were fixed on the road, but his expression suggested his head was somewhere else entirely, perhaps being driven on this road twenty years before. 'We're nearly there,' he said.

'Nearly where?'

'I'm sorry you had to be part of it. It wasn't your fault. But someone has to pay for your husband's role in this.'

'He wasn't that sort of cop.'

'You're all that sort of cop,' Sutherland said. 'I've watched you, all of you. And people like Iain here. You're all the same. In each other's pockets.'

Pennycook had been crouched in his seat, his eyes fixed on Sutherland. At the mention of his name, he stirred and sat upright. 'What the hell are you planning to do? Kill us all?'

Grant could see now that the blue lights were a line of patrol cars, a roadblock. There were signs and flashing lights.

ROAD CLOSED. POLICE – STOP. She could see figures placed strategically behind the cars, presumably armed officers. At first, she thought they'd misjudged the situation, but then she realised they'd deployed a stinger across the carriageway with the aim of bringing the SUV to a halt before the roadblock.

'For fuck's sake,' Pennycook squealed, 'just fucking stop. You can't get past that.'

With a sudden jerk, Sutherland twisted the steering wheel to the left and pulled off the road, bouncing over the kerb onto the rising ground beyond. Grant caught a glimpse of the commotion on the road behind them, then they were crashing through woodland, branches striking the side of the vehicle, wheels bouncing on the uneven terrain.

They passed between two trees into a more open area, and for a moment Grant thought they were safe, that Sutherland would finally slow down, realising there was no way out.

Sutherland slammed his foot down harder on the accelerator, throwing her back into her seat. He was heading towards the largest of the trees in the thicket. Grant threw herself forward, trying to grab his hand.

It was already too late. The car skidded and veered to the left, but not enough to avoid the tree. Grant instinctively closed her eyes, as if she could shut out the inevitable reality.

The impact, when it came, was like nothing she'd ever experienced.

CHAPTER SIXTY-NINE

Alec McKay nodded to Ally who, as always, was standing behind the bar polishing glasses. Ally gazed back at him for a moment, then nodded as if acknowledging McKay's right to be in the pub.

McKay walked across the room and stood in front of Craig Fairlie's table. 'Quiet today.'

'You know how it is. Tourist season more or less over. All the glamorous celebrities have gone home.'

'Pint?'

Fairlie tapped the nearly full glass on the table. 'I'm good.'

McKay fetched himself a fizzy water, which Ally served without a word. As he rejoined Fairlie in the corner, McKay said, 'Hell of a mess.' He gestured towards the newspaper on the table. The front page was devoted to the fatal crash on the A9, although for the moment the details remained limited. There was mention of a police operation and multiple fatalities, but the names of the victims hadn't so far been released.

'Quite a lot swept under the carpet,' Fairlie observed.

'I don't know how long we can keep it that way. Especially when it emerges that Iain Pennycook was one of the victims.'

ALEX WALTERS

'Should give his campaign a boost anyway.' Fairlie stopped and took a mouthful of his beer. 'Sorry. Don't mean to sound flippant. Not in the circumstances.'

'Gallows humour. We all need it. Especially in this job.'

'I can imagine. But this must be closer to home than most.'

'You might say that.'

'How is Helena anyway?'

McKay was silent for a moment, as if contemplating how to answer the question. 'She's fine. Well, she will be fine, they reckon. Some broken bones. Lots of bruising. But no internal damage. She's not in a great state, but she'll recover. Physically, anyway.'

'Physically?'

'She's struggling with the idea that Rory might not have been the white knight she always thought he was.'

'Is there much evidence of that?'

'I'm guessing no one's going to be digging too deeply after all these years. Which may make it worse for Helena. The not knowing.' McKay had told Fairlie some of the story – as least as far as he'd understood it from Helena in her hospital bed – when he'd set up this meeting.

'Are you seriously suggesting nobody's going to investigate any of this?'

'There'll be something,' McKay said. 'Probably something that doesn't reflect well on the Serious Investigations Team, I imagine, as well as anyone else they can drag through the mud. Why didn't we spot Sutherland earlier? How did he get away with it for so long?' He shrugged. 'They're reasonable questions. But I have a feeling nobody's going to make much effort to dig into the history. There's not much to be gained and plenty to lose. Rennie and Farrow are both dead, as is Sutherland himself. Sutherland's confession that he was involved in O'Donnell's killing changes the narrative, but there's no lingering question about Clark's role. He was there and he was involved in the murder. The fact that Pennycook and his mates tried to erase Sutherland from the picture and place Clark in the frame by himself isn't likely to alter his sentence, even if he recovers. And that's not looking likely. So all nicely cut and dried.'

'Why are you telling me all this?'

'Because you're an old friend, Craig.'

'Aye. And this place is the Ritz.'

'The way I see it, no one's going to be interested in joining the dots on this one.' McKay laughed. 'Sutherland wasn't even a cop, though that's not a distinction the media are likely to spend too much time on. It was something he'd successfully blurred himself over the years. He had a fake warrant card in the name of a retired cop that looked pretty authentic. We think he might have used that identity to inveigle his way into Hugh Preston's trust, and he'd probably have wielded it if he'd been stopped in the hospital before he killed Brian Renton.'

'Nice of you to share these details with me.'

'I'll deny every word of it if anyone asks, obviously.'

'You think the O'Donnell story's going to be swept under the carpet.'

'I think it's likely to be kept inside the police family, let's put it that way. We've a new Area Commander arriving who won't be keen to rock the boat, given everything that's happened in recent years.'

'So you want to blow the whistle?'

'If I were blowing the whistle, I'd do it properly. I understand you get protection that way. Not that it actually seems to protect anyone who does it. But that's not my style. I'm just having a chat with an old mate.'

'Who happens to be a journalist.'

'Is that what you're up to these days? Who knew?' McKay took a sip of his water. 'I'm going to be rushed off my feet over the coming months. It'll be a while before Helena's fit to work. She might even decide this is the point to take early retirement.'

'Not Helena.'

'Maybe not. But this has hit her hard. And on top of that, we've finally persuaded Ginny to take compassionate leave to help care for Isla. The final straw was Isla's mother threatening to come up and help them.'

Fairlie looked puzzled. 'Wouldn't Isla welcome that?'

'You've clearly never met her mother. Neither have I, for that matter, but Ginny's told me enough to convince me that Isla really wouldn't. Not while she's undergoing her treatment, anyway, and Christ knows how that might turn out. So Ginny's off for the foreseeable too, and muggins here's left running the show. Not for the first time.'

'Sounds like the end of days,' Fairlie commented.

'Feels like it sometimes. But we keep buggering on. Or at least I do. I want to help Helena. I don't want her twisting in the wind over what Rory might or might not have done. What he might or might not have been.'

'You think I can help?'

'Not for me to say. But there's a story there, in the whole O'Donnell case. I think maybe a bigger story than any of us realises. You're a hack. It's what you do, chase up stories. I could probably give you a bit of help. But off the record, you understand.'

'Naturally. And if I succeeded in chasing up this story, as you put it, would you really want me to make it public?'

McKay was silent for a moment, as if considering the question. 'It depends what you find, I guess.'

'If Rory Grant really was bent, I couldn't sit on that. I'd have to tell the whole story.'

'That's why I hesitated for so long before I called you. But I think Helena would want to know the truth, even if it turns out not to be the truth she wants to hear.'

'I'll give it some thought,' Fairlie said. 'It won't be easy.'

'You've got sources,' McKay said. 'Contacts. You know people who were part of Pennycook's scene back in those days. You can do things I couldn't without attracting attention. There's a chance you might find something the official files won't tell me.'

'Like I say, I'll give it some thought.'

'You do that.' McKay looked around. 'I better love you and leave you. I've too much to do, and I want to get out of this place before the rush starts.' He pushed himself to his feet. 'Take care, Craig. And keep me posted.'

ALSO BY ALEX WALTERS

The DI Alec McKay Series

***

ACKNOWLEDGEMENTS

Thanks as ever to all those who made this book possible, particularly as ever to Helen for her ideas, support and endless patience.

And thanks as ever to all at Bloodhound Books for their work on the book - especially Betsy, Fred, Tara, Abbie and Shirley for their input and support.

ABOUT THE AUTHOR

Alex has worked as a consultant and advisor in numerous organisations across the UK and internationally, including police forces, prisons, probation services and other parts of the criminal justice system. He is the author of numerous crime novels with series set in Mongolia, Manchester and the Peak District, as well as several standalone thrillers. His DI Alec McKay series, published by Bloodhound Books, is set in the Scottish Highlands where Alex now lives.

A NOTE FROM THE PUBLISHER

Thank you for reading this book. If you enjoyed it please do consider leaving a review on Amazon to help others find it too.

We hate typos. All of our books have been rigorously edited and proofread, but sometimes mistakes do slip through. If you have spotted a typo, please do let us know and we can get it amended within hours.

info@bloodhoundbooks.com

Printed in Great Britain
by Amazon

58266181R00209